OPERATION NIGHTFALL: THE WEB OF SPIES

KARL WEGENER

FJK-KW Press

Operation Nightfall: The Web of Spies

CONTENT GUIDANCE: This novel is inspired by the events which occurred between 1945 and 1952 during the Polish, anti-communist insurrection. It contains depictions of war, combat, violence, and torture. Please read with care.

To my wife, Jody. Forever and always.

"From Stettin in the Baltic to Trieste in the Adriatic, an iron curtain has descended across the Continent. Behind that line lie all the capitals of the ancient states of Central and Eastern Europe. Warsaw, Berlin, Prague, Vienna, Budapest, Belgrade, Bucharest and Sofia, all these famous cities and the populations around them lie in what I must call the Soviet sphere, and all are subject in one form or another, not only to Soviet influence but to a very high and, in many cases, increasing measure of control from Moscow."

Winston Churchill, "The Sinews of Peace," presented on March 5, 1946, Fulton, Missouri

CONTENTS

Glossary of Terms, Abbreviations, and Cultural References

BBFPS
Acronym for British Baltic Fisheries Protection Service, an MI6 front organization that carried out covert operations in the Baltic Sea region.

Black market
An underground or shadow economy.

Blyskawica Submachine Gun
A Polish submachine gun produced for the Polish Home Army. Adapted from the British Sten gun, it was the only weapon mass-produced covertly during WW2.

Book cipher
A cipher in which each word or letter is replaced by a code that locates it in a specific text, or key. This method of encoding messages requires the sender and receiver have an identical copy (i.e. same edition) of the key book.

Bornholm
A Danish island in the Baltic Sea north of Poland.

Brush pass
A clandestine tradecraft method where an item is surreptitiously passed from one intelligence agent to another as they walk past each other.

Cheka

The Cheka was the first in a long succession of Soviet secret police organizations. Under the direction of Vladimir Lenin, the Cheka carried out mass arrests, imprisonments, torture, and summary executions of political opponents of the communist regime.

CIC

Acronym for Counterintelligence Corps. A U.S. Army Counterintelligence Corps was a WW2 and early Cold War era intelligence agency within the United States Army.

Counterrevolutionaries

In Soviet Russia, any person who was against or perceived to be against the workers' or communist revolution.

Coxswain

The person in charge of a boat's navigation and steering.

Dead drop

A method of espionage tradecraft used to pass items or information between two individuals using a secret location, thereby avoiding direct meetings.

E-boat

E-boat was the British and Western Allies designation for a class of fast attack boats operated by the German Navy, the Kriegsmarine. The "E" designation stands for enemy. The Kriegsmarine referred to this class of boats at Schnellboot or S-Boot, meaning fast boat.

Ersatz coffee

A coffee substitute, usually made from roasted grains or nuts including acorns, soybean, barley, or chicory root.

GCHQ

Acronym for Government Communications Headquarters, the signals intelligence collection service for Great Britain.

GRU

GRU is the abbreviation for **G**lavnoye **R**azvedyvatel'noye **U**pravleniye and translates to the Main Intelligence Directorate. The GRU was the foreign intelligence agency of the General Staff of the Soviet Armed Forces.

Maskirovka

A Russian military doctrine, developed early in the 20th century covering a broad range of military deception activities including denial, deception, camouflage, misinformation, and disinformation.

MGB

MGB is the abbreviation for the **M**inisterstvo **G**osudarstvennoy **B**ezopastnosti, translated as the Ministry for State Security. It was the precursor to the KGB and conducted foreign and domestic intelligence gathering and counterintelligence operations.

MI5

Acronym for the Security Service, Britain's counterintelligence and security agency.

MI6

Acronym for the British Secret Intelligence Service or SIS responsible for covert, foreign intelligence collection and operations.

Morse code

Morse code is named after Samuel Morse. It is a system whereby text characters are encoded into signals of two different durations, referred to as dots and dashes or dits and dahs.

Nick and Nora Charles

Fictional characters created by novelist Dashiell Hammett in his novel, The Thin Man. The characters were also adapted for a series of films from 1934 – 1947, and for radio from 1941 – 1950. Nick and Nora solved murder mysteries while engaging in sharp and witty conversation.

NKVD

NKVD is the abbreviation for **N**arodnyi **K**ommisariat **V**nutranyk **D**el and translates to the Peoples Commissariat for Internal Affairs. The NKVD was the interior ministry of the Soviet Union and included the secret police. Its main function was to ensure the security of the Soviet Union, and it did so through political repression, mass arrests, deportations, and executions. It carried out Stalin's purges during the 1930s. During WW2, the NKVD formed 53 Rifle Divisions and 28 Rifle Brigades. They were initially responsible for rear area security but took part in offensive operations during the Battle of Stalingrad and the Crimean offensive. After WW2, NKVD units were used to suppress partisan insurrections across the Baltic, Ukraine, and in Poland where they faced especially fierce opposition from the Polish Home Army.

Ottendorf cipher

A form of a book cipher, where the ciphertext is made up of numbers in groups of three. The numbers correspond to specific positions within a text, typically a book, and usually refer line, word, and letter.

Polish Home Army

The Polish Home Army, or Armia Krajowa was the main resistance movement during the German occupation of Poland in WW2. Although it was officially disbanded on 19 January 1945, many Home Army units continued to operate against the Polish communist government and against Soviet troops stationed in Poland.

Puck

Pronounced "Putsk," Puck is a town in northern Poland situated on the south coast of the Baltic Sea.

Quo Vadis: A Narrative of the Time of Nero
A historical fiction novel written in Polish by Henrik Sienkiewicz. Set in Rome during the reign of Nero in 64 AD. Quo Vadis is a love story about a Christian woman, Lygia and Roman patrician Marcus Vinicius. The novel was first published in installments in 1895 and published in book form in 1896 and has been translated into over 50 languages. The book is said to have contributed to Sienkiewicz's Nobel Prize for literature in 1905.

Radioteletype
A network of electromechanical teleprinters connected by a radio link.

Radium
A chemical element used in luminescent paint on watches, clocks, and instrument dials enabling them to be read in the dark.

Red Army
The Red Army, whose official name was the Workers' and Peasants' Red Army was the army and air force of the Soviet Union from 1922 until 1946, when it officially was renamed The Soviet Army.

Rezident
Russian word for the senior Russian spy operating within a foreign country.

Rezidentura
Russian word for the base of clandestine, espionage operations within a foreign country.

Special Operations Executive, SOE
A clandestine service and the precursor to MI6, set up in 1940 by Winston Churchill. The mission of the SOE was to conduct espionage, sabotage, reconnaissance, and aid resistance groups within German-occupied Europe during WW2.

Sten Gun
A British submachine gun used by British and Commonwealth soldiers during WW2. The Sten was also distributed to resistance groups during the war. The Polish Home Army produced a variation of the Sten, which eventually evolved into the Blyskawica Submachine Gun.

Tak Tochno
A Russian phrase for, "Yes sir!"

The Thin Man
A detective novel written by Dashiell Hammett which was first published in a condensed version in Redbook magazine in 1933 and then as a full novel in 1934.

Trotskyites
The name for supporters of Leon Trotsky, a leading figure during the Russian revolution and ultimately a political foe of Soviet leader, Josef Stalin.

UB
UB is the abbreviation for **U**rząd **B**ezpieczeństwa and translates to Security Office. The UB, which operated from 1945 to 1953, was the Polish secret police, espionage, and counterintelligence service. Its officers were referred to as Ubecy.

Zloty
The zloty or Polish Zloty is the official currency and legal tender of Poland. It is subdivided into 100 groszy.

Part One

Part One

Chapter One

The Incident

As Lieutenant Colonel Yuri Sokolov's green Russian staff car moved slowly along the narrow forest road, it came upon a sharp bend, a spot where the road turned back onto itself at a nearly 270-degree angle. He knew immediately this was the spot where the incident occurred. His source described the location to him perfectly and said he should see it for himself. There had been increasing cases of vandalism. Windows on government buildings had been smashed, and party officials had been harassed and threatened. But this was the first direct attack resulting in loss of life in the Gdansk Pomerania region of Northwest Poland. There had been attacks near Warsaw but that was over four-hundred kilometers to the southeast and Sokolov was troubled that violence was now in the region. But that was the reason why he was here.

His source described an act of violence so brutal it would stoke fear amongst the Polish militia and the security services. Their fear would lead to distrust and anger towards the local population. They would never know whom they could trust, and they'd turn their distrust and anger into retaliation and retribution. It was predictable. In Sokolov's mind it was a natural human reaction. He had seen it time and time again and had used distrust and anger to his advantage throughout his career.

Sokolov leaned forward from his seat in the rear of the vehicle, motioned to his driver, and said, "Pull over there. Over there on the right, next to that large tree," pointing to a fir that stood at the edge of the road.

There were two vehicles up ahead blocking the road, and he counted a group of six Polish militiamen moving through the trees on either side. A young officer, who looked not more than a teenager stood in the middle of the road and barked out orders to the men.

"Search among the trees," the officer yelled. "They can't have gone far."

Sokolov's driver slowly moved the vehicle to the side of the road next to the tree and waited for further instructions. The Russian looked around satisfied, and said to his driver, "I'm going to take a look around. Please turn the car around and wait for me. I won't be long."

"Yes, Comrade Colonel," the driver replied.

Sokolov opened the rear door on the driver's side and slid out of the vehicle and onto the road. He stood up, adjusted his belt, and pulled down on his uniform tunic, running his hands over it to smooth out any wrinkles. He slid his sidearm holster to a comfortable position on his right hip, and then reached up to adjust the wireframed spectacles that had slipped down his nose. He pulled out his soft field cap tucked into his belt and carefully put it on, cocking it to one side. He glanced down at his watch which bore the slogan, "Death to Spies" on its face. It was seven past nine in the morning. Then he took a deep breath, smelled the scent of pine and fir, and then slowly exhaled as he prepared himself for what he knew he would find.

Shutting the door behind him, he began his walk up the road. The gravel surface crunched under his heavy boots. The road was deeply rutted from the farm and forestry vehicles that used the road daily, and he had to raise his arms to his side, much like a high-wire artist in a circus, in order to balance himself and keep from falling.

He walked past the two militia vehicles and stopped to survey the scene directly ahead of him. Not more than ten meters in front of the vehicles lay the bodies of two militiamen. They were not moving and appeared to be dead.

He continued walking down the road and stopped just short of the first body. He squatted to take a closer look at the victim, a young man who couldn't have been more than eighteen or nineteen years old. His face was covered with blood, and the top of his head had been peeled back. His hair and a large flap of skin from his forehead and scalp lay on the road next to him, exposing the skull underneath. His body was still partially underneath the motorcycle he was riding, but his legs were bent into unnatural angles and appeared to have been broken when the machine skidded on the gravel road and fell atop him.

Sokolov stood up again and walked directly in front of the young man, looking down at him. He noticed other wounds. The first was a puncture wound to the man's neck. *How odd*, he thought. Then he saw there were two similar wounds on the man's chest, and they were easy to discern even though his uniform jacket was saturated with blood. He bent over the body to take a closer look at the wounds. *Incredible. This man's been stabbed! These wounds were made with a knife. A very sharp, double-edged knife*, he thought. The man had not been dead for very long. Sokolov had seen enough death to know how a body reacts. The wounds looked very fresh, and Sokolov estimated they were no more than thirty minutes old. *Killing with a knife*, he thought. *Now that is an especially cruel act. The person who did this wanted to inflict pain. Hmm.*

"Hey! You there! Stop! What are you doing there?" the young officer shouted in Polish as he turned around to see Sokolov standing over the body of his fallen comrade. He pulled out his weapon and shouted, "Step away! Raise your hands where I can see them," and then with his weapon drawn, he walked briskly towards Sokolov, breaking into a fast trot. "Raise your hands, I say," the Pole repeated. Sokolov eyed him calmly as the Pole approached, now running flat out.

Just like a dog who mistakes his master for an intruder, the Pole realized his error, but a little too late, finally recognizing Sokolov, a Lieutenant Colonel in the Soviet Army's Main Intelligence Directorate, or GRU. The young officer skidded to a stop, with gravel and dirt flying in his wake, and stood directly in front of Sokolov, panting from his sprint, his arm stretched out with the semi-automatic pistol in his hand pointed at the Russian's head.

"Kindly lower your weapon please," Sokolov said to the young officer, speaking to him in Polish, never taking his eyes off him or from the pistol in his hand as he looked him up and down, noticing how his ill-fitting uniform hung limply over his rail-thin body. *This boy is in deep water. He's in over his head,* he thought. *And someone needs to fatten this boy up or give him a smaller uniform.*

"I'm sorry Comrade Colonel," he stammered, as he attempted to speak in Russian while still pointing the weapon at Sokolov, until he finally slowly lowered it to his side. "I didn't know it was you. I didn't recognize you from a distance. I'm sorry and beg your pardon. We just arrived here, and . . ."

"Please speak in Polish. I understand and speak the language myself. I lived in Poland when I was younger," he added as he tried to calm the young officer. "Now, take a deep breath and tell me what happened here."

The officer holstered his weapon and took several long breaths in an effort to compose himself before he was able to continue. "We were chasing a group of suspected Home Army soldiers, the insurgents. Two of my men, these two here," he said, pointing to the dead men in the road. "They were in pursuit on their motorcycles. We were only a few minutes behind them, following them up the forest road and then we came upon this . . ." and his voice trailed off.

Sokolov looked over at the second man. As he stared at the man, he detected something terribly wrong he hadn't noticed before, but even from a distance, he immediately knew what had happened to him. The man was lying in the road only about five meters from where Sokolov stood. He saw the man's motorcycle further up the road on the right, lying on its side, crashed in a heap another ten meters from where the man lay.

Sokolov squinted through his glasses and looked carefully at the man in the road once again. He had seen this type of killing, an execution really, many times before, and immediately realized what was so terribly wrong. The man lying on the road up ahead was headless. Something or someone had decapitated him. Sokolov looked all around and finally his gaze turned to the right side of the road where he saw the man's head. It had rolled and had come to rest at the base of a small fir tree sapling. It sat upright, with a look of shock still apparent on its face.

The Russian had seen many men killed since he began his service during the Revolution with Stalin's secret police, and he was personally responsible for his fair share. Since 1941, he served alongside the Red Army, initially commanding an NKVD infantry battalion before accepting an appointment in 1945 as an officer within the newly formed GRU. He had fought against the German Army all the way from Moscow to Poland, and despite his personal history with death, and after seeing thousands of dead men on the field of battle, he was no longer bothered by it, but was constantly amazed, and never surprised, by the many ways men could find to kill other men.

Three years after the war with Germany ended, Sokolov was once again hunting counterrevolutionaries. But this time they weren't Trotskyites or rebellious members of the Red Army officer corps. Now his job was to hunt down and eradicate the last remnants of the Polish Home Army, an insurgent fighting force whose allegiance to the Polish government in-exile posed a direct threat to the Moscow-friendly, and Soviet-backed communist government in Warsaw.

"Lieutenant," he said turning his attention back to the Polish militia officer.

"Nawrocki, sir. Lieutenant Pawel Nawrocki, Polish Militia. Comrade Colonel, sir!"

"Lieutenant Nawrocki, please continue with your search of the area, but I don't think you'll find the perpetrators here. They are gone. So, I'm just going to look around for a bit if that is all right with you. I do not want to interfere with your work. But I do want you to know that you'll have all the necessary resources of my office to catch whoever did this. Anything you need. Do you understand?"

The Pole nodded.

"So, please carry on, and after I've looked around a bit, we can compare notes, so to speak. Is that acceptable to you?"

"Yes, Colonel. Of course. And I assure you we will catch whoever is responsible."

Sokolov paused for a moment and then said, "Yes, I'm sure you will." *This boy is so out of place. How did he rise to lieutenant so young?* He continued to look Nawrocki up and down when an idea came to him. "One more thing Lieutenant. If I may suggest, have your men look for spent shell casings. Most likely you would find them up the road a bit. If you and your men would kindly look up there," he said waving vaguely in the distance, "Search twenty, maybe twenty-five meters or so. Whoever did this would have set up a crossfire to create a killing zone. They would have positioned themselves on each side of the road. Any casings you find will help us determine how they were armed, and who they were, although I am sure it is as you say they were from the Home Army. And tell your men they are also looking for any evidence as to how long whoever did this was lying in wait. There might be cigarettes, discarded food items. Anything like that to give us some idea as to who and how many men, or women for that matter, were hiding here. Conduct your search, and have your men assemble back here with anything they have found in, shall we say, fifteen minutes? Do you understand?"

"Yes, Colonel. Completely." Sokolov's presence had taken Nawrocki by surprise, and he wondered how the Russian knew of the attack. *An informant*, he thought. *Or perhaps it was the district commander?*

"Good, now carry on please."

And with that the lieutenant saluted, turned, walked down the road about ten meters and called out, "Men, gather here. Quickly," pointing to a spot on the road where he wanted them to assemble.

Good, that will keep them occupied for a few minutes, Sokolov thought. They are so young, especially the lieutenant, he thought. They were boys during the war, and this is probably the first time they have seen such violence, he thought. Well, they all will have to learn quickly.

He then turned his attention away from the militiamen and directed it to the headless man in the road. *So, how did this happen here? How did they set this up?* he thought as he walked over to the headless man and stood next to the body. He stared at it for several minutes, all the while thinking, *there are no gunshot wounds. The head has been completely severed.* He noticed how the blood beneath the body had pooled up and then seeped into the road surface, creating a rust-colored tint. *This is obviously the spot on which he died.* He looked further up the road and saw the motorcycle, which lay crumpled on its side. He could see large divots in the road where the gravel had been torn up by the motorcycle. It apparently continued its journey along the road riderless, skidding out of control until it came to rest along the roadside.

Stepping over the body, he walked over to the motorcycle to inspect it more carefully, and he could see it was riddled with bullet holes, the frame, engine, and tires, all shot to pieces. Spent shell casings littered the forest floor around the motorcycle frame. He reached down to pick one up and examined it closely. It appeared to be a nine-millimeter casing, which would have been standard issue. He looked down at the forest floor and counted more than twenty spent casings. *Submachine gun. Standard weapon, probably the Blyskawica, or perhaps a Sten. Definitely Home Army,* he thought. *But there were no gunshot wounds on the man,* and once again he returned his gaze back toward to body. It was then that something else caught his eye. There was an object wrapped around and dangling from a large tree to his left, which stood directly across the road from the headless corpse.

Sokolov walked back up the road and as he got closer to the tree his suspicions were confirmed. He could see remnants of wire, cut hastily, but still dangling from the tree. *A taut wire trap*, he thought. Upon reaching the tree he could see two large nails had been driven into the tree on each side. The wire was still wrapped around the nail heads, but the rest of the wire itself had been cut and removed from the road after the damage had been done. He then looked at another large tree, this one directly across the road, and could see similar wire remnants still wrapped around the tree. He had a theory now, and he walked across the road to confirm it.

He inspected the tree carefully and saw the small harness and wooden block on the tree's far side. This device would allow a person to pull the wire taut across the road – wire that was intentionally strung at neck level. The wire was thin and virtually impossible to see when traveling at a high rate of speed. But it was deadly. Anyone traveling on a motorcycle or even within an open topped vehicle would be decapitated when they hit the wire. *Bastards*, he thought.

Sokolov surveyed the area immediately surrounding the tree. The undergrowth was trampled down, and he deduced the perpetrator had been waiting, knowing the militiamen on motorcycles were coming up the road. As he carefully scanned the area, he looked down to see if the perpetrator had left anything behind, anything at all that might provide a clue as to their identity. He looked down in the area directly behind the tree and something caught his eye. There was a brief glint, a flash of light, and about one meter behind the tree he saw what appeared to be a small, shiny object on the forest floor. It was nearly obscured by the dense growth, but the occasional ray of sunlight illuminated the object. He brushed aside the undergrowth and reached down to pick it up.

An earring? he thought as he held it in his hand. He raised the earring to his eye and inspected it more closely. *So, was our assassin a woman?* he wondered. This did not surprise Sokolov at all. His experience during the war taught him that women could kill as effectively as men. Slowly twirling it around with his fingers, he examined the earring's color and shape. It was a clip-on style of earring. *The killer may not have pierced ears*, he thought. A red flower, possibly made of a ruby, but more likely a red emerald, was affixed to the earring. Set in the center of the flower was a small diamond. It was a poppy, the national flower of Poland. Sokolov knew it would take considerable force to quickly raise the wire and make it taut across the roadway. Even though the wire was taut, the force from the impact of the rider would have jolted her, and the earring must have popped off as she held onto the harness. *She probably didn't even notice when it happened and then in the rush to leave the scene, it was left behind*, he thought.

Sokolov gave the earring one last look before placing it into the front pocket of his tunic. He turned once more to face the bodies lying in the road. He could now see the skid marks from the men's motorcycles, and it became perfectly clear to him. He knew exactly what happened on this isolated forest road.

"Lieutenant," he shouted. "Gather your men here."

Upon hearing Sokolov's shout, the Pole called for his men to follow him back up the road to where Sokolov stood. Within just a few minutes, the lieutenant and his militiamen stood in a semi-circle around the Russian, waiting for him to speak.

"Did you find anything, Lieutenant?" Sokolov asked.

"No sir, nothing. No spent casings. No food. No sign anyone was ever here. The men we were chasing, they appear to have vanished."

"So, you have no idea how many men might have been here, waiting, hiding?"

The Pole paused, swallowed, and said, "No sir. As I said, we didn't find anything up the road."

"Very well," Sokolov replied. "And tell me, how was it that you happened to pursue these men on this road? You said they were insurgents, Home Army soldiers. Is that correct?"

"We received a tip – an anonymous message in the form of a written note."

"I see. When did you receive this note and what did it say?"

"We received it early this morning. It was tacked on the station door, most likely before dawn. It said a group of insurgents were hiding in a barn on one of the newly formed collective farms outside of Puck. I radioed to Lukaszewicz," he said pointing to the headless man in road. "I told him to investigate the report, but not take any action until we arrived with our squad of men," he said pointing to the militiamen standing behind him. "I told him our squad would meet him in less than ten minutes. He was just to observe them. We were just a few minutes away when Lukaszewicz radioed to me again that a group of four insurgents had opened fire on him and on Officer Bankowski. That is him right there," pointing to the second man lying in the road. "He said after they opened fire, they left the barn in a small service vehicle. He reported that he was following them and had just turned up this forest road. I radioed back and said we would be there to support him as soon as possible. It took us approximately ten minutes to reach this location, and this . . . this is how we found them. They were . . . slaughtered."

Sokolov stood there, taking in the information the Pole had just given him. He thought for several seconds, considering what he had been told, analyzing the evidence from his own observations, and an image of what happened began to emerge in his mind's eye.

"I have a clear idea as to what happened here, Lieutenant. Well, let me explain. You also know what happened here. You can see it very clearly. But let me tell you how it happened and make a very educated guess as to why it happened. Would you like me to share my thoughts, Lieutenant?"

"Of course, Comrade Colonel. You have much more experience in these matters."

Sokolov gave the lieutenant a sad, ironic smile, and he nodded in agreement. "Yes, unfortunately I do have considerable experience," he replied. "So, here are my thoughts. It's just a working theory, mind you, but I think it will turn out to be an accurate depiction of the events as they transpired here. There was only one person here, it's possible there were two, but I think just one. And the person was waiting alongside that tree over there," Sokolov said, thrusting his arm out to point at the tree to his right where he had found the wire harness. "Do you see it?" he said a little louder this time to make sure the Pole and the militiamen could see the tree at which he was pointing.

"There is a device attached to it, an apparatus of sorts, and it is still hanging from that tree, you can still make it out from here, no?" Once again, he turned to the young Pole and to the militiamen to see if they were following along with him.

"Yes, I see it," the lieutenant replied, and the other men murmured their acknowledgment as well.

"On that tree, you will find a harness for a taut-wire trap," Sokolov continued. "Do you know what that is?"

The Pole swallowed hard, and shook his head no.

"In that case you will want to learn more about such traps, Lieutenant. They are very commonly used by terrorists and there was a person standing there, waiting in hiding behind that tree," he said emphatically. "This person was the lone accomplice to the Home Army soldiers your men were chasing. Your comrades on their motorcycles passed by the tree, this person pulled on the harness and a thin, but very sturdy strand of wire was pulled tautly across the road. The wire was positioned at neck level, and anyone, such as your men who were riding on motorcycles, when they hit the wire . . ." and then Sokolov quickly drew his hand across his throat, the universal sign of death by decapitation.

The militiamen murmured amongst themselves, their faces registered shock.

"It happened very quickly, Lieutenant," Sokolov continued, and the eyes of the assembled men grew wide, as if they were young children listening to a ghost story being told to them while sitting around a campfire in the dark of night. "At least for one of them."

"The first man here," Sokolov said pointing to his body, "What did you say his name was?"

"Officer Lukaszewicz, sir."

"Yes, Lukaszewicz. He was the first to hit the wire and he would have been killed instantly. The force of the impact with the wire sliced his head cleanly off, but the inertia from the speed of his motorcycle meant that it continued on up the road where it crashed. His body was thrown off the motorcycle from the force of hitting the wire, and I'm sure it tumbled a few times, until it came to land in the middle of the road while his head simply rolled off to the side and landed next to that small sapling."

Several of the militiamen closed their eyes, their heads hung low as Sokolov continued his story.

"Now the second man, you said his name was Bankowski? Is that correct?"

"Yes sir," replied the lieutenant, his face now pale.

"Well, he was following closely behind Lukaszewicz, and was probably no more than six or seven meters behind him. Therefore, he had a perfect view of what had happened to the poor bugger, and he could clearly see what was about to happen to him. So, he tried to duck his head. Perhaps he even tried to put his motorcycle into a slide to avoid the wire. But speed was his enemy too. He was traveling too fast to completely escape the wire. He was almost successful, but not quite. The wire clipped the top of his head, taking off part of his scalp," Sokolov said, pointing to the flap of scalp still lying in the road. "His motorcycle slid along the road, but he was trapped underneath it. But the wire, it didn't kill him. No. I believe the person hiding behind the tree did that. With both riders down, that person emerged from behind the tree and dispatched poor officer Bankowski, but very cruelly. He was probably still alive, although injured from his fall. As you can see, his legs are broken. But if you look closely at his wounds, you will be able to immediately see what happened to him. The person behind the tree dispatched him with a knife. Two punctures in his chest and one in his neck. This poor man? He didn't die so quickly. He slowly suffocated from the wound in his neck, choking on his own blood."

The lieutenant took a deep breath and looked as if he were going to be sick, but he regained his composure, reached into his trouser pocket to pull out a handkerchief, and wiped his face and forehead.

"Are you all right, Lieutenant?"

"Yes sir. I'm fine. It's just difficult . . ."

"Yes, I know it's difficult, but stay with me. Let me continue. Neither of us found any evidence that there was more than one person here. So, if there were others involved, they would have stopped their vehicle somewhere up the road and come back to the scene on foot. and shot up the motorcycle just for show and to render it useless. It's probably beyond repair. I found empty casings nearby and they definitely point to the Home Army. While they were doing this, the perpetrator cut the wire and removed it from the scene, and only left the harnesses behind. And then they all left the area together, climbed back into their vehicle and sped off. And there is one more thing," Sokolov said as he reached into his tunic pocket to pull out the earring he had found. "I found this item next to the tree over there. It's likely that a woman may have been the person behind the tree. And it is also likely it was this same woman who killed your comrades here today."

The militiamen stood in silence for several minutes, taking in all Sokolov had said.

Finally, the lieutenant spoke up. "A woman sir?" he asked softly.

"Yes, a woman. They are more than capable, I assure you, so make sure to write it up that way in your report, Lieutenant. That is how it happened. You are looking for a woman who is aiding these insurgents," Sokolov said as he placed the earring back into his pocket.

"Yes, Comrade Colonel."

Sokolov looked at the Pole, appraising him carefully. "I also said I could tell you why it happened Lieutenant. Would you like to know why this happened?"

"Of course, sir! Why do you think this happened?"

Sokolov paused for a moment to gather his thoughts. He wanted to select his words carefully. He knew the lieutenant and his men were young and inexperienced, but he also knew they needed to grow up quickly. There could be no time for coddling.

"This all happened because your house is a filthy mess, and you need to get your house in order Lieutenant."

"Sir? I, I don't understand," the Pole stammered with a bewildered look on his face.

"You were set up. This note you received. I do not know for certain, but I believe the same woman who murdered your men wrote the note. This was a trap. They planned to lure you up here and make an example of you. You're lucky only two men died here today," Sokolov said, his words hanging in the air in the now silent forest. Sokolov walked over to the Pole, put his arm around the young officer's shoulder, and led him away from the rest of his men. They took a half dozen steps together and then stopped. Sokolov turned to face the lieutenant and as he looked at him, he couldn't help but think, *He's just a boy too. He can't be more than twenty. But it is time for him to grow up. It's now or never.*

"You have to act, Lieutenant," Sokolov whispered. "You cannot be weak. Incidents like this are bad for morale, you see. This incident . . . you see it sets a very bad example, a terrible precedent. Something like this can and will encourage others, Lieutenant, and we do not want that to happen."

Sokolov paused and looked at the Pole directly in his eyes. "Something is rotten here. You have to find this woman and everyone else who is behind this. And make certain you clean up anything rotten in your own house, inside the militia. Trust no one. Insurrection is like a cancer. It has to be cut out to be destroyed. Do you understand?"

The Pole shook his head. "I'm not sure where to begin," he said, looking confused.

"You can begin by finding this woman. Even if it means rounding up everyone in the town. She is the key. Find her and eliminate her and eliminate everyone else who is helping her or who would even think of helping her. Round up everyone and do not stop questioning them until they give you the answers you want."

Sokolov paused, firmly grabbed the young lieutenant's shoulders, shook him, and spoke to him with a rapid staccato. "If you don't do it, I will do it for you." He let go of the lieutenant's shoulders, and he brought his arms back down to his side. "Do we understand each other?"

"Yes, Comrade Colonel," the Pole stammered.

Sokolov inched forward to where he stood chest to chest with Nawrocki. He was so close he could feel the heat from the lieutenant's body. "Good. I'm glad we have had this conversation, and we understand one another, Lieutenant. Fighting against enemies of the state is all new to you, but not to me. I've been at this since you were in diapers. I've seen this all many times before and I know how this will play out if you don't take action."

Sokolov abruptly turned and started to walk back to his staff car. He had taken barely a half-dozen steps when he stopped, turned around and called out once more to Nawrocki, "Lieutenant! This is the only time I will tell you. You are the one who needs to act. You don't want me involved; I assure you. If I have to get involved in this little insurrection of yours, I will do whatever is necessary to win. And I always win Lieutenant, no matter how many people have to die. Keep that in mind."

Chapter Two

And So, It Begins

Ada Bialik was lost in thought as she looked out the attic window onto the narrow footpath below. Even at this height and distance, she could see the path was worn from constant use. It was lined with wildflowers that swayed gently in the breeze of the warm, early autumn morning. She began to relax, a sense of calm washed over her, and her thoughts began to drift as she contemplated the scene below. She could see bees moving from blossom to blossom, gathering pollen and then flying off to their hive which sat at the edge of a large forest located about one hundred meters to the south of the cottage. As they moved off to return to the hive, they were replaced by another flight of bees. She closed her eyes and imagined how the bees repeated the process over and over, wave by wave, gathering pollen and taking it back to the hive to create honey.

She looked out onto the footpath and saw it connected to a narrow cart road that ran from east to west. She watched two farm workers from the collective walk along the cart path towards the fields directly to the north where they grew sugar beets. From her vantage point, she watched as a team of men and women in the field began to harvest the crop. It was a labor-intensive process where two big men wearing harnesses struggled to pull a plough through the rows in order to expose the roots of the plants. Normally, such a plough would be pulled by a team of horses or other draught animals, but the war took its toll on beasts of burden too. Mechanized farm equipment was also scarce, so manpower would have to suffice.

As the men toiled, a second group of workers followed closely behind to grab each sugar beet plant, pull it from the earth, shake the soil off the roots, and then lay out each plant into rows where a group of women following close behind used the sharp blade on their beet hooks to slice off the leaves and the tops of the roots, leaving only the beetroot behind. Finally, a second group of women picked up the individual roots and tossed them into a cart they were pulling.

Bialik watched in fascination as the workers slowly made their way up and down the rows of plants. *Who are these workers*, she thought? *Where did they come from*? She made a mental note to herself to visit with the workers, find out more about them, their habits, where they were from, and how they came to be here on this collective farm, all with the hope that she could trust and befriend at least one of them. *I will need a friend there*, she thought. *That is essential.* Looking out onto the farm she noticed a small building; it looked like a type of barn. *Hmm, that could be useful too,* and she made another mental note to investigate the barn and discover who had access to it and how often it was used.

It was a peaceful scene, but Bialik knew she could not allow herself to be distracted by it. *Focus,* she kept telling herself. *Remember why you are here*, she repeated to herself over and over. Her mind returned to her one desire, the single focus of her being that had driven her for more than three years since the war with Germany ended, and a new war took its place – revenge. Now that she had arrived in the town of Puck, she would finally be able to carry out her mission. She started to think about what she needed to do to put a plan into action but realized something had intruded into her thoughts. *Is that a voice I hear? Of course ... I am not alone.*

She thought she heard someone in the room speaking. It was a voice coming from behind from where she stood. It was a man's voice, and he seemed to be speaking to her, but she couldn't quite make out the words. She turned slowly and looked back across to the room's entrance. It gave her a start at first, but she quickly recognized the tall, gaunt man wearing an ill-fitting brown suit standing at the doorway at the far end of the room. She had been looking outside into the bright sunlight, and her eyes needed to adjust to the darkness, but slowly his figure came into focus, emerging from the shadows. She could see his lips moving, mouthing words, saying something to her. *What was he saying? Was it a question perhaps?* She blinked her eyes and took a deep breath. *Focus,* she thought. *Always pay attention to your surroundings.*

"It's a beautiful view, isn't it?" said the man as he stood in the doorway.

"Excuse me? What did you say?" His voice had startled her, but its sound helped bring her back into the moment, and she remembered that she wasn't alone at all. The man had been standing there all this time. "Oh, yes. Yes, it is quite beautiful," she answered as her mind processed his words.

"Your housemates will not arrive until next week, not for another three days," the man said. "But since you are here early, you can have your pick of any room in the house. The rooms downstairs on the first floor are more comfortable. It's so dark up here, even though we have electricity running again," he said looking up at a single bare bulb that hung in the middle of the loft. "This attic space also becomes very warm in the summer, and I fear too cold in the winter. Not to mention the kitchen and bath are also downstairs. Personally, I think you'll be more comfortable on the first level, don't you think?" he added.

Bialik looked around the space again and her gaze returned to the footpath below. The room was sparsely furnished, but it would be adequate for her. It was a long, rectangular room, with a small stove fireplace situated directly in the middle. There was a narrow bed near the door where the man stood, with bedding and blankets stacked neatly on top, and it was flanked by a small table with an oil lamp sitting upon it. There was a low dresser on Bialik's left, and a larger, tall wardrobe to her right. In the corner near to the window and exit door where she stood, was a table and two chairs. That space could also serve as her workplace, where she could read, write, and plan. An empty bookcase stood on the other wall, across from the table.

"Oh. No, thank you. This room suits me, I think," she replied. "I think it will be quieter up here. I can prepare the daily lessons over there," she said pointing to the table. "And I can see the farm and almost the entire town from here. It's a pleasant view," she said, pointing back to the end of the room, where two windows flanked a doorway which led to a set of stairs, constructed to provide egress from the house. *Probably some new Party rule. The stairs were new, recently added,* Bialik thought. *They were probably installed to comply with some new safety regulation the Party insisted on implementing,* she surmised. "It is a lovely view," she repeated. *The stairs make it easy for me to come and go as I please, without anyone seeing me. It's also a convenient escape route. It's important to have multiple ways to enter and exit,* she thought.

"Very well if that is what you wish, it is settled. You'll take this room," the man replied, watching Bialik carefully as she remained standing across the room from him. Housing came as a perk with her position, and she knew she was fortunate. Poland had been decimated by warfare since 1939, with nearly two-thirds of all houses destroyed, and even now, three years after the end of the war, homelessness was rampant, hunger was widespread, and people were still digging out from underneath the rubble. She didn't know what happened to the previous occupants of this cottage and didn't want to think about them. It would only anger her, and she knew she was quick to anger. She had to keep her head clear. *Focus on the mission,* she repeated to herself.

The man standing across from Bialik was Mateusz Kaczmarek who also held the official, but lengthy title of Deputy District Commissar for Education. He was the individual responsible for reestablishing primary education in Puck, and throughout the newly formed administrative district. He also served as headmaster of a new elementary school in town, Hero Ludwik Wiśniewski

Primary School, named for a local communist who was among the first to be rounded up and executed by the Germans in 1939. Kaczmarek personally selected Bialik from a list of applicants who recently completed the mandatory party training for teachers, a program designed not only to ensure compliance with rules and doctrine of the new regime, but to weed out anyone who might be disloyal. Loyalty, above all, was a trait prized most by Party leadership. After meeting Bialik, Kaczmarek walked away impressed by her calm demeanor and her dedication to learning and teaching.

The Germans and the Russians both had done their best to try to eradicate Polish culture during the war years, and that included all but dismantling the education system which, before the war, was one of the best of any nation in Europe. Reichsführer Himmler himself ordered that children be educated only to grade four. They should be able to write their name, but reading wasn't necessary. Counting to five hundred was the only arithmetic required. The primary role of education, according to Himmler's edict, was to foster honesty, politeness, and obedience to all Germans.

With the exception of selected trade and vocational schools, the Germans also abolished all forms of higher education in Poland for non-Germans. But that didn't stop resourceful Poles from continuing their studies. During the war, thousands of students, including Bialik, attended underground universities, where academics presented lectures in apartments and other secret meeting places, risking deportation and death, in order to continue their education and complete their studies.

"I knew the war wouldn't last forever, and I knew I would survive," Bialik told Kaczmarek at her interview where they first met. "So, I was willing to do anything necessary. I wanted to be ready for the day when the war ended. And I want to do my part to help Poland rebuild," she said, her green eyes blazing with intensity as she looked at Kaczmarek who sat across the table in a tiny office at the University of Warsaw. He was impressed with her determination, perseverance, and grit, knowing full well that she risked her life in order to complete her studies. *She is the kind of teacher who can inspire our children*, he thought as he concluded the interview with an offer of employment.

That was more than a month ago, and Bialik jumped at Kaczmarek's offer to teach Kindergarten beginning with the autumn term. Her students would be six-year-olds, attending school for the first time, mandatory for children of that age. It was their first step into Poland's resurrected compulsory primary education system, a system which would keep them occupied until they were at least eighteen. From there, they would either move onto university or attend a technical or vocational school which would give them the skills necessary to master a specific occupation or trade to begin their adult life.

Bialik turned away from Kaczmarek and returned to the window. She placed her hands on the two latches and pushed it open. The air inside was stale as the room hadn't been opened for months. She stuck her head outside and took a deep breath of fresh air and looked out onto the surrounding area. She felt the warm sun on her face.

"That's a good idea. Get some fresh air in here," Kaczmarek said. "I also have a few things for you. I have a temporary ration book." He walked over to stand next to Bialik. He held a small booklet in his hand and handed it to her. She looked down at the tiny, brown booklet, with food items such as bread, flour, sugar, and salt, along with the rationed amount, written in blue ink. She ran her fingers over the official stamp on the cover.

"You can pick up your permanent book next week at our school office. We can issue it to you on Monday, but this will allow you to pick up a few items. We don't want you starving before school starts," he added with a smile. "Oh, and I have this for you. It isn't much, but it will help carry you through," he said reaching down onto the floor to pick up the small basket he had carried with him.

"There is some coffee. Real coffee. Don't ask me where I got it. You don't want to know," he said softly, but with a sly smile. "And there is some sugar, flour, and salt. It's just enough to get you started," he added as he rummaged through the basket. "There is a small amount of soap," he said, picking up a small bar of homemade soap wrapped in a cloth. "It's not very elegant, but my wife thought you would appreciate it. Oh, and here are a few fresh eggs. I collected them this morning. My wife and I have a few chickens and they've just started to produce for us."

"Oh, my goodness. This is too much," Bialik exclaimed. "I can't even remember the last time I had an egg. And coffee! This is extremely kind of you." Bialik looked at the bounty contained in the basket. "I know how difficult it is . . ." she said as her voice trailed off. "Food is scarce," she said but Kaczmarek immediately interrupted her.

"No, we mustn't talk about shortages and about what we don't have. We survived a war," he said emphatically. "It is also not as bad here as it is in the cities. Here in the country, we can grow food. Besides, the only way we will be successful is if we put the war behind us and work together. That means sharing what we have with each other. We have a chance to create a new Poland and you will play a vital part in that effort, Comrade Bialik. It starts with educating the children of Poland and you will be their first teacher. I know you understand how important that is."

"Yes, I do," she said as she closed the window and walked back into the center of the room. "Thank you, comrade. I take my duties very seriously and I promise you, I shall not disappoint you," she replied, immediately wondering whether she would be able to live up to such a promise.

"I know you won't," Kaczmarek replied. "Alright, I shall leave you to it," he said as he moved towards the door to leave. "Is there anything else I can help you with?" he asked. Bialik watched as he stared at the three suitcases that contained everything she owned. Was it her imagination or was he particularly curious about the red suitcase? She didn't want him to touch it and had insisted on carrying it up the stairs to the attic herself, while he carried the other two. She wondered if she had inadvertently drawn too much attention to it.

"No, thank you," Bialik replied. Now all she wanted was for Kaczmarek to leave. "I can manage fine. You've been very kind. Thank you."

Kaczmarek looked at her and nodded. She noticed how his gaze seemed to linger on the red suitcase, but he finally moved towards the doorway and then abruptly stopped. *Now what*, she thought.

He turned and said, "Oh, I almost forgot. My wife asked me to invite you for supper this Sunday. Six o'clock. I presume that will be acceptable for you?"

"Sunday? At six o'clock? Why yes, that would be wonderful," Bialik replied. "I look forward to it. Thank you again." *Now, please go,* she thought.

Kaczmarek turned once again to leave when Bialik called out to him.

"Comrade excuse me. But where do you live?"

"Of course, how forgetful of me," he laughed, shaking his head at his own absent-mindedness. "I live just a ten-minute walk from here. Let me show you," he said, and he strode back across to the far end of the room, opened the door, and stepped out onto the small landing.

"Come, here. Let me point it out to you. You know where the school is, do you not?" Bialik nodded her head yes. "Well, I live in a small house directly across the street from the schoolhouse. If you take the path to the road there," he said pointing to the farm road, "You see it, yes? Take that road and head east, that is to your right. The farm road connects to the main road leading into Puck. Once you reach the main road, turn right, and stay on it. The school and my cottage are just a short walk away, no more than ten minutes. You'll be able to find it, I am sure. If you have difficulties, just ask anyone in town. Everyone knows who I am," he added.

"Thank you, Comrade," Bialik replied. "I am certain I will be able to find it. And thank you again for your invitation. It is very kind of you and your wife. And for all of this too," she said pointing to the basket filled with food and staples.

"I look forward to getting to know you, and all of the new teachers," Kaczmarek replied. "I'll see you Sunday at 6pm sharp. I will leave your key to the house on the hook by the door downstairs. Make sure you lock up at night and whenever you leave. It's relatively safe in our district. The militia does an excellent job of patrolling, but you should still be on your guard. Now, I must be off," he said, nodding his head to Bialik as he exited, closing the attic door behind him.

Bialik watched Kaczmarek depart and listened to his footsteps as he descended the stairs. She could hear him close the door downstairs and she knew she was now alone. It was time for her to get to work. She had much to do.

***

Bialik spent the rest of her morning unpacking and organizing her belongings. During a time when such items were scarce, she had managed to accumulate clothing on the black market. Her wardrobe, which consisted of four dresses, five blouses, three skirts, one navy, one brown, the other a dark green, a sweater, and a light blue winter coat all fit in the smallest case. A second, and larger suitcase case held her underwear, socks, makeup, and a few toiletry items. But it also contained a dark blue turtleneck sweater, work trousers, a military-style field jacket with liner, and a pair of heavy boots that were also packed inside. She always told people she enjoyed hiking and walking in the forest, foraging for mushrooms, or other wild edibles that could supplement a wartime diet. It was an answer that always seemed to suffice whenever she was questioned about her need for such heavy clothing.

On the inside of the second case, tucked into a zippered pouch, were a notebook, several pencils in need of sharpening, and a single book, a rare first edition of *Quo Vadis: A Narrative of the Time of Nero* by Henryk Sienkiewicz, published in 1896. She had one copy and hoped that the second copy of the very same first edition was still in safe hands. She felt the book's heft as she held it in her hand, its pages dog-eared from use and its spine partially cracked.

Bialik could still vividly recall the last time she had opened the book. It was more than three years ago when she was instructed by her handler, the woman who recruited her, to go underground and remain in hiding. At their final meeting, the woman who went by the name of Felicja Nowak told her, "Go to ground and stay out of sight. You must live to fight again on another day." She was instructed to make contact when she was absolutely certain she was safe and not under surveillance and initiate that contact at a specific time during the early morning hours.

Later today, most likely in the late afternoon, she would have reason to open the book once more. And that would set everything into motion. So, in preparation for the task to come, she gathered up the book, the pencils, and her notebook and placed the items in a neat pile on the table near the window.

She carefully hung all her clothing in the tall wardrobe. There was ample room. She then unpacked her remaining personal items, first unfolding and then carefully refolding her underwear, socks, and other smaller items which she then placed in the drawers of the small dresser.

The only items that remained were her toiletries, and she removed them from her suitcase and placed them on the small nightstand next to her bed, sliding the oil lamp over to make room. She picked up the small handmade bar of soap Kaczmarek gave her earlier. It was still wrapped in a thin cloth, and she lifted it to her nose. It smelled of lavender and perhaps even rosemary and she was filled with gratitude for this gift. She longed for some proper shampoo but reckoned she would have to do without for quite some time.

With all of her clothing and personal items now in place, she slid the two empty suitcases underneath her bed to store them. She could now turn her attention to the third suitcase, the case that piqued Kaczmarek's curiosity when she carried it up the steps into the attic. She decided it should go on the bottom shelf of the wardrobe, but quickly discovered it was too large to fit inside. So instead, she decided to slide it underneath her bed. As she moved it to the bed, she looked down at it and noticed how the red leather had faded. The case now bore deep scratches and gouges from years of heavy use. She decided to cover it up with two extra blankets she had found on her bed. *This will have to do for now. At least it is out of sight. It's the best I can do, but I must find a more secure location as soon as possible*, she thought.

Closing the wardrobe, she turned to look around at her living space. *My new home. At least for now.*

The only thing left for her to do was store the food items from the basket Kaczmarek had left with her. She grabbed the basket, took it downstairs, and stored everything in the small pantry located next to the kitchen. She figured once her roommates arrived, she would work out with them how they would all share their rations. *At least we'll all have ration cards*, she thought. *Hopefully, we'll be able to pool our resources.* Hopefully.

Finished, she thought. *Now what?* She looked down at the watch on her wrist. The watch and a pair of earrings were the only keepsakes she had left to remember her mother. She ran her index finger around the bezel, set with small European cut diamonds, with rubies at twelve, three, six, and nine. She tried to remember everything she could about her mother. But the more she tried, the more difficult it became to remember the sound of her voice, the color of her eyes and hair, her scent, the softness of her skin.

She recalled the last time she saw her mother. Bialik was about to escape into the tunnels beneath the Warsaw Ghetto and her mother had volunteered to stay behind to cover her retreat and that of other insurgents fighting the Germans. Her mother's last words to her were, "Trust your instincts." Bialik turned to leave and just as she was about to disappear into the darkness, she turned back one last time and saw her mother mouth the words, "I love you."

But now, the harder she tried to remember, the more elusive the memories seemed to be. It had been too long. This was both a blessing and a curse. As her mind flashed to her mother, she tried to imagine her, standing before her, but now with the watch around her wrist. The image began to fade as Bialik recalled how she had sold everything else that had belonged to her mother on the black market, including several rings, two pairs of diamond earrings, and her mother's heavy winter coat. It was the only way she could survive.

She sighed and just let the memories go. They were too sad. She checked the time once again, and the delicate hands of her watch, painted with radium that glowed in the dimly lit room, displayed 11:45. Bialik decided she should walk to the market in Puck to pick up a few additional items. She wanted to use her new ration card and the trip into town might also give her a chance to locate Kaczmarek's house and help orient her to her new surroundings. She saw the key hanging from a small hook next to the door, just as Kaczmarek had said. She grabbed it along with the now empty basket he had left with her, and she exited the cottage, but held the door open before closing and locking it. She wanted to test the key first. It worked, without difficulty, so Bialik closed and locked the door, jiggling on the door handle to ensure it was actually locked tight, and headed off for town.

Bialik walked briskly, but despite her pace, the trip took her just over twenty minutes, longer than Kaczmarek said it would take. *No matter*, she thought. *Now I know*. By the time she arrived, it was almost a quarter past noon. Her brow glistened with sweat, and she dabbed her forehead with the cloth handkerchief she always carried in her pocket.

She wanted to get to the market before it closed so she headed in the direction where she thought it to be. She stopped along the way to ask directions. and confirmed she was on the correct path. She walked past the 13th century Gothic Church of Saints Peter and Paul and marveled at how the structure seemed to survive the war completely intact. Finally, after walking another ten minutes, she came upon the municipal market, and she was pleasantly surprised by what she found.

Bialik saw rows of vendors, and she entered the market square and began to walk up and down each row, looking at all the items for sale. She saw how some vendors had simply stacked crates of fruits and vegetables and sat in front of their goods on crates tipped over on their side. Some had brought their goods to market in wagons and dropped the wagon gates to display their products. Others stood behind tables they had set up, with selected items laid out on the tabletops while the bulk of their inventory remained stacked behind them. A few enterprising individuals had gone to the trouble of erecting multicolored canopies made from scraps of whatever material they could find, which created a festive look. In all, the market was surprisingly well stocked with vegetables, mainly cabbage, carrots, and potatoes. There was no meat, but she had been able to survive with far less. *Kaczmarek was right. It is better here than in Warsaw.*

She stopped in front of a small stand selling produce, and upon looking it over she decided this would be where she would make her purchase. A woman, Bialik judged her to be in her seventies, watched carefully as she looked over and selected a few vegetables to take back with her. She placed a small head of cabbage, some carrots, and a few potatoes into her basket. The woman continued to stare at her, but Bialik simply smiled. She decided to take a friendly approach. *No sense making enemies on my first day.*

"I'll have to weigh everything. And I'll need your ration card," she said to Bialik, looking her up and down. "I don't know you. You are new here."

"Yes, I just arrived very early this morning," Bialik replied cheerfully. "On the 6:00 a.m. train from Warsaw. I'm a kindergarten teacher at the new primary school."

"Ah, the old German school," the woman said, her face hardening a little more.

"It's now named Hero Ludwik Wiśniewski Primary School."

"Hmm. Yes, so we've heard," she replied and started to weigh out the produce Bialik had selected. "He wasn't a hero, you know."

"What? Who?"

"The Wiśniewski boy. He wasn't a hero. He was a troublemaker, but I don't suppose he deserved what he got from the Germans," the woman replied. "They strung him up. But they did that with almost everyone in Puck when they first came here. So, by that standard, everyone was a hero and should have a building named after them."

As she listened to the woman, Bialik absent-mindedly fumbled with the coins in her purse, rolling them around with her fingers. "You must be from here. You lived here during the war?" she asked, as the woman carefully weighed the vegetables and placed them back into Bialik's basket.

"Yes, I'm from here. I was born here, and I've lived here all my life, including during the war. The Germans killed my husband and two of my sons. They didn't get me though, or my youngest boy, but now the Russians have him. And then communists took my farm. There are other people working on it, living on it now. And you, you're a teacher you say? Well, you are living in the cottage that my husband built by hand. He built it for my son and his wife. But they're both dead now. The communists took that from me too. They said I no longer needed it, and they would put it to good use. I hope you'll enjoy living there," the old woman said, with a mixture of contempt and sadness.

Bialik stood silent in front of the woman. *So, now I know who once owned the farm and cottage. And I now know what happened to them.* "I am very sorry for your loss and for everything you have had to endure, Mrs. . . . what is your name? I'm Ada. Ada Bialik, and I hope that we can be friends. I'm just trying to do what we all are trying to do now. Live."

The woman said nothing and gave Bialik a cold stare.

"How much do I owe you for the vegetables?" Bialik asked, not knowing what else to say.

"Twelve zloty."

Bialik carefully counted out the coins in her purse and handed the woman the correct amount. The woman glared at her and then took her money without counting it.

Bialik returned the woman's stare until she realized there was nothing more that could be said other than, "Goodbye. I hope to see you again soon," and she turned and began to walk back to the cottage.

She had only taken a few steps when the woman called out to her, "Zajac. That is my name. Ela Zajac," she said.

Bialik turned back to face the woman and smiled. "It's a pleasure to meet you Mrs. Zajac. I hope to see you again soon. And I meant what I said. I hope we can be friends."

The Polish woman nodded her head but said nothing. Bialik gave her a wave, turned, and hurried home.

***

After she stored the goods from the market in the pantry, she grabbed a small paring knife from the kitchen and then went upstairs to her loft. She sat down at her table and set about sharpening the four pencils lying in front of her. The paring knife, although not terribly sharp, was sufficient for the task. Bialik patiently sliced off the dull ends from her pencils, carving away at the wood to expose the lead, and forming each pencil into a sharp point, a task that took her less than ten minutes. Inspecting her work, she was satisfied. Each pencil was now sufficiently sharp, and she would be able to write with them.

She reached across the table for her notebook, opened it to a blank page and began to write a message she would transmit in the early morning hours after midnight. It would be the first time in years that she had communicated with her handler, so she wanted to keep it brief. Operational security demanded it regardless. She knew any communication from her would create alarm. Was the message authentic? Was it really her? Had she been compromised and was she under the control of enemy security services? She knew she was about to set off a firestorm.

She stuck to the basics, not wanting to give away too much information in the body of her message. She would not reveal, for example, her precise location. Not yet. Her reticence was born out of concern for her own safety and security, and in the end, her brief message contained a scant twenty-nine words. Bialik put down her pencil and read her completed work. *Good,* she thought. *This will be enough for now.* And then, she started to encode her words into a seemingly random set of numbers, using an Ottendorf cipher, the way her handler had taught her to do it.

She worked slowly, ensuring each character in her message corresponded to either a specific page number, a word number, or letter number contained in her cipher key, her very rare first edition copy of Quo Vadis. In order to decode the message, the individual on the receiving end would need to possess an identical copy of the book, another copy of a very rare first edition of Quo Vadis. She completed her work and then checked it. She checked it three times to ensure that it was correct. Satisfied, she closed her notebook, picked it up along with her book and placed the items on the bookshelf on the other side of the room.

Later that night, after a dinner of a single egg that she fried up along with a single potato and a bit of cabbage, Bialik decided to prepare for bed. It was still early in the evening, only about 8 o'clock, and the sun would be setting soon. But the sky was clear, so she knew twilight would last for another two hours, and the moon would be full tonight. She also knew she had to be rested for the task ahead of her, so she decided to close her eyes for just a bit, to rest and calm herself. Ever the light sleeper, Bialik knew she would be able to wake herself up after a few hours. She would not sleep until dawn. Not tonight. There was too much at stake.

After washing her face and cleaning her teeth in the small bath downstairs, she returned to her loft. She decided against changing into her night clothes. It was an old habit, and it was inconceivable for her to do what she needed done if she had dressed for bed. Instinctively, she had to be ready for anything, and bedclothes would not do. Instead, she sat for several minutes on her bed, brushing her hair, thinking about what she was about to unleash. Brushing her hair was a small act of normalcy during a time when nothing could be considered normal. And then she remembered she had forgotten to do something very important. She got up and walked to the door and latched it shut, locking it from the inside. She then returned to bed, and she turned down the covers and wearing the clothes she had worn all day, she slipped underneath. Within minutes, she was asleep.

***

Bialik was awakened by the light from the full moon as it shone through the window, brightly illuminating the room, and casting long shadows. It was so bright, she first thought she must have slept through the night until morning. She moved her wrist close to her face so she could see her watch. The dial read 2:30, the beginning of the two-hour window she had to accomplish her task based on her handler's instructions. It was time.

Slipping out of her bed, she knelt down alongside it and slid the heavy red suitcase out from underneath. Tossing the blankets covering it aside, she picked up the case and carried it to the table, where she let it fall down with a dull thud. And then she opened the case to reveal the contents inside.

Everything was neatly in place, exactly as she remembered it, exactly as she had placed it years before. She pulled out the long wire aerial, wrapped tightly in a coil and unwound it. Using nails that had protruded from the rough beams, she carefully strung the aerial across the ceiling, making her way over to the window. It took her several minutes to extend the wire to its required twenty-five feet. During the war, attaching the aerial was the most time-consuming task and was one of the reasons why life expectancy of wireless operators was so short. She was out of practice, but she finally had the aerial properly in place, and then she connected the receiver's ground wire to the metal stove in the center of the room. She reached back into the case and pulled out the six-volt battery pack, plugged it in and powered on the set.

Reaching into the case, she pulled out her headset and put it on over her ears. She then connected the transmitter keypad, selected the proper crystal for the transmit frequency and flipped the switch to 'send.' She could hear the white noise, the hiss, pop, and static as she tuned the set to the frequency she knew would be monitored. Satisfied that she was ready, she pulled off her headset and walked over to the small bookcase on the other side of the room where she pulled out the notebook containing the message she had encoded. She returned to the table, pulled up her chair, donned her headset one more time, took a very long, deep breath, and began transmitting.

Tap, tap, tap, tap, tap, the sound of the keypad striking filled the room as she transmitted her message, three times in rapid succession, using Morse code. Although it had been years since she last operated her wireless, and she felt a bit rusty, it all came back to her very quickly. She felt alive.

Chapter Three

Tap, Tap, Tap, a Voice from the Past

Nine hundred miles away, at a remote, wireless intercept station located just outside the small hamlet of Poundon in Buckinghamshire, England, a sleepy radio operator bolted upright when she heard the first few beeps, the unmistakable sound of manual Morse code being tapped out and transmitted over the air. She immediately turned on her tape recorder. She had started her shift over three hours ago, and was sitting at her workstation, bored stiff as she scanned her assigned frequencies over and over, starting at the bottom of the frequency range and going to the top, and then returning to the bottom and scanning to the top all over again, and again, and again. She was waiting for something to happen, waiting for anything to happen, wanting desperately for someone, anyone to talk to her. She listened intently to the transmission, and she was shocked at what she heard. The operator instantly recognized who was behind the transmission. She immediately recognized the sender's 'fist,' the idiosyncrasies in the way a sender transmitted code as distinctive as a speaker's voice, or a fingerprint. She began to transcribe the message, carefully copying down every digit, exactly as it was transmitted.

The transmission lasted for only four minutes. The sender repeated the message three times, and after the operator heard the sign off, she rewound her tape, and she carefully listened to the recording while checking the accuracy of her transcript. Satisfied she had correctly transcribed the message, she ripped the thin paper from her copy book, got up from her position, and walked up to the shift supervisor, who sat overlooking the long bay of other radio intercept operators, each of them quietly going about their work.

"Ma'am, this just came in. I just checked it for accuracy, and I thought you should see it at once."

The supervisor looked up from her desk. She was busy reviewing other agent transmission transcripts, highlighting sections that she would use to create her evening summary report. "So, what is this?"

"It's Lygia," the operator replied.

The supervisor's face registered shock, she shook her head in disbelief, and she immediately dropped everything she was doing to look over the message in her hand. "Lygia? That can't be possible. How . . . are you sure?"

"Yes. I am as sure as I can be. I recognized the sender's fist immediately. It's been years, I know. But it's something you don't forget. And all the markers are there, the sender inverted specific characters, just as always. On purpose. Deliberately. I've noted it all on the transcript. It all points to Lygia. I am absolutely certain of that."

The supervisor's thoughts raced as she looked over the transcript in her hand. "This will have to be decoded. And although I'm sure you've transcribed it correctly; it will need to be checked. Bring me the tape please. And your copy book. I'll need your complete book. You can start another."

"Yes ma'am," the operator said. "What do you think it means ma'am?"

"It's not our job to worry about what it might mean. There are others who get paid to concern themselves with that."

"Yes ma'am. I'll fetch the tape and my book and bring them to you directly."

***

Alicia Betancourt was already seated on the leather sofa in James Banbury's office when he walked in shortly after 8:00 a.m. He shot her a surprised look, but in reality, Betancourt often started her day sitting there, waiting for him to arrive, so she could call his attention to some matter that required his immediate action.

This morning was a little different though, because she had arranged with the service mess to deliver a large pot of coffee, and the shiny polished silver carafe, along with two cups, saucers, spoons, and fresh cream and sugar, which were neatly set up on a table in front of his desk. It was all there waiting for him, hence the surprised look on his face. He knew something was up.

It was barely six months ago when Banbury had been promoted to director of the Northern Department in Britain's Secret Intelligence Service, MI6. Betancourt was in charge of the Baltic Section, and she also served as his number two. They had known each other for years, serving together within the Special Operations Executive during the war and now in MI6. They often joked they were "work spouses," and even their respective real spouses would laugh at the joke.

"You're here awfully early Alicia, but I'm happy to see you didn't come empty-handed, so I thank you for all of this," he quipped, eyeing the coffee service set up on the table. "How did you know? Mary and I were out too late last night at the theater."

"I didn't know, and I'd have poured you a whiskey, but I thought it was a bit too early. Well, perhaps not for you," she said, "but definitely for me," which caused Banbury to raise an eyebrow as he looked over at her. He hung up his topcoat and tossed his Trilby on the shelf of the small closet next to his desk. Closing the door, he sat down in his chair and pulled it forward and looked at Betancourt with a worried look.

"That sounds ominous. What do you have for me? Is everything alright?"

"That depends on your outlook on life. Are you an optimist or a pessimist? Do you believe in the new world we have created, or would you prefer to blow it apart and start all over?" Betancourt replied. She tossed a folder marked "Most Secret" onto his desk and it landed on the blotter in front of him.

"What's this?"

"Read it, and I'll pour you a coffee. You still may want to fortify it with a spot of whiskey though."

Banbury sat down at his desk, opened the file, and began to read. Betancourt set a cup of steaming coffee, with two sugars and a splash of cream, on his desk. As he read, his face clouded. The document was only a single page, so he quickly read it, and then he re-read it to make sure he fully comprehended its meaning.

"When did this come in?" He reached for coffee in front of him and raised the cup to his lips, taking a sip.

"Early this morning, shortly after 2 a.m., London time. There's a one-hour time difference of course."

"And who transcribed this?"

"Alma. Alma Westcott, sir."

"That's a stroke of luck. She's been on this since forty-four. Who was the supervisor on duty last night?"

"That would have been Pierce sir, Wendy Pierce. We can trust both of them," Betancourt said, anticipating what he was about to ask next.

"Yes. I suppose we'll have to. We don't have a choice, do we? But instruct them that no one else is to see any of these transcripts."

"Already done sir."

"Good. And who decoded this?"

"I did. It was coded using a book cipher, from a special first edition, of which there are only two known copies. I have one, although it took quite some time to find it this morning. It hasn't been used in years. I also have the tape and the operator's original copybook. The transcript was sent via radioteletype. Everything else arrived via courier this morning. I've left instructions to hand deliver any future transcripts and tapes to me, and only to me. Nothing is to be transmitted via radioteletype."

"What about our friends in GCHQ? Is it possible they also intercepted this message?"

"It's possible," Betancourt replied, "But I think it is doubtful. The frequencies we use, and the frequency Lygia used last night, are not normally monitored by them. And they've allowed us to keep our own intercept sites, knowing full well that we operate on our side of the street, and they, on theirs."

Banbury nodded his head in approval. "Make some discreet inquiries, nevertheless. I want this kept tight, close to our vest. We may need to bring them in at some point, but not now. And when is our reply due?" He asked, but he already knew the answer.

"We have twenty-four hours from time of receipt, sir. And the clock is ticking."

Banbury sat back into his chair and let out a long sigh, "Right. Very well."

They sat in silence for the next few minutes, sipping their coffee. Finally, Betancourt broke the quiet and said, "What shall we do next Colonel?" using Banbury's military title, his preferred form of address.

"The first thing you and I shall do is reply to this message. I want it sent out tonight by Pierce and Westcott. They are the only two to be briefed on this. No one else at the Poundon site is to touch this. At least for now. Understood?"

"Completely. And what's the second thing?"

"Tell your husband Edward he'll have to dine at his club tonight. You and I are taking a trip to Germany, so grab your emergency travel kit. I want to be in the air before midday."

"Germany? What on earth for?" she asked.

"We need to meet with Luba Haas."

Chapter Four

Into the Fog

The Polish officers acknowledged Sokolov with a nod when he entered the interrogation room. The room had no furnishings except for two chairs. Its walls were bare. There were no windows, and the only light came from two lamps which hung from the ceiling. It was one of a half-dozen similar rooms located inside a large rectangular warehouse which stood just a few blocks from the quay in Puck. On the outside, the building looked like any other warehouse. What was on the inside, however, made it very different.

Originally intended to store finished lumber products, the Polish Department of Security, the *Urząd Bezpieczeństwa* or UB had other ideas for it. They decided it should serve as its local headquarters, interrogation center, and prison.

"So, what has he told you? What does he have to say for himself?" Sokolov asked the senior officer as he looked at a man who was probably in his early twenties seated in a straight-back chair. His arms were tied behind his back and his legs bound tightly to each leg of the chair. His head had fallen forward. He was now unconscious, a state brought on by the relentless beatings he had received over the past two days since he was brought in for questioning by the UB. His eyes were black and blue, and swollen completely shut, his face was misshapen and bloody, and blood trickled down from the corners of his mouth, and from his nose, staining the front of his shirt.

The UB worked in teams of three. There was a senior officer, who acted as lead interrogator, and two other junior officers who acted as enforcers. When a prisoner refused to answer a question, or didn't answer a question truthfully or satisfactorily, the enforcers would inflict stronger measures, starting with slaps to the face, punches to the gut and kidneys, and always escalating to full-scale beatings.

"He works on one of the new collective farms near Puck," replied the senior UB officer. The two other officers stood on either side of the seated man. They were still breathing heavily, each of them had been taking turns working over the poor, helpless sod seated in the chair. They were taking a break, and rubbed their leather-gloved hands, which were painful and sore from pounding the man senseless.

"His fellow workers turned him over to us. They told us they saw him talking to a man in uniform, a soldier, last week. They yelled at the soldier, told him to keep away from the farm, they wanted nothing to do with him. But a few days later they saw him again. The same soldier came back and was seen talking to our friend here," he said pointing to the man in the chair. "His job was to maintain the equipment stored in the barn, and make sure the barn was locked up every night. He was the only one with a key to the lock on the barn doors. So, it had to be him. He is the man who gave aid to the Home Army. He is the one who hid the insurgents in the barn, gave them refuge there."

"And why him? Why would he do this? Did he give you any reason as to why he would want to do this?"

"He said his older brother fought with the Home Army against the Germans. He died in forty-four, in Warsaw."

Sokolov nodded. He understood the man's motivation. He recalled how when he served outside Warsaw in August 1944, the Polish underground in the form of the Home Army, had mounted an offensive to wrest Poland's capital from German control. It was the largest operation ever mounted by any resistance group during the war, and they were counting on help from Allied forces. But the Russian Red Army halted its advance from the East and refused to enter the city, allegedly on orders from Stalin himself. Stalin wanted the Polish Committee of National Liberation to form a government in Poland loyal to him. So, he allowed the Poles to slug it out against the Wehrmacht for over sixty days on their own, and they were eventually crushed by the German counteroffensive, destroying the city of Warsaw in the process.

"Did he give you names of any others?" Sokolov asked. "Was he working with anyone else? Who else is still out there?"

"He said there were four Home Army soldiers, but he didn't ask their names. He said he didn't want to know who they were. And he wouldn't tell us anything else. He claimed he knew nothing else. He said all he wanted to do was to help them, and said he was working alone. So, we had to use – stronger measures," he said pointing to the two UB officers. "But he has refused to talk and give us anything more. He insists he acted alone. He said he was approached by a single Home Army soldier asking for help, and he helped him because he hoped someone would have helped his brother. He said that is why he let them hide in the barn."

"He confirmed there were four," Sokolov said. "Were they all men? Were any of the four in the barn women? Was there a woman with them?"

"He hasn't said anything about a woman. He did confirm there were four and that's all we know. At least for now. That's also what the militia reported. They reported they were chasing four insurgents, but there was no mention of a woman being among them."

"And what about your so-called 'informant' at the collective?' Have you questioned him?"

"We didn't need to. He is the farm manager. He reported to us that his workers saw soldiers, insurgents in the area."

"He informed you prior to the attack? You had knowledge of the attack? Did you notify the militia about this?"

There was a long, uncomfortable pause until the Polish officer replied, "No. We did not."

Sokolov glared at the UB officer. "You didn't tell the militia about this?"

"No Comrade Colonel. It was an oversight on our part. We've taken steps to ensure it doesn't happen again."

"Hmm," Sokolov scoffed. "What about the note. The so-called, 'anonymous tip?' Do you have it?"

"Yes, the note was left in the early morning hours before dawn. Here it is," the UB officer said as he picked up a torn sheet of paper from his desk and handed it to Sokolov. "It simply says, 'Home Army soldiers hiding in the barn on the Dubinsky Collective.' That's all it says."

Sokolov stared down at the handwritten note. It was written in neat, block letters, written the way a child might when practicing penmanship. He considered it for a minute and then tossed it back onto the desk. "If you haven't already done so, question the militia," he said. "And make sure you question that Lieutenant. What's his name? Nawrocki? Was it him who found the note?"

"Yes, Colonel. We'll question him today, but he is well known and connected in the community. His record is unblemished."

"I don't care who he knows or what he's done in the past. It's all too convenient, it's too easy. The militia receives an anonymous note. From whom? As a result of this note, the militia sends out a team of men and two of them are now dead. Interview everyone in that station house if you have to. Someone must have seen something."

"Yes, Comrade Colonel. We will keep at it."

Sokolov glared at the officer and said, "And what measures have you taken to correct the communication problem between the UB and Militia?"

"The officers, the individuals responsible have been reassigned to other duties."

"Hmm, I can only imagine," Sokolov scoffed. "And what about this one?" he added, nodding his head at the man in the chair. "Does he have a name?"

"Lewandowski. Jan Lewandowski. He has lived in the area his entire life. His parents still live here."

"Have you rounded them up? His parents? Any other siblings or relatives in the area?"

"Yes, we have them, and they are being questioned now. It's just his mother and father. They own a small shop in Puck. His father is a cobbler, repairs shoes. His mother is a seamstress. But I don't think they'll be of much help to us."

"One never knows. You'll have to keep at it. Keep questioning them. Don't release them," Sokolov said as he walked forward and stood directly in front of the man in the chair. He lifted the man's chin and stared at his bloodied face.

"Jan Lewandowski. Can you hear me, Jan?"

There was no reply.

Sokolov let go of the man's chin, his head slumped forward, and dropped back onto his chest. Sokolov squatted and positioned himself close, so close they were now face-to-face, and he leaned forward, his face now just inches away from the bloodied prisoner in the chair.

"Jan," he said softly. "Do you know what your name means? Do you, Jan? Your name, 'Jan,' it means 'a gift from God.' Did you know that, Jan? Did you? Can you hear me, Jan? Do you believe in God, Jan?" Sokolov stood and stepped back to look down at the Pole. "Hmm. Well, we will all soon find out if you do, and you'll find out if God listens to you."

Sokolov tugged on his uniform tunic to straighten it, let out a deep breath, and turned to leave the interrogation room. He opened the door and was about to depart but then paused, held the door open and stood in the doorway. He turned back to face the UB officer and said, "I am just here as an advisor of course. This is your investigation and your problem, but I can tell you that everything that has happened here has the attention of people who are at the highest levels back in Moscow. They are watching, very closely."

"We will get results. We will find out who is responsible," the UB officer replied, looking defiant.

"Yes, I've heard that before Comrade. I do have a suggestion for you, in my role as an advisor of course, if you care and are interested enough to listen."

The Pole glared at Sokolov before grudgingly nodding his head, "Yes, go on Colonel. What is your recommendation?"

"You need to make an example of him. You need to get the attention of the people and let them know you are serious, that you are not playing games. Do you understand?"

The UB officer nodded.

"Send him into the fog," Sokolov added. "Make him disappear. And let everyone who lives in his tiny town know about his crimes, and what will happen to people who commit such crimes. And when you are finished with his parents, make them disappear too. The town will need to find another cobbler and seamstress. That will get people's attention."

***

Sokolov sat in the back seat of his car and fumed for the entire hour-long drive from the UB prison to the Soviet garrison. *At least we have men in place, inside the UB*, he thought. *I'll place more men there and run the damn operation myself if I have to.*

As they drove, his driver glanced into the rear-view mirror to check on Sokolov. He knew from experience Sokolov was furious. He didn't know what happened inside the UB prison, but he also knew to keep his mouth shut and keep his distance. So, they rode in silence to the Soviet garrison. He dropped Sokolov off in front of the old barracks building used by the German army during the war which now housed his office. Sokolov got out of the car, slammed the door without saying a word to his driver, and ran up the stairs into the building.

He walked down the hallway to his office, pulled out a key, inserted it into the lock on the door and entered. He had only taken a few steps inside when he stopped suddenly, and his face registered a look of shock.

"Yuri! Don't look so surprised! It has been a long time, friend."

Sokolov stood there dumbfounded. Sitting in the chair next to his desk sat Major General Dmitri Kutuzov, deputy head of the GRU, waiting for him.

"Dmitri? When did you? How did you?" Sokolov stammered.

"I ordered the desk sergeant to let me in," Kutuzov replied.

"What are you doing here?" asked Sokolov. He didn't take Kutuzov's presence to be a good omen. They hadn't seen each other since before the battle of Stalingrad, more than seven years earlier. They had a history, but Sokolov couldn't imagine what would bring him here now.

"It's been too long, and I wanted to see how you are getting on here," Kutuzov replied, raising a bottle of Moskovskaya Zitrovka. "Let's celebrate our reunion."

Over the next hour, the two old friends made short work of the bottle and it now sat nearly empty on Sokolov's desk along with two small mugs, one made of tin, the other ceramic. Sokolov felt the effects of the vodka as he watched the ash from Kutuzov's burning cigarette fall onto his desk and a cloud of smoke fill his office. The light from the single bulb over the desk interacted with the smoke to create a dense, yellow fog. The ash tray on the desk was overflowing and the room reeked from the stench of the Belomorkanal cigarettes Kutuzov smoked in succession. Warmed by drink, he sat and stared at Kutuzov. *He's had enough*, Sokolov thought. *I always could out drink him. I only have to wait him out and I'll soon find out why he's here.*

"Another?" Kutuzov asked as he reached forward to grasp the bottle, before serving a healthy pour into the ceramic mug from which Sokolov had been drinking. He did the same into his own grey tin mug, and then placed the bottle back onto the desk. The two men raised and clinked their cups together before downing the vodka in a single gulp. Kutuzov took a final draw on his cigarette, stubbed it out into the ash tray causing ashes and discarded butts to fall out onto the desk, and then lit another, inhaling deeply before the smoke caused him to wheeze and go into a coughing fit.

"Those things are going to kill you, comrade," Sokolov said shaking his head, knowing full well Kutuzov would never give up smoking. They had known each other since the late 1920s, and survived the purges together, Sokolov by being the enforcer, and Kutuzov by being politically adept enough to stay one step ahead of the next purge.

"What, these?" Kutuzov replied hoarsely, looking down at the cigarette he held in his hand. "Not a chance. If the Nazis couldn't kill me, I can survive these. Besides, what good is life without a few vices, right?"

Sokolov could only smile. They were unlikely friends. Kutuzov was smooth and polished, which combined with his innate ability to lead men, helped him rise through the ranks. Sokolov was rough and coarse. He was known for his temper and controlling it had always been a problem. Sokolov's rage became uncontrollable after he lost his wife Katya and son Ilya during the revolution.

Kutuzov knew the story. As Katya and Ilya walked home after a visit with her parents on the outskirts of Veliky Novgorod, a skirmish broke out between elements of the White Guards and the Red Army charged with protecting the city. They were caught in the crossfire and died in a hail of bullets. While one bullet is as good as another, it was impossible to know which side fired the fatal round.

But Sokolov blamed the White Guards, the counterrevolutionary force who fought against the Bolsheviks. He wanted revenge and joined the Bolshevik security police, the Cheka, and he found a place where his grief and anger were acknowledged and rewarded. During the Revolution, he helped carry out the Red Terror, the orchestrated campaign of political repression and targeted assassinations aimed to crush political dissent and all threats to Soviet power. Leaning on his reputation for ruthlessness, he forged a career as an enforcer and assassin and eventually became an executioner for the NKVD, handpicked for the job by none other than Stalin himself. But his best quality, at least in the mind of Stalin, was loyalty. His other flaws would be overlooked. Unquestioned loyalty to Stalin, which never wavered, became Sokolov's trademark.

Sokolov picked up the bottle and poured another round for the two of them, giving himself only half of what he had poured for his friend.

"So, why are you here, Dmitri? Puck isn't the kind of place where you usually visit."

"I'm here to visit an old friend."

"Yes? And?"

Kutuzov stubbed his cigarette but this time he didn't light another. He leaned back in the chair and stretched his arms, let out a yawn and rubbed his eyes.

"Just say what's on your mind Dmitri."

Kutuzov looked back at his old friend and then leaned forward, placing his forearms on the desk that separated them.

"Moscow is very concerned about the troubles here in Poland. This rebellion, insurgency, or whatever one chooses to call it."

"Tell me something I don't know, Dmitri."

"They are concerned about how it looks, and the impression it gives off. They do not wish to appear to be too heavy handed and they want to ensure you manage the situation carefully. The old ways may not be appropriate here."

"Not appropriate?" Sokolov replied. "Since when? What has brought this on? After millions of deaths, are you saying the Party has finally developed its conscience? I find that hard to believe."

"Be careful old friend. I would keep such thoughts to yourself."

"So, you've come here to admonish me?"

"Oh no. Not at all. I only ask that you not go too far. Your methods can sometimes be considered . . . excessive. And this has held you back. I merely ask you not go too far in putting down this rebellion in your area. That's all."

"If you are referring to my involvement in the Katyn execution, I only did what I was ordered to do. It is what I have always done.

I always did the jobs nobody else wanted or had the courage to do. I always did what was asked of me and never expected anything in return. And what's all of this about impressions and how it looks? What does that even mean?"

Kutuzov let out a long sigh, looking for the right words to share with his friend. "Your involvement at Katyn was buried long ago. Literally. But the perceptions are real. We are still allies with the West, although that situation is changing daily. What I am saying Yuri, is very simple, if the Poles come down hard on their own people, that is one thing. If we do it, it is another matter entirely. Make it look like it is their idea. Make them do the dirty work."

Sokolov nodded. "I understand. And as you are aware, we have penetrated the Polish security services. And it is just the beginning. By the time we are done, the Poles will be saying the sky is green and the moon is the sun. We can make it look like anything we want."

Kutuzov laughed as he reached for the bottle one last time and divided the remaining contents into the two cups on the desk. "Good, my friend. I knew you would understand. Now, there is one other bit of information I need to share with you."

"What's that?"

"We have a highly placed source. One who is extremely reliable. This source has been working for us since before the war started."

"And what is this source saying now?"

"Our source has very specifically told us your area in the North will become a focal point for the Polish insurrection and the incident that occurred here is a precursor of events to come. We also suspect it is extremely likely the insurgents are working directly with our former allies in the West. We believe it is part of a larger effort to undermine our influence across Eastern Europe. We have gone back to our source and asked for information to confirm our suspicions, and to identify any individuals working directly with the West. I will personally make sure you receive any new intelligence information from this source as soon as I receive it. You will be able to set up and run counterintelligence to defeat our adversaries. Do you understand what I am saying to you?"

"Yes, of course I understand," Sokolov replied impatiently.

"Then, once again, I ask you to control your impulses. Keep them in check. There are larger forces at play here."

Sokolov sat in silence, weighing what his old friend had told him. "This seems like a gift from you. I'm not accustomed to it. You've never gone out of your way to warn me before."

"You can think of it as a gift if you want, but I am merely passing along advice to an old friend. It is the least I can do to thank you for years of loyalty and service to the Party. And to me. I'm sure you will use this information wisely," Kutuzov said as he raised his cup to his lips one final time and downed his drink in one gulp.

Chapter Five

Breaking Silence

Bialik had been trained by her mother and her SOE handler Felicja Nowak on how to use firearms and how to use a knife for silent killing. They trained her in hand-to-hand combat and self-defense techniques. She learned how to encode messages and transmit and receive them using the wireless. They trained her in basic tradecraft. She knew how to detect and avoid surveillance. She knew how to set up and retrieve information from dead drops. But for her to carry out her mission, she lacked one important skill. They hadn't trained her how to identify, gain the trust, and recruit people sympathetic to her cause.

She needed to find someone who would be willing to help her. She had to make contact with the insurgents, and she was flying blind. She was on her own with only her instincts to guide her. She alone would have to figure it out.

The insurgency had been going since the end of the war, for more than three years and Bialik wanted in. Bialik knew if she could make contact with the forest soldiers, the remnants of the Home Army who fought against the communist government and Soviet occupiers, she could help them. She'd show them the wireless set and tell them how she could communicate directly with British intelligence. And she would convince them they should throw their support behind the forest soldiers. She was confident the British would help them with arms, ammunition, money, just as they had during the war. And if she were able to do all of that, it would give her the satisfaction of knowing she had fulfilled her mother's wish – to stay alive and keep fighting. She just needed to make contact.

Bialik knew there was a fertile field of potential sources who might help her because nearly everyone living in and around Puck had some sort of grievance, some personal axe to grind. But she needed to find a source with a motivation deeper than hunger and deprivation. That wouldn't be enough for what she would ask her source to do. Everyone was hungry, and basic staples such as flour, sugar, salt, meat, and clothing were all in short supply. No, she wanted something more. She wanted someone special. She wanted a deeper commitment. She wanted someone who was driven by personal loss, a desire for vengeance for sure, but most of all, a desire to see Poland free from outside influences, namely the Russians. Above all, Bialik hated the Russians. She hated them for allowing the Germans to crush the Warsaw uprising in 1944, causing her mother's death. She could never forgive them for this.

Bialik had her suspicions as to who might help her but there was only one way to find out. She had to put herself out there and risk exposure. Everyone who lived in Puck heard the rumors. Bialik heard them too. There was a small network of people who provided direct aid to the insurgent soldiers. She needed to tap into it. She needed to find them, whoever they were. But she had to be discreet since any inquiries about the activities of the forest soldiers could be construed as subversive and dangerous. She was not from Puck; she was an outsider. Worse, she was from Warsaw, so she had to be very careful about what she said, and with whom she spoke. It's not as if she could walk up to the first person she saw and ask, "Where are these forest soldiers hiding? Can you take me to them?"

She had to take her time. She would feign disinterest or at most would display only an idle curiosity. She had to always be on her guard, for in the short time since the communists had taken over, they had created a surveillance state where neighbors spied upon neighbors, and family members were known to have turned over other members of their own family to the security services.

Bialik shopped nearly every day, buying only what she needed for one or two days and during her forays into town, she would listen in on conversations. It was mainly gossip, chatter about who was carrying on with whom, who was mad at whom, complaints about the chronic shortages of food and clothing, and the day-to-day drama of town life.

"Nadja threw her husband out the other night, did you hear?"

"No what happened?"

"He came home stinking drunk from the pub, so she said she'd had enough, pushed him out the door and he slept in their barn all night."

"Oh no. Has he left? How will she manage?"

"She's taken him back, but he's still sleeping with the chickens and pigs," and the two women squealed with laughter.

So Bialik put herself out there. She began to gently probe, asking questions, acting curious, but dispassionate and acting as if she really didn't care. It started as a casual conversation at the market with Iwan Dawidowski, the old man who sold butter and eggs.

"I heard someone damaged several militia vehicles last week," Bialik said.

"Hmm," Dawidowski scoffed. "I try not to listen to such things. Rumors, that's all they are."

"Perhaps. But you hear of these things all the time," Bialik replied.

"I don't pay any mind to it. I have too many other troubles to think about."

"That's probably a good idea," said Bialik. "It's best to stay out of these things. Still, someone in town must be helping them. I wonder who?"

"Hmm," Dawidowski replied gruffly. "Well, I can't say for certain, but I'm pretty sure there are a few people right here in this market who are involved in it. They're up to their ears."

"Really?" Bialik replied, feigning surprise and acting shocked. "That's terrible."

"I suppose I can't blame them," said Dawidowski. "Some people here have lost more than others. They've lost family, their homes, some have even lost their livelihood." Dawidowski looked around to see if anyone was listening and then whispered. "We shouldn't be talking about this. But there are people here in the market," he said nodding his head over his shoulder in the direction of the market center, "if I had to guess who's helping these cursed soldiers, that's who I'd say was helping them. But I don't want to talk about it."

It might have been a clue, or it could have been malicious gossip, but Bialik knew her persistence would pay off. Be curious, ask questions cautiously, and remain patient. Whoever was supporting the insurgents would eventually come to her. Her persistence and patience were rewarded on her next visit to Ela Zajac's market stand.

Zajac watched Bialik picking over the produce, selecting the very best items, a small head of cabbage, some potatoes, a few onions, and then she walked over to her and said, "The word going around is that you have been asking a lot of questions."

"Questions?" Bialik looked up and replied. "What questions? I don't know what you are talking about."

"You know exactly what I mean," Zajac whispered, looking about to see if anyone was listening to their conversation. "You have been asking about the soldiers. The forest soldiers. Those kinds of questions can get you into trouble. You're an outsider here. Everything you do draws attention." Bialik didn't reply.

Zajac eyed her skeptically and continued, "You shouldn't ask about such things. There are people here, your neighbors, people whom you may think of as friends, or even work colleagues you cannot trust. You cannot trust anyone. There are many here who would report you to the security services and you'll be dragged off in the middle of the night – teacher or not – it doesn't matter. Your position and status, your party membership, even your friendship with the headmaster, the commissar, none of that will help you with the likes of them. You wouldn't be the first party member to disappear, you know, and you won't be the last. They'd sell their own mother out for extra rations or to curry favor with the security services. Or they'll do it just out of fear because they don't want to be the one dragged off in the middle of the night. You mean nothing to them."

Bialik stood there in silence, rolling a small yellow potato in her hand as she considered her next move, contemplating what Zajac had said, and mulled over how she should respond.

"I'm merely curious, that's all," she whispered while looking intently into Zajac's eyes, trying to get a true measure of the woman and what she was saying to her. She wondered if she had hit a nerve and had found her source.

"Are you curious what it's like to starve to death in a Siberian labor camp?" Zajac replied. "That's where your questions will take you if the wrong person hears them."

At that moment another customer walked up to the stand, and began to look over the produce for sale, picking out several fat onions and placing them into the sackcloth she was carrying.

"Wait here. Don't leave," Zajac whispered to Bialik. "I'll be right back after I take care of this person."

Bialik moved to the far end of the stand and pretended to be interested in the apples stacked neatly in the bin. She waited patiently and watched Zajac help the customer, a pleasantly plump woman, wearing a dark grey overcoat and a bright red babushka who appeared to be in her mid-fifties, pick out the very best produce, all the while chatting her up about the weather and when the first frost might occur. Finally, after an interminably long wait – it was only five or six minutes – but it felt longer, the woman handed Zajac her ration card and payment. Zajac reached into the pocket of her apron where she carried her money, counted out the woman's change, and then reached back into her pocket for her stamp, and finally stamped the woman's card.

"Thank you for coming today," Zajac said. The woman merely nodded her head in acknowledgment, briefly looked over at Bialik and smiled, and then shuffled off to a nearby stand that sold fresh farmer's cheese. Zajac watched the woman carefully as she moved away to continue her shopping. When she was finally convinced the woman was out of earshot, Zajac turned and moved over to where Bialik was standing.

"If you know what is good for you, you'll drop these questions," Zajac said. "You are young, and you have your whole life ahead of you. You have a good position and you're a party member. You have too much to lose."

"There are many things you don't know about me," Bialik replied. As she continued, her voice rose with intensity. "And just so you know, I've already lost everything that ever mattered. So, I will have to decide what is good for me and what isn't. You of all people should understand that, given the sacrifices you've been forced to make."

Bialik watched and waited as Zajac stood with her hands thrust into her apron pocket. She weighed whether or not she should say more to Zajac. Who would be the first to blink? Who would be the first to trust? Would it be her? Who would make the first move?

"What makes you think these soldiers would want to have anything to do with you?" Zajac asked.

Bialik looked around to see if anyone else was within earshot and then replied, "You seem to know a lot about them. That is what my instinct tells me anyway. I may be wrong, but I don't think I am. So, if you know how to contact them, and my gut tells me you do, I would like to meet with them. I support their cause and I want to help them. I have resources. I can make sure they receive the supplies they need. So, if you know them, I'm asking you to help me, because we cannot be overly concerned with comfort, keeping our bellies full, or holding down a good position, not when others are sacrificing so much for us. We've given up too much and it's time for us to say, 'no more.'" Bialik paused for a moment and then continued. "On the other hand, if you don't know them, or know how to contact them, I'm sorry I misjudged you. Of course, if you tell anyone of our conversation here today, I shall deny every word, and I know the authorities will believe me, because I am, after all, a member of the Party. But," she added, "I don't think it will come to that. I don't believe I have misjudged you at all."

Bialik wondered if she had overplayed her hand. Had she miscalculated? It became a faceoff between the two women.

"How do I know I can trust you?" Zajac asked.

"Right now, at this very moment, you don't. But we've both laid our cards on the table. It seems we have to trust each other; don't you think? So, I suppose I should be going now," Bialik said. "How much do I owe you for the potatoes, these onions, and this small cabbage?"

"I'll need to weigh everything," Zajac replied, as she took the items from Bialik and carried them over to the small scale where she placed first the cabbage, then the potatoes, and then the onions, recording the weight and writing down the price on a slip of paper, which she started to slip across the wooden counter that separated her and Bialik. Before Bialik could pick up the paper, Zajac pulled it back, and wrote something else on it. She gathered up Bialik's purchase and placed the items into a brown sack, along with the slip of paper.

"Let's call it twenty today. That will be sufficient. I'll need your ration card please," Zajac said.

Bialik pulled the coins from her purse and counted out the correct amount. She placed the coins on the counter along with her card, which Zajac promptly stamped, while the coins remained untouched. Bialik picked up her ration card and returned it to her purse. She then reached into the bag with the vegetable, retrieved the note, reading it quickly before handing it back to Zajac.

"No notes," she said. "Never write anything down. You'll have to remember everything I say to you. Now, destroy this and throw the pieces away. I will tell you how and when we need to communicate."

Zajac took the note from Bialik and began to tear it into tiny pieces. There was no turning back now. Bialik had committed. If she were wrong about Zajac, one of them would wind up dead.

"It was my oldest son's best friend," Zajac said.

"What? I don't understand."

"My oldest son's best friend – from before the war. He just appeared one day, here at my stand. He asked for my help. He said he was with a group of soldiers who were continuing the fight. I remembered him. He and my son would play together all the time. They were inseparable. I knew there was nothing I could do to bring my son back, but if I helped this young man, it would help me keep the memory of my son alive. Do you know what it is to live only for memories? So, that's why I agreed. I agreed to help provide them food, whenever I can. And information too. Nobody pays attention to an old woman. I tend to be . . . invisible if you know what I mean. They think I have nothing, only memories, so I am of little value. Or so they think."

"Does anyone else know for certain you are helping the soldiers?"

"No, but I am sure there are those who may be suspicious."

Bialik remembered her conversation with Dawidowski.

"There are too many people here who want to stick their nose in your business," said Zajac. "That is why when I heard you were asking questions around town . . . well, I assumed the worst."

Bialik let out a long sigh and replied, "You are correct. There are people in town who are suspicious of you. I suppose they are probably suspicious of everybody though. But you have to be careful. And yes, I can completely understand how you feel. I also live for memories, and I want to create new ones. I want to keep your son's memory alive. But you have to trust me. We have to trust each other. That is what it is going to take. Can you trust me enough to help? Will you put me in touch with the soldiers who are hiding in the forest?"

Zajac nodded affirmatively.

"Good. Now listen carefully. This is what I want you to do."

***

They had arranged to meet on a busy forest trail popular with locals. It was a public spot, and it wasn't out of the ordinary for either of them to be there. The townspeople all used the trail to access areas in the forest where they could forage for wild onions, herbs, and of course, mushrooms, a delicacy prized by those who had the knowledge to discern which varieties were safe to eat and not risk poisoning themselves and their dinner companions.

Bialik was walking up the trail to their meeting spot when she saw Zajac in the distance, alone, but busying herself, harvesting what appeared to be wild dill, or perhaps it was some other herb, but it didn't matter. Their seemingly random encounter, running into each other on the trail, now gave them a pretext for meeting, and she was pleased to see Zajac had kept up her end of the bargain by showing up, ahead of time. *She's reliable. That's one less thing to worry about*, she thought.

As she approached the bend in the road where they had agreed to meet, Bialik called out, "Hello!" Zajac looked up and waved but said nothing until Bialik walked up to her.

"Do you know how many people walk along this trail?" Zajac asked. "I've already seen a half dozen or more from town in the brief time I've been waiting for you. This isn't a private location. From what you said, I thought you would want to meet in a place where nobody could overhear our conversation. You said I was to be careful, and this is where we meet? We could have met in my cottage, but this place . . . I don't know."

"That's why I picked this spot. We're hiding in plain sight," Bialik replied.

"Hmph. In that case, I don't understand why we just couldn't talk at my vegetable stand. Or I could invite you to my cottage for tea," said Zajac, not bothering to hide her irritation. "Why bring me all the way out here?"

"You come here all the time, don't you?" Bialik asked.

"Yes of course, but I still don't see why . . . "

"Just finish picking your herbs," Bialik replied, cutting Zajac off mid-sentence, "and when you are done, join me. I'll be waiting for you over on that fallen tree over there. Do you see it?" she said, pointing to a spot about twenty meters off in the distance, and slightly to their left. "I'll be waiting for you there and I'll explain everything."

Bialik didn't wait for a reply from Zajac, and she quickly walked away, taking long strides until she reached the fallen tree. She turned around to see if Zajac was behind her, saw that she hadn't moved from her original spot, and wondered whether or not the old woman would follow and join her, or if this entire effort had been a waste of her time. She removed the cloth satchel from her shoulder she had brought with her and sat down on the fallen tree and watched patiently as Zajac finished collecting herbs. *It is dill*, she thought, and then after several minutes, Zajac began at last to slowly walk into the forest, eventually reaching the tree where she sat down next to Bialik.

"Have you set up the meeting?" Bialik asked.

"Yes, in two days, just as you asked. But I still don't understand why we are meeting all the way out here, in nature," Zajac replied, seemingly put out by having to walk into the forest to have a conversation.

"When I was younger, before the war of course, my parents used to take me to a spot just like this," Bialik replied, taking in a deep breath, and inhaling the heavy scent of pine and the musky odor of moss. "Can you smell it. This is how a forest is supposed to smell, isn't it?" They sat in silence for several minutes, and she continued. "My father taught me how to pick mushrooms. He and I would go deep into the forest while my mother would forage for wild onions and fresh herbs. Every Sunday, on a day just like today, we would go out together. We'd fill our satchels and baskets with mushrooms, wild herbs, berries, and wild vegetables, and then we'd return home where my mother would prepare the most delicious meal. Sometimes we'd have meat, sausage, pork, but often not. But it didn't matter. It was always delicious. And after dinner, my father would play his guitar. He was quite good, you know. And my mother would sing. She had a beautiful soprano voice, and I would sing along until it was time for bed. I remember it like it was yesterday. But that was so very long ago now."

"What happened to them?" Zajac asked softly.

"Father was called up when the Germans and Russians invaded in thirty-nine. It was early September, and I remember the day my mother and I saw him off at the train station in Warsaw. He left us on September 6. He told us not to worry, that he would be home soon. And then we received word he had been killed fighting near the Bzura River. They told us he was killed on September 16, so he only lived another ten days after we kissed him goodbye."

"And your mother? What happened to her?"

"Mother and I stayed in Warsaw and eventually she took up arms as part of the resistance. Mother died in forty-four. She was killed in the Warsaw uprising in October of that year. The Russians stopped their advance and refused to cross the Dnieper river. They even refused to allow the British and Americans to resupply the Home Army. They allowed the Germans to massacre us, and we knew then what the Russians would have in store for us. They wanted their own government in Warsaw, not a government aligned with the Western Allies."

"I'm sorry."

"You needn't be sorry. I'm not the only person who lost their parents, or their family during the war. You've lost your family too, and you continue to suffer. So, I tell you all this not to earn your sympathy, but to merely inform you I am invested in the struggle. And I will not quit the struggle until I see a return, a payback for my investment. That's what I want to get out of it. A sense of payback. Do you understand?"

"Yes, I do," Zajac replied.

"My father taught me how to pick mushrooms, but my mother taught me many other things, things that will keep us alive. She taught me, for example, how to make sure I haven't been followed by anyone. I will teach you how to do that to. That is why we are meeting here, in this lovely spot. I know I haven't been followed," Bialik said. "This is also a natural place for us to meet. And anyone who sees us out here wouldn't suspect anything. They'd just see us doing what they would be doing, foraging for herbs, berries, and mushrooms. Whatever we can find, just as everyone else does when they are here. I've brought us something to eat and drink too." Bialik reached into the cloth satchel she had placed on the forest floor and pulled out a small hunk of cheese, some bread, a small knife, along with two glasses, and bottle of wine. "You see, anyone passing by would also see us eating, enjoying a pleasant autumn afternoon, just as they might do out here, in the quiet of the forest. They might even wave to us or stop and say 'hello.' We blend in, and that's what is important."

Bialik offered the bread and cheese and handed Zajac the small knife. "Here help yourself to something to eat. Go ahead. I'll pour us some wine and then I want you to listen carefully, because your life, my life, may depend on what I'm about to tell you."

Zajac tore off a chunk of bread and cut a slice of cheese as Bialik poured each of them a glass of wine.

"Thank you for setting up the meeting with the soldiers," Bialik said as she took a sip from her glass, "Now, let's talk about dead drops and how we shall communicate."

Always protect your sources. That was the rule, and Bialik knew she could not place Zajac in any more danger than necessary. She'd be sick if anything happened to her. She only needed her to set up the first meeting with the forest soldiers. But she also decided that Zajac could be useful in case of an emergency, or as an alternate means of communication with the soldiers. Bialik would continue to buy items from Zajac at her stand, but they would never, under any circumstances, use the stand as a place to talk about operational matters. So, she set up a simple signaling system.

"There is a bench sitting near the corner of Milynska and Zamkowa Streets. Do you know where I am talking about?" Bialik asked.

"Yes, I walk by there every day on my way to the market."

"Exactly. And I walk by every day on my way to school. It's also a natural spot for us to stop, coming or going. If I need for you to pass along information to the soldiers, I will mark the left side of the bench with a single stroke using this," she said holding up a thick piece of chalk, the kind of chalk she used every day in her classroom. "It will be a vertical mark. I will only do this if it is absolutely necessary and have no other means of contacting the soldiers.

"And then what?" asked Zajac.

"The mark means that I have information that I will need for you to take to the soldiers. I will have placed that information in a package in the wall that runs along the outside of St. Catherine's Church on Milynska Street. There is a large tree that is directly opposite a small alcove in the wall. Do you know the spot?"

"Yes, of course I do."

"Good. The alcove is the spot where people light candles in memory of loved ones, and people still do that," Bialik said. "Simply step inside the alcove and light a candle. Now this is the critical part. In the lower left corner of the alcove, you will find two loose bricks. I'll have placed the message behind the two bricks. You'll need to bend down to see them. All you need to do is remove them and retrieve the message. Make sure you put the bricks back in place after you've retrieved the message. Do you have any questions?"

"No, I understand what I am to do."

"Good. I only expect to have to contact you in case of an emergency. But check every day for a mark on the bench, retrieve the message, and carry out my instructions. Do you understand?

After you've retrieved the message and carried out my instructions, make a single, vertical mark on the right side of the bench. If I do not see a mark, I will know you have not been able to retrieve the message."

Zajac sat in silence, took a sip of wine, and asked, "What if I need to contact you. How do I do that?"

"If you need to contact me, leave a horizontal mark on the bench. I will be in touch."

***

It was two days later when Zajac guided Bialik to a spot on the edge of the forest clearing. Just a few minutes after they arrived, a tall man in uniform walked out into the clearing from the tree line on the other side. As he walked forward, he raised his hand, beckoning them to meet him in the clearing, and the two women stepped out from where they stood and walked towards him until they all met in the middle.

Bialik knew the man only by his sobriquet, Wulkan, and he knew her only as Magda, another layer of operational security Bialik insisted upon that offered some, if minimal, protection of their true identities.

"Welcome. I'm the commander of the soldiers fighting in this area," he said as he waved a hand behind him. Bialik could barely make out the outline of figures hidden in the trees behind him, but she could see they were heavily armed.

"Are you armed?" Wulkan asked.

"Always," Bialik replied, as she slowly lifted the hem of her skirt to reveal a scabbard strapped to her right thigh which encased a long, double-edged knife.

His eyebrows raised in surprise and then a smiled and said, "Impressive. Do you know how to use it?"

"Yes. I was trained by the very best and this is my weapon of choice."

The commander nodded his approval. "Follow me. I won't take you to our camp for security reasons, but we have set up another location where we can sit down. Ela tells me we have much to talk about."

***

Bialik saw the chalk mark on the bench and two days later, she was sitting next to Zajac, on what they laughingly called, "their log."

"So, what is it you have for me?"

"I have it on good authority the Russian army is building a garrison at the western edge of town," Zajac replied. "They've already started construction. Eventually they will build a rail line to the garrison, but that will take some time."

"From whom did you hear this?"

"From the railway station chief. He's particularly fond of the wine you give me. It's a weakness of his and once he has a glass or two, you can't shut him up."

Bialik smiled. "So, they are building a new Soviet army garrison there. What else did the station master tell you?"

"Yes, they'll be moving in a battalion from what he tells me."

"A battalion?"

"Yes, the station chief said it was a motorized infantry battalion, and a company of engineers, who've already moved in. They are the soldiers who are overseeing construction. They've hired Polish labor to help. They don't pay them squat, but men have to work, so they take what they can get. They've broken ground to build barracks first, but they also are building storage for ammunition. In fact, there is supposed to be a delivery of ammunition in two weeks. Exactly two weeks from tomorrow. The rail ministry doesn't want the responsibility of holding volatile cargo here at the station, so they've pressed the Russians to move it as quickly as possible and the Russians agreed. They also don't believe the militia can keep it secure, so they plan to move the shipment early in the morning after it arrives. They'll have to cart the ammunition by lorry over the forest road since the rail line won't be ready for months. They just had a big meeting about it yesterday."

"And the station chief, he told you all of this?"

"Yes. He likes to talk. It makes him feel important. All it took was a little wine."

"You need to stay away from him I think," Bialik replied. "At least for the foreseeable future. I don't want you getting caught up in the aftermath."

"The aftermath? What is it you plan to do?"

"The less you know, the better," Bialik replied. "This is very important information and you've already done enough. You've put yourself at risk and I cannot ask you to do more. So, please do as I ask. Stay away from the station chief. Do you understand?"

Zajac nodded and said, "I don't know what you are planning, but if it is like the last time when the militiamen were killed, the Russians and Polish security will rain down bloody hell on the town. It will be much worse than before. More people will disappear."

"I'm sorry, but it has to be done. I only need for you to arrange a meeting for me with Wulkan as soon as possible. I will take care of everything else."

Chapter Six

All Roads Converge

Luba Haas arrived at her office at her usual time, at just a little past 8 a.m., and the duty officer told her she needed to attend an important briefing in the main conference room. As she entered the very room where her new life began three years ago, she stopped dead in her tracks. James Banbury was the last person in the world Luba Haas had expected to see. He was sitting on the far side of that large, and now familiar conference table, huddled in quiet conversation with Alicia Betancourt, another person whom Haas hadn't seen in years.

The moment Haas entered, Banbury looked up at her and smiled. He stood up to greet her and extended his hand. But Haas was completely blindsided by his presence, and she froze. Banbury's hand hung awkwardly in mid-air, and he realized she would not return his handshake, and while still smiling, he slowly withdrew it, drawing his arm down to his side. Haas watched him as he tugged on the sleeve of his impeccably tailored blue suit, allowing the proper amount of the French cuff of his starched shirt to show.

"Hello Luba," he said softly. "It's good to see you again." He said it in such a way to indicate he actually meant it, that he was happy to see his old charge once again. "You remember Alicia Betancourt, of course," he added, turning to his number two as she rose from her seat. Haas glared at Betancourt but said nothing. Haas had known Betancourt since the early days of the war. They had undergone SOE training together but were never close and were definitely not friends. Haas could never understand how someone like Betancourt could rise through the ranks of the SOE, and now MI6, having fought the war from behind a desk, while she and hundreds of agents spilled their blood across Europe.

It had been more than three years since Banbury and Haas last met in a small café in Bremen, and that encounter hadn't gone down very well. Banbury had wanted Haas to return to London, but she wanted to stay in Bremen. Haas could never understand how Banbury could be such a staunch defender of the service, and he couldn't comprehend why she insisted on seeing a mole behind every desk at MI6. She was never suited for headquarters life and Banbury could never fully understand the mindset of a field agent. So, they disagreed, they argued, they parted, and they let go of their shared past and years of wartime service. In the end, they both knew the best decision was for each to go their separate ways, and Haas's time at MI6 ended that day.

During the intervening years, Haas recruited and now ran a small, but increasingly valuable network of agents operating in the Russian sector of Berlin, and across the Russian zone of occupation. She did this all from the confines of her office within the 323rd U.S. Army Counterintelligence Corps Detachment, the CIC, tucked away in the Hotel Zur Post, a short walk from the main train station in Bremen. She regained the same swagger she had during the war, when she was Britain's longest serving agent, and one of its most highly decorated.

But now, she also displayed a confidence and a maturity that grew out of not only the fact she was older but was part of a team that constantly had her back. She was no longer "a loner, and a law unto herself," as British spymaster Vera Atkins once described her. Haas's time at MI6 ended three years ago, but after taking a job with the CIC, her career was once more on the ascendancy.

Since arriving in Bremen, Haas recruited a small network of well-placed German spies, most of whom were former Nazis who escaped punishment at the end of the war and were needed to keep the engine of government running in post-war Germany. They regularly reported on troop movements, tactical readiness, and the military construction projects of the Group of Soviet Occupation Forces in Germany. Haas' agents also shared important economic intelligence that gave a true picture of conditions in the East. It was difficult enough for the Germans in the Western zones, but in the East under the Russians, it was far worse.

Unlike her former colleagues at MI6, the U.S. military brass valued her, loved what she was doing, and she thrived on their attention. Off-duty, she became a regular, and well-known member of the lively Bremen cocktail circuit that existed throughout the British zone and within the American enclave. She rekindled her ability to make small-talk and chit-chat, something she dreaded during her time in London.

In the three years since the end of the war, a growing number of women were making their presence known in Occupied Germany. Senior officers were beginning to bring their wives, while others found companionship among the growing number of German women who worked for the Allies. But none of them compared to Luba Haas. She'd long ago given up wearing combat fatigues to work, although the word on the street was that she still kept a 9-inch Shanghai knife strapped to her thigh.

Despite shortages and rationing, she was able to acquire fabrics and material through the British and American military exchanges, and she now favored bespoke suits or swing dresses, all made just for her at a small shop in the Altstadt section of Bremen. The shop proprietors were only happy to copy the latest designs from Paris, using photographs Haas gave them ripped from the latest copies of Life, Look, or Vogue Paris magazines.

Her transition from a war time agent of the British Special Operations Executive was now complete. She had found a new home, built a new life, and men, even powerful men, dazzled by her beauty and charm, wanted to claim her as theirs. The same scene repeated itself night after night. Whenever she entered a room, American and British officers would be drawn to her like a moth to a flame, and she would find herself surrounded by men fawning for her attention.

"Luba, you look magnificent tonight, can I fetch you something to drink?"

"Cigarette, Luba?"

"Do you need a light, Luba?"

"Luba, tell us that story of how you outwitted the Gestapo in France?"

So, Haas would tell the assembled men and women how she convinced a Gestapo officer in France to release two SOE agents and a French officer from prison by claiming to be Field Marshall Montgomery's niece. She threatened serious consequences if the men were not let go. The officer relented, and with the help of a two-million-franc bribe, the three men were released into Haas's custody.

In the past she would have grown bored with it all. But now it was different. She thrived on it, she relished it, and she used it to her advantage. She knew she had allies, something she never had during her time in London with MI6. Every last man, and more than a few women wanted her, and she would tease and lead them on until they would finally give in to her.

"I need to get on that next flight to Berlin, Colonel," Haas would ask confidently, but with a warm and enticing smile. "I know you are just the person who can make that happen, aren't you?"

And if they resisted, she persisted.

"Why do I need to go? Because I heard the Soviets are constructing a new garrison near Potsdam and I need to see it by air to confirm the reports. Colonel, be a dear, I know you can help."

And finally, after an officer had given in to what she asked for, agreed to her request, after all the seductive back and forth with his hopes now raised, he would try to pounce.

"Luba, please join me for dinner." Or,

"Luba, I'm planning a few days in Paris. Wouldn't you like to see Paris with me?"

But her answer was always the same.

"No, I'm so very sorry, but you know that's impossible." Or,

"But Colonel, I've been to Paris many times. I was there when it was liberated."

And her refusals always ended with some version of, "Besides, you know I am spoken for. I'm with someone now, and I am very, very happy."

Yes, Luba Haas was indeed spoken for, although that didn't stop high ranking officers, and even a few junior ones from trying. She was spoken for by a man many believed was punching above his weight when it came to matters of love, but newly minted U.S. Army Major Caspar Lehman, who everyone including his men called him "Cap" for short, was indeed the object of her desire.

On the surface, it was an odd and incompatible pairing. Haas was exotic and glamorous. When Luba Haas entered the room, all eyes were immediately on her. Whereas Lehman, a soft-spoken lawyer from Louisville, was of average height and build, neither handsome nor ugly, and came across as shy and reserved.

But Lehman was able to capitalize on his ordinariness. He could naturally blend into any background and situation, and that is what made him so dangerous. People always underestimated him. He had a knack for seeing people for who they were, both good and bad. He could read people and possessed an uncanny ability to determine if they were telling the truth.

Born in Bremen, Germany, Casper Lehman was three years old when his family moved to the United States just before the Great War. He paid for his college education by working part-time in his family's landscaping design business. He spoke fluent German, Russian, and French, and when the war broke out, a well-connected fraternity brother from Louisville recommended Lehman for the intelligence services. He trained at Camp Ritchie in Western Maryland and became one of the "Ritchie Boys," selected because of their knowledge of the German language and culture. He would go on to serve with distinction in Northern

Africa and Italy, was in the second wave to land at D-Day, fought in what became known as the Battle of the Bulge, and was among the first U.S. Army soldiers to liberate the death camps at Landstuhl and Dachau.

Lehman had an impeccable, distinguished war record, but it wasn't his record that made him attractive to Haas. Luba Haas served with many courageous men during the war, and she married the bravest man she ever met, only to lose him in an act of unimaginable brutality and cruelty.

What attracted Haas to Lehman was that after all the campaigns, from Northern Africa to the beaches of Anzio and Normandy, from the frozen forests outside Bastogne to the death camps where the limits of depravity were stretched to the limit, Lehman could still find beauty watching the sun rise and set. He could still smile while watching small children laughing and playing, he could relish the sensuousness and simple pleasure of eating oysters, or freshly baked bread slathered with butter and honey, and he could lavish kisses that were so gentle and soft it could make the angels weep. After everything Lehman had witnessed and endured, he still possessed the one element that set him apart from all the other men who clumsily came on to her — his humanity.

That humanity is what Luba Haas loved most about Caspar Lehman, and that is what drew her to his side. And then Lehman doubled down by exuding a genteel civility, by valuing Haas, not for her beauty, but for her passion, for her intellect, and her fearlessness. He wanted her so badly, but he insisted upon "courting" her, with all his charm as a Southern gentleman, never taking anything for granted, never assuming anything, always working hard to build and earn her trust and respect. Luba Haas had become Lehman's "*podruga zhizni*," a Russian phrase he learned from his mother that roughly translated to "life companion," but had a deeper meaning of "soul mate." After three years, they were now inseparable, partners not only in life, but partners on the job where they came to rely heavily on each other.

It wasn't always that way. Back in April 1946, Haas was an unwanted MI6 castoff, dumped into the unit Lehman commanded, a newly formed counterintelligence corps detachment in the backwaters of Bremen. He was forced to take her on, the orders came straight from the very top, from Eisenhower himself. He was ordered to credential her as a badge carrying agent of the CIC, and work with her to capture a former Gestapo officer responsible for the death of thousands of slave laborers, including they would find out, her husband.

But over time, they found a way to work together and trust each other. She immediately fit in and earned the respect of every man in the detachment, they accomplished their mission, their success launched their life together, and they became the U.S. Army's version of Nick and Nora Charles, the fictional crime-solving couple from the popular 'The Thin Man' series of films. But while Nick and Nora's exploits were fictitious, a product of Hollywood, Lehman and Haas encountered real villains within the shadowy world of counterintelligence.

They discreetly moved in together and shared a small, but very tidy flat a mere fifteen-minute walk from the office where they worked. It wasn't exactly regulation, technically there were rules against such fraternization, but the CIC had a long tradition of acting as "an army within the Army," and Luba's status as a fully credentialed counterintelligence agent, coupled with her success in the field caused everyone, up and down the chain of command, to look the other way.

However, on this morning, none of that mattered. The tension was palpable as Lehman slipped past Haas, who was blocking the doorway, and entered the conference room. As he slipped past her, he gently placed his hand between her shoulders, giving her a soft touch as if to say, *don't worry, my love. I'll explain everything once someone explains it to me.* Haas shot a look at Lehman as if to say, *you'd better have a good explanation for this mister.*

"James, it's good to see you again. It's been quite a while," Lehman said. "I just got off the horn with the G2 in Frankfurt, Colonel Richardson. His flight has been scrubbed due to ground fog there, but he wants us to go ahead with our meeting. I told him I'd brief him later to bring him up to speed, but he already seemed to know why you are here. He said I was to give you our full cooperation."

Lehman paused, and after a moment of awkward silence continued, "So, why are you here James? Why all the secrecy?"

Banbury cleared his throat and looked across the table at Lehman and then at Haas.

"Thanks Cap," said Banbury. "I spoke with Richardson yesterday and he indicated he was on board and would give us his full support. So perhaps we should just sit down, and I'll be happy to explain our presence here. Oh, and let me introduce the head of our Baltic section, Alicia Betancourt," he added as they took their seats on opposite sides of the table. "She plays a very important role in what I am about to tell you."

"We're all ears," Lehman replied as he took a seat motioning for Haas to sit next to him. Haas sat down with a huff and continued to glare at the two Brits across the table. She wasn't sure at whom she was angrier, Banbury for showing up in her life once again, or Lehman, for not telling her Banbury was planning to make an appearance. *Cap had to know about this in advance*, she thought.

"What I am about to tell you is top secret," Banbury began. "You've both been briefed on Operation Nightfall, the operation to leave agents behind in Poland, in case they were needed in the future. Well, there has been an interesting development. One of the agents you recruited, Luba, has communicated with us."

"Go on," Lehman said, as both he and Haas leaned forward, anxiously wanting more information.

"Two nights ago, well actually it was in the early morning hours, we intercepted a coded message. It seems that one of your agents has returned from the dead, or at least has come out of hiding."

"Which agent?" Haas asked.

"The agent that we know as Lygia. It seems he, or she is very much alive."

"What about the others?" Haas asked. "Have you heard from the other three?"

"Up until a few days ago, we had assumed they were all compromised, killed, or lost," Banbury said. "Since the Russians have taken control, thousands of Poles have been detained, executed, or shipped off to labor camps in Siberia. They have a word for it, you know. *Tuman*, is the Russian word I believe. As you know, the word means fog in Russian. The idea is they are sent into the fog and made to disappear. But now, after all these years, we seem to have an active agent in Poland."

"So, what do you want from us?" Lehman asked, cutting to the chase and interrupting Haas before she could ask any more questions.

"As you can imagine, after we received this message . . . well suffice to say the message created quite an uproar at headquarters. But, after some careful thought, we believe this communication, this bolt out of the blue gives us the raison d'être to accelerate certain plans, which up until now have been withering in limbo and looking for a reason to exist," Banbury replied, as he looked directly at Haas, and then turned to Lehman before he continued, "But no longer."

"Yes, and?" Lehman asked, waiting for the other shoe to drop. "What do you need from us?"

"Lygia's reappearance may give us the opportunity to relaunch Operation Nightfall and include it within a larger set of plans and operations, all of which seek to thwart Soviet advances in Europe. This planning all began under the previous Prime Minister, Mr. Churchill. Mrs. Betancourt here has begun training a cadre of agents and resistance fighters. They are still several months away from being ready to go. However, before we consider any operation in Poland, there is still an important piece missing, a pesky detail that we need to get sorted out."

"And what's that?" Lehman asked.

"We need Luba's help. She's the only person alive who actually knows Lygia. We need her to verify the person we're dealing with is . . . what is the saying you Yanks like to use, the real deal?"

"What about the message?" Haas interjected, "Lygia was trained to insert certain errors into her coded messages, as a check. There should have been markers in the code. And the sender would also have a distinctive way of transmitting code."

"Yes, her message included the markers," Betancourt said. "I decoded it myself using the Quo Vadis book code. The message contained inverted and transposed characters, repeated phrases, everything. The individual who intercepted the message on our side recognized the sender's fist, the cadence and the rhythm of the code. The unique identifiers were all there. Our operator swears it is Lygia."

"Okay," said Lehman, "Let's assume for the moment that it really is this Lygia person. Why now? After all these years, why come out now?"

"We don't have an answer for that," replied Banbury. "We can only surmise that the agent has been in hiding, waiting for the right time and place."

"It could be a trap. It smells like one, anyway," Lehman said.

"It has a certain odor about it, I cannot disagree," Banbury said. "But it could also be an opportunity."

"What was in the message?" Haas asked. "What did it say?"

"I have a copy right here for you," Banbury said as he reached under the table and pulled out a leather attaché case, placed it atop the table, opened it and pulled out a one-page document. He placed it on the table and slid it in front of Lehman and Haas for them to examine.

Lehman and Haas looked down at the document in front of them and read.

Established secure location.

Will advise location after confirmation.

Established routine contact with friendlies.

Need medical supplies, weapons, ammunition, funds.

Request immediate assistance and further orders.

Request confirmation per plan.

The room fell silent as Lehman and Haas read the message and began to realize its implications.

"I know what you are probably thinking," Banbury said. "We responded to the message, per plan, in part to simply buy some additional time. All we said in our reply was we were working on the request for supplies and so on and would provide an initial plan in one week. The clock is on, and we now have five days to formulate such a plan and put it into action."

"How is it that Luba is the only person who knows who Lygia really is?" Lehman asked.

"Well," Banbury started to explain when Haas immediately cut him off.

"I didn't trust anyone at SOE headquarters," Haas interjected. "We had our entire circuit in Poland rolled up. And I had suspicions, serious reservations about certain SOE officers and with the company they kept."

"It was an extraordinarily difficult time for us, to say the least," said Banbury, trying his best to remain calm and cool. "The operational situation in Poland was very difficult. Our allies, the Russians, weren't helping us there in forty-four. They had their own agenda, and they effectively sabotaged the Home Army. Their inaction effectively allowed the Germans to crush the Warsaw uprising."

"There were too many coincidences," Haas continued. "Every time we worked with headquarters to coordinate delivery of ammunition or supplies, we lost agents. All of a sudden, the

Germans became incredibly good at identifying and eliminating our people. Better than they ever had been before. There had to be a leak somewhere. So, for Nightfall, I insisted that I would be the only person with direct knowledge, and direct contact with the agents. I recruited them, I met with them, I trained them. They all communicated with London via book code, using the Polish book, Quo Vadis, and I set that all up too."

"We've never been able to identify any source of a security breach from our side," Banbury said.

"I know who it is," Haas replied. "It's those damned schoolboys from Eton. Those proper English gentlemen playing games as spies. You know who they are, James."

"I share your concerns, Luba, and I've communicated that to you in the past. But the truth of the matter is there is no smoking gun, and we cannot find any evidence that points to them conclusively, or to anyone else for that matter, no matter where they attended school," Banbury replied.

"You haven't looked hard enough and you're unwilling to consider it could be one of your own," Haas retorted, and Banbury shook his head in exasperation.

"Wait, wait, wait," said Lehman. "Everyone, please calm down. Please." Lehman looked back and forth at Banbury and Haas like a schoolteacher breaking up an argument between bickering students. "We're getting nowhere by arguing. What I'm trying to understand is the full situation here, so bear with me," he said, looking once more at Haas as to indicate, *please, enough.*

"We have taken what we believe are the necessary steps to ensure operational security," Banbury stated. "From our side, there are only a handful of people outside of this room who have any knowledge of Nightfall, and the bigger operation we intend to launch."

"And who might they be?" asked Lehman.

"They are C, the chief of intelligence, to whom I report directly, the home secretary plus two of his most trusted aides, the foreign minister and two of his most trusted assistants, and the prime minister, of course."

"That's quite a handful," said Lehman.

"We do have to inform our superiors, just as you do, Cap. But, that's it. That's the list. And none of those people will be briefed on an actual operation, until we're ready to take action. They don't know who, how, or when. They know nothing. We've kept it that way, because. . .," as his voice trailed off. "We've kept it that way to provide not only operational security but plausible deniability. And nobody on your side knows any of the operational details either. At least, not yet."

Both Haas and Lehman immediately understood the implication. If such an operation were to fail, leadership could disavow all knowledge of it, chalk it up to rogue, or overzealous elements.

"Well, then. Okay," Lehman said, staring at Banbury. "I think we understand completely."

They all settled into a tenuous silence and once again, Lehman broke the stillness and spoke out.

"So, you have a message," said Lehman, "Purportedly from an agent that is only known by Luba. Why do you need to contact this agent in the first place? The agent has been silent for years. Why do you even need this person?"

"We considered that possibility," Banbury replied. "But the presence of an agent, trained by one of our own, who has a knowledge of our methods of operation, who has the means and capability to securely communicate with us, and who has established contact with various resistance groups, remnants of the Home Army, the "friendlies" described in Lygia's message to us, such an asset is a missing piece that we do not currently have in place. Even if we were to go ahead and insert our new agents and fighters, they would have to establish contact with the various factions fighting the Soviets and Polish communists. If Lygia is real, we believe it enhances our chances for success. Lygia, presumably, has a detailed understanding of the current situation on the ground and we do not. Unfortunately, there is only one way to find out."

"We believe it has to be done in person," Betancourt added. "After all, as unlikely and difficult as it may be, it is possible for an experienced wireless operator to mimic another operator. And it is easy enough to insert the other identifiers if Lygia has been compromised or coerced to do so. So, in our view, the only way to be sure it is our agent is to set up a meeting to verify that it is the real Lygia, the person whom Haas recruited."

"I'll do it," Haas blurted.

"Luba, wait a minute here. Not so fast," said Lehman. "We can't risk starting another war."

"We aren't starting another war," Haas replied angrily. "We're trying to finish the last damned war. That war didn't end for Poland when Germany surrendered. We. . . they . . . are still fighting. It's the same enemy, but they're wearing a different uniform."

"Luba is right," Banbury said. "Even before the war ended, the Soviet-installed government declared the anti-Nazi resistance illegal. Those were the pro-Western groups who were working with us, such as the Home Army. They were offered guarantees of amnesty if they laid down their arms, but it was all a lie. Most of them were arrested and thrown into jail. Many of them were sent off to Soviet prisons and have never been heard from again. But try as they might, the government there has not been able to crush dissent. So today, there is an active and ongoing armed resistance that is attacking Polish state-run institutions and even Soviet facilities. I'll leave it for the historians to decide, but three years later, as far as we're concerned, the situation in Poland is that the country has descended into an all-out civil war, and we intend to do everything we can to help them topple the current regime and restore a democratic form of government there."

Once again, a tense silence fell over the room. It was Lehman who finally broke it.

"I don't like it. It's very risky, and besides," Lehman said softly, "I'm not even sure this is our fight. We have a new organization that's supposed to be doing this, fighting these battles, engaging in this kind of war."

"If you are referring to your new Central Intelligence Agency," Banbury replied, "I can tell you they are completely on board with this. We don't always see eye-to-eye on the details, but we're in complete agreement about the endgame – stick it to the Russians any chance we get. They are providing much of the funding for this operation and others as well."

"Well, if it's all the same, James, I'll need to hear that from someone on our side," Lehman replied. It was now his turn to express sarcasm and though he didn't feel good about it, it was the only way for him to vent his frustration with the situation. He knew when he was being railroaded into agreeing with a decision that had already been made well above his pay grade.

Silence once more, but this time it was Banbury who broke it.

"Luba, I know you said you would do it, but I want you to hear us out completely. I want you to hear our plan. Before you commit, let's have Alicia here brief you on the high-level details of our plan and then make your decision."

Lehman let out a long sigh and sat back in his chair. He looked over at Haas and reached into his trouser pocket for the Zippo lighter he had carried with him since December 1944. Pulling it out of his pocket, he absent-mindedly began to flick it open and shut, and the clicking sound began to fill the room. He had long since quit smoking, but the lighter remained. It was a gift from a buddy who died on the first day of the Battle of the Bulge, a possession with which he couldn't part.

Haas looked over at Lehman, she wanted his approval, yet he looked away. "In the end, it's your decision Luba," said Lehman.

"You're the only one who can make it," and then he continued to flick his lighter open and shut.

"Go ahead," Haas said. "What's the plan?"

"Very well," Banbury replied and then he turned to Betancourt and said, "Alicia, please tell Luba and Major Lehman what we have in mind."

Betancourt placed her forearms on the conference table and leaned forward. She looked them both directly in the eyes and said, "So, what do you know about fast boats?"

***

Lehman and Haas had a quiet dinner together at their favorite Gasthof just a few blocks from their flat. They sat, mostly in silence, picking at their food, and if anyone were to ask them, neither of them would be able to remember what they had ordered.

"You're awfully quiet tonight, Herr Major. You too, Fraulein Haas. Is everything okay?" asked Gaby, who regularly served them. "Did you not like the food tonight?"

"No, Gaby. Everything is fine. "We're just tired, I guess," Lehman replied. "It's been a long day. I'll just take the check please."

Haas took a long draw on her cigarette and then stubbed it out in the ash tray on their table. She had not given up the habit as Lehman had.

"Let's go, Cap," she said.

Lehman settled the tab, helped Haas with her coat and the two left the restaurant and walked in silence, arm-in-arm, back to their flat. When they arrived, they each hung up their overcoats in the small wardrobe standing in the entryway and entered the main room of the flat.

Haas left to go into the bathroom to get ready for bed. Lehman walked across the room to the large oak wall cabinet that served as storage for items like glassware, china, and silverware, all items they had managed to accumulate during their time together. The cabinet was the first item of furniture they purchased together. It was of typical German design, tall, made from oak, stained a medium oak brown color, and highly functional.

The cabinet also had a place to store liquor and Lehman opened the compartment door, reached inside, and pulled out a bottle of rare bourbon from the George T. Stagg Distillery he had received from his sister, along with a glass and poured himself two fingers. This bourbon was impossible to come by in Germany. It couldn't be found in the U.S. Army "class 6" stores, the liquor stores, so he rationed it very carefully. He saved it for special occasions and disasters, and today was one of those.

He bent down to the lower shelf of the cabinet where a Grundig shortwave stereo receiver sat and turned it on, listening to the hum from the receiver's vacuum tubes as they warmed up. The radio was tuned to a station in Paris that played American jazz and Lehman and Haas had spent hours listening to music together. Haas preferred the likes of Tommy Dorsey, Duke Ellington, and Ella Fitzgerald. But Lehman loved the brooding, complex sounds from artists such as Miles Davis or Charlie Parker. But by far his favorite was Louisville-born Lionel Hampton, whom Lehman had seen perform live in New York before the war, when Hampton toured with the Benny Goodman orchestra. He stood in front of the receiver and took a sip of bourbon as sounds began to emerge from the radio.

Who is this, he wondered? Sounds like Gillespie.

He took another sip and closed his eyes and music began to fill the room.

"I wish you had told me in advance he was coming," said Haas, now standing in the doorway that led into their bedroom. She was wearing a not too revealing, but just revealing enough silk negligee. Lehman looked over at her and gave her a smile.

"Drink? I'm pouring the good stuff," he said.

"I'm parched," Haas replied, and Lehman moved to the end of the cabinet and pulled out the bottle and another glass. He poured two fingers worth and held the glass up for Haas. He wanted to see her walk across the room.

"If I had told you, would you have shown up?" he asked.

"No, of course not," she replied.

Lehman chuckled at that. He loved her honesty, and he tossed back the remaining bourbon in his glass. He poured himself another. This time, a short round.

"So where does this leave us?" he asked.

"It's just one operation, Cap. In and out. Be quick, get out, return home," she replied.

Lehman looked at her and took another sip.

"Alright then. You'll go. I'll stay. And I'll be here when you return."

Haas raised her glass and Lehman responded by raising his and they each finished their whiskey, looking intently into each other's eyes.

"Let's go to bed, Cap."

Lehman put his glass down on the cabinet, took the glass from Haas and placed it next to his. He took her hand and they slowly walked into the bedroom together.

***

It was about an hour later, and they were lying together in each other's arms. Haas had just fallen into a deep sleep, and Lehman still could hear the jazz coming from the radio in the other room. As he drifted off to sleep, he moved closer, nuzzled her neck, felt the beat of her pulse against his cheek, smelled the perfume in her hair, and he took a long deep breath to imprint her scent and this precise moment in time upon him. The music began to fade into the background, and all he could hear was the steady rhythm from the sound of her heart beating.

Chapter Seven

No Turning Back

Bialik crouched low with one knee on the ground at the edge of a line of trees that overlooked the large clearing. It was a moonless night, and traveling on foot in near total darkness, she had finally arrived at the collection point. She had been to this spot before, but tonight it was different. Her previous meetings were held outside the camp. For operational security, she had never set foot inside the camp. She and the commander agreed the camp's exact location didn't need to be revealed to her. But tonight, because of the nature of the mission ahead of them, that would change, and she would enter the camp that hid the forest soldiers.

She had left her flat at 3 a.m., sneaking down the outside staircase that allowed her to come and go as she pleased, moving quietly so as not to awaken her flat mates. She traveled alone in the darkness, through the dense forest. The journey had been difficult. As she navigated her way, she was glad she decided to wear gloves because more than once, tree roots and thick underbrush reached up to grab her, tripping her and causing her to fall. The gloves at least offered some protection, preventing her hands from being scraped and cut up, but they couldn't help her face, as she made her way through the forest. Low-hanging branches scraped and cut into her cheeks and forehead. She now waited in the darkness for the signal from the soldiers on the other side of the clearing. That was the plan. She was not to move forward until she received their signal. She did her best to wipe the blood away with her gloved hands. Bialik wondered how she would explain the cuts and bruises on her face to her colleagues at school, but that would have to wait, at least for now.

She was breathing heavily as she peeled off the bulky rucksack she had lugged through the night and dropped it to the forest floor with a thud. She had tied all of its contents together with thick twine and then wrapped everything in a woolen blanket she also tied tightly with twine. This prevented the contents from banging together and making any noise. Finally, she tied a basket to the outside of the rucksack – it was too large to fit inside. The basket was to play an important part in the operation she and the soldiers would carry out later on this early morning. If everything went according to plan, she would be back in her flat by 8 a.m.

The clearing was irregularly shaped but formed a kind of rough circle bordered by tall trees all around. It was a rare open space within the thick forest. Evergreens dominated the forest, but there were deciduous trees mixed in as well, mainly smaller birch trees whose white bark stood in contrast to the dark bark of the pine and fir trees that towered over them. The edge of the clearing was covered by heavy brush on all sides.

As Bialik looked out across the clearing, she knew what lay ahead. She had been to this spot before. But the early morning darkness made it nearly impossible to see anything clearly. *It was true*, she thought. *The darkest night really does occur just before dawn.*

She continued to wait, looking for the prearranged signal. She listened carefully for sounds of movement from the other side, but she could only hear the wind blowing steadily through the branches of the trees above her. Her labor had caused her to work up a sweat. Her body had warmed during her transit but now she was cold, and she shivered in the cool breeze that swept through the trees.

Finally, her wait ended. She could just make out a flash of light coming from the opposite side of the clearing. Then she saw another flash, and two more in quick succession, and then a long pause, until finally, there were two more quick flashes of light. It was the prearranged signal and now it was her turn to respond.

Using the torch in her hand, she quickly flashed three times, indicating all clear. She was ready to move out.

She reached down to her feet, grabbed the large rucksack, and placed it over her shoulders. It was bulky and seemed heavier than when she had set out. It was filled to the brim with tins of food, some medical supplies, and other items she had been able to pick up on the black market, items she traded using the extra ration coupons she received because her position as a teacher gave her extra privileges.

Bialik slowly rose from her spot, and although her eyes had become accustomed to the darkness, it was still nearly impossible to see on the cloudy, moonless night. Ever so slowly, she began to move across the clearing toward the tree line on the opposite side, making her way carefully so as not to stumble in the darkness. The clearing was more than thirty meters across at its widest point, and the grass in the clearing nearly came to her knees. Fortunately, the terrain was relatively flat with little undulation, she was strong and although she was tired, she was able to reach the tree line on the opposite side after only a few minutes. Once there, she was immediately greeted by three men, each of them wearing Home Army uniforms. Without a word, two of the men reached out to Bialik and pulled her into the forest, while the third stood watch to make sure she hadn't been followed.

"Did anyone follow you?" asked one of the young men.

"No," Bialik replied. "There was no one. I am sure of that."

The young soldier looked at her skeptically and called over to his comrade, "Jerzy, stay behind for five minutes just to be sure." He then turned to Bialik and said, "Let's go. The commander is waiting for you."

Bialik and the two soldiers moved out. They didn't offer to help her with the rucksack. In the forest, everyone was equal. Man or woman, it didn't matter. Everyone pulled their own weight.

The soldier's camp lay another three kilometers ahead, under the thick forest canopy, and it took the three of them over twenty minutes to navigate their way. Bialik was thankful there was a narrow, but well-worn path, and this made travel with her heavy load just a little easier. Nevertheless, she was breathing heavily and covered in a fresh sheen of sweat when the trio came upon the camp.

The camp was home to over one-hundred soldiers, most of whom would take part in the operation today, and it covered an area of nearly one square kilometer. Narrow forest trails crisscrossed throughout the camp and the trails could be accessed by a network of trenches and bunkers, more dugouts than true bunkers, all carved into the earth and concealed with evergreen branches held up in place by hand hewn logs and tree limbs. The network of trenches formed the camp's defensive perimeter.

As they approached, Bialik could hear the unmistakable sound of rounds being chambered into rifles and machine guns from unseen men guarding the perimeter. The trio immediately stopped and waited. They heard a voice call out, "Burza," the Polish word for "tempest," and immediately the soldier accompanying Bialik replied, "Huragan," or "hurricane," the sign and countersign for the day. The voice ahead of them called out, "Pass," indicating they were now free to move forward, the challenge and response had been accepted.

Crouching low, Bialik and the soldiers moved forward another ten meters where they slipped into a long trench occupied by three soldiers, two manning a heavy machine gun, and the third armed with a rifle. The soldier with the rifle, who immediately recognized the trio, said, "Follow me," and led them down the trench to a spot where it connected with yet another narrow trench that led to the interior of the camp. "You know the way. The commander is waiting," he said, and the trio continued forward another hundred meters where they came upon steps, constructed with heavy logs that had been placed into the earth. They exited up from the trenchworks and moved into a small clearing where a former logging cabin stood, which now served as the commander's headquarters.

"We'll leave you here," the soldier said to Bialik as they reached the cabin entrance, and he and his comrade turned around and retreated back into the trenches. For one last time, Bialik peeled the heavy rucksack from her back and dropped it to the ground, as a tall man, the commander known only by his sobriquet Wulkan, entered the cabin.

"It is good to see you again. I see you've brought us a few items," he said looking down at the rucksack. "We thank you for everything you are able to do."

"I've brought some medical supplies and a bit of food. I've received a reply from British intelligence, and I am expecting much more from them. They have promised ammunition, weapons, and money. I'm organizing the drop off and pick up. We can talk about the details after this morning's operation."

Wulkan nodded, "Good. If today's raid goes well, we should have plenty of ammunition for the near term. But we always need more. What we need most are men to fight."

"The British are training soldiers to join us. They said in their last communication with me, they would be arriving soon but didn't say when exactly. I will let you know as soon as I receive any information."

"Alright," Wulkan replied, "I want to learn more about this, but now, we need to move out." He looked down at his wristwatch. "Our men are already in place along the road where the convoy will pass. I have a vehicle waiting for us. The ambush site is a good distance from us, and we only have thirty minutes to get there."

***

Their plan was simple. Stop the convoy, steal the weapons, ammunition, and anything else contained in the vehicles. Wulkan suggested they could cut down a tree and block the road. But Bialik had another idea. Instead of barricading the road, she would act as bait by kneeling in the road, pretending she had tripped and fell, blocking the convoy from moving.

"The sight of a lone woman in the road will not cause them alarm," Bialik explained. "It will catch them off guard."

"It's risky," Wulkan replied after Bialik laid out her idea. "They might just run you over. Then what?"

"I'll have to take that risk. I'll do my best to roll out of the way and then you and your men can open fire. Set up a kill zone and take them out with the crossfire. But remember, we are trying to capture their vehicles and the cargo. So, try not to shoot them up too much because we need to drive them off."

The ambush site was a section on the forest road where the grade was steep, a switchback where the road took a sharp turn to the left and back to the right. Drivers would have to slow their vehicles as they negotiated the sharp turns, and downshift to a lower gear to compensate for the steep grade.

To make the ruse complete at the ambush site, and to make it appear that she had fallen in the road, Bialik scattered the mushrooms she had foraged the day earlier onto the road. She tipped over the basket she had brought with her and then she waited. Finally, she could hear the sound of the approaching vehicles.

Bialik looked back into the forest and then down the road. The forest soldiers were ready. They had set up two machine guns only ten meters up the road from her position. She wouldn't have much time to get out of the way if she weren't able to stop the vehicles. If the machine gun positions opened fire, she would have to duck as quickly as possible and roll out of the way.

The rest of Wulkan's men, totaling almost fifty, were under cover in the forest directly across from her, on both sides of the road. Bialik could hear the vehicles moving closer and closer and she moved into her position. She knelt down onto the road, smudged some dirt onto her arms, legs, and face to appear as if she had truly stumbled in the road, and then she waited.

She looked up and saw the column of vehicles inching their way around the bend in the road towards her. She now had a clear view of the entire column, and she could see a total of four vehicles. An open-topped Gaz-67 four-wheel drive vehicle, the Soviet equivalent of the U.S. Army jeep was at the front, followed by two Gaz-MM medium-duty lorries, each loaded up with crates of ammunition and weapons, and a second Gaz-67 brought up the rear. The lead vehicle had a driver, and passenger in the front, and a third man in back, armed with a PPSh-41 submachine gun, a deadly "burp gun" the Soviets nicknamed "papasha" or "daddy." The trailing vehicle had only a driver and a single armed guard, also armed with a submachine gun. The Gaz lorries only had a driver, so the column totaled seven men. The Russians were badly outnumbered.

As the vehicles approached, Bialik began her act. She scrambled to pick up the mushrooms strewn across the road and place them into her basket. She looked up as the column moved closer and closer, and she grabbed frantically at the mushrooms on the road, until the vehicles slowed down and finally stopped just a few meters from where she knelt.

The passenger in the front seat, a young corporal, who from the looks of him, was from the Caucasus region of the Soviet Union, stood up and shouted out to Bialik.

"*Devochka*! Girl! What do you think you are doing? Get out of the road!"

Bialik simply looked back at the corporal and continued to gather the scattered mushrooms.

"Wait here," the corporal said to his driver, "I'll take care of this," and he dismounted the vehicle and strode quickly over to where Bialik was kneeling in the road. He stopped just a few steps from Bialik.

"Get out of the road or we will run you over," the corporal shouted. "Do you understand me?"

"I tripped and fell. I was only gathering mushrooms."

The corporal decided he would have none of it.

"Get out of the way," he screamed as he moved forward, reached down, and grabbed Bialik by the hair and began to pull her to her feet. At that instant, the first shots rang out from either side of the road, startling the corporal. He swung around and instinctively reached for his sidearm just as one group of forest soldiers poured out from both sides of the forest road and swarmed the convoy, spraying the lead and trailing vehicles with automatic fire, killing the drivers and the armed guards, while a second group attacked the two lorries, firing into the cabs, killing the drivers.

The corporal had his sidearm out of its holster and was about to return fire when Bialik struck. She pulled her knife from its scabbard and her first blow struck the corporal on his right groin, at the point where the legs meet the abdomen, and with a vicious twist, she severed the femoral artery. He looked down at Bialik and his mouth opened in a scream, but no sound emerged because Bialik struck once more, this time her knife plunged into the corporal's soft upper belly, just below his sternum and ribcage, and she angled the blade upwards towards his heart, twisting the blade as she pushed upwards. The Russian struggled, he reached out with both hands, and tried to grab Bialik and throw her onto the road when she struck again, this time in his neck. She plunged her knife deep into the jugular notch, the soft spot in the neck at the top of the sternum, and once again she twisted the handle to inflict as much damage as possible and severed his windpipe.

Bialik watched as the corporal fell to his knees and murmured something unintelligible. He was dying and Bialik watched as he slipped into shock. His hands instinctively reached up to his throat just as Bialik withdrew the blade. He tried to stop the flow of blood, but even he knew it was too late for that. Bialik's face bore no emotion, only a cold stare as he fell forward face first onto the road, dead.

Bialik looked down at the Russian, the knife in her hand hanging by her side as the forest soldiers pulled the Russian soldiers out of their vehicles and dragged their bodies into the underbrush at the side of the road. She could hear Wulkan order the main body of the men to return to camp while a small contingent of men were ordered to drive the captured vehicles to a narrow logging road about five kilometers up the road. That was the spot where they would unload the ammunition, weapons, and other cargo. As quickly as they appeared, the main body of soldiers slipped back into the forest and disappeared. The two soldiers who had stayed behind along with Wulkan ran over to where Bialik stood and waited for his order.

"Toss his body into the brush with the others and cover them up. I want to make it hard for them to find the bodies. But make it quick. We need to move out," Wulkan said to Bialik who stood in silence, continuing to look down at the dead Russian. "Did you hear me, we need to move out," he repeated.

"Yes, I heard you," Bialik replied. She knelt down and wiped off the bloody blade of her knife on the dead Russian's uniform, and satisfied it was clean, returned the knife to her scabbard. "Get him out of here. Get rid of him."

The soldiers grabbed the Russian by his arms and legs, lifted him up, and carried him over to the edge of the forest where they tossed his body into the heavy brush. Bialik and the commander watched in silence.

"That was close," Wulkan said. "Too close. I thought we might lose you. Are you okay? You're not hurt, are you?"

"No, I'm not hurt at all. I'm fine," Bialik replied irritably. "I was never worried about him. He was mine the minute he stood over me."

"That was obvious," Wulkan replied. "Nevertheless, I am glad you came out of this unhurt. We cannot afford to lose you. You are too important."

"You don't have to worry about me. I'm up to the task. I'm in for the long fight, and I can handle myself."

"That's not what I worry about," Wulkan replied, looking over into the brush where the body of the dead Russian had been tossed. "I worry you may enjoy all of this a little too much," he added as Bialik gave him a cold, hard stare.

"I take no joy in this commander if that is what you mean. I'm not proud of having to kill like this. I'm only doing what is necessary. Now, as you said, we have to leave. Let's get out of here."

* * *

After unloading the vehicles of their cargo, the insurgents drove them west along the forest road, taking the same route the Russians in the convoy would have taken. They drove for a few kilometers to a spot where the road narrowed, where they stopped and parked the vehicles alongside each other, completely blocking the road from both directions. They grabbed the jerrycans stowed away in the back and emptied the cans of fuel on and around each vehicle. They removed each fuel cap and stuffed fuel-soaked rags inside the fuel line and set the rags ablaze. Within minutes, dark plumes of smoke could be seen from Puck, a distance of more than twenty kilometers to the east.

The smoke could also be seen from the Soviet garrison to the west, and when the convoy failed to arrive on time, the garrison commander dispatched a squad of some twenty infantrymen to search for the missing men and their vehicles. The local Puck fire brigade, concerned a fire was already spreading through the forest, went out to investigate the smoke. They were already on the scene when the Russians pulled up in two half-track vehicles. Thick black smoke billowed up into the sky and the smell of burning fuel made it difficult to breathe and nearly impossible to see.

"Who's in charge here?" shouted a tall Russian junior lieutenant as he jumped out of the front of his half-track vehicle and ran towards the fire brigade and burning vehicles. He pulled out a dark green handkerchief from his pocket to shield his mouth from the fumes and acrid smoke.

"That would be me," replied a slender, bespeckled man in his early fifties with a droopy mustache, wearing grey overalls with a dark grey overcoat bearing the insignia of the fire service. "I'm the brigade commander and I'm in charge here," he said with a sense of pride, all the time eying the Russian warily.

"What happened to the men and cargo? There was a detail of soldiers. They were responsible for guarding the cargo. They never showed up at our garrison. Where did they go?"

"I don't know anything about that. We came up the same road as you, but from the opposite direction and we saw no men. Not a soul. We arrived just before you and this is exactly as we found the vehicles," the brigade commander replied. "The vehicles were all engulfed in flames, but as far as we could determine, there was nobody inside. As for cargo, the vehicles all appear to be empty."

"You found no sign of the soldiers? Or the cargo?"

"No," he repeated, this time more emphatically, growing tired of being interrogated by the Russian. "As I said, this is exactly as we found everything. It would appear these vehicles were driven to this spot and deliberately set on fire. What was it you said they were carrying?"

"I didn't say, but these vehicles here," the lieutenant said, pointing to the lorries, "were transporting a shipment of ammunition and weapons to our garrison armory."

"Well, these vehicles were almost certainly empty when we arrived. They were not carrying anything more explosive than the petrol in their tanks."

"How could you know that?"

"It's an educated guess from handling hundreds of vehicle fires. But I know that because there have been no secondary explosions. If these lorries were carrying ammunition as you say, the fire would have caused the ammunition to explode and blast everything to the heavens. There would be very little left of them. Once the fire is out, we'll have to inspect them carefully, but I'm reasonably certain whoever did this drove the vehicles to this spot, and deliberately set them on fire. The vehicles were probably doused with fuel. You can see the empty petrol cans over there," he said pointing to the side of the road where they lay.

"We have to find our men," the lieutenant replied nervously. "Are you certain you saw no sign of them on your way here? I can't believe you saw nothing?"

"As I said, lieutenant," he replied growing tired of the lieutenant's questions, "We didn't see anyone or anything on our way here. Whoever did this drove the vehicles to this location and left the vehicles in the middle of the road. That was done on purpose. Deliberately. It appears they wanted to block the road, and they have done that for certain. You and your men cannot travel further to the east, and we cannot travel any farther west. Not on this road anyway, at least until we put out the fire and push these vehicles out of the way. Once we have the fire under control, we'll be able to definitively say if there are any bodies in the vehicles. But as far as your men are concerned, my guess is they are back there somewhere," he said pointing down the road towards the east. "Or, they may be out there," he said, pointing to the forest.

"We have to get the road cleared," the Russian said, getting angrier and more impatient by the moment. "We have to search for our men."

"You'll be able to pass as soon as we get the fire under control."

"Why aren't you trying to put the fires out? Why aren't you pumping water onto the flames?" The lieutenant inquired as the firefighters cleared the brush from each side of the road and hastily dug out an earthen berm between the burning vehicles and the forest.

"You don't know much about vehicle fires, do you? Well, I do. I saw enough vehicles on fire during the war. And I know what happens. You see lieutenant, the reason we can't pump water onto the fire is because it could cause the fire to spread into the forest, and then we'd have a much bigger problem. Instead, we're pumping water around the vehicles, we're removing the heavy brush, eliminating as much flammable material as possible from the roadside. That is what those men are doing there and over there," he said pointing to the firefighters on both sides of the road, who were busy digging a fire break using picks and shovels. "You'll have to be patient. I want the road open too, but I'm not going to burn down the forest. We have to wait until the fuel burns off. Once the fire runs out of fuel, that is when we can put water onto the vehicles. But if we did that now, we'd risk setting this entire forest on fire." The lieutenant looked helpless, not knowing what he should do when the fire brigade commander said, "We could use your help."

The Russian nodded. "Just tell us what to do," he replied, feeling relieved he and his men would be useful.

"Have your men help us dig the fire break. We have additional tools on our truck."

Over the next hour, the fire consumed most of the remaining petrol in each vehicle and the flames subsided. The fire brigade commander called out to the Soviet lieutenant, "Pull back your men and vehicles at least twenty-five meters. When we're ready, you and your men can help us clear the roadway. I'll let you know when."

The lieutenant gave the orders, and his men, their faces and uniforms completely covered with soot and grime from digging the fire break around the vehicles, were only too happy to pull back. They looked on from a relatively safe distance as the firefighters finally poured water onto the vehicles, causing them to hiss like dragons as the cool water from the tenders hit the hot vehicle frames. *So, this is what hell is like*, the Russian lieutenant thought, as clouds of pitch-black smoke billowed up. The air smelled and tasted of burnt rubber and petrol.

It took nearly another hour before the fire brigade commander finally called out, "You can move forward now lieutenant. We need your help to pull these vehicles out of the road."

One at a time, the soldiers and firefighters attached a grappling hook and line to the frame of each vehicle, and using the Soviet half-track, pulled the charred vehicle remains to the side of the road, opening a single lane. The road was finally cleared.

***

The Soviets had deployed a force of over five hundred men from their garrison, the complement of nearly the entire motor rifle battalion. They had slowly made their way from their garrison to the west of Puck and had scoured the road and the adjacent tree line for any signs of their missing comrades. Dozens of Polish militia officers, along with a company-sized unit of Soviet Ministry of Internal Affairs infantry troops moved along the road from the east. In total, seven hundred men had combed the entire length of the forest road, a distance of twenty kilometers, when they finally joined up. It was an east meets west operation, but there was no celebration when the two forces joined together.

Standing only a few meters from the edge of the road, a Polish militiaman called out.

"I've found something," he shouted and as he pulled back a pile of tree branches and debris to reveal whatever he initially thought was hidden underneath, the look on his face went from excitement to horror as he discovered it was a body. Finally, in the early afternoon on the day after the ambush, the missing soldiers were found.

***

Their bodies had been lined up neatly on the road when the green Russian staff car slowly drove up. Two Soviet officers stood over them in silence, talking quietly amongst themselves. Just a few meters away, Lieutenant Nawrocki paced nervously. When they saw the car, the Russian officers ceased their conversation and came to attention. They knew what was coming.

Nawrocki immediately recognized the car and his stomach churned at the prospect of meeting the vehicle's occupant. The staff car finally stopped. The two Russians and Nawrocki could see the occupant in the rear seat speaking to the vehicle driver, issuing instructions, and finally, after the instructions were made clear to the point where there could be no misunderstanding, the rear door opened, and Sokolov emerged. He stepped out of the vehicle, placed his service cap onto his head, tilted it to one side, pulled down on the front of his tunic, adjusted the holster bearing his sidearm to a comfortable position, and walked over to the three men.

Nobody said a word. Sokolov walked over to where the first body lay in the road, looked down, and then slowly moved down the line, inspecting each body. When he came to the last dead man, he knelt down to take a closer look. He pulled open the dead man's tunic and noted the puncture wounds on his upper thigh, his belly, and finally his throat. His face reddened, his jaw clenched, and he slowly rose, looking back to his left down the line of bodies, taking it all in.

"So, Lieutenant Nawrocki. We meet again on this same forest road," Sokolov said without looking at the Pole. He didn't bother to hide his disgust and anger.

Nawrocki attempted a reply, but he couldn't muster a sound. Not a single word came from his mouth. He knew the stakes had been raised and the conflict had been escalated. The Russians would now enter the fight with full force and with vengeance on their mind. He worried not for his own safety, but for his mother's and whether he would be able to protect her.

"Lieutenant. I'm sorry to say that you have had your chance. I told you that you had to clean up your house and this is the result. You have failed." Sokolov paused once more to look down at the line of dead soldiers laid out in front of him until his gaze finally fell upon Nawrocki. "Now, I'm afraid you're going to have to do it my way."

Chapter Eight

Chelsea

The neighbors who lived near the thirty-five room Victorian mansion in the fashionable Chelsea district considered it to be among the ugliest buildings in London. But to those who served in British intelligence, the mansion and the grounds surrounding it were considered a bulwark against communism. Important work was conducted inside its walls, and it was a lowly file clerk, tired of hearing disparaging comments about the building in which he worked, who first referred to the unsightly edifice to his supervisor as "The Citadel." The name stuck.

Located on the corner of Royal Hospital Road & Tite Street, it was viewed as an eyesore and drew the ire of members of the Chelsea Society, an organization whose stated aim was to protect the historic fabric of Chelsea and preserve and enhance the district's unique character.

The mansion's exterior combined features of the Queen Anne revival style, which included the traditional red brick façade and white window sashes, and the Italianate style, with a flat, hipped roof bordered with clamshell, clapboard siding. But what took the design over the top in the eyes of the neighbors were the nearly three dozen brick panels placed haphazardly around the building's exterior, each of which featured carvings created from stone depicting sheaves of wheat, sunflowers, pineapples, dogs, cats, and several panels showcasing common waterfowl. The masons who constructed the building were given carte blanche to decorate the exterior, apparently without restraint to their creativity or good taste, and they held nothing back.

Construction of the mansion began in the late 1880s and the design inconsistencies were due, in large part, to the mercurial temperament, and to the rise and fall of the fortunes of the mansion's original owner, an investment banker named Fitzroy-Hume, who made and lost said fortune several times in the rubber trade. When the ninety-nine-year-old Fitzroy-Hume died without an heir and without a will after the market crash of '29, he left a mountain of debt behind for his widow to manage. She sold the house off at a fraction of what it was worth just to settle his debts and pay-up taxes he owed to the Crown.

After the Widow Fitzroy-Hume sold it, the house had a series of owners who over the next decade let it slip into decline until Lloyds Bank took possession in the summer of 1939. When the war began, the rising need to house and accommodate the influx of officers and staff charged with organizing Britain's defense, allowed the bank to sell the house to the British government.

In early 1940, it became home to members of the Royal Navy. But after the end of the war, the mansion fell into the hands of MI6. While thousands of men were mustered out of the service and returned to civilian life, the men and women of Britain's secret services were just getting started. They were engaged in a new war, the so-called Cold War. It was just beginning, and the intelligence services were on the front lines of this conflict. They were only too happy to put the building to good use. It mattered not to them the building was considered by some to be ugly.

Like most buildings in London, the mansion suffered damage during the Blitz, but not enough to bring the structure down and the joke in and around the neighborhood was the building was so hideous, even Goering's air forces couldn't bring themselves to waste precious bombs on it.

To make matters worse, the house was now surrounded by a five-meter-high wrought iron fence topped with rolls of concertina wire, a security feature that was added during the early years of the war. When MI6 took over, lamp posts were placed every ten meters along the fence and provided constant illumination of the mansion and surrounding grounds at night. Such security measures wouldn't have been out of the norm during the war, even for government buildings in an upscale district such as Chelsea. But now, three years after the end of the war, the concertina wire reminded the locals of events they would prefer to forget.

Finally, in the summer of 1948, signs began to appear, bearing the name of yet another government agency, the *British Baltic Fishery Protection Service*. The signs were placed on the fence every ten meters or so, an attempt to make it perfectly clear who the building's occupants were.

Along with the signs, a small, rectangular brick blockhouse was built and this new structure, which served as the guardhouse to provide access control to the mansion grounds, was located just outside of the front entrance, facing Royal Hospital Road. The blockhouse bore another smaller sign, which displayed the acronym for the aforementioned agency, the *BBFPS*. Two guards were always on duty in the blockhouse. They manned their post seven days a week, twenty-four hours a day. Everyone entering or exiting the compound had to pass through this security check point. A second gate, located at the rear of the compound behind the building could provide additional access, but it was always locked shut. It was only to be used in cases of emergency.

Residents in the neighborhood were mystified why a maritime agency, with an apparent mission to look after British fishing interests in the Baltic, would need such elaborate security. There was indeed something fishy going on at this location, and it drove the neighbors within the Chelsea district mad. They were further agitated by the constant stream of visitors and vehicles coming and going from the mansion at all hours of the day and night. Apparently, fishing in the Baltic was a 24-hour a day operation that required around the clock protection.

Complaints made to elected officials about the constant noise caused by vehicles coming and going were largely ignored. A local MP, who on one morning tried to force his way onto the mansion grounds, hurled the ultimate statement of class and privilege to the guards manning the front gate, "Do you know who I am?" before being summarily restrained and escorted off the property.

Later that day the very same MP received a visit from a very senior member of the intelligence service. The senior official was Lord Huxley himself, the number two to "C," as the head of MI6 was called. Huxley promptly informed the indignant MP that while every effort would be made to minimize noise, there was serious business going on the grounds of the mansion, and he would be well advised to turn his attention elsewhere, or certain aspects of said MP's social life and sexual proclivities might see the light of day.

"You wouldn't dare," the MP shouted.

"Try me," was the terse reply, and the matter was promptly put to rest.

***

So, it was just a few minutes past 5:00 a.m. on a dark, cold morning in early November, with a steady drizzle of rain falling, when a black four-door sedan turned onto Royal Hospital Road and headed toward the Citadel. The car pulled up to the building's front entrance and waited until a guard, a tall man in his late fifties with closely cropped gray hair, wearing a heavy, full-length black slicker with the collar pulled up high to block the wind and rain, exited the stone blockhouse. His name was Caldwell and he had served in Burma with the Royal Marines during the war and was hired by MI6 as a security man. Caldwell walked over to the vehicle, tapped on the driver's side window and the driver rolled it down and flashed a laminated identification badge.

"Good morning, Harry," Caldwell said, immediately recognizing the driver. He was expected, but they still had to go through with the questions, "And who do we have with you today?"

"Good morning, Mr. Caldwell. I have our special delivery package," Harry replied.

Caldwell reached into his slicker and pulled out a small torch which he turned on and illuminated the interior and the rear seat of the vehicle and saw a single passenger, a very attractive woman, in her mid to late thirties he judged, dressed in green combat fatigues. The woman squinted and raised her arm to shield her eyes from the bright light.

"I'm sorry about that ma'am," Caldwell said as he lowered the torchlight, "Welcome to the Citadel. We're expecting you. Harry here will drive you to the side entrance of the building where they will escort you inside for your meeting with Mrs. Betancourt and Colonel Banbury later this morning. They are not here yet, but they usually arrive before eight. Harry will also help you with any gear you have and will get you settled into your room. Welcome to the Citadel."

Turning back to the blockhouse, Caldwell shouted out, "Mr. Rowan, please open the gate," and a smaller and much younger man exited the building, walked over to the heavy wrought iron gate, lifted the latch, and with a grunt, pushed the heavy gate open to allow the vehicle to pass through.

"Until next time, Harry. Cheers," Caldwell said. Harry nodded in response, put the vehicle into gear, drove onto the compound, turned to the left, and slowly drove to the side entrance where he would drop off his very important passenger, the so-called special delivery.

As the vehicle passed through the gate, the younger man, Rowan, peered intently into the rear of the sedan trying to get a better look at whomever might be inside. Although it was dark and rainy, the security lights around the fence illuminated the car sufficiently enough for him to make out the figure of a woman. He noted she was dressed in British combat fatigues and could also make out her rank – flight officer in the RAF. *Blimey*, he thought. *A woman, dressed for combat?*

The vehicle passed through, Rowan closed the gate behind it, and he and Caldwell both returned to the relative warmth of the guard shack to finish out their overnight shift, which would end at 6 a.m. sharp.

"Did you see? There was a woman in the car," Rowan said incredulously. "I wasn't expecting that. So that was the special delivery tonight, eh? And all the way from Germany. Imagine that. I wonder who she is?"

"And how would you know about any of that?" Caldwell replied, looking sternly at his young charge.

"People talk. You know how it is."

"Hm, Is that so? Which people are those?" Caldwell said angrily, his voice rising. Rowan remained silent. "You're new here so I will just tell you how it is, Mr. David Rowan," he said using Rowan's full name to admonish him the way in which a parent admonishes a young child. "You and I have one job here. Our job is to keep out people who have no business coming into this compound and only let in those that have a reason for being here. You and I don't have a need to know about what goes on inside this fence. That's why we're out here. So, you best put it out of your mind. You didn't see anything tonight, and if you did, you best forget all about it, understand?"

"Yes. I understand," Rowan replied. He could feel his anger rising. He didn't appreciate the rebuke, but he bit his tongue. He would remain quiet and not press the matter. But he wouldn't forget about this. *Someday, I will get back at you*, he thought. "Would you like for me to begin preparing our shift log?" he said, quickly changing the subject. "I've also volunteered for burn detail again," he added. "I'll need to get over to the furnace straight after we're relieved."

Caldwell looked at Rowan for a few seconds, wondering what was going on in the young man's mind. Why would anyone volunteer for burn detail? "Hmm, aren't you the eager beaver. Yes, go ahead and get the log started. Just get it ready for me, and then you can head over to the furnace. There'll be more than enough work for you there. I'll finish the log myself."

"Thanks Mr. Caldwell," Rowan said.

***

Haas peered through the rain-streaked windows of the vehicle trying to get her bearings as it drove onto the mansion grounds. Her driver, apparently his name was Harry, slowly maneuvered the sedan towards the left side of the building. It was a short drive and he stopped underneath an elaborate porte-cochere, which provided shelter against the rain and led to a marble staircase to the right of the vehicle. As Haas looked out of her window, she saw the door at the top of the staircase open, and a woman, dressed in a woolen two-piece, single-breasted suit, a victory suit that was still considered fashionable, step out from inside the building and wait there patiently. Haas looked her over. She looked like she was in her mid-twenties, she was tall and slender, with auburn hair, parted on her left, and swept to the right, cascading into soft waves that fell just above her shoulders. Haas noted she wore heels, at least three inches in height which made her appear even taller as she stood at the top of the staircase.

"Here we are ma'am," Harry said. "I'll fetch your gear from the boot. That's Miss Jenkins at the top of the stairs there. We'll take you up to your accommodations. I believe you'll have some time to get settled in. I'm sure it's been a long night for you, ma'am. Jenkins will fill you in on your schedule for the day."

Harry applied the parking brake and turned off the engine. He hopped out of the sedan and ran to the other side where he opened the right rear door, "Here you are ma'am. As I said, I'll fetch your gear and I'll bring it up to your room." He waited, holding the door open for Haas as she slid across the rear seat and exited the vehicle.

"What is this place?" asked Haas, to nobody in particular, but Jenkins replied.

"Well, officially you are now on the grounds of the offices of the British Baltic Fishery Protection Service. But we call the building and the grounds surrounding it the Citadel."

"Yes, that's what the chap at the front gate called it," Haas replied, looking intently at Jenkins.

"There's a bit of an amusing story behind that," Jenkins said as she descended the staircase towards Haas. "And I'll be happy to share it with you. Good morning, Mrs. Haas. My name is Jenkins," she said extending her hand as she introduced herself.

Haas and Jenkins shook hands. *Firm grip* thought Haas. "Please call me Luba."

"It's a pleasure to meet you, Luba. And I am Natalie, although everyone here calls me Jenkins. Now, if you would please follow me inside. I will show you to your quarters. They are on the top floor. You have a beautiful view of the surrounding area from the small balcony, I might add. Hopefully the weather will clear, and you'll be able to see the sunrise over the city."

Jenkins turned sharply and climbed back up the stairs to the door, which she held open for Haas. "Do you have all of her gear?" she shouted back to Harry.

"Yes, I do Jenkins," he said as he hoisted a green duffel bag and a small backpack over his shoulder.

Haas entered into the mansion and gave the interior a quick look. The entry led into a large foyer, lined with plaster walls, painted an off-white color, and ornamented with a chair rail and dark mahogany paneling underneath. Jenkins and Harry followed her into the foyer, and once the trio were inside, Jenkins took the lead. Haas noted the many tapestries and paintings, most of which depicted scenes of the English countryside, all neatly hung from the picture rail which ran along the wall. She briefly glanced upwards and noticed the elaborate cornice and crown molding at the top of the walls. The ceiling was also made of plaster and decorated with dozens of carved ceiling roses, all arranged in a symmetrical pattern.

"Please follow me, Luba. There's a lift through that archway."

When they arrived at the lift, Jenkins slid the gate open and motioned for Haas to enter first. She turned to Harry and said,

"Just drop the gear inside the lift here, Harry. We can manage from here on."

"But I was told I should . . ."

"No buts Harry. We have it from here," Jenkins said. "We're big girls and we can manage."

Harry stared at Jenkins, and she returned his stare with a glare that caused him to sigh, partly in frustration and partly in defeat. He wasn't high enough in the pecking order to take her on. He carefully placed the duffle and backpack into the lift chamber, turned to Haas and said, "Take care ma'am."

Having watched the encounter between Harry and Jenkins with interest, Haas gave Harry a simple nod of acknowledgement as Jenkins slid the lift gate shut and locked it into place, moved the elevator lever forward and up they went until they reached the top level of the house. Harry could only watch as the two women ascended and eventually disappeared from his view. The lift moved slowly, but once it reached the top floor, Jenkins locked the machinery in place, slid open the gate and with a wave of her hand, motioned for Haas to exit.

"Harry seemed disappointed," Haas commented. "He seemed intent on taking my duffle upstairs."

"I have found his enthusiasm to be a bit much," Jenkins replied. "And Colonel Banbury has asked me to limit your contact with the staff here. Operational security and all that. There are only a handful of people working in this building who are fully briefed and cleared for the operation you are working on. We hope to keep it that way."

"There are two apartments on this level," she said. "Your quarters are to the left. I'll be staying in the quarters to the right, just down at the end of this hallway."

"Oh, are you a full-time resident here, or has James assigned you to keep watch on me?" Haas said, partly as a challenge, but also as an attempt at humor. "I wouldn't put it past him," she said laughing. Haas wasn't sure how Jenkins would take her comments.

Jenkins smiled and said, "Oh no Luba. It's not like that at all. You're right, I don't normally live here. I can't afford the neighborhood. It's quite posh you know. No, I have a small flat that I share with a roommate. But while you are here with us in London, I am at your complete disposal. My job is to make sure you have anything you need and make your stay here as pleasant and comfortable as possible. Consider me your personal aide. Now, let me show you to your quarters." Jenkins picked up the duffel and backpack and headed down the hallway to the quarters assigned to Haas.

The pair walked down the wide hallway and when they reached the open doorway, Jenkins motioned for Haas to enter, "Please, after you." Haas entered into the room and was initially caught off-guard. The quarters were not what she had expected. If she didn't know otherwise, she would have thought she was stepping into one of London's finest hotels.

Jenkins shut the door behind them, and they walked through the wide alcove which led into a large sitting area, which was decorated with two plush sofas and matching armchairs. Haas immediately noted the low mahogany table which set between the two sofas. The table was topped with a crystal decanter filled with whiskey, along with four glasses, which completed the room's furnishings. She also took note of the liquor cabinet against the far wall, which appeared to be fully stocked.

"Whiskey? And a proper bar. How did you know?" Haas quipped.

"Colonel Banbury told me you were fond of Macallan. I presumed that was still the case, no?"

"Of course, but I've also acquired a keen taste for Kentucky bourbon."

"Noted. I will see what I can do to round out the selection for you," Jenkins replied with a smile. "Your sleeping quarters are in this next room," she said leading the way into a large room with a four-poster, canopied bed on the far wall. "There is an ensuite bath and toilet here to the left, and to your right a small balcony. You do have a lovely view of the neighborhood. And there is a small table with chairs set up on the balcony. It's a lovely spot to relax after a long day. Or, so I am told," Jenkins quickly added as she walked over to the tall wardrobe which stood next to the door leading to the bathroom. She dropped the duffel and backpack in front of the wardrobe and opened it wide to reveal the contents inside.

"What's all of this?" Haas asked as she stepped forward to inspect the clothing hanging inside the wardrobe.

"I know you have probably only brought along tactical gear."

"Those were Banbury's instructions, so yes."

"I took the liberty of arranging some other clothing for you," Jenkins replied, running her hand across several dresses, suits, blouses, and overcoats. "I had to estimate your sizes and I think I am close, but we have a tailor and seamstress who can alter any item as necessary. I've selected some clothing to make your stay here in London a bit more comfortable. You can't exactly go traipsing around Piccadilly in your combat uniform, now, can you? And, you can decide which, if any, of these items you wish to take with you when you are inserted, in-country."

There was a long pause as Haas considered the implications of what Jenkins had just said.

"My initial understanding is that it is to be a simple operation. Or at least it was. Two or three days at most. Make contact. Determine the authenticity of the source, make the decision to terminate or continue, and then extraction."

"The Colonel and Mrs. Betancourt will brief you on the current state of the operation, so you should address any questions and concerns directly to them. I'm just, as they say, following orders, and doing what I've been told to do. But," she whispered looking around to see if anyone was listening even though she knew they were the only two in the room, "I can tell you nothing has fundamentally changed about the mission. I believe the Colonel and Mrs. Betancourt simply want you to be prepared for all contingencies," she said, breaking into a smile.

Once again, Haas carefully considered what Jenkins was saying to her before replying. "As I recall, James did say to bring only work clothes, and that he'd handle the rest."

"Quite."

"Look, I don't want to get off on the wrong foot with you, Natalie. I don't want to be any trouble for you. James and I have a history, you know?" Haas said.

"Well, I can only imagine. You two worked together for a long time. Luba, let me be perfectly candid. This assignment is an honor for me. I'm familiar with your war record. We all are. It's remarkable. You served longer than any agent in the field. You survived. You're a legend, especially among the women. The men . . . well, I think they still probably think of you as a threat. That's why the colonel wants me to keep you under wraps, so to speak."

"I understand completely. As far as the men are concerned, they always saw things differently. I'm not sure they wanted us during the war, but they were smart enough to realize that women had a part to play. But it was a long time ago now, and nobody really wants to think about all of that any longer, don't you think?" Haas replied. "We all did our bit, right? What choice did we have?"

"No, you don't understand," Jenkins said. "I was in training with the SOE when the war ended. I never got to deploy despite being slotted for Germany. But the war ended, and SOE was disbanded almost immediately, and with that we all had to return to our lives. There no longer were any real operational roles for women. I wanted to stay on, but the only job I was offered was secretarial, in the typing pool."

"You're here now, it seems," said Haas. "Hopefully your work gives you meaning. And it's better to be on the inside, don't you think?"

"It's largely administrative, but I hope that will change. And yes. I am grateful for the chance. Mrs. Betancourt has been very supportive of women in the service, as has Colonel Banbury. But, it's not the same as it was during the war. I still dream about parachuting behind enemy lines as you did."

A sharp knock at the door startled both of them.

"Ah, that would be breakfast," Jenkins said, regaining her composure. "I've arranged for the kitchen and the housekeeping staff to bring us something this morning. They're bringing up coffee, that's your preference I understand, some bread, butter, jam, and pastries. I'm sure you must be famished. I thought we could take the time to review your schedule for the day ahead. It's chock-a-block with activity. Also, I might add, and this is only if you wish, you may take your meals here in your quarters, at least while you are here and not training in the field. They will be very happy to accommodate you. Now, just let me get the door and have them set-up our meal in the sitting room. Please feel free to freshen up and join me whenever you are ready. Take as much time as you need. I'll be waiting in the next room," she said as she turned smartly toward to apartment door, leaving Haas alone with her thoughts.

Good, this will give me time to do a quick check for listening devices, Haas thought. Old habits die hard. Haas had no reason to believe her room was bugged but clearing a room to ensure there were no listening devices planted was what she had been trained to do.

She began to methodically search the room, starting with the obvious hiding locations such as lamps, light fixtures, and the electrical outlets. She carefully examined the paintings hanging on the wall, running her hands along the frame, and removed each of the paintings from the walls. She reached into her pocket, pulled out a small knife and slit open the paper backing in order to see inside. Nothing. Finally, she examined every piece of furniture, starting with the bed, moving to the dressing table, and eventually the wardrobe, looking carefully for places where a device could be hidden. Again, nothing. At least that she could find.

Unless I've lost my touch, I don't think the room is bugged, she thought as she walked over to the door and entered the sitting room to join Jenkins. Now. Let's see what I'm getting myself into.

Chapter Nine

Soho

It wasn't the kind of establishment Peter Avery would normally frequent. But this was a meeting he wouldn't be having at his regular club, the Oxford and Cambridge University Club. He was a Cambridge man after all and he preferred to conduct meetings within the club's comfortable confines, inside the rooms with darkly paneled walls, padded, plush carpets, and filled with the sound of hushed voices, glasses clinking, or the crack of billiard balls in the background. But, in fact, he hadn't set up this meeting at all. This meeting was set up by a man whom he never had met, a man who went by the name of Alex.

So instead of enjoying the comfort and familiarity of his club, he instead had to travel from his office to a less than desirable part of Soho, which also served as one of London's red-light districts. He exited his taxi and tossed the driver an extra quid for his trouble.

"Thanks, guvnor," the driver replied. "Enjoy your afternoon," he added with a wry smile.

Avery simply tipped his hat to the driver, pulled the collar up on his overcoat, and started walking. As he walked to his final destination, he had to stifle a laugh as he walked past several lines of row houses, most of which still showed damage from the war, and he noted a considerable number of them had their doorbells marked, 'Model.' *Model. A model. Indeed*, he thought.

When he opened the door to The Crooked Limb, a dark, working-class pub on Old Compton Street, he drew a few odd looks from two old men who were seated at the bar and a pair of tradesmen seated at one of the tables situated in front of the pub. But they apparently decided he wasn't worthy of their attention because they quickly returned to their number one priority, the

125

drink in front of them. He stood in the doorway for a moment and looked to his left into the darkest corner until he saw a man who was sitting alone at a small table. The man had placed an umbrella on the other side of the table. A dark Fedora was placed on top of the umbrella, these items served to indicate the table's sole occupant was saving a spot for someone. This was the identification signal they had agreed upon. *So, this is Alex*, Avery thought. *Probably not his real name.*

Alex didn't smile and displayed only casual indifference upon seeing Avery. He looked up in Avery's direction and nodded his head very slightly to offer some form of acknowledgment. He then picked up his hat and placed it on his side of the table. This was the signal to proceed, their meeting could go on as planned. Now all he had to do was to wait for Avery to join him.

Suddenly, Avery heard a voice of a woman call out, "Hey, you! Close the damn door! I'm not paying to heat up the whole bloomin' neighborhood," but he couldn't see where the shouting came from. So, he took a step inside and closed the door behind him. It was a surprisingly heavy wooden door and its weight blocked out not only the light, but the sounds of the world outside. He was inside now, he looked around and he finally saw a barmaid glaring at him. *The source of the shouting,* Avery surmised.

"That's better, mister," she said and then quickly turned her attention back to pulling a pint of what appeared to be a dark lager.

Avery may have been out of place in her pub and in Soho, but he was not intimidated by the barmaid, her patrons, or the area's reputation. He was lean and athletic with a square jaw, cleft chin, and stood at just over six feet tall. Women, and quite a few men, thought he had the look of a Hollywood movie star. His hair, which he combed straight back was thick and full. For a man in his mid-forties, he was fitter than men half his age, and unlike most of his deskbound colleagues in the Foreign Office, where he headed up the American Department, he took physical activity seriously. He worked out regularly, lifting weights and running. He was also a lifelong boxer, having picked up the sport as a young lad at Eton, and he continued to practice the sweet science as a student at Cambridge. During the war, while serving as a logistics officer at the Royal Navy Barracks in Portsmouth, he won the middleweight division title in the Army and Navy Boxing Championship in 1944.

Avery was a man who knew how to handle himself and would back down to few men. But he always possessed added confidence when he carried what he considered to be his great equalizer, his service weapon from the war, a Webley & Scott Mk I semi-automatic pistol, which he had tucked away neatly in the side pocket of his overcoat. He slipped his hand inside his pocket and repositioned the pistol in the event he needed to quickly draw and use it. Touching the handle calmed his nerves and he stood at the doorway for just a few moments to compose himself and gather his thoughts before walking over to the woman pouring pints behind the bar.

"A pint of bitter please, and another of whatever he's having," he added, nodding to Alex sitting in the far corner.

She looked over at Alex sitting alone quietly.

"Him? He hasn't been drinking much of anything," the barmaid replied as she carefully pulled a pint for another patron. "He's been nursing that drink for nigh on an hour now." When she finished her pour, she finally looked up at Avery, standing before her wearing a Saville Row bespoke black virgin wool overcoat with a red pocket square. "My, aren't you something to look at? Aren't you lovely. I don't get many gentlemen the likes of you in here," she said as she eyed Avery up and down, and she gave him an approving and borderline lascivious smile.

"I'm here to visit with an old friend," he said melodramatically, playing along with the barmaid, as he absent-mindedly fiddled with the knot of the red tie that perfectly matched the pocket square of his overcoat.

"An old friend, yeah. That's rich," she said with a chuckle.

"Well, let's freshen him up anyway, shall we?" He pulled a sovereign from his trouser pocket and placed it on the bar. "Just keep the tab open, luv." Avery glanced down at his wristwatch and noted that it had been almost two hours since he left the Foreign Office to set out for Soho, via a most circuitous route. First, he walked to the south and turned onto Victoria street where he walked for nearly thirty minutes, stopping from time-to-time to look in shop windows, not really paying attention to the wares on display, but looking to see if he could see the reflection in the window glass of someone, anyone, loitering and watching and keeping pace with his movements. He even ducked into a small bookstore where he purchased a travel book describing the sights and places to visit in Wales. He had no intention of traveling there anytime soon of course, but once again, the diversion helped him to determine whether or not he was being followed.

After exiting the bookstore, he walked for another four blocks, where, upon seeing a passing taxi, he hailed it down, telling the driver to head to Soho. He instructed him to drop him off three blocks from the pub. He exited the taxi and took a look around. Once again he was satisfied nobody was following him, and he made a beeline straight to the pub.

"Aye guv. You keep throwin' these on my bar and you can have anything you want," she said as she picked the coin up to examine it closely. She slapped it back down onto the bar with a loud thwack and Avery watched as the woman slowly, and skillfully drew two pints, tilting each glass at a forty-five-degree angle and producing just the proper amount of head on the top of the glass.

"Here you are," she said when she finished, and placed each pint directly in front of Avery. "Let me know what else I can do for you."

"Thanks, I shall do that," he replied, not wanting to think about the other possible meanings of her words. Avery picked up the glasses and slowly made his way to the table where Alex was sitting.

"Mr. Avery. It is good to finally meet you in person," Alex said. "I've read all about you, and feel I already know you, but it is good to match a face to a name," Avery sat down and placed the two pints on the table. He slid one pint over to Alex, slipped off his overcoat and draped it over his chair and looked at him carefully. Alex was a slight man with a pale complexion. Avery judged him to be in his late thirties, younger than he was and wasn't sure what to make of this. He wondered if they were sending out the second team, and if he no longer rated their top man.

"It took you longer than I anticipated," Alex continued, his Russian accent revealing to anyone listening that he wasn't a local. "I was beginning to worry about you. Were you followed?" he asked, lowering his voice so as not to be heard.

"Followed? No, that's why it took me so long to get here. In the past, I rarely met with my, erm, contacts. We communicated almost entirely through drop sites. So, I took extra precaution. I wanted to make sure this meeting would only be between the two of us. And I must say, you've picked an interesting location to meet."

"I thought it best to meet in a place where nobody would expect us."

"Well, you've certainly done that," Avery said, lifting his pint glass to his lips and taking a sip. "Hmm, this isn't half bad," he remarked and set his glass down.

"I want to be perfectly clear with you Mr. Avery, just so you completely understand the rules under which I've been ordered to operate."

"Yes, go on."

"You've worked with us for a long time now, haven't you Mr. Avery? Sixteen years, isn't that correct."

"Fourteen. I began working with your people in 1934, when I was at Cambridge." As a student, Avery was well known on campus for his progressive leanings. And with the world economy in tatters, war on the horizon, Avery believed everyone who might be called to military service should get involved in politics. He became a communist and was recruited by the NKVD, who encouraged him to give up his political aspirations and pursue a career in the foreign service instead.

"Ah yes," Alex replied. "And through the years, you've provided us with invaluable information. But recent events have raised concerns. So, I've been told to keep you on, what is it you say, a short leash? My superiors are very concerned the events which transpired in Cairo are not repeated. Please understand I am a man of great patience and understanding, and I also appreciate we are meeting for the first time, but what is that expression? My hands are tied, so to speak."

Avery didn't say anything, but he knew exactly which events Alex was referring. He'd been assigned to the embassy in Cairo immediately after the war. His work was demanding, requiring long hours and late nights. He had to leave his wife Madeline largely on her own and it strained the marriage. There were rumors circulating around town she had been having an affair with a French diplomat. He began drinking heavily, showing up late for important meetings, or missing them entirely.

The Russians became increasingly concerned. He missed meetings with his handlers, and they were about to drop him. He had become unreliable. The final straw that broke the proverbial camel's back occurred at an embassy party hosted by the British ambassador. He'd gotten pissed and created a scene and he threw a champagne glass across the room at a low-level American embassy staffer in attendance whom he thought was being disrespectful. He had to be physically restrained and escorted from the embassy by security staff.

It was only after Madeline had interceded on his behalf that Avery's fortune began to change. She felt at least partly responsible for his erratic behavior. So, she called her father, a peer of the realm and former career diplomat who still carried weight within the Foreign Office, and the two of them were able to convince the British ambassador Avery was ill, that the stress of his job in Cairo was contributing to that illness, and he needed to return to London immediately to seek proper medical care. The ambassador, only too happy to get rid of Avery and make him someone else's problem, immediately agreed and within a week, Avery was back in London.

Madeline, supposedly after receiving a stern talk from her father, agreed to drop her affair, give the marriage another go, and she immediately became pregnant. Avery decided not to look a gift horse in the mouth and didn't question the pregnancy's timing, or the child's paternity. The two were, from all outward appearances, happy to be back together and looked forward to the birth of their child.

This all had a positive effect on Avery. He seemed happy to be back in London, cut back on his drinking, and applied himself at his new assignment within the Foreign Office. With his improved attitude and relative sobriety came forgiveness. And just as it is with many bureaucracies, it's easier to promote a bad egg than it is to sack them. Within just a few months after his return to London, he was appointed as special assistant to the foreign secretary, a position which afforded him access to many of Britain's most sensitive secrets. He then took over as head of the American Department, once more reporting to the Foreign Secretary himself, and suddenly, a treasure trove of highly classified information and reports, including British plans for Eastern Europe, crossed his desk daily which described a growing number of joint, clandestine operations between SIS and America's newly formed CIA. Avery saw anything and everything that crossed the Foreign Secretary's desk that could affect the relationship between Britain and the U.S.

There was just one thing left for him to do. He had to repair the relationship he had with his Russian handlers, the botched assignments, missing or showing up drunk for meetings. His new position gave him the perfect opportunity to make amends. His Cairo handlers indicated, if and when he was ready to resume contact, he was instructed to acquire a post office box to which only he would have access. He was further instructed to place a specifically worded announcement in the Daily Mail and include the post office box number. From there, he only had to wait for a response. It had been only three weeks ago when Avery placed the peculiar announcement, a quote from the Russian poet Pushkin, who was celebrated as a socialist god by Stalin himself, and patiently waited for a reply.

```
Better the illusions that exalt us than
ten thousand truths.
B6252
EW1 Whitechapel
```

He didn't have to wait long. Just two days after the announcement appeared, Avery received his reply on a note typed on white paper, delivered in a plain white envelope with no return address, which set today's meeting into motion. Now, sitting across from the Russian, Avery nervously took several quick swallows of his beer and glanced nervously around the pub. He reached into the breast pocket of his coat and pulled out a thick envelope. He placed the envelope on the table and slid if over to Alex. "This," he said, "should allow you to lengthen the leash. I believe it will also make your wait worthwhile."

Alex looked down at the envelope before picking it up and placing it in the pocket of his overcoat, which he had draped on the chair next to him. "I must say, this is unexpected Mr. Avery. I merely wanted to meet with you for the first time, to get to know you, and set some ground rules. We know there were difficulties in your last assignment in Cairo, and do not want to add to your pressure. But if the contents of this envelope are of the quality you have provided in the past . . . well, I'm pleasantly surprised and I am sure my superiors will be very pleased."

"They will be pleased. Of that I am sure," he replied. "You see, activity is heating up, especially in the Baltic, and specifically in

Northern Poland, near the coast," he said, looking around noticing that they had drawn the attention of several patrons sitting a few tables away from them. Avery glared at their prying eyes, causing the patrons to turn their heads, averting his gaze, and once again, they returned to the solitude and companionship of the drink before them.

"I made copies of the relevant cable traffic for you," Avery continued. "It seems our SIS friends have made contact with a Polish agent, someone whom they presumed was lost."

"Lost? What do you mean?"

"I'm saying they have a sleeper agent operating in Poland and this agent has resurfaced. This agent, whoever it is, has created quite a kerfuffle. The agent was recruited during the war by the SOE and has been dormant until recently. But they are planning to make direct contact with the agent within the coming weeks. This is just the first step. They are also planning a bigger operation in Poland and throughout the Baltic. Everything in the Baltic is being run through a front organization. They have a compound over in Chelsea. Their ultimate aim is to undermine, and eventually overthrow the current Polish government. Many of the operational details are laid out in the cables I've provided. I don't have all the information. Yet. But I can get it. And, I don't yet know the identity of the sleeper agent, but I can get that information too," Avery said as a smile of satisfaction spread across his face.

"We shouldn't talk more about this here," Alex replied nervously. "I'd like to review the information you've provided, and we can set up another meeting in a better location. A place where we can talk more freely. Agreed?"

"Yes, but there's something else you should be aware of Alex. You need to know this now. Today. You need to act quickly."

"And why is that?"

"Again, you'll find this in the cable traffic, but the Americans are also involved in the operation. To be more accurate, they've given their tacit approval, and even though the CIA will not be directly involved, they're providing money to support the operation."

"The Americans. This so-called CIA? They are a fledgling organization. They have only rudimentary capabilities."

"They've agreed to look the other way, so to speak, and allow the U.S. Army to provide other resources."

"What resources?" Alex asked, and then shrugged and said, "Yes, I know, it's all in the cable traffic you provided."

"Just yesterday, at 4:30 a.m., an American counterintelligence agent arrived in London. The agent is a woman, and she's currently staying at the SIS facility in Chelsea. Her name isn't mentioned in any of the cables, but I know who she is."

"And how do you know this?"

"Back in 1944, I provided your colleagues information about the SOE agent network working in Poland and specifically in and around Warsaw. Your people gave the information to communist insurgents. The very same information fell into the hands of German army intelligence, the Abwehr. Once the information was in the Abwehr's hands, they were able to make short order of the SOE network in Poland."

"I don't understand. What does this have to do with their current operation?"

"The SOE agent who set up the network in Poland apparently also set up the sleeper network. A network of deep cover agents, leave behinds, as we like to call them. They are only to reveal themselves and come out when they are ready to become operational. It appears they are planning to send this agent back into Poland. If we follow this woman, she'll be able to lead us directly to the insurgents."

"This is all very interesting information Mr. Avery," Alex replied. "I will of course have to verify this information before we commit to anything."

"Dammit man, don't you see? The SOE agent in Poland, she's now working for the Americans. It's the same woman. Oh, for heaven's sake, it's all in the cables I've given you, Alex," Avery said with exasperation. "Read the damn cables and you'll be able to crack this operation wide open."

Alex sat across the table from Avery in silence for a moment. He ran his index finger absent mindedly in a circular motion over the top of his glass, as he considered his next move.

"Let me ask you, can you meet again in two days' time? At 2 p.m.?" he said finally.

"Yes, I should be able to get away. But where?"

"You're familiar with Primrose Hill?"

"Yes, of course."

"Good. There are two benches on the south end of the park, not more than fifty meters from the Primrose Hill bridge. Do you know it?"

"I know where the bridge is. It connects to the zoo and to Regent's Park."

"Yes, that's correct. I'll be sitting on the bench closest to the bridge. Meet me at that bench at 2 p.m. I will provide the locations of suitable dead drops, along with further instructions on how we shall conduct our business together, how we shall communicate, and what to do in case of an emergency. Meet me there, and please make sure you are not followed. Can you do this?"

"Yes, I most certainly can," Avery replied. "I will be there."

"Good. And Mr. Avery, I seemed to have misjudged you. I will read the cable traffic you have provided. I promise you. And please, keep the information coming to us. Now, let us finish our drinks, leave this charming establishment, and go about the rest of our day. I have much work to do and not much time in which to do it."

Avery leaned back in his chair and let out a long, deep sigh of relief. He stifled a smile because he wanted to appear calm and cool in front of the Russian. But on the inside, he was bursting with happiness. He was on top of the world. Peter Avery was back.

Chapter Ten

Full Disclosure

Haas entered the sitting room and Jenkins invited her to take a seat on the sofa opposite from her. "Coffee with milk and one sugar, isn't that correct?" she asked as she poured coffee from what appeared to be a silver-plated carafe.

"You know a considerable amount of detail about me," Haas replied.

Jenkins laughed nervously and smiled. "Colonel Banbury has told me many things about you. And I've had access to all of your personnel files, covering your service with the SOE and with SIS after the war ended."

"I didn't realize my file included how I take my coffee."

"I've tried to learn as much as I could about you," Jenkins replied handing a cup to Haas.

Haas reached over to the table and picked up a spoon. She then sat back onto the sofa and stirred her coffee with a sad, pensive look as she thought back on her time with the SOE and MI6. "In that case, you know I left on less than friendly terms," she said.

"I don't know all of the details of course. I know there were petty jealousies and insecurity on the part of a number of the male officers, especially those who never dared to set foot on the battlefield during the war as you did. Colonel Banbury shared the highs and lows with me. But honestly, none of that really matters, certainly not as far as I am concerned. We have a mission to accomplish, and you are the lynchpin. Without you, the whole operation is at risk, not to sound melodramatic, mind you."

Haas sipped her coffee and sighed. *I'm back in it up to my ears now*, she thought. "Right," she said. "You're right. None of that matters now. We do indeed have a mission to accomplish, and I'm famished. Let's eat and go over what's ahead for me today. You said I will be busy."

***

After her breakfast, Haas returned to her room. Jenkins would come and fetch her for her first scheduled appointment of the day, a meeting with Banbury and Betancourt in his office. She had about an hour to kill, so she decided to shower and change from her fatigue uniform into one of the items of clothing Jenkins had left for her.

She turned on the hot water and the room immediately steamed up. She tested the water's heat with her fingers, and fiddled with the water nozzle until it was at a perfect temperature, before stepping in. The shower was luxurious, and she stood underneath it for nearly ten minutes, and the hot water helped loosen her shoulders, stiff and sore from the tension she carried with her. Finally, as was her usual practice, she turned the nozzle to cold. She took in a sharp breath and shuddered as the icy-cold stream of water cascaded over her. She felt goosebumps rise as she quickly rubbed her hands over her body. But the cold shower had served to invigorate her and any fatigue she had felt was now gone. She turned off the water, grabbed one of the heavy bath towels hanging on the brass rack adjacent to the shower stall and dried herself off. Once dry, she wrapped the towel around her and returned to the bedroom, where she opened up the duffel bag containing her clothing. She rummaged around the bag until she found underwear to put on. She'd have to forgo hosiery, as she hadn't packed any stockings, but she did pack several pairs of flesh tone colored anklet socks. *These will do for the moment*, she thought. *I'll see if Jenkins can acquire stockings for me.*

She walked over to the wardrobe and opened the doors wide, once more revealing the contents inside. What to wear, she thought as she rifled through the items, pulling out dresses, blouses, and skirts, carefully inspecting each item. Her eyes were drawn to a casual, dark blue A-line dress with a floral print and button-down shirtwaist. Still on the hanger, she held it up to her body, and noticed that it fell to just below her knee. As she removed the dress from its hanger, she also noticed the label indicated the dress was made in Poland, and that it came from a shop in Warsaw. It was standard practice to wear clothing from the country into which an agent was inserted. The last thing an agent needed if they were detained was to be wearing clothing from London. She opened the buttons on the shirtfront and slipped her arms into the sleeves, slid the dress over her head until it fell down naturally upon her, and rebuttoned the front, smoothing out the fabric with her hands. She closed the wardrobe to look at herself in the mirror hanging from the door and turned around to see that it fit her perfectly. *So, this is what they're wearing in Poland these days*, she thought. Satisfied with the way she looked, she opened the door to the wardrobe once again and turned her attention to the footwear Jenkins had supplied.

There were a half dozen pairs of shoes lined up neatly on the bottom shelf. None of them could be described as beautiful, but they all had a similar design and appeared to be practical. Each pair had a blunt toe box with a two-inch stacked heel. Haas immediately noticed that, with exception of the soles, none were made of leather. Leather was still in short supply, as it had all gone to support the war effort. Instead, these shoes all were made of some sort of heavy fabric, three pair were dyed black, the remaining three pair, brown.

She picked up a pair of black, lace-up oxfords, and inspected them closely. Turning them over, she noticed what appeared to be a factory stamp on the sole. *Polish-made. Good*, she thought. She ran her fingers over the uneven stitching that ran along the outer edge of the sole. She then examined the insoles, and noticed they were made of stiff fabric and not the soft leather used in the German shoes she now regularly wore. These shoes were not meant to last for years. But no matter. She'd need to wear them for a far shorter period of time. She made a mental note to tell Jenkins the target exploitation group, the team of individuals who collected and then replicated articles of clothing and other items from within denied areas, had done an excellent job. She would definitely look the part while in Poland.

Haas sat down on the edge of the bed and slipped on her socks and shoes. She loosened the laces so she could more easily slip her feet in, and then pulled the laces snug before finally tying them, right foot first, then the left. She stood up and took a few steps around the room. *I'll need to get used to these,* she thought, *they're very stiff.* She walked over to her duffle bag, pulled out a brush, and returned to the mirror and ran the brush through her hair a few times. She decided to forego makeup. *No need for that,* she thought, as she continued to run the brush through her hair until she heard a sharp knock at the door. *That would be Jenkins.*

All right, here we go, she thought.

***

Jenkins escorted Haas back to the lift which they rode down to the first floor of the mansion. Upon exiting they turned to the right, passed through a short hallway, and entered what was once a large ballroom that was now a beehive of activity. They turned and walked along the right side of the room nearest to the mansion windows. Haas noted the curtains were wide open to allow for as much sunlight as possible. She also noted every light and lamp in the room was switched on. As they continued to walk, Haas saw there were four rows each containing two long tables, lined up end to end, positioned in the center of the room. She watched as five men and three women seated at the tables pored over what appeared to be aerial photographs. Atop each table was a large wooden box with a translucent surface which appeared to be lit by bulbs inside which cast an eerie, fluorescent glow. Haas looked on as one of the women placed what looked like a transparent image of an aerial photograph on the box's flat surface and began to carefully examine the photograph through some sort of viewing lens.

On the far side of the ballroom, a man and woman stood next to a large easel which had several aerial photographs mounted on what appeared to be thin cardboard. They each took turns pointing out various features and objects. Haas couldn't discern what the objects were, but she could see the pair were engaged in a quiet but animated discussion.

All the activity in the room intrigued Haas so much, she stopped dead in her tracks. She counted a total of twenty-two men and women working and noticed the room's walls were lined with maps of the eastern portion of Germany, which was the Soviet controlled sector, the greater Baltic region, and more than a dozen maps of Poland in varying scales and size.

"What is all of this?" she asked Jenkins.

"This is our target analysis section," explained Jenkins as she walked over to Haas and stood next to her. "We have a team of multidisciplinary analysts compiling information from multiple sources."

"Multidisciplinary? What does that mean?" Haas asked.

"What we do here is combine intelligence from different sources with a goal of gaining a more complete understanding," Jenkins explained. "For example, we run regularly scheduled aerial photo reconnaissance missions throughout the entire Baltic region. Our team of imagery analysts help identify potential threats to the agents we've placed in the field. We also have a team of analysts who regularly review reports and transcripts of radio intercepts," Jenkins said pointing over to a group of six men and women seated behind desks against the far wall. "And that group over there," she said pointing to another group of four men and women, "reviews and compiles our human and open-source information. Unfortunately, within those disciplines, we are limited at present to routine diplomatic cables and a collection of print publications from the state-run media within the Soviet zone of control. Receiving timely information from our agents is difficult at the present time. And of course, the Soviets and their client states have definitely shut down any remnants of a free press. However, we are developing agent sources all the time. And as far as the state-controlled press, there is still useful information to be had, as long as you know how to intelligently interpret the tea leaves of bureaucrats. The state press always wants to tout accomplishments. It's up to the analysts here to apply the appropriate grain of salt to whatever the state publishes."

"That's remarkable," said Haas. "What I would have given to have had access to such information during the war."

"Indeed. Colonel Banbury has said as much. He's been the driving force behind this, insisting we have our own analytical capabilities. We even have our own weather forecasting team which collects data from around the UK and Europe to provide our agents with a custom forecast. They also calculate high and low tides, moonrise and moonset, and other valuable information. You'll have the opportunity to meet and spend time with the entire target analysis team, and you'll help guide them as you prepare for your mission ahead. But now, let's get over to the Colonel's office. There is a lot to discuss there too, and we don't want to keep him waiting."

"Right," Haas said. "Let's not keep James waiting," as she and Jenkins resumed walking through the ballroom, down a short hallway, and then entered into a small library, whose walls were lined with bookcases from floor to ceiling.

"Colonel Banbury's office is right here," Jenkins said, pointing out a heavy oak door to her left. She walked up to the door and knocked firmly. But she didn't wait for an invitation to enter, and she opened the door and held it open so Haas could enter the room first.

Banbury was seated behind his desk and looked up from a stack of papers he had been reading when Haas and Jenkins entered the room.

"Ah, Luba! Welcome to the Citadel," he said rising up to greet Haas. "And welcome to London of course. I trust Jenkins has been taking good care of you?"

"She most certainly has," Haas replied, looking over at Jenkins. "She's even seen to it that I am suitably attired."

"I can see that. I'd say she has done a rather excellent job. You definitely look the part."

"I do look the part, don't I? I thought this was to be a quick in and out mission, but from the amount of clothing Jenkins has provided indicates I should prepare for an extended stay. What's going on James? And what is all of this?" Haas asked, looking around Banbury's office. "Perhaps you should start over from the very beginning," Haas said. She seated herself in one of the two chairs in front of Banbury's desk. "Let's get down to business, shall we? And where is Alicia? I thought this was more or less her show?" Banbury looked at Jenkins and nodded his head indicating she should take the other seat.

"While you were flying in last night, Alicia had to travel down to Portsmouth to pick up a very important package. She's on her way from there now and will be joining us shortly," Banbury replied as he sat down. "So, let's begin. What I am about to say to you is of course classified, top secret. We've brought you back to London to enlist your support with Operation Nightfall, an operation you helped launch in 1944 when you served in the SOE, which involved recruiting leave-behind agents in Poland. Before I go into all that, tell me, what do you know about the current situation in Poland? Have you been able to establish any contact with your family in Gdansk, either officially, or unofficially?"

Haas winced at the mention of her family members. She had grown up in Poland, in Gdansk, and lost contact with her family in 1944. Her letters initially went unanswered, then they were returned, marked 'addressee unknown.'

"No," she replied. "I've heard nothing from my mother, nor from my aunts or uncles. Two cousins were working for the resistance when the war ended, but they've all disappeared. As far as I know, they are all gone."

"I'm very sorry Luba," Banbury said slowly. He took in a deep breath and continued, "As I am sure you are aware, the situation in Poland is very difficult. Today, there is an active and ongoing armed resistance that is attacking Polish state-run institutions and even Soviet facilities. I'll leave it for the historians to decide, but it's been three years since the end of the war and as far as we're concerned, the situation in Poland is that the country has descended into a low-level civil war. The communist government is struggling, and we intend to do everything we can to help topple the current regime and restore a democratic form of government there.

"Go on," Haas said. "I'm aware of all of that."

"Quite," Banbury said, clearing his throat. "We of course thought Operation Nightfall was dead. It had been over four years since we received any communication from any of the leave-behinds, the agents you recruited in 1944. After such a long time, we naturally presumed any agent you had set up had either been rounded up or killed by the Russians or the Polish security services. Until of course, we received the radio transmission, quite out of the blue, from the agent we know as Lygia."

Haas nodded impatiently. She waited for the other shoe to drop. *Get to the point, James*, she thought.

"So, what this is," he said as he swept his hands in front of him, referring to the mansion and their surroundings, "is effectively a charade. Technically, and from all outward appearances, you are sitting in the headquarters building of the British Baltic Fisheries Protection Service. However, everyone working in this building is a member of the SIS. Every last man and woman down to the cooks and the chambermaids."

"Yes, Jenkins told me as much," Haas replied. "But what is the purpose of such an organization, and what does that have to do with the mission at hand, and me, specifically?"

"I'm coming to that. Since Lygia has miraculously returned from the dead, we wanted to take advantage of the situation. So, it was a logical decision to place Operation Nightfall within a much larger set of operations we are running from this building, code named Labyrinth. There are a myriad of sub-operations, targeting the different Baltic states, all with their own code names. You do not have a need to know about these operations, but I can tell you they all are run from the Citadel. So, to answer your question, the BBFPS is a cover organization. It's a front. Our goal is to train agents and armed insurgents, and once properly trained, we will insert them in-country, Poland for example, where they are to link up with the anti-Soviet and anti-communist resistance groups operating there. We'll train them, arm them, and support them until we roll back communism in Eastern Europe."

"Those are lofty goals, James. Does Britain have the wherewithal to see it through?"

"To be perfectly honest, I don't know. But I wouldn't be doing this if I didn't think we had the ability to achieve our objectives. The Americans are also helping us, they are providing funds and other forms of support, sharing of intelligence for example. We won the last war, and I know we can win this one. Eventually."

"Hmm. Well, you know where I stand on the issue, James," Haas said. "So, have you had additional transmissions from Lygia since we last met in Germany?" Haas asked.

"Yes, we have. Lygia is on a roughly twice weekly transmission schedule and has made contact with local resistance fighters. They've been very active, with attacks on the local militia and an especially daring ambush of a Soviet ammunition supply convoy. We've been able to confirm both attacks through other sources of intelligence, principally signals intercepts. The Russians are not very happy, neither are the Polish security services. There have been reports of mass arrests in and around the area where Lygia is operating, a small town in the north, Puck? Do you know it?

"Yes, it's not far from where I grew up. It lies about sixty kilometers or so to the north if I'm not mistaken."

"That's it," said Banbury. "In the most recent transmission, Lygia reported to us yesterday that the insurgents hit the UB jail in Gdynia and as a result, more than forty detainees escaped. From what we gather, the Russians are absolutely furious, and their anger goes all the way back to Moscow."

"This is a dangerous escalation, James. I can't believe you're going to take on the Red Army in Poland. There is no way you can send enough men or weapons," said Haas.

"No, we're not going to do that," Banbury replied. "This is ultimately a Polish fight. We are merely trying to make the fight end to our advantage."

"Hmm. So, tell me once more why I am here," said Haas. "What is it exactly you want me to do?"

"Your main mission objective is simple: Confirm whether or not we are communicating directly with Lygia. Everything indicates we are, but we have no way of verifying Lygia's identity. You are the only one who knows who Lygia is. We here don't even know if Lygia is a man or a woman, although I have my suspicions." Haas sat across from Banbury, said nothing and gave him an inscrutable look. "We also need you to buy us some time."

"Time for what?"

"We plan to regularly deliver ammunition, weapons, and other necessary supplies. But it will take us time to fully develop that capability. We're very concerned about recent insurgent attacks on members of the Red Army. So, we need to convince Lygia and the insurgents, which we believe are remnants of the Home Army, to limit their attacks to Polish targets only. Oh, I don't care if they target a Russian soldier from time to time. But, no more large-scale attacks on the Soviets. Polish targets are fine, but the Soviets are off-limits, at least for now. I don't want to provoke the Russians too much before we establish our agent network and can provide a steady flow of arms and fighters to the insurgents."

"What makes you think Lygia will listen to me, James?"

"You recruited Lygia, and you'll have to use your powers of persuasion, just as you did with the SS and Gestapo when you convinced them to release two SOE agents they were holding."

"Different times, James. Plus, I was able to bribe them with two-million francs. Money talks, but I don't think Lygia is motivated by money. Lygia is motivated by something far greater; freedom."

"I understand. Therefore, you will be going in with a cache of money. They'll be able to use it to locally procure supplies. Hopefully that will be enough to mollify them because in addition to weapons and ammunition, we're not ready to supply the insurgents with what they most want."

"And what is that?"

"What they most want are more fighters. More men to throw into the fight. We won't be ready to do that until early next year. We've just started training our first cadre, and we hope to place them in the field, into Poland by April or May 1949. Next year."

"Alright James. I'm going to need more than what you've given me here, but we'll work out a plan. Together. Just as we did in the old days," she said with a smile. "I will buy time with Lygia until you are able to get all of your ducks in a row. Satisfied?"

"Completely."

"Good. Now, please continue. Tell me what on earth this operation has to do with fish in the Baltic."

"I'm glad you asked that question, Luba," Banbury said, "The BBFPS also operates out of a field office located in Kiel, Germany."

"Kiel? That's off the beaten path. What's so special about Kiel?" Haas asked.

"Ah, now you are getting to the heart of the matter. And this is how our grand charade will affect you," said Banbury, his eyes flashing with excitement. "During the war, how did we insert you and other agents behind enemy lines?"

"There were many ways. On foot. By air. I parachuted into France. We all did."

"Quite right. But that won't be the case this time. This time, you'll not be traveling by air, but by boat."

"By boat?" Haas replied incredulously.

"Are you familiar with E-boats, Luba?"

"No, but I have a feeling I'm about to learn all about them."

"The Germans called them S-boats, which is short for *Schnellboot*, meaning fast boat, but our Royal Navy referred to them as E-boats. The E stood for 'enemy.' Not very creative if you ask me. But these boats have two very important capabilities. First, they are extremely seaworthy, even in the heavy seas of the Baltic and North Sea. They can take a real pounding in all sorts of weather. Secondly, they are very fast. That's why the Germans called them fast boats, which is a much more appropriate designation. These boats are capable of sustaining speeds of greater than forty knots, and quite frankly, they can outrun anything currently in the Soviet Navy."

"I see. And operating boats under the premise of protecting British fishing rights in the Baltic gives you the perfect cover," Haas said.

"Precisely," Banbury said as he sat back in his chair and smiled. "Now, there are a few things you should know about Jenkins here. She is here to be your personal assistant, but she possesses a number of exceptional skills you are probably not aware of."

"Oh? Such as?" Haas replied, glancing over at Jenkins who blushed with embarrassment.

"For starters, she speaks fluent Polish. And she's become quite proficient with explosives and firearms. She also knows her way around the wireless. She trained with us in the SOE, but the war ended before we could deploy her. After the war ended, we've been searching for the suitable assignment for her."

"*Mówisz po polsku*? You speak Polish?" Haas asked.

"Yes, my mother was Polish, my father English," Jenkins replied.

"Why didn't you tell me you were Polish?" Haas asked.

"It didn't come up and you didn't ask. You know, never volunteer too much information, right?" Jenkins replied.

"Ah, touché," said Haas.

"My father was an academic. He lectured in the economics faculty at the University of Warsaw in the 1920s. That is where he met my mother. They fell in love and got married. I was born in Warsaw, but thankfully my parents had the prescience to return to Britain less than a year before war broke out."

"The two of you will have plenty of time to swap stories," Banbury interjected. "Jenkins will be our point person in Poland, and the two of you will deploy together. Assuming Lygia is legitimate, Jenkins will take over and manage Lygia's case file. Regardless, and even in the event our asset Lygia goes belly up, Jenkins will establish connections with the insurgency, and direct operations herself from the field. Luba, we need you to share your unique insights with her, the tricks of the trade. You were our longest serving agent during the war, and we hope you'll be able to share your survival skills, train Jenkins up, take her under your wing."

"You cannot teach luck, James," Haas replied. "But I will do everything I can to support her." Haas reached over and clasped Jenkins' hand and gave it a tight squeeze. "We'll have each other's backs. Are you familiar with that expression, Natalie? It's what my American colleagues say all the time. You're in for a rough time, you know that, right?" Haas added, continuing to squeeze Jenkins' hand.

"I know what I'm in for," she replied.

"I hope so, my dear. I truly hope so. James, do you have any more surprises for me? Do you have any good news?" Haas asked.

There was a knock on the door before Banbury could formulate a reply. Haas, Jenkins and Banbury all turned as the door opened, and Alicia Betancourt entered the room, followed by a tall man wearing what appeared to be the uniform of the British Navy. But his uniform was devoid of an insignia of rank or any other designation. Haas carefully looked the man over, up and down. He was about six feet tall with a lean body, chiseled face, and a salt and pepper beard. He looked to be in his late thirties, but Haas couldn't be sure. His closely cropped hair was definitely a premature gray, but still revealed flecks of blonde. What stood out to Haas were his eyes. They were steely blue gray in color, like the color of the sea.

"Ah, Alicia, your timing is perfect," Banbury said, once again rising from behind his desk to greet her and the man. "How was your trip in from Portsmouth?"

"Uneventful. Everything went according to plan."

"Yes, I see you've brought the package. Everyone allow me to introduce Captain Hans-Friedrich Ruger, formerly of the *Kriegsmarine*, the German Navy, but now very gainfully employed by our side. In fact, we have also enlisted the assistance of a half-dozen of Captain Ruger's fellow sailors in our operation here."

Banbury walked out from around his desk to shake Ruger's hand. Turning back towards Haas and Jenkins, he said, "Captain Ruger, you know our Miss Jenkins of course, but may I introduce you to Luba Haas?"

Haas remained seated, extended her hand, and Ruger reached out to give Haas a firm, but warm handshake.

"It's a pleasure, madam," Ruger said to Haas, and he seemed to resist his urge to bow and click his heels together. "Fraulein," he said nodding his head to Jenkins.

"Captain Ruger, I was just explaining how we've developed an innovative way to transport cargo into and out of Poland. Luba, Captain Ruger here has been invaluable. He's an expert on fast boat operations as he commanded a German squadron during the war. Captain Ruger knows the North Sea and the Polish coast like the back of his hand. Luba, meet your E-boat captain."

Part Two

Chapter Eleven

Acceptable Risk, Acceptable Loss

It was just a few minutes after 2 a.m. when Haas, Jenkins, and twenty-one Germans under the command of Captain Ruger boarded an E-boat and departed from the small port at Nexo, on Bornholm Island, Denmark. Once they cleared the harbor, they proceeded out to sea bearing northeast for ten minutes and then made a sharp turn to the northwest and increased their speed to thirty knots.

Although Ruger was in command of the vessel, two British naval officers, Commander Charles Radcliffe, and Lieutenant Commander Henry Baker were also onboard. They would not be joining the actual operation. It was 'C,' the Chief of MI6 who insisted the officers be added to the team, to observe the preparation and training. Their job was ostensibly to consult and provide advice, but in reality, their purpose was to ensure the number one rule within all bureaucracies was followed – cover your arse.

They had been training for a week now and today was their final run. They had it all down now. The crew practiced lowering the landing craft and holding it stable for the landing team. The landing team practiced making their way over the rail and assuming their positions. Once the helmsman observed everyone was on board, the landing craft could get underway. After a week of training, they could do this in total darkness in less than their goal time of six minutes.

At precisely thirty minutes out, Ruger received a coded radio signal from London. During the actual operation, this radio message would be the signal for the E-boat to enter the territorial waters claimed by Poland. But today, it was just the same exercise they had been repeating over and over. They were practicing landing and infiltrating Haas and Jenkins into a denied area, onto a spot on a beach on the coast of Poland.

Upon receiving the signal, Ruger ordered his helmsmen to increase speed to forty knots and turn back towards Bornholm on a bearing that would take them to the eastern side of Salene Bay, located on the northern side of the island, to the spot where steep cliffs overlooked a broad stretch of rocky beach.

The beach on Salene Bay was merely a replica of what they would find in Poland. The target analysts back at the Citadel selected this particular stretch of coastline on Bornholm because it closely resembled a beach north of Ostrowo, Poland where the real landing would take place. Both beaches possessed numerous rock formations that jutted from the sea, which presented a potential hazard if not navigated properly. Each area of coastline possessed a shallow, silty bottom shelf, which extended out for more than one hundred meters. Once the landing team reached the shelf, the depth at low tide was no more than a meter and a half. It was shallow enough to wade ashore. The shoreline along both beaches teamed with long strands of fucus vesiculosus, a stringy brown seaweed commonly known as bladderwrack, so named because its round vesicles filled with air, resemble a bladder. Bladderwrack could grow to a length of five feet, and its holdfast, the rootlike structure which connects it to the ocean floor, made for another potential hazard for the landing party. The landing craft pilot had to navigate through the thick strands of seaweed without the boat's outboard motor propeller becoming entangled and fouled.

On the actual landing day, Haas, Jenkins, and the landing team would meet up with Lygia in person. If, at any time during the operation, they came under fire from Polish security or other forces while on the beach, the seamen in the second boat would provide covering fire allowing both boats to retreat to the E-boat waiting offshore. But the goal of this mission was to erase all doubt about Lygia. If Haas could identify and determine Lygia was the genuine article, the mission would go forward. If Lygia turned out to be an imposter, part of an elaborate trap, the mission would be aborted. Their orders were clear in this case. It would fall to Jenkins to terminate Lygia and they all would immediately return to the E-boat.

They had worked out precisely how they would enter Polish territorial waters. They needed to quickly, but silently and stealthily, deploy the small boats that would take the landing party ashore. Today's drill was to have been their seventh and final landing, having already successfully and without incident completed their practice landing each of the past six days. By now, the crew, and most importantly Haas and Jenkins, although tired from the daily drill, possessed a high level of confidence they could successfully execute the mission.

The weather conditions, always problematic on the Baltic, and especially challenging in November, had been good. For the past week, the early morning hours had been generally clear, with good visibility. A week ago, during their first practice landing, the moon was at its brightest, but now they were in the final day of the waning crescent phase of the moon.

Early in the morning as they departed Bornholm, the moon appeared in the sky as a mere sliver. The sky was cloudier than the previous six nights, and this meant they had to execute the operation in almost total darkness. This all fit into the plan, however. After today, they had a four-day window to launch their E-boat from Bornholm, transit across the Baltic, enter Polish waters, and deposit Haas and Jenkins onto the shore. The actual operation and landing would occur during a new moon phase, a time during which there is no moonlight at all.

Predicting the weather involves both science and art. Timing out the arrival of a front is always tricky, especially so during November in the Baltic. And on the final day, the seventh day of their practice runs, the weather prognosticators misjudged the arrival of a very fast-moving front by several hours. The weather, and everything associated with the operation was about to take a turn for the worse.

By the time the E-boat had reached its destination, a point of roughly two kilometers offshore from Bornholm, the wind and waves had noticeably picked up. The crew lowered two 7-man rubber landing crafts into the water as the E-boat was rocked by large waves whose crests broke into spindrifts. The wind had shifted and now came out of the northwest, drawing in colder Arctic air. The windspeed increased to between forty and fifty kilometers per hour. Gusts now exceeded sixty, a force of between six and seven on the Beaufort Wind Scale. Ruger and Radcliffe watched from the E-boat bridge as a team of four men struggled to keep the boats steady, holding tightly onto the lines, as the rubber boats were tossed violently by the waves and crashed repeatedly into the hull of the larger E-boat. Haas, Jenkins, and a crew of twelve Germans were assembled on deck, awaiting their turn to climb over the side onto the now slippery rope ladders and make their way down to the rubber boats below.

"Captain Ruger, the weather is not going to cooperate today," Radcliffe said as he observed the struggle below him, "It's your call of course, but I wouldn't object if you called this off."

"We've been in far worse seas and conditions," Ruger replied. "Besides, we don't know what the conditions will be next week. They might be worse. It's your people who need the experience."

"Very well, Captain. As I said, it is your call."

Haas and Jenkins stood next to each other on the deck and clung to the boat's rail. They each carried a *Blyskawica* sub-machine gun equipped with a 32-round box magazine, wrapped in oil cloth to keep the weapon dry for as long as possible, which they slung over their head and shoulders so they would have both hands free for climbing. Both of them wore a thick, belted rubber poncho, which was tied at the waist. Their webbed belt, wrapped around the waist and over their poncho, bore a case containing two additional magazines, a canteen, and a small first-aid kit. Under the poncho, they each wore lined, heavy, zippered overalls which provided them some protection from the cold and covered up their civilian clothing which they wore underneath. Two waterproof duffel bags, which would be lowered to their boat once they had boarded, carried their additional clothing. Each bag also held one hundred thousand Polish zloty, the rough equivalent of twenty-thousand pounds, which could be used to purchase supplies, but most likely bribes.

The rain, now driven by the heavy wind, stung their faces and Haas and Jenkins struggled to keep their balance as the E-boat pitched and rolled in the sea. They were flanked by two German sailors, an older former petty officer, and a young seaman, whose job was to ensure the boarding party safely made it down to the landing boats below. The boat's helmsman and two sailors had already successfully climbed down into the boat. Jenkins would be the next to go over the side.

"I'll see you below," she shouted to Haas as the Germans helped her over the rail and she descended the ladder. She lost her footing several times on her way down, as the ladder's rungs were made slippery from the driving rain. A heavily armed sailor immediately followed Jenkins over the rail. He would take a place next to Jenkins in the boat.

Finally, it was Haas's turn. She looked off into the darkness and waited for the tap on her shoulder, the signal to board. As she readied herself to climb over the rail, a young sailor came up alongside her and stood with her against the railing.

"Who are you?" Haas asked, looking over at the German. "I haven't seen you before, have I? You haven't been on the previous drills." She had to close her eyes as a strong gust of wind blew rain across the deck.

"My name is Häupler. Dieter Häupler. I'm taking Schiller's place today. He's sick. But don't worry, I know what to do. And I've also been in far worse weather than this."

Haas opened her eyes and looked at the German. She could barely make out his facial features in the near total darkness but could see that he was young. *He has to be in his early twenties,* she thought, *but he looks like a boy.*

"And how is it you've been in the service so long to see weather conditions worse than this?" Haas asked.

"I joined the German Navy on my sixteenth birthday, in 1943 and I've served with Captain Ruger all that time. I've seen a lot."

That makes him just twenty-one, Haas thought. He has his whole life ahead of him and he's going to be sitting next to me in a damned rubber boat.

"I'm sure you have. Well, you picked a fine day to volunteer," said Haas. She felt the tap on her shoulder and looked to her left to see the sailor motioning her to begin her descent into the darkness below. "I'll see you on board, Dieter Häupler," and she hoisted herself up onto the slippery rail, turned her body, grabbed onto the slick rope ladder, and began her descent.

"Yes," Häupler shouted to Haas, looking down at her as she climbed the ladder. "And don't worry."

"I'm not worried," Haas shouted back. But it wasn't true. She wasn't looking forward to this.

By the time the landing party finished boarding, the Baltic was acting like a butter churn as waves rose, crested, and toppled over themselves, turning the sea into a white foam. The lines were cast off and the boats began to slowly make their way to shore. They rose up and down, water crashed over the bows, which drenched everyone and everything onboard.

Each boat was designed to fit seven people. It had three rows of wooden seats, each of which could accommodate two people, and a helmsman sat aft. The boat was only three meters long and two meters wide and it felt cramped when fully loaded.

Haas sat in the first row near the bow. She would be the first to disembark, and Jenkins sat behind her in the second row. Häupler sat next to Haas and another sailor sat next to Jenkins, and the last two sailors in the party were seated in the third row. A helmsman sat aft and manned the outboard motor and tiller. It was his job to ferry them to shore.

"Everything good? Are you ready to go?" Häupler shouted.

"Yes, I'm fine," Haas replied with her eyes tightly shut as she held onto the wooden bench seat with all her might. The waves rose to a height of greater than one and a half meters and the helmsman struggled to maintain control in the rough seas. As they made their way towards the shore, the waves seemed to swell higher, taking the boat up until it was nearly vertical and then it finally reached the crest and fell, crashing back into the water.

"Don't worry," Häupler shouted. "I've been through much worse. We'll be ashore soon." Häupler had barely gotten his words out when at just that moment, a nearly three-meter-high wave seemingly came from nowhere and struck the boat's starboard beam. The boat began to tip precariously, and it nearly capsized, and the quick acting helmsman managed to turn leeward, the proper course of action, but not before a second wave hit the boat. The force from the wave caused Haas and Häupler to lose their hold. They took the brunt of the wave and were thrown overboard into the sea.

The moment Haas hit the icy water she was immediately struck by another wave which pushed her down into blackness. It was so dark underwater she couldn't see her hands, arms, or legs. She felt as if she were sinking, weighed down by her equipment and clothing. She became disoriented. As she struggled to swim, she couldn't tell if she was swimming up towards the surface, or downwards to her death.

Don't panic. You're a good swimmer, she thought. *You know how to swim, just do it.* She cast off the equipment holding her down and pulled her weapon over her shoulder and let it fall into the sea. Next came her web belt and she immediately felt lighter. She needed to get her bearings and determine which way was up and which was down. But it was too dark, and the water continued to swirl around her. She was running out of breath. She extended her legs to see if she could touch the bottom of the beach shelf, but she could feel nothing. *We're too far out,* she thought.

Stay calm, she kept saying over and over to herself. *Use your instincts and swim.* She kicked her legs and pulled with her arms using all the strength she had, swimming in the direction of what she thought was the surface, not knowing, but hoping she had made the right decision. Her lungs burned as she strained against the weight of the water, kicking, and pulling. She felt herself getting weaker. *This is it. This is where I will die. This is how I will die.*

Suddenly, she felt a hand grab a handful of her poncho and began to pull her. At first, she panicked and tried to fight, kicking and flailing her arms at the unseen force pulling her through the water. She felt herself moving faster through the water as a second hand grabbed onto her, seemingly propelling her towards the surface. Haas then felt someone behind her. An arm slipped around her neck. She couldn't see who it was in the inky water, but suddenly she felt someone swimming alongside her, accelerating her pace to the surface. *Häupler?* She felt a surge of hope and continued to kick in the water with all her strength.

Finally, she broke through the surface and gasped for air. Another wave crashed over her, and she felt herself sinking once more as she swallowed sea water. But the swimmer at her side refused to let her go and they bobbed back up to the surface together. She coughed up sea water as she felt the arm slip away from her neck. Her instincts kicked in and she began to tread water, bobbing up and down. She gagged and coughed up more seawater as she tried to take in large gulps of air, desperately trying to fill her lungs with oxygen. She turned around in the water to look for her rescuer. And for just a brief second, she caught a glimpse of Häupler's face. His eyes sparkled and for a moment, she thought she saw him smile as if to say, "See, I told you it would be all right." He was bobbing up and down, struggling to stay afloat when another large wave hit. His eyes grew wide, first with surprise, then shock, and finally fear. The wave crashed over him, pushed him down, and he slipped below the surface of the water.

"Haas! Haas! Where are you? Haas!" It was Jenkins screaming in the darkness, and Haas could hear her as she called out her name, over and over.

"Over here! I'm over here," Haas screamed as she bobbed up and down in the darkness. Amidst the roar of the rain and the waves, she could hear the outboard motors from the two boats. She squinted her eyes and, in the darkness, off to her right, she could just make out the shape of one of them. It could not have been more than ten or fifteen meters away, and it was moving in circles, the crew frantically searching for her. Haas screamed with all her might, "Jenkins, over here! I'm here. To your left. Starboard, dammit! Look to your left. I'm off your starboard side!"

Jenkins was kneeling over the side of the boat, frantically searching for Haas and Häupler when she spotted her and screamed at the helmsman, "There she is! Off our starboard side! Over there!" she pointed.

Haas continued to tread water. She could hear the boats approach her; their outboard motors whined as the coxswains pushed each craft forward at full throttle. Seconds felt like eternity and then she felt hands grabbing at her, pulling her back into the relative safety of the small boat. The last thing she remembered before she passed out from exhaustion was Jenkins yelling to the coxswain, "Take us back! Now!"

***

Haas sat alone in an oversized and well-worn leather chair in a large open room with a soaring cathedral ceiling with heavy exposed wooden beams. She reflected on what had happened earlier in the day. The room served as a gathering space, a social meeting room, within a thirty-room beachside hotel on Bornholm

Island, where she, Betancourt, Jenkins, the crew of German sailors, and other hangers-on had been lodged for the past ten days.

They were the only guests in the hotel; it was normally closed during the winter months. But the owners, a middle-aged Danish couple who lived in an adjacent house year-round, were only too happy to rent out the entire space at high-season rates, with the proviso they keep mum about anything they saw or heard amongst the strange mash-up of guests.

It was Betancourt, along with a stern-looking officer from the Danish intelligence service who warned the owners and their assembled staff that any mention of the group's presence, other than the official cover story – the attendees were part of a conference on fishing practices in the Baltic – would be punishable by hefty fines and imprisonment. Betancourt even went so far as to require the owners and the twelve staff members who agreed to work during what was normally the off-season, to sign an official looking document, totally unenforceable under Danish law, stating they would never divulge any information about their guests. They were required to take any knowledge of the presence of these winter guests to their grave. So, without question or protest, each of the compliant Danes signed the document, and on paper at least, any details of the operation's participants and their activities would remain secret.

Haas now sat in a chair positioned diagonally across from a floor-to-ceiling stone fireplace where the flames roared and the fire crackled and popped. It was one of two chairs, which combined with the low coffee table and an enormous matching leather sofa, made a comfortable seating area in front of the fire. Behind her there were tables, and Haas imagined how they might be occupied by guests during happier times, during the summer months when the hotel would be filled to capacity with Danes on holiday. She imagined their faces as they sat there drinking, playing cards, and singing songs as someone played the antique grand piano nestled in the far-left corner.

Haas looked out of the large bay window to her left, which overlooked a broad beach, and she could see the heavy rain coming down in sheets. The rain was driven by gusts of wind which howled from the northwest and pelted the windowpanes, causing them to rattle. Off in the distance, in some other room of the hotel, she heard the chime from a clock strike four times.

She sipped hot coffee from a heavy mug she cradled with both hands. Her drink was fortified with a healthy pour of whiskey – the bottle sat on the table next to her – and this was her third cup and third pour. Now, after nearly an hour of sipping and sitting in the chair in front of the fire, she had regained the feeling in her hands, but just barely. Her mind was numb too, but that wasn't brought on by the cold.

"How are you, Luba?" It was Betancourt. Haas didn't hear her enter the room and she didn't see her sit down on the sofa across from the chair where she sat. Jenkins, Ruger, and Radcliffe sat next to her on the sofa, and they all stared at Haas. She didn't hear them either. They all looked grim.

"I'm fine," Haas replied softly. "I'll be alright," she said taking another sip from her coffee. "What happened to Dieter Häupler? What happened to him? Have you found him?"

"No, not yet. Our Danish friends have notified the local authorities. The weather is too bad to mount a search. They'll start looking when the weather breaks. But . . . he's presumed lost."

"He saved my life you know," Haas said in a flat tone, but she felt her anger rising. "I wouldn't be here now. I wouldn't be sitting with you, drinking this hot coffee spiked with this excellent whiskey if it weren't for him," she said looking at the mug in her hand. "He told me not to worry. He said he'd survived conditions far worse than today."

"Häupler served the final two years of the war with me," Ruger offered. "There were many days when we thought we would never see another sunrise. But he was correct about today. We've been through far worse."

"His being correct isn't going to bring him back," Haas retorted angrily. "We didn't have to be out there today. We had done this drill successfully six times over the past week. One more drill won't make a difference between success and failure."

"Luba . . ." Betancourt started to speak.

"Did he have a family?" said Haas, interrupting Betancourt.

"Yes. He was from Kiel," Ruger replied. "I know his parents. They are longtime family friends. They both survived the war, and they still live there. He had an older brother, who didn't make it, however. This will be difficult for them, especially his mother. She came to me when Dieter enlisted. She begged me to, what is it you say, pull some strings, and get him assigned to my command? I told her I couldn't guarantee anything, of course. Assignments are made based on the requirements of the service. But I was able to use my influence and he was assigned to my boat. But as for today, he knew the risks. He knew what he was getting into. He wanted to be here, and he wanted to be on that boat today."

"That doesn't make it any easier to take," Haas replied. She shook with anger and refused to look at Ruger, or at any of them.

"It's quite unfortunate," said Radcliffe, "and from my point of view, this is one of the reasons I suggested the transfer be made farther out at sea, using a fishing boat as the transfer vessel."

"That's all well and good, but we don't have a boat, a dinghy, or a bloody canoe available," Betancourt snapped. "And we do not have the luxury of time. We're going to land on a beach near Ostrowo because that is where we have arranged to meet Lygia. This operation is going to take place within the next four days, and that is final. It is all set. The wheels have been put into motion and the meeting with Lygia has to take place. Is that clear?"

A silence fell over the room, interrupted only by the crackle of the fire.

Haas set her coffee mug down onto the table next to her chair and turned to look at Betancourt.

"We're all just cogs in a wheel. Grist for the mill. That's all we are, aren't we, Alicia?" Haas said.

"Don't get high and mighty with me, Haas," Betancourt replied, her frustration boiling over and visible. "It was an unfortunate accident. It was tragic, I'll give you that. But that doesn't change anything. This mission is going forward. Nothing today has changed that."

Haas picked up her mug, tilted it back and drained the last gulp of coffee and whiskey before slamming it back down onto the table.

"It must be a great comfort to be able to rationalize away the loss of life the way you do, Alicia. What is the calculation, exactly? One life? Two? Three? How many? Is there a number when you start to care?"

"What's gotten into you," Betancourt replied. "Have you lost your nerve, Haas?"

Hass let out a laugh so loud it startled everyone in the room. "Lost my nerve?" she said, barely getting the words out as she was still laughing. "No. Not hardly." And then just as suddenly, her face turned darkly serious. "No, Alicia. I have not lost my nerve. I'm not going soft on you. But the difference between you and me Alicia is that I'm the one who must look them in the eye, just as I did today as poor Häupler slipped below the waves. It's always like that. While you're sitting back comfortably in London or wherever it is you hang your hat, people like me have to see the look on the victims' faces when their life fades away. But you wouldn't know about that. You and those like you just continue to make your calculations," said Haas, spitting out the words as she glared disgustedly at Betancourt.

"We all have a job to do. We all have our role to play, Haas. I play mine and you play yours. And it does sound to me like you're getting soft," Betancourt replied. "Let me make it perfectly clear to you what the calculation is. There is a number I care about, and it is one. One individual. And that one individual is you. It all boils down to you because, whether I like it or not, and I don't, you are the only person on earth who can tell us if we are throwing our hat behind the real Lygia. You've set yourself up to be the savior. So, it's quite simple really. We will do everything possible to put you on a beach in Poland. That is the mission, and we will execute it. We will put you on that beach near Ostrowo so that you can do your job. That's the only calculation I care about. I'm doing my job. The question is, will you do yours?"

"I'll do my job, Alicia. And do you know why? It's because I have actual skin in the game. For you, this is just an exercise, an abstraction. It's a ticket you need to get punched to further your career. For me, . . . Never mind. You have nothing to worry about. You won't have to lose any sleep over it. You never have and you never will." Haas rose out of her chair to stand and looked at the trio sitting across from her. "You'll all be able to continue on your merry way, continue to make calculations of risk, and when something goes awry, like it has today, you'll be able to chalk up the next unfortunate accident as an acceptable loss, just as you always have," Haas said as she turned and stormed out of the room.

As Betancourt leaned back into the sofa and watched Haas depart. Jenkins turned to her and asked, "Is she going to be alright?"

"I think so. I certainly hope so. She's very capable, very resourceful. But . . ."

"She seems very emotional," said Jenkins. "Is she always like this?"

"She's always been that way. But we only need one thing from her. After that? That's why we have you," Betancourt said and quickly turned her attention to Ruger.

"Captain Ruger, I need you to get your boat and men ready. I have to provide London an update on today's events, But I fully expect we'll receive our orders to sail within the next forty-eight hours. We have a date to meet Lygia on the Polish coast and I don't want to break it. So, I suggest you get to it. And take Commander Radcliffe with you. I'm sure he'll be able to help you in some way."

Ruger and Radcliffe looked at each other, a bit uncomfortably, and rose to leave the room.

"I shall carry out your orders ma'am," Ruger said and then he turned to Radcliffe. "Shall we, commander?"

Betancourt didn't bother to look up at the men as they exited. "God, what do you have to do to get a drink in this place?" she commiserated.

"I'll fetch you a whiskey," Jenkins quickly replied. "I could use one too," she said rising to head over to the dining room where the staff had set up a small bar.

Jenkins scurried off to the bar and returned to the sofa in under a minute with two glasses and a full bottle of whiskey. She poured a glass for Betancourt and handed it to her before pouring one for herself.

"There's another bit of information I need to tell you, and I don't know if this is good news or bad," said Betancourt as Jenkins settled deeply into the sofa.

"I'm all ears."

***

As Jenkins knocked softly on Haas' door. She murmured, "Luba. It's me. Jenkins. You didn't come down for dinner, so I brought you something to eat."

"Come in. The door isn't locked," Haas replied. Jenkins opened the door and reached down onto the floor where she had set a tray. She picked the tray up off the floor, pushed the door all the way open with her foot, and entered the room and found Haas lying on her bed, her head propped up with pillows.

"I'll just put this here for you," Jenkins said as she placed the tray down onto the edge of the bed.

"That's very kind of you to bring me something. You didn't have to do that. I was planning to raid the kitchen later in the evening after everyone had gone to sleep."

Jenkins remained standing in front of the bed, looking as if she wanted to say something and was about to speak when Haas blurted, "Was there something else?"

"Yes," Jenkins replied. "Betancourt has made some changes to the operation. I need to tell you about them."

"Wonderful," said Haas. "I can hardly wait to hear them. What else?"

"There's been a new message from Lygia. I don't think it is good news, but I want your thoughts."

Chapter Twelve

The Invisibles

Kamenev watched as the thin trail of blue smoke from a burning cigarette slowly curled upward towards the ceiling of the Rezident's office. It was the first time he had ever been alone with Vitali Serov, the Rezident himself, the chief of Soviet intelligence operations in Great Britain, and he was uncomfortable. His discomfort hit him the minute he opened the heavy door and walked into Serov's office. Here he was, deep within the Soviet Embassy in London, inside the Rezidentura, the base of operations for Soviet intelligence. It was a section within the embassy where only a select few of the diplomatic staff had access. The Soviet ambassador himself could not enter the Rezidentura unless invited, and he was rarely invited, and Serov's office was its innermost sanctum.

Serov was a veteran of the many iterations of Soviet intelligence services. He cut his teeth during the waning days of the Cheka shortly after the revolution and served in the alphabet soup of agencies which followed: the GPU, OGPU, NKGB, NKVD, and now, the MGB, the Ministry of State Security. A wiry, studious looking man who, despite a rumpled appearance which made him look like a university professor, Serov had a meticulous eye for detail and an extraordinary memory. But it wasn't skill alone that propelled his rise through the ranks.

There was a rumor floating around the Rezidentura that Serov kept files which purportedly contained the details, the good and bad, the likes and dislikes, the habits, the strengths and weaknesses of every intelligence officer with whom he worked. And stories about Serov, containing some facts, a few bits of conjecture, and many fabrications would often be told in the early morning hours after a long night of drinking. Soviet MGB officers, in their cups after consuming too much vodka, whispered one such story amongst themselves about how back in 1938 while serving as an assistant to the Rezident in Lisbon, Serov leaked selected information from a file he kept on his boss. His boss was suddenly recalled to Moscow, and he disappeared. Never to be seen again. Liquidated. The more vodka consumed, the wilder the stories became, until the myth of Serov and the power he wielded with his files grew into legend. Serov had a reputation of being ruthlessly ambitious. He was always looking for leverage and when the moment was right, he wouldn't be afraid to use it to further his career.

Serov also had a reputation for being especially hard on young, inexperienced officers like Kamenev. So, watching the smoke rise up to the ceiling and fill the room was like a game and it offered Kamenev a distraction, something to occupy his mind as he watched the Rezident carefully read the report he had so painstakingly put together. As he sat in front of Serov's desk, he wondered what he had done to merit such special attention. Why had he called him in? Why was he awakened at 3 a.m. yesterday, rousted out of bed by a low-level staffer, told to dress and immediately report to his supervisor?

When he finally arrived at his supervisor's office, Kamenev found him to be equally bleary-eyed from a similar rousting. His supervisor ordered Kamenev to prepare a report that would go to the Rezident himself. He was to author a detailed report describing every meeting, everything discussed, every action he had taken with two agents he was running. He had twenty-four hours to prepare the report and he was to present it, along with himself to the Rezident himself in his office. Finally, some twenty-four hours later he was sitting in front of Serov, and he had no idea what he had done to bring such attention to himself.

As the lowest ranking person in-country, it was not customary for an officer of his stature to work directly with the Rezident. But as it turned out, Kamenev was either blessed with good luck or the misfortune of being assigned as the officer who would run Peter Avery, or 'Homer' as he was known inside the MGB. The more seasoned, experienced officers within the Rezidentura were of the opinion Homer was washed up, unreliable, and had outlived his usefulness. So, the job fell to the new guy. It fell to Kamenev.

The cigarette continued to burn in a heavy crystal ashtray on Serov's desk. As he sat waiting for him to complete his reading, Kamenev watched how Serov would pick up the cigarette from the ashtray and place it to his lips. He looked on as Serov inhaled deeply, held the smoke in while squinting, holding the report up closely to his eyes, appearing to scrutinize every word he read before he finally exhaled, blowing the smoke across his desk towards Kamenev.

As Kamenev sat there, he became fascinated by how meticulously and gently Serov placed the cigarette into the ashtray. And he was amazed how the ash on the cigarette, now close to five centimeters long, remained attached to the butt and hadn't fallen off into the ashtray, onto Serov's desk, the floor, or onto his clothing. He was amazed at how Serov never took his eyes off the report he held in his hand. He never fumbled for the cigarette as he reached for it, and he never failed to place it in the exact same spot in the ashtray. But most of all, Kamenev was astonished to see how Serov had been able to do this six times. He had smoked six cigarettes, one after the other, stubbing each of them out just before they were about to burn his fingers, lighting another one, and continuing to read, while not one fleck of ash found its way outside of the ashtray.

Finally, after the sixth cigarette had been stubbed out, Serov finished the report. He carefully checked each page to ensure they were in their proper order, placed the report inside a folder on his desk, and closed the cover. He removed his wire rimmed spectacles and placed them on the desk. He rubbed his eyes, and briefly massaged the bridge of his nose where the spectacles sat, and where over time, they had created angry, red indentations.

Serov replaced his spectacles, leaned back in his chair and looked across his desk at Kamenev, who sat stiffly on a hard, wooden chair. The desk was part of a suite of furniture which originally came with two different, far more comfortable chairs. Kamenev heard stories how the Rezident had them replaced with a pair of stiff wooden chairs, with straight backs, hard wooden seats, and no arms. He heard stories how the Rezident wanted anyone who sat across from him to sit stiffly, straight up in the chair, with no place other than their knees to comfortably place their hands and arms, because he wanted them to be as uncomfortable as possible in his presence. After nearly an hour alone with the Rezident in his office, Kamenev could say from personal experience the stories were true. He was uncomfortable.

"Do you know why I called you in here to meet with me today, Kamenev?"

"I, I presume you wanted to evaluate my work, Comrade Rezident," Kamenev stammered out in reply.

"There is an expression and I wonder if you've heard it. I believe it is an American saying, and it is a silly one at that. 'It's better to be lucky than good.' Have you heard of it? Do you know it?"

"I cannot say I do, Comrade Rezident," Kamenev replied.

"I think it is a ridiculous notion of course, because in life, and especially in our chosen profession, one has to combine good fortune and superb skills. One has to be both lucky and good. And it seems that you, my young friend, have the good fortune to possess both. You are now sitting on top of a proverbial goldmine. Do you understand what you have done?"

"Not completely. I'm only doing what I believe is expected of me."

"Yes, you are correct. You are doing your job. But you've done more than what was expected. You see, everyone within the Rezidentura thought you drew the short straw when you were assigned to babysit our agent Homer. I overheard their comments. I could hear them laughing behind your back, acting as if they had pulled something over on you. I have to admit, I may have even shared their sentiment. But, based on the information I've just read in your report, it seems that our Homer is enjoying a sort of renaissance in his career. He has provided you not only useful information, but intelligence that is actionable and timely. Mind you, you did nothing to cultivate Homer. He's been on our payroll for years since his days as a student at Cambridge. And if you weren't the junior officer in-country, he would have been assigned to someone else. But then, he was the one who dropped this information into your lap like a Christmas present. You are his handler. The officer in charge. All of that makes you lucky. You were there at the right time and place. But, your other source," Serov said, leaning forward and tapping the folder containing the report three times with his index finger. "This 'Richmond,' this man whom you recruited, the man who works inside the MI6 operation itself, now that took skill to develop. And foresight. You knew we would need to verify the information Homer provided. And Richmond has done just that. Luck and skill have conspired and for you, it's a job very well done, comrade. Well done."

"Thank you, sir," Kamenev replied, letting out a long sigh of relief. He knew this meeting could have easily gone in another direction.

"So, tell me, Aleksandr Vladimirovich," Serov said, using Kamenev's first and his middle or patronymic name, the name of his father, a sign of formality and respect. "Tell me a little about your new source, the man we have codenamed Richmond."

"He is a simple man, Comrade Rezident, and he occupies a relatively low-level position. He's a security guard at an MI6 facility in Chelsea."

"Security guards often have excellent access to information. They can go virtually anywhere within a facility, unseen. They are expected to be everywhere, and they become invisible."

"Yes, that is especially true in the case of Richmond. He usually works at the main gate to the facility, so he sees everything and everyone entering and leaving. But I've encouraged him to take the initiative. He's volunteered to perform additional duties, including burning classified documents at the end of the day. It's a task no one wants to do, and when he volunteered, his superiors immediately agreed. This is how he came to acquire the material I cited in my report. He pulled draft cables and files concerning the British operation, codenamed Nightfall from the burn bag and provided them to me, to us," Kamenev said, quickly correcting himself.

"He secreted the physical documents out of the facility?" replied the Rezident. "That is very risky, and it is my only criticism of your work, Aleksandr Vladimirovich. Give him a miniature camera. And provide a camera to Homer too. It's too dangerous otherwise. I will authorize the expense."

"Yes, Comrade Rezident. I will take care of that immediately and see they are both trained on how to use the equipment."

"Make it happen as quickly as possible."

"I will," Kamenev replied, his voice rising with excitement.

"And tell me. Why Richmond? How did you derive such a codename for him? Does it hold any significance?"

"Ah, well that is rather simple. There is a tube station named Richmond. That's the location he passed on the information to me, at the station, during the rush to work early one morning. The crush of people made it easy for us to literally bump into each other. We used a simple brush pass technique, and he passed on the documents to me as I gave him an envelope stuffed with pound notes."

Serov picked up a cigarette pack from his desk, and upon discovering it was empty, opened the top drawer to his desk. He retrieved a fresh pack, tore off the cellophane and foil wrapper, and pulled out a cigarette, and placed it to his mouth. Kamenev reached into his pocket, pulled out a lighter, and lit the cigarette.

"Ah, thank you," said Serov taking a long drag from the cigarette and then blowing out the smoke. This time, he blew the smoke out of the side of his mouth, and not in the direction of Kamenev. "Please continue. Tell me. What are his motivations? Is it just the money? Or is it something more? What makes this Richmond tick?"

"I have a complete file on him, Comrade Rezident, if you'd like to read it. I can fetch it for you?"

"No, no. I want to hear it from you directly. I want to see how much you really know about this man."

"Well, then," Kamenev said as he composed his thoughts. "As I said, he is a simple man. Very humble background, so the money is helpful, but it is not his only motivation. He's originally from Birmingham and grew up there in council housing. His father worked in the pits and drank away whatever he made. His father abandoned the family when Richmond was only an infant. When he was seven, his mother contracted tuberculosis and could no longer care for him. She eventually succumbed to the disease, and he was taken in by his maternal grandmother who raised him. He enlisted in the army when he was seventeen, that would have been in March 1945, and he spent two years in service. Discharged honorably, but bitterly. He blamed his mother's death on the various austerity measures the government was forced to put in place."

"How did you come to recruit him? Where and when did you meet him?"

"We met at a huge Party rally late last year. I had only been in-country for perhaps, only six weeks? Again, it was one of those situations where they gave me the assignment to attend the rally because I was the junior man. And I was surprised, but very pleased at the number of people who attended the rally."

"Yes, the Communist Party of Great Britain has grown considerably among the workers," said the Rezident. "I daresay, their membership rolls are their highest now. It shouldn't come as a surprise. Despair, discontent, and loss of hope are the elements which drive revolutions. And do you know what has helped us the most, Aleksandr Vladimirovich?"

"Well, I believe the trade unions have been supportive of us, Comrade Rezident," Kamenev replied."

"Oh yes. Yes, they have helped us, but what has helped us the most are this country's policies, such as lack of medical care for the masses and allowing poor living conditions to flourish. The slums are appalling."

"Yes, sir, they are indeed."

"Did you know where the first rent-strike in this country occurred?"

Kamenev shook his head.

"It occurred in Birmingham, the very city where your agent grew up. A woman named Jessie Eden organized 50,000 households and led a successful strike. We didn't have to lift a finger to help her. It was back in 1939, long before your time here. No, with conditions as they are in this country, it's no wonder your man is willing to help us."

Suddenly, Serov's demeanor changed. His face brightened and he broke into a smile. "But I am being rude, inconsiderate. Why don't you take one of the chairs over there," Serov said pointing to two wing-back chairs on the other side of his office. In between the chairs stood a small table. A bottle of vodka and several small crystal glasses sat on top. "We can enjoy a drink together. Please, take a seat and make yourself comfortable."

Kamenev stood up and looked to where the Rezident had pointed. He wondered what brought on such civility and began to wonder Serov's file on him might contain. *Was this a trap?* he wondered.

Not knowing what else to do and having little other choice, Kamenev finally said, "Thank you Comrade Rezident." He walked the few short steps to the chair as Serov stuffed the fresh cigarette pack into his coat pocket and followed him over. Holding his cigarette in his left hand, Serov deftly opened the vodka bottle with his right and poured two drinks.

"Here you are Aleksandr Vladimirovich," sliding the glass across the table. "To your health," and he raised his glass to toast Kamenev.

Kamenev picked up the glass and replied, "And to yours," and the two men downed the shot in one gulp. *I need to limit myself to only one drink. Well, maybe no more than two*, he thought.

Serov poured another shot for each of them and said, "Please sit. Be comfortable and continue."

Kamenev sat down, noting the chair's plush fabric, and sank comfortably into the soft seat cushion. He placed his fingers around the glass of vodka, twirled it slowly in his hand, composed his thoughts and continued. "I could see from the moment we met he was drawn by the cause and could be useful to us, assuming he could channel his anger and occupy a proper position. He's very clever. So, when a position opened at the MI6 facility in Chelsea, a security guard job, I thought there might be an opportunity. I had been monitoring their hiring. They regularly place hiring notices in the local newspaper. I had initially hoped to find a low-paid secretary or clerk. But I thought a security guard could work too. So, I encouraged him to apply for the job. He did, he was hired, much to my surprise by the way, but I think the fact he was a veteran helped. He was so happy to have found a solid job. He was elated in fact. We met for drinks the night after he took the position. He thanked me for my help, and that is when I took the chance. I asked him if he would be interested in being part of something bigger, and he said, 'What do you mean?' I told him he could help to ensure a safer world, a better world. And in the process, he could earn a few extra pounds for his efforts. We talked about his hopes, his dreams, and I offered him the assistance of the Soviet Union."

"I know you have put him through our process to ensure he's not a double agent, yes?" Serov asked.

"Of course, Comrade Rezident," Kamenev replied, now flustered at the thought the Rezident might think he was too inexperienced and would cut corners. "He was interviewed, interrogated by Comrade Popov, my superior. We also gave him small tasks to perform, which he did perfectly. It's all in my report, Comrade Rezident. Would you like to read it?"

"No, no. That is not necessary. Please continue."

"Yes. Well, let's see. Where was I? Yes, I recall I told him with our help he could achieve anything he wanted, and he would be able in some measure, to exact revenge on the country and system that allowed his mother to die. The compensation he receives from us is not what motivates him, although I am sure it helps to augment his meager salary. He is moved to act by a much deeper motivation. And that, Comrade Rezident is the short version. The long version is in his file. You see, like me, he's the lowest man in his organization. So, I thought he would be overlooked and wouldn't be noticed. He is, as you say, invisible."

Serov stubbed out his cigarette in a crystal ashtray on the table next to the vodka bottle. He fished out the pack of cigarettes from his coat pocket, pulled one out and placed it between his lips, waiting for Kamenev to light it for him once again.

Kamenev quickly responded. He lit the cigarette and sat back in his chair, not sure what else to say. Serov smoked and stared at Kamenev for several minutes in silence, a silence which had become awkward until he finally announced, "You definitely will be noticed Aleksandr Vladimirovich. You will not be invisible."

"In what way? What do you mean, Comrade Rezident?"

"I asked you earlier. Do you know why I called you in to see me today? Stop," Serov said holding the palm of his hand up. "Let me answer the question for you. You are no doubt aware of the challenges we are facing in Poland, yes?"

"Of course, Comrade Rezident. There is a violent rebellion occurring."

"Yes, and your two sources, the two agents you are running, the one who was dropped into your lap and the other whom you have recruited, have provided us with a smoking gun. Of course, we have had our suspicions. But it is clear from your report, from the information you have collected, the British have their grimy hands in this. They are attempting to roll back the progress we have made and in doing so, they not only jeopardize the security of the Soviet Union, but they also risk another war in Europe. Naturally, this has the attention at the very highest levels in Moscow. The very highest. And you, my young friend Aleksandr Vladimirovich, have caught the eye of Chairman Stalin himself. That is the reason why I brought you in here today. You have been noticed, at the highest level, and it is my job to see that you do not get burned as you fly so close to the sun."

Kamenev swallowed hard; Serov's words rang in his ears. "At least we have the means to catch them in the act. We can stop them before they go any further."

"Oh no, my young friend. We are going to let this play out. We are going to set a much bigger trap and lure them straight into it. We're going to do everything we can to help the British. Why help them, you are probably thinking? The reason is simple. They are going to lead us directly to the leaders of the rebellion, and to any other sleeper agents they might still have who are working for them in Poland. And then we'll gather them all up and after we're through with them, after we've sucked them dry of every bit of information they have, we will throw their emaciated carcasses into the fire, and they will curse their mothers for bearing them and bringing them into this world."

Chapter Thirteen

Fortunate Souls

Everyone living in and around Puck was now under suspicion. The UB blanketed the town with surveillance after the last attack carried out by the forest soldiers. Every telephone line was tapped. Every conversation was being listened to. Informants were everywhere. People were being followed. The UB hadn't been able to put a stop to the forest soldier's attacks on government buildings and on the people, who served in it, so they doubled down. Mass arrests became the UB's calling card, so Bialik and Wulkan agreed to put a hold on new attacks, at least until the pressure died down.

"They can't arrest everyone," Bialik said to Wulkan at their last meeting. "This will pass. We just have to be patient."

"They don't need to arrest everyone," he replied. "They just need to arrest the right people. They only need to find the people who can lead them directly to us."

When carrying out mass arrests, the UB were sometimes supported by Polish militia or the Polish army, but usually the task would fall to Soviet NKVD troops. They would block off a street at both ends with armored vehicles to prevent anyone from escaping. Then, UB officers, the *Ubecy* as they were known, would then go door to door, house-to-house, rousting occupants from their sleep in the early morning hours, the preferred time of day for conducting these operations. They'd throw them in the back of one of the waiting lorries and cart them off to the regional prison in Puck.

The arrests produced two types of ex-prisoners, the fortunate and the unfortunate.

After three or four days of confinement, a few fortunate souls, only a handful, but a highly curated group out of those who had been arrested, would finally drag themselves back to their homes. They had been released and when asked, they would tell of their ordeal to their friends or to family members. It was always the same story, told over and over. Only the date, the time of day, or the names of those arrested would change. The fortunate souls would describe the interrogations, the hours of intense questioning, the cold, damp cells. How they were deprived of sleep, fed only water, or barely enough food to keep them alive. How they were forced to stand for hours, how they were tied up into contorted positions until their circulation was cut off, denied the use of a toilet until they had no choice but to soil themselves and wallow in puddles of their own urine or excrement.

Their voices became hoarse as they began to mumble and describe the beatings and torture, they received at the hands of the UB. How far would a limb bend before it would break? How long could a person hold their breath while three men hoisted them upside down and held their head under icy water? How long would a body convulse after receiving a jolt of electricity from wires connected to a bank of automobile batteries? The fortunate souls knew the answers to these questions and to many more and willingly shared them with anyone who had the stomach to listen.

They were the fortunate souls after all, and they knew it. At least they were alive.

But as they neared the end of their stories, something unusual always happened. They would look around the room nervously. They looked over their shoulders because even within the confines of their own homes, they no longer felt safe. They had lost their sense of security. They knew there was no escape, even when they were in rooms where they had lived out their lives. Familiar rooms. Rooms with memories. But now the memories were gone, replaced by panic and fear. Their eyes would frantically search around the room, looking for a face hiding in the shadows, straining to see someone who might be lurking behind them and listening in on their conversation. And then, when their frantic search yielded nothing, they would cast their eyes downward and whisper in a voice so quiet they could barely be heard. They told how the other prisoners were dragged away, how they had heard their screams in the distance in the early morning hours or late at night, or perhaps they had even witnessed the act themselves. They heard how these unfortunate souls were thrown into cattle cars; bundled onto a train headed East, and how they were being shipped off to Russia, to Siberia, never to be seen again. The fortunate souls would have been consigned to the same fate if they hadn't cooperated and told their captors and tormentors what they wanted to hear. This was the price of admission to a select club of survivors.

Tell us who they are. Who is helping the insurgents, the cursed soldiers? Just give us one name, that's all you have to do, and we can clear all of this up. One name and you'll be allowed to return to your home. One name and you'll be free to live out your life. That's what you want, isn't it? Just give us a name and your troubles will be over. That's all you have to do.

The fortunate souls continued to hear those words from unseen interrogators over and over in their mind until they would sob uncontrollably, first out of fear they might be grabbed once more from their bed in the middle of the night, and then out of guilt and the despair that comes from knowing they had sentenced a friend, or a colleague, or perhaps it was a family member, a brother, mother, sister, or a father. They would forever know someone, who based on their words of confession, had disappeared into the fog, never to be seen or heard from again. They knew the line between survival and death had become blurred and they would forever question whether or not they were fortunate.

**

Bialik had always assumed she was being watched. She expected it, in fact, and despite having developed a job with routine hours, she tried to be less predictable. She would leave her flat at different times every day. She would vary her route, or she would suddenly stop in one of the local shops, thus requiring anyone following her to either stop until she left the shop or continue to walk past her and try to resume surveillance once she returned to the street. She might stop on a street corner and before crossing, stop and pull out the compact from her purse, seeming to check her make-up while using the mirror to look behind her to see who may be following. And today, Saturday, market day, was the third time during the past week she had noticed the man.

The first time was on Monday, when she saw him across the street from the main entrance to her schoolhouse. It was early, 7:30 a.m., and the only people usually found on the streets near the school were students scurrying to class. The older students always congregated in groups in the school's large courtyard as they awaited the bell to call them into their classrooms, girls on the right and boys on the left. Someone older usually accompanied the younger children, usually it was the mother, sometimes a grandmother, or occasionally it was a sister or brother who would walk alongside their younger sibling. But rarely, if ever, were the children accompanied by an older man. At this time in the morning, able-bodied men would already be at work. It was not customary for a man to be on the street at this time of day, and this man stood out. He was definitely out of place.

Bialik saw him standing alone on the street corner directly across from the school's main entrance. He wore a long, black leather coat and a dark Fedora pulled down to one side, covering part of his face. A lit cigarette dangled from his mouth. *If he's Ubecy, he's certainly playing the part*, she thought. She could only see one of his eyes, and at this distance it was impossible to discern their color, but there was no doubt in her mind he was looking at her. *So, this is it*, she thought.

At first, she thought she should challenge the man, walk across the street, march directly up to him and ask, "What are you doing here?" But she thought better of it. He might summarily arrest her on the spot. So, she turned into the schoolyard and as she walked towards the building, she could feel his gaze boring a hole in her back. She walked quickly down the pavement which acted as an invisible wall, separating the older girls and boys, keeping them on their proper side as if it were a rule they were required to follow. She walked up the four brick steps leading to the building and opened the door, but not before turning around to see the man throw his cigarette on the ground, and slowly but deliberately grind it out with his left foot, staring at Bialik the entire time. He continued to stare at her as he pulled the collar up on his leather coat, and then he turned abruptly to his left and walked away.

She saw him a second time on Wednesday evening near Kaczmarek's house. It was shortly after 8 p.m., and she had just finished an enjoyable dinner that his wife had prepared. She had planned to excuse herself and leave – it was a school night and she still had to get home in the dark - when Kaczmarek encouraged her to stay a little while longer.

"I shouldn't be saying this to you," Kaczmarek said as he poured Bialik the last drop of wine from the second bottle they had opened. "Of all the teachers at our school, you are my favorite."

"You're right, Comrade Commissar. You shouldn't say such things. You mustn't have favorites," Bialik replied, feeling discomfort as she wondered how Kaczmarek would react if he knew her secret. He would be crushed to find out she wasn't a committed communist and was actively working to undermine the regime. But would he turn her in? *Probably. Yes. He would have no choice*, she decided. "We have many highly skilled teachers at the school. I am just one among many."

"But it's true. Your students are the happiest in the school. And they all perform well on their exams. You're a credit to our school and to your profession. I'm very proud of you."

"It is lovely to hear you say that. I care for my students deeply and want only the best for them. And I also greatly appreciate the generosity you and your wife have shown me. I don't know how I shall ever be able to repay you, but now I really must be leaving.

It's dark out and I need to be on my way. Thank you so very much for a lovely dinner."

"You repay me every day with your teaching. You repay all of us," Kaczmarek said, beaming with pride at her.

Bialik gathered her belongings and said her goodbyes to Kaczmarek and his wife. She had just stepped out their front door and turned onto the sidewalk to begin her walk home when she saw a figure in the shadows across the street. Although it was dark, she could tell it was him. Even in the darkness she knew he would be wearing the same long leather coat and Fedora tipped to one side. She continued to walk in the direction of her flat, glancing over her shoulder to see if he was still behind her. He was. She debated whether to return to Kaczmarek's house, but what would that accomplish? What would she say? What reason could she give for having fallen under surveillance, even though every person in town was under suspicion? It would raise too many other questions and she decided against it. She also didn't want to implicate Kaczmarek, a man who had taken her under his wing and showed her so much kindness. So, as she continued walking and for the next ten minutes, the man continued to follow her. He followed her all the way to the farm road which ran in front of the house in which she lived.

She debated whether she should start to run but decided against it. She picked up her pace on the farm road, walking faster and faster, until she could finally see the footpath which cut across the field and led to her flat. She looked over her shoulder when she reached the head of the path and gazed back at the man one last time. He had stopped in the middle of the roadway not more than twenty-five meters from her and lit a cigarette. Suddenly, as she turned away to walk up the footpath, she was temporarily blinded by the headlights of a small car on the farm road ahead of her. The lights flashed twice as if it was some sort of signal, and this caused her to finally break out into a run up the path all the way to her flat, running up the three flights of stairs. She fumbled with her keys in the dark, desperate to insert the key into the lock, and after an agonizing few seconds, she was finally was able to open the door. She rushed inside, closed and locked the door behind her and with her back against the wall, leaned over to look out of the window. She saw the car move slowly up the farm road, come to a stop in front of the footpath and then slowly move on. She couldn't see because of the dark, but she thought she heard a car door open, the sound of muffled voices, a car door slamming shut, and then the whir of a car motor as it picked up speed, growing fainter as the car drove off.

It's possible she hadn't picked up on the surveillance earlier in the week, but it was on a Saturday as she entered the city market to shop when she saw him for the third time. He was standing across from the main entrance, watching as people came and went. She definitely could tell it was him even though she didn't look directly at him. There was no doubt. As she walked into the market, she could see out of the corner of her eye how he was wearing his now familiar leather coat and fedora, raked sharply to one side. She wondered, *Is he here for me?* Her question was answered as the man threw his cigarette to the pavement and began to move in her direction. He was following her again.

The market was packed and more crowded than usual. As she wound her way through the crush of people, Bialik sensed the mood was subdued, somber, and everyone seemed on edge. Even the queues for meat and dairy products were longer than usual and a scuffle broke out between two men, one accusing the other of jumping the queue. The fight was immediately broken up by six men in plain clothes, who seemingly appeared from nowhere. They grabbed the men and hustled them off to jeers of contempt from the people standing nearby.

"Just return to your shopping, everyone," shouted one of the plainclothes officers, as the men were led away in front of the shocked onlookers, "There's nothing here that concerns you. Everything is under control."

But the people assembled in the market that morning had other ideas. A chorus of jeers and boos rained down on the plainclothes officers as they attempted to exit. A group of a dozen or more men formed up into a human wall and attempted to block the way out.

"Let us pass immediately," shouted the officer in charge. "Unless you want to find yourself in prison."

The market suddenly fell silent and the officer in charge reached into his coat and pulled out his service weapon. "I will use this," he said as he waved his pistol ominously at the men blocking their exit. "Now, let us pass. Now I said!"

At the sight of the drawn pistol, the men blocking the way grudgingly broke down. They stepped aside and opened a narrow path to allow the UB officers to pass. One of the men who had blocked the path spat on the ground in front of the officers as they quickly hustled the men away. The other men spat on the ground once the officers had passed, yelling and cursing at them as they led the men they'd arrested away.

Damned Ubecy, Bialik thought as she stood and watched the events unfold. She then resumed winding her way through the crowded market, and she finally reached the aisle where Zajac's stand stood. As she turned the corner to enter the aisle she suddenly froze. The stand was empty, Zajac was nowhere to be found, and two men in plainclothes standing only a few meters away saw Bialik and began to slowly move towards her. *What is this*, she thought as she quickly turned to look in the other direction down the aisle. Three more men stood at the very end of the aisle and began to make their way through the dense crowd, pushing people out of the way as they attempted to move closer.

She turned around, intending to make her escape in the direction from where she came, but once more, there he was. The man. She saw him up close, standing not more than ten meters from her and waiting for her. *This is it*, she thought. *But they won't take me without a fight*, and she dropped her basket, hiked up her skirt and reached underneath. She grasped the handle of the knife strapped to her thigh and removed it from its sheath. It took her no more than five or six strides before she stood face-to-face with the man. He was taller than her by nearly a foot and he was amused by Bialik's aggressive stance, as if the confrontation was some sort of joke. He sneered at her and then started to laugh, and it was at that precise moment, with the man's mouth wide open in laughter that Bialik crouched low and struck. The man gasped for breath, first with surprise, then with shock, and finally in horror as Bialik plunged the knife through his leather coat, deep into his solar plexus twisting upwards towards his heart as the blade went in.

The man unleashed a string of curses as he attempted to gain control of the knife now impaled in his belly. *What? He's Russian?* Bialik thought with astonishment as she immediately recognized the Russian curses. This discovery sent Bialik into a rage. *This is for my mother, you bastard*, and she pushed and twisted, attempting to deliver a killing blow to the man, who no longer sneered at her. He looked at Bialik and she could see the fear in his eyes as his life slipped away from him.

"This is for every Pole whose life was cut short fighting for freedom," she shouted as she continued to push and twist and then it was she who sneered at the man when finally, and with every ounce of her strength, Bialik ripped the knife out from the man, causing more damage, shouting, "Long Live Poland!"

He looked down and clawed his leather jacket open and he could see the blood stain on his shirt grow larger and larger. He had no more curses to utter, no more sneers to display. His eyes rolled back, his body went into shock, and he fell face first onto the pavement.

It all happened so fast it took several seconds for the people in the market to comprehend exactly what they had just seen. The man fell at the feet of a young woman who couldn't have been more than twenty. She was pushing a small pram with a sleeping child tucked neatly inside. As the man's blood pooled on the pavers underneath him, the young woman finally realized what she had witnessed. She screamed, which led to more screams from the crowd, and they gathered in a circle around Bialik and the man, looking on and not sure what to do next. Then came the shouts from the five plainclothes officers, who now stood in a group at the end of the aisle a mere ten meters from Bialik. They all pulled pistols from underneath their coats and one of them shouted, "Stop! Grab that woman!"

Bialik stayed crouched low and moved the knife back and forth between each hand in front of her, swiping at the growing crowd encircling her, and they immediately backed off. They had already seen what she could do and wanted no part of this crazy woman with a knife. The crowd began to rush away from Bialik in the direction of the approaching plainclothes officers, blocking their path. As the crowd surged, bodies fell in the street and were nearly trampled as the panicked mass pushed away from Bialik towards the men attempting to capture her, creating a logjam in the narrow market aisle. The logjam gave way, and the crowd broke through, sweeping the officers up and carrying them off in a human wave. One of the officers fell and was trampled by the screaming crowd.

Bialik continued to crouch and swirl, flashing the knife menacingly at anyone who might approach her. She could hear the shrill whistles coming from the officers of the Polish Militia as they rushed to the scene to restore order. *Escape*, she thought. *But in which direction? And to where?*

"Let her go," a voice boomed from behind where Bialik stood. "And let me through." It was Wulkan, dressed in his Home Army uniform, the sight of which seemed to rally the crowd. He emerged from a throng of people, and the crowd immediately recognized him and gave way, creating a narrow path for him as he moved forward. The crowd began to chant, *"Wolność za Polskia,"* "Freedom for Poland," over and over, first in a soft whisper and then louder and louder. Bialik whirled around to see him waving his hand and beckoning to her. "Come! Quickly," he cried out to her as the crowd parted just enough for Bialik to rush to Wulkan's side. Bialik hiked up her dress once again, this time sheathing her knife while trying to look as calm as possible, looking at no one in the eye.

"Come with me!" he said to her as the crowd closed ranks behind him. "Hurry, I have a car waiting," he said as he quickly strode out of the market with Bialik at his side. "We're parked in the alley up ahead," he said pointing to the narrow street up ahead used by the market vendors to deliver goods.

"How did you know?" Bialik asked, struggling to keep up with him.

"We have our informants too," he replied. "They've taken Zajac, but we're not totally blind."

"Ela? No," Bialik cried, and then she added, "That man I killed. He was Russian."

"I know that too. The NKVD has infiltrated the UB. They are the one's pulling the strings now. Hurry, we must move quickly."

Bialik could see the small car up ahead. Two of Wulkan's men, armed with machine pistols stood watch, ready to take on any UB officers in pursuit. As they neared the vehicle, one of the men jumped into the driver's seat and started the car, while the other held the door open. Wulkan pulled Bialik's arm and flung her through the open door. She slid across the seat and hit her head with a thump on the opposite door. Wulkan dived into the car, falling on top of Bialik as he yelled, "Go, go, go," and slammed the door behind him. The engine roared and the car's tires squealed on the cobblestone street. The other of Wulkan's men jumped into the front passenger seat with a thud as the driver sped away from the market. Shouts and cries of "Freedom for Poland" and "Long Live Poland" rang out.

"Where are we going?" Bialik asked as she pulled herself out from underneath Wulkan.

"We are going to where you've hidden your wireless. We're going to need that."

"What about Ela? Is she . . . still alive?"

"We don't know. We're trying to find out."

"I need to stop at my flat," she said as she looked out the window of the vehicle, realizing the direction where they were headed. "I'll need to pick up some things."

"Do you have your codebook?"

"It's hidden with the transceiver."

"Good. We're only picking up your radio and codebook because it's too risky to go to your flat and we don't have time for that. Besides, the UB and Militia are probably already searching your room and tearing it apart as we speak. We have clothing for you to wear."

"So where are we going?" She knew, but she wanted to hear it from him.

"You're coming with us. You'll join us at our camp. I'm afraid your teaching days are over."

***

It was after 10 p.m. and a single desk lamp burned, illuminating the desk but creating dark shadows in the rest of the room. Sokolov sat at his desk reviewing multiple interrogation reports for the people arrested at the market. A half-empty bottle of vodka and two glasses stood on the right edge of his desk.

The reports Sokolov read stated the number of people at the market two days ago was about two hundred. *A best estimate*, he thought. In the sweep that occurred afterwards, the UB along with Polish Militia arrested more than forty unfortunate souls who they believed would have been in a position to witness the attack on Junior Lieutenant Gennady Petrov. According to the reports Sokolov read and re-read, the people were arrested because they were in the immediate area of where the stabbing occurred and should have been able to provide detailed eyewitness accounts of what transpired. *How would they* know? he wondered. *They just picked up anyone they could. Probably those who were the slowest and couldn't run fast. The ones who were nearly trampled*, he thought, shaking his head in disgust. And despite being held under harsh conditions, the detainees revealed not a sliver of information. They even refused to give their captors information they wanted to hear, and the statements they gave about what they saw had a remarkably similar ring to them.

"I didn't see anything. I couldn't. I was facing in the other direction."

"It all happened too fast; I didn't see who did it. I only saw the poor man lying on the ground."

"I didn't recognize her. I've never seen the woman before."

Sokolov's attention was broken by a sharp rap on his office door. "Come. Enter," he said, never looking up as the door opened and Junior Lieutenant Maxim Grigoriev entered. Grigoriev closed the door behind him, walked directly to Sokolov's desk and stood at attention.

"Junior Lieutenant Grigoriev reporting as ordered, Comrade Colonel," he announced.

Without looking up Sokolov replied softly, "Stand at ease, Lieutenant." He continued to read through the interrogation reports on his desk and when he finally had enough, he looked up at the lieutenant who stood nervously in front of him. "I have read through the various interrogation reports, and it is a mystery. Everyone we have detained saw everything and nothing at the same time. Can you explain this mystery to me?"

"Sergeant Zaitsev and I were stationed near the vegetable stand. We saw our subject enter the aisle and we moved towards her. She saw us and attempted to flee back in the direction of where Lieutenant Petrov was positioned. She attacked him and her actions incited the crowd and as we tried to move in to help Petrov, they turned on us. There were too many of them and we were swept away by them. I, myself was actually lifted from the ground. Zaitsev fell down and was trampled."

"Yes, so I've read. He'll recover," Sokolov said. He seethed with anger, glaring at Grigoriev. "So, lieutenant, please explain one thing to me. Your orders were to simply follow the woman.

That's all. Stay in the background. Follow her and observe her activities. Confirm our suspicions about her. You were supposed to be discreet. And instead, your actions led to a near riot. And now the woman has gone to ground. She has disappeared."

"Comrade Colonel, permission to speak freely." Grigoriev said nervously.

"By all means. I cannot wait to hear what you have to tell me."

"It was Petrov's idea," Grigoriev stammered. "He wanted to rattle the woman. He wanted to get under her skin."

"To get under her skin. And what purpose would this serve?"

"He said if the woman knew she was being followed and in danger of arrest, she would become careless. She would make a mistake; she would become fearful and bolt. He said she would then lead us to the insurgents."

Sokolov continued to glare at Grigoriev for several minutes before he responded. "It seems Petrov was an extremely poor judge of character. He is the one who made the mistake and unfortunately, he is no longer here to defend his actions, so I am afraid it has fallen to you. You will take command of our little group inside the UB."

Even though the room was cold, Grigoriev began to perspire. A bead of sweat trickled down his forehead and into his right eye, causing him to squint uncomfortably. "I will not disappoint you Comrade Colonel."

"Hmm," Sokolov scoffed. "Let's hope not. Now, I want you to return to the UB. I will send a replacement for Zaitsev. He'll report to you in the morning. When you get back to the UB, your job is to do one thing and one thing only. Keep the Poles in check. You are to do nothing about tracking down the insurgents until you hear from me. You may continue to interrogate and collect information, but you are not to take any action until I give you the explicit orders to do so. Is that clear?"

"Yes, Comrade Colonel sir!"

"And Lieutenant, one last item. There will be no more improvising," Sokolov said emphasizing each word. "Unfortunately, there's no war going on so I cannot send you to the front. But I still have Siberia. Do I make myself clear?"

"Yes sir! *Tak tochno*! Perfectly clear!"

Sokolov glared at Grigoriev and said, "Now, get out of here and return to your unit."

"Yes sir!" Grigoriev saluted, turned on his heel and quickly marched out of the room, the door slamming behind him.

Coming from the far-left corner of the room, Sokolov heard the sound of a match being struck, and it briefly illuminated the figure of Kutuzov lighting a cigarette. He had been quietly standing in the darkness, observing and listening as Sokolov dealt with Grigoriev. Kutuzov walked to the chair in front of Sokolov's desk and sat down. He leaned forward and poured each of them a vodka. "You will have an NKVD infantry battalion at your disposal, Yuri. And it will be augmented by a motorized rifle battalion from the 20th Guards Army. They are eager to avenge the loss of their comrades who fell in the ambush. The units are deploying to the field tonight for training maneuvers. Or at least that is the information we are leaking out. In reality, they will be in place to move on the insurgents. You'll have more than a thousand men, which should be more than enough to handle a few dozen remnants of the Home Army."

"Once your source confirms the date and time, I will order Grigoriev's team to observe the landing and pickup. They will be stationed at a discreet distance from where they will land at Ostrowo. Their orders will be to follow the landing party and report to us the location where they take them. Fortunately for us, we had the good fortune of arresting the old woman, Zajac. She gave us the identity of the sleeper agent during her . . . uh, interview. So, the circle is closing, Dmitri. The noose is tightening. We follow the landing party, and they will lead us to the insurgent camp. That's the only thing she wasn't able to give us before she died."

"Are you satisfied your man Grigoriev will do his job? That he won't become overzealous?"

"He will do his job, or he will be looking out onto razor wire from inside a labor camp in Siberia. And the man I'm sending in as a replacement will keep Grigoriev in check. So, I am very confident they will do as they are ordered."

"Good. It will be good to have this mess cleaned up. I want you to crush them, Yuri. Crush them with all your might," Kutuzov said as he tilted his head back and downed the glass filled with vodka in one gulp.

Chapter Fourteen

A Little Extravagance

The more time Catherine Ring spent with David Rowan, the more suspicious she became. It wasn't that she didn't like him. She definitely did. She enjoyed spending time with him. She thought he had a pleasant smile and kind eyes. His facial features were soft and delicate, and while she wouldn't have described him as conventionally handsome, she was nonetheless attracted to him. At least that's how she felt when she met him for the first time.

But over time, his actions caused her to become suspicious. After seeing Rowan regularly for several months, she came to believe he wasn't being entirely truthful with her. His demeanor changed and she feared he was hiding something. And that is when it all came crashing down.

Ring liked Rowan because he wasn't coarse around the edges like the other working-class men at the Citadel. During her time with him, she never heard him utter a curse word or profanity in her presence or in front of the other women. At first, he seemed shy to her, perhaps a bit uncomfortable around women, but in an endearing sort of way. He struck her as a man who probably lacked experience, but she found his demeanor to be charming, and his confidence grew throughout their brief relationship. He always acted gentlemanly towards Ring. He wasn't overbearing and didn't try to push drinks on her. Instead, when they met for the very first time, he offered to buy her dinner.

Once weekly, usually on Thursdays, the women from the Citadel's typing and secretarial pool would go out for drinks after work. It gave them a chance to blow off a bit of steam and exchange office gossip out of range from the prying eyes and listening ears of management. Although there were no official rules governing such gatherings, it was clear these weekly social events were intended to be for the workers only, and the senior Citadel officers rarely, if ever attended. If on a rare occasion they did, their presence made it an early evening for everyone.

The women usually met up at a pub just a ten-minute walk from the Citadel, named The Shoulder of Mutton. It was a working-class pub located in a shabby, run-down building which dated to the late eighteenth century, but somehow managed to survive the Blitz with only a few pock mocks caused by exploding ordnance. Its shabbiness extended to the interior as well, with low ceilings, creaky floors, and crumbling plaster walls yellowed from years of tobacco smoke. But friendly proprietors, an efficient staff and an eclectic local clientele made up for what it lacked in outward beauty. They were very happy to serve the women who worked at the Citadel, who would sit and nurse their drinks, because they brought in male patrons from the compound. Their male counterparts included a regular set of five to six men from the guard section and a smattering of other working types who would drop in – maintenance men, groundskeepers, and sometimes one of the cooks – all of whom were free with their money and would offer to buy the women drinks and flirt suggestively with them in the hope their efforts would be rewarded later that evening. The men usually went home disappointed, vowing to never waste their money on this particular group of women again, until the next Thursday rolled around and once more, they would all be back at it.

It was at exactly 7:00 p.m. when Ring first noticed Rowan on one of her usual Thursday evenings. She knew the precise time because she heard the clang from the large clock which stood next to the bar and it chimed seven times, right on the hour. The women had been there since before 6:00 p.m. and Ring had been sitting there, nursing her drink, a strong Kentish cider. She was listening to her colleagues chattering on about the latest gossip going on at the Citadel.

"Didja hear the night watch officer caught Missy Tucker and that Ashton bloke in the file room together?"

"No! When? What happened?"

"Last Friday. They were supposedly 'working late.' At least that's what Missy told her husband! The watch officer thought he heard something, and when he opened the door, there she was, with her skirt all hiked up around her waist, getting amongst with Ashton."

"No!"

"Yes, it's the god's honest truth, I tell you."

That was the moment when she caught Rowan staring at her. When she returned his stare, he abruptly looked away and for the next fifteen minutes they played a little game. He would look at her, she'd catch him, he'd turn away, and so it went until Ring decided enough was enough. She picked up her glass, marched over to the table where he sat alongside several of his mates from the guard section and said, "You're the new fellow they just hired to man the front gate, aren't you?"

"Aye, ma'am. Yes, I am."

"Ma'am? How old do you think I am? My mother is a ma'am," she replied in mock offense as his table mates laughed heartily. "I'm a miss."

"I'm sorry," Rowan stammered in response. "I meant no offense, ma'am . . . I mean miss. Miss! Sorry!"

Ring looked at him, gave him a smile, then a laugh and said, "Well aren't you going to invite me to sit down?" She stood there waiting for his answer while his table mates laughed.

A short, stocky man sitting next to Rowan elbowed him roughly in the ribs and yelled out, "She's got your number, mate! Miss, let me introduce you to the new man. David Rowan is his name, and as the new guy, he's buying a round for everyone here." The others continued to laugh as Rowan's face turned red from embarrassment. But he ignored the taunts and laughter and slowly stood up and looked directly at Ring.

"I have to apologize for my friends here. I hope you'll forgive them. But they obviously don't know how to act in polite company. Poor upbringing, I suppose," he said softly, which only drew more laughter and taunts from the rowdy bunch. "There's a free table over there," he said pointing to a tiny table with two empty chairs on his left. "Would you like to join me there?"

Ring looked at the table which was indeed empty and replied, "Certainly! I'd be delighted," and she strolled over to the empty table and sat down, waiting for Rowan to join her. He picked up his drink and made his way over to join Ring while his mates looked on, laughing and carrying on.

Rowan pulled out the other chair and sat down, placing his pint in front of him. "Would you like to get something to eat? We could go somewhere else if you like, but they say the food is pretty good here," Rowan said to her, trying to make himself heard over the noise in the pub. In fact, unlike many other pubs in the neighborhood, The Shoulder of Mutton actually served up excellent food, which included a decent shoulder of mutton, hence the name, along with other pub staples such as shepherd's pie, lamb kidneys, and steak and kidney pie.

"I'd love to. I'm starving," Ring replied, "But only if we can go Dutch," she quickly added. She didn't want him to get the wrong idea about what dinner might mean or lead to.

"I'd be honored if you'd let me treat you tonight. I'm celebrating a bit," he replied, looking at her hopefully.

"Celebrating? And what would you be celebrating?"

"I've been on the job for over a month now, and I really like my work. I haven't spent a lot of money. I've been saving it up and I thought I'd splurge a bit. That's all. Won't you let me treat you tonight?"

Ring looked back at him skeptically at first, and then she saw the earnest look on his face and in his eyes. "Oh, alright. I suppose so. That's very kind of you, but don't go getting any ideas about this."

"Oh no, absolutely not," Rowan stammered. "It's just that I could go for a proper meal myself. I have a few bits and bobs back at my flat, but truth be told, I'm not a very good cook. So, I'm doing myself a favor too, you know," he said with a smile and they both had a good laugh together. For the next several hours, over several drinks and a dinner of roast mutton which they shared, the two chatted and shared their respective stories of how they found themselves to be in London, working for MI6. And then Ring heard the clock strike ten times.

"Oh my," Ring exclaimed. "I need to be getting on. It's very late."

"May I see you home? We can hail down a taxi."

"Absolutely not," she replied. "No, I'm just going to pick up the bus on the corner, but you can walk me there."

"I'd like that if that is alright with you. I want to make sure you get home safely."

"That's very sweet of you," Ring replied.

And that's how it all began.

Ring became Rowan's first real girlfriend. They started by meeting up at the pub every Thursday evening. Ring found it easy to talk to Rowan and she enjoyed his company, but she never thought it to be a serious relationship. She just wanted to enjoy their time together without a lot of strings attached. But her suspicions became aroused when she noticed how he always had more pocket money than the other working men at the Citadel. On Thursdays at the pub, he'd always buy a round, which by itself didn't raise any red flags, but then he wanted to take her to fancier restaurants.

"I'm tired of the pub fare," he said. "And I want to take you somewhere nicer."

"What's wrong with the food here," she would reply. "Besides, all my girlfriends are here. I don't want to go anywhere else."

But Ring's concerns about his spending raised to a new level when Rowan started bringing her gifts. It started innocently enough with him bringing her a set of handkerchiefs, but then it escalated to a silk scarf and other items of clothing, and then one night he upped the ante.

"What's this?" Ring asked as he slipped the box to her from across the table.

"Open it."

Ring looked down at the thin rectangular leather box in front of her. She could tell from its shape it was most likely a bracelet or possibly a necklace, but when she opened it, she gasped. What she found inside took her breath away. The box held a white-gold, filigreed, art deco-style bracelet with a single seventy-four facet step-cut diamond in the center. Even in the dimly lit pub, the diamond flashed a parade of kaleidoscopic colors. Ring continued to stare at the bracelet, not knowing what to say. Finally, she looked up at him and spoke.

"David, this is absolutely beautiful. But I can't have you buying me items like this," she said quietly. There was a part of her that wanted to accept the bracelet. It was breathtakingly beautiful. But she wasn't ready to take this relationship to that level. And she worried about the money and where it might be coming from. During routine security and counterintelligence briefings, they had it drilled into their heads to be watchful for someone living beyond their means. If someone suddenly came into money and their spending habits changed, it could be a sign they were selling secrets to foreign adversaries.

She cleared her throat and continued. "It isn't right. You should be saving your earnings and not spending it this way."

"You like me, don't you?" he replied. "And you like the bracelet don't you."

"Well of course I like you. And this . . . this is beautiful. But it just isn't right."

"What's not right about a bloke wanting to give his girl a gift?"

"Look David," she replied, reaching for his hands across the table. "It's not that I don't appreciate it. I do. Truly I do. But I know how hard we all work, and none of us is getting rich working at the Citadel."

"I may have come into a little bit of money."

"Oh? Really? But that's all the more reason you should be saving it and not wasting it," Ring replied. He had piqued her curiosity. "And you say you may have come into some money. From where? You told me you came from a poor family."

"I, I had a distant relative who passed. And he left me a small inheritance."

"A distant relative? Who? Who would that be? This bracelet must have set you back a small fortune," Ring replied.

Rowan became angry. "Never mind. If you'd rather I not spend my money on you, maybe I'll just ask one of the other girls out. I'm sure they won't have a problem if I take them out for a meal, bring them flowers, or buy them a bracelet," he said in a huff as he reached back across the table and snatched the bracelet back. He snapped the case shut, slipped it back into his coat pocket and stood up. "It's my money, and I'll spend it whatever way I see fit," he said angrily, and he stormed out of the pub into the night, leaving Ring sitting there in silence.

That's how it ended.

**

It was on a typical Monday morning when Ring, busy typing a cable scheduled to go out later that day, was approached by her supervisor who walked over to Ring's desk. She looked down at Ring and waited until she stopped typing.

"Catherine, would you please come with me?"

"Of course, miss, but I should finish this cable first," she said looking up at her supervisor, noting the look of worry and concern on her face. "Is something the matter?"

"Margaret can finish that for you," the supervisor said turning to the woman who sat next to Ring, who also was wondering what was going on. "Margaret, would you please finish this draft cable for Catherine. Place it on my desk when it is finished." And then turning back to Ring, she repeated. "Please come with me. Now, please."

Ring pushed her chair back from her desk and slowly rose, now aware all the eyes in the room were focused on her.

"Please everyone, get back to work. There is nothing to concern you here," the supervisor said. "Catherine, this way please." Ring stepped alongside her and the two exited the secretarial pool and walked down the hallway together until they came to a small office, usually unused but not today. The supervisor opened the door and waved for Ring to step through. Two men, one tall, the other short, but both unsmiling and inscrutable sat behind a small table. The tall man motioned for Ring to take a seat in the chair across from them. He nodded to the supervisor who gave Ring a quick, but worried glance as she left the room, closing the door softly behind her.

"Miss Ring, my name is Darby, and this is Mr. Harbisher. We're with the counterintelligence service and we have a few questions to ask you if you don't mind."

Chapter Fifteen

A Slight Change of Plans

A very didn't like meeting in person. He always thought it was too risky to meet Alex, no matter what precautions they took. He knew Alex, as a member of the Soviet embassy staff, would be under constant surveillance and any physical meeting in London was fraught with danger. Meeting out of the country was impractical, so instead, he preferred to pass information to Alex via the extensive drop site network they had set up across London and in the nearby countryside.

But on this one occasion, the information he needed to pass to Alex was so important, so perishable, he knew he would have to risk a physical meeting, so he called the emergency phone number Alex had provided him, a number which rang in the office of Brower & Baker, solicitors located in East London, solicitors who only served one client. The protocol was simple. Call the number. Ask to speak to Mr. Hammersmith and he'll be given instructions as to where and when to meet.

Avery stepped into the red telephone box located three blocks from his office. He inserted coins into the telephone and dialed the number. The line rang twice before it was picked up and Avery heard the voice of a youngish sounding woman on the other end of the call.

"Brower & Baker. How may I help you?"

"Um, hello. I need to speak to Mr. Hammersmith."

There was a short pause.

"Mr. Hammersmith, you say?" came the reply.

"Yes, I need to speak to Mr. Hammersmith. It's quite urgent."

"Can you stay on the line for just a moment sir? I will be right back with you."

Avery stood in the red box and looked out onto the street, watching the cars, taxis, buses and lorries as they navigated their way through the heavy London traffic. He turned to look onto the sidewalk, checking both directions to see if anyone was watching him, not that he could do anything about it. It was several minutes before the woman came back onto the line.

"Hello?"

"Yes?" Avery replied.

"Mr. Hammersmith is not available. He's at the skate park on Clapham Common and will be there until 3 p.m. You can reach him the day after tomorrow. Do you understand?"

"Yes. I do. Perfectly. Goodbye."

Avery hung up the receiver and took a deep breath. The meeting was set. 3 p.m. at Clapham Common at the entrance to the skate park in two days.

The prospect of meeting was weighing heavily on Avery's mind, and it came as a shock when, while walking home from work on the day before the meeting was to take place, a man he had never seen before roughly bumped into him on the sidewalk just a block from his home.

"Oh, I am so very sorry sir," the man exclaimed in a thick Russian accent. "Please pardon my clumsiness," he said as he reached out and placed his left hand on Avery's shoulder, while with his right hand, he swiftly placed a small envelope into Avery's coat pocket.

"See here," Avery complained. "What is this? What are you doing, man?"

"I'm so very sorry. But there is an emergency," the man whispered. "I'm a friend. A colleague of Alex. Alex must cancel your meeting. He sends his apologies. Read the message. Please. It's urgent," he said as he turned and walked away. Avery watched, dumbfounded and not entirely certain as to what just happened. He watched the man, clearly a Russian, who said he was a colleague of Alex, walk briskly down the street. Up ahead, a black car turned the corner in his direction and stopped. The man picked up his pace and began to trot, heading towards the car when the door opened, the man jumped in, slammed the door behind him, and the car sped up the street heading towards Avery. Avery watched in astonishment as the car passed him by. As the car drove by, he could see the man who had accosted him, sitting alone in the back seat. A driver and another man, each dressed in dark suits and overcoats, were in front and they completely ignored Avery, as they drove by, as if he weren't even there.

Avery reached into his overcoat pocket and felt the small envelope. Still in shock, he turned and resumed his walk home, which was just a scant few steps away. He inserted and turned his key to open the door and he stepped inside.

"Is that you dear?" A voice called out from the kitchen. "Peter?"

"Yes. I'm home," he replied as he closed and locked the door behind him. He was still shaken from what had just happened.

"I'll fix you a drink. Hang up your coat and I'll meet you in the parlor."

"Yes . . . yes, dear. I could definitely use a drink," Avery said as he opened the coat closet on the left side of the foyer where he stood. "I'll be right there," he said as he retrieved the envelope and opened it. He pulled out a single sheet of paper, which was folded in half and opened it.

```
34 Tanner Street, SE1
No. 6
Southwark
Tuesday, 2PM
```

Avery just stood there looking at the note. It was not an address or location he recognized. But clearly the man who gave it to him was Russian. He could tell from his accent. Was he actually a friend and colleague of Alex? The way in which this message was passed to him was completely out of line with the protocol he and

Alex had set up. And what was this emergency? Was this some sort of trap?

"Is everything alright, dear?" his wife Madeline said, with drinks in hand, startling him. "I thought you'd be in the parlor. What's wrong?"

"Oh, what? What? Oh yes. I'm sorry. It was a rather dreadful day at the office, I'm afraid," he said as he continued to look at the note in his hand.

"What's that?" she asked, referring to the note in his hand as she stood on her toes to give him a peck on the check.

"Oh, it's ah, nothing dear. Nothing. Just a reminder of something I have to do at the office tomorrow."

"Well, try to put it out of your mind, my love," she said. "Dinner will be ready in half an hour. You can finish that drink and then get ready."

"Yes. Yes," he said, his thoughts still processing what had just happened on the street in front of his house and what his next steps would be.

"Are you sure you're alright dear?"

Avery took a long gulp from his drink. He turned to Madeline and looked at her lovingly. She was several months on now and beginning to show. "Yes. Absolutely smashing, my love," he said smiling as the action he needed to take became clear in his mind.

Chapter Sixteen

A False Sense of Security

"Come in, enter," Banbury said. He looked up as the door opened. The two MI5 agents, Darby and Harbisher entered, walked over, and stood in front of Banbury's desk.

"Let's use the sofa," Banbury said pointing to the other side of his office. "We'll be more comfortable there. Please sit. Can I get you fellows anything? Coffee, tea? Something stronger? It's a bit early in the day for me," Banbury said looking at his watch, "but I could be coerced."

Darby and Harbisher sat down on the sofa. It was Darby who replied, "No thank you Colonel Banbury. That won't be necessary. We know you are very busy. But we wanted to go over our counterintelligence report with you."

"Yes, of course," Banbury said taking a seat in a large, overstuffed armchair opposite the two agents. There was a healthy distrust between the two intelligence services, born in part by the natural competition and rivalry that often exists between bureaucracies, but also due to feelings by leadership and the rank and file within each organization that the other didn't know their arse from their elbow. And even though they were supposedly both playing for the same team, so to speak, neither organization trusted the other. MI5 officers thought their counterparts in MI6 were prissy, amateurish, dilettantes. And MI6 thought MI5 officers were knuckle-dragging hooligans with no sense of finesse. But Banbury, upon learning his entire operation was in jeopardy because of the discovery of a mole within his organization had no recourse but to make nice and cooperate.

"So, what do you have for me?" Banbury said, anxious to get to the heart of the matter and not waste time.

"Thanks to your assistance throughout the investigation, sir," Harbisher began, "We've been able to roll up everyone involved. David Rowan is in custody, of course, and we were able to get his handler as well. We arrested a member of the Soviet Embassy staff. His name is Aleksandr Kamenev, a relatively low-level member of the diplomatic staff who has only been in-country for about a year. He has the title of cultural attaché, but he's MGB for certain. The Home Secretary has notified the Soviets that Kamenev must leave the country within ten days. Pity we cannot detain him to try to get more out of him. And I am certain the Soviets will extract their pound of flesh and expel one of our chaps from Moscow, a tit-for-tat retaliation. That's the way these things usually work."

"Yes, quite right," Banbury replied, taking the information in. "Tell me, what is your assessment. Do you think they took the bait?"

"Only time will tell, sir," Darby interjected. "But it was a stroke of genius sir to feed the Russians bad intelligence. Thankfully, we had the time to do that. Once we caught Rowan at one of his dead drop sites trying to pass information on to the Russians, he broke pretty quickly. You should have seen the look on his face when we caught him, red-handed with his hand in the trap. It was simple at that point to get him to agree, in the hopes of getting his sentence reduced, to help us and pass along the false information your team provided. Nabbing Kamenev only strengthened our hand, in my opinion. I believe it gave credibility to the information Rowan passed on to them."

"Hmm. I certainly hope you are correct," Banbury replied, mulling over in his own mind whether or not he thought Darby's opinion held water. "What about the woman. Our secretary, Miss Ring? What am I to do with her?"

"Oh, she's not involved," Darby quickly answered. "She was seeing Rowan socially, but she knew nothing about his extracurricular activities. She actually turned down a pretty lavish gift he presented her. That's what caused the two of them to break up. Rowan was miffed she wouldn't accept it. No, sir. The only thing she's guilty of is being a little slow to act. She said she was going to report his lavish spending, and his living beyond his means. But she never quite got 'round to it. So, I would say what you do is entirely at your discretion. But I would say a slap on the wrist and admonishment to be more forthcoming in the future should be sufficient. But that is entirely up to you, sir."

"Yes, well. . . I shall consider your recommendation, Darby. And I thank you both for your discretion and diligence. You've rooted out a very bad apple in our midst, and I shall make it known to my superiors of your superb work. We're about to put some very valuable assets in harm's way and with this wrapped up, our operation can now go ahead as scheduled. So, unless there is anything else . . .," Banbury said as his voice trailed off.

"No sir, not at all," Darby replied. "You have anything else to add Harbisher?" Harbisher shook his head no. "Good, then we'll be on our way sir. Here's a copy of our report for your files."

"Very good, gentlemen. Thank you very much. You know the way out, I presume?" Banbury asked as he stood up and headed back to his desk. He had to get a message off to Betancourt that the mission was still on, per the plan, and on schedule. The landing at Ostrowo would take place in three days at 0430 local time.

***

Avery stood in front of the door to 34 Tanner Street, number 6. The building was one of a set of row houses, all private dwellings. He had arrived a few minutes early and it was just before 2:00 p.m. He tested the door handle and found it was locked. That's when he noticed a button marked with the numeral six. He waited for a few minutes, checked his pocket watch which now read precisely 2:00 p.m., and he pressed the button. He could hear a buzzer going off from somewhere inside the residence. He waited, and after just a few seconds, he heard a loud buzz which unlocked the door. He opened the door and stepped into a small entryway which lead to a set of stairs directly in front of him. It was dark, with only a small overhead bulb illuminating the stairwell.

"Mr. Avery? Thank you for coming," said a voice that came from the top of the stairs. Avery looked up and, in the darkness, he saw the Russian. He could just make out his features in the darkness, but it definitely was the same man who bumped into him on the street in front of his house. "You're precisely on time," the Russian said.

"It always pays to be prompt," Avery replied.

The Russian smiled and said, "Please join me upstairs. There is someone here you will want to meet. I know he is very anxious to meet with you."

"Right," Avery said as he began the long climb up the narrow stairway. When he reached the small landing at the top, the Russian held the door opened for Avery and motioned for him to step inside.

"May I take your coat and hat Mr. Avery?" the Russian said. "I'll just hang them here in this wardrobe."

Avery removed his hat and overcoat, handed the items to the Russian, and waited.

"Please, follow me sir," the Russian said, and Avery followed him into the narrow row house, through a sparsely furnished front room and down a narrow hallway which opened into a large sitting room, where in the corner sat a thin man wearing spectacles. Avery recognized him at once and was momentarily taken aback by his presence.

"Allow me to introduce . . .," the Russian said, but Avery cut him off.

"I know who this is. I recognize you," Avery exclaimed. "Comrade Serov! This is an incredible honor."

Serov got up from the chair in which he had been sitting and greeted Avery. "Mr. Avery," Serov replied, "The honor is mine. You've been a great friend to the Soviet Union, and I wanted to meet with you myself. There is some risk in my being here of course. We had to take a number of extraordinary measures to elude your surveillance. This house, for example, has been long reserved for a one-time use, so it has in all likelihood never been under surveillance. And through several leaked communiques and the creative use of a body double, your colleagues believe I returned to Moscow yesterday for a brief meeting at the Kremlin. I think we've taken all the necessary precautions. I am satisfied, so please, sit down," Serov said, pointing to a sofa. "May we offer you some refreshments?"

Avery took a seat on the sofa and Serov returned to the chair in which he had been sitting.

"No thank you, Comrade Serov, I'm fine."

"Please. Call me Vitali."

"Yes, of course. Thank you, Vitali Petrovich."

"Ah, you know my full name," Serov replied, feigning surprise, knowing full well there would be a dossier on him.

Avery had read Serov's file many times. It outlined everything known about him, such as his first and patronymic names, along with many things unknown and left for conjecture. But to meet the man in person. He was as starstruck as a teenager meeting a matinee idol.

"Why yes, of course," Avery said. "You are well known in my country's intelligence circles. And I must say, there are dozens of my fellow countrymen, colleagues in the service who would give their eye teeth or more to be here with you right now. Imagine this. Here I am sitting next to the Rezident himself. I am utterly thrilled to meet you. But, tell me. What has happened to Alex? Is he alright? He hasn't been harmed, has he?"

"Ah yes. Alex. He's fine of course, but I'm afraid he was detained by your compatriots. Unfortunately, one of his other sources has acted in quite a careless manner and he allowed himself to get caught with his hand dipping inside the cookie jar. Isn't that what you say? And, our Alex has been caught up in it all. He was detained but released and has been given just a few days to leave your lovely country, Mr. Avery. So, I decided to take the risk and meet with you myself. I understand from Alex you had information which is so urgent that it could not go through our normal channels."

"Yes, I have details about an upcoming operation. There will be a landing in Poland to insert two agents into the country."

"I am aware of it," Serov replied. "We have just received information that it has been delayed. By a month."

"What? A month? No, that is absolutely not true," said Avery. "It's scheduled to take place this week. That has always been the original plan. On Friday morning, the 17th, at 0430 local time. That is what I wanted to tell Alex. There has been an operation to pass along false intelligence to you. But I know with absolute certainty the operation will take place this week. I knew the information could not wait, which is why I asked to meet with Alex in person."

Serov sat for a moment, stroking his chin as he contemplated what Avery just told him. "Do you have proof to back this up? Not that I don't trust your word Mr. Avery, but it would be helpful to have something concrete."

"Of course, I do," Avery replied as he reached into his pocket and placed a small canister of film on the table in front of Serov. "It's all here. I photographed the cable traffic and other documents. You'll see in the photographs all the details. You've been fed disinformation. The operation is happening. You can count on it, and you have to act on this information."

Serov looked at the film canister. He turned to Avery, nodded, smiled, and said, "Oh, we will Mr. Avery. Please be assured we will definitely act on the information you have provided. We are grateful for your service to us."

Chapter Seventeen

The Lovely Couple

At just after midnight on Friday the 17th, the E-boat came to a full stop in a thick bank of fog roughly two miles off the northern coast of Poland and waited. They were in international waters, but that would change. At 3:30 a.m. the boat moved again and took up a position about two kilometers off the Polish coast, about a mile and a quarter. They were now in Polish territory. Then, at 4 a.m. local time, the landing party climbed over the E-boat's rail and made their way down the rope ladder and into their rubber landing boats, just like they had practiced. The rendezvous with Lygia was set for 0430 local time.

Once the landing party and their gear was aboard the two landing boats, the sailors cast off the lines and the boats headed towards the coast ahead. Amongst the gear and supplies loaded on the second landing boat was a new wireless set, which was to replace the WWII vintage set Lygia had been using. The newer set was lighter, smaller, and much easier to set up and tune. This would help any operator evade Polish or Soviet radio detection-finding units intent on locating illicit communications emanating from Polish soil.

There was no moon or stars visible in the sky as low hanging clouds blocked their view. It was pitch black and she could barely see the back of Jenkins' head as it bobbed up and down and from side to side as they made their way to the beach ahead.

Haas sat in the darkness next to a German sailor as their boat bounced across the water. This time, she didn't want to know his name. She wanted to know nothing about him. She said nothing to him when they stood together on the deck of the E-boat as they waited for their turn to board the landing boats below. She said nothing to him when he took his place alongside her. When he

215

tried to speak to her just before they cast off, to make small talk to pass the time until they reached the shore, Haas would only look ahead and say, "It's better if we do not speak."

After she uttered those words, Haas thought she detected a look of sadness on his face. But it was too dark to tell, so they rode together in silence. The only sounds they heard were the low-pitched chug of the outboard motor, the splash from the sea surrounding them, the occasional thump from the rubber boat as it hit atop the surface of the water, and the sound of the surf crashing on the beach ahead.

Haas hung on tightly to her seat. She knew what it was like to be thrown overboard and was determined to not go through that experience again. When she closed her eyes, she immediately saw Lehman's face. She missed him. In her mind's eye, she could picture his smile and hear the sound of his voice with his peculiar Louisville accent, a gentle drawl she found so unusual and captivating. She had learned British English and had worked with the British for years; she was accustomed to hearing a wide variety of English accents. But Lehman's accent was nothing like she ever encountered.

She enjoyed listening to how he would pronounce certain words. Oil became "awl." The "i" vowel sounded more like "ah." And like most southerners, certain "s" sounds were replaced by a "z." So the word greasy became "greazah" when Lehman said it. When she first heard him speak English, she became confused because he would add an "r" to certain words, such as the world wash, which he pronounced "warsh." But she loved how, unlike most of the other men in his unit, he spoke slowly, carefully articulating his words, drawing the syllables out. One would never know from listening to him speak English that it was not his first language. For when he spoke German or Russian, the languages of his father and mother, all of his Southernisms and Americanisms disappeared, and he spoke just as a native would. No one would be able to detect he grew up in Kentucky, having moved there with his parents when he was a small child. In the early morning darkness, Haas could hear his voice speak to her. In her mind she could hear him speaking, catching a word here or there; they were fleeting words and snatches of conversations they recently had. She missed him.

It was just three days ago when Haas arrived in Kiel for a short layover to take on fuel, supplies, and make sure the E-boat was ready for its mission to Poland. Tensions were running high after losing Häupler, and after discussing it with Banbury, Betancourt decided to give Haas some time off when they arrived in Kiel. So, Haas immediately had a call patched through from the BBFPS office in Kiel directly to Lehman's office in Bremen. The phone only rang once on his end when he picked up.

"Lehman here," he answered curtly.

"Hello Major Lehman," she said seductively when he answered. "Have you missed me?"

"Luba? Is that you?" Lehman replied, nearly knocking over the cup of coffee on his desk. "Yes, of course I missed you. Where the hell are you?"

"I'm in Kiel for three days only. But I have the next forty-eight hours off before I have to report back. That means, at least for the moment, I don't have anything to do. Betancourt wants me out of her hair for the time being, so I was thinking of making a short visit to you in Bremen. But, with the train schedules being what they are. I don't think I can get there and back in time."

"That's not a problem, Luba. I can come to you. I can leave this afternoon. It's just a few hours' drive and I can be in Kiel by early evening. I can be there tonight. Leave it to me. I'll book a hotel room for us. How can I get a message to you?"

"It will have to go through Banbury's office. Call him and they'll pass the message along to the BBFPS office here in Kiel. I'll just wait here until I hear from you, and then I will call you back."

"Banbury's office," Lehman scoffed. "I really don't like the idea of him getting in the middle of our business."

"It's the only way to get a message to me, Cap. But don't worry. His staff will patch you through to me. It won't be a problem, trust me."

"Okay. If you say so. How much time did you say you have?"

"Two nights. So, get here as soon as you can."

"I will. Just wait there for my call. I'm going to pull some strings and get us a honeymoon suite."

"Oh? Is there something else you want to say to me?"

"I love you, Luba."

"I love you too, Cap. I'll wait for your message."

"And you'll be able to meet me at the hotel?"

"I'll be there, but you'll have to tell me which hotel. You'll have to tell me where to meet you," she replied laughing.

"I'll let you know as soon as I figure it out. And, don't worry. I know a guy," he said with a laugh.

"You know a guy? Is it the same guy I know?"

"One and the same. I'll give our man a call. He'll be more than happy to set us up. It's noon now, so I should be able to make it there by early evening at the latest."

"I can't wait to see you. I'll wait for your call. Hurry."

***

Haas and Lehman's guy was a German named Ernst Richter, a man who on the surface ran a respectable import-export business, but in reality, was up to his eyeballs in shady deals on the black market. He became a CIC source after Lehman and his men caught him with a shipment of more than one hundred cases of single-malt whiskey intended for the British officers' mess. High-end whiskey was the kind of product Richter was known for. His specialty was luxury. If someone needed caviar and champagne for a special celebration, no problem. Looking for a 1928 Chateau Mouton Rothschild, look no further. Richter could deliver any vintage in whatever quantity you required. Want to dazzle your paramour with a diamond bracelet by Cartier, or with fragrances such as Jean Patou's "Joy," Dana's "Tabu," or Chanel No. 5? Not a problem. Richter could quickly and discreetly slip these elegant items into your pocket. If you wanted anything from gourmet food or fine wines, jewelry, perfumes or haut couture dresses and gowns, Richter was your man. He could provide anything and everything of luxury – for the right price. Richter was about to become Lehman's guy.

Lehman, Haas, and a company of U.S. Army military police descended on the building and took Richter and a half dozen accomplices, including the lorry drivers into custody, and brought them back to Bremen for questioning. After several hours of pressure tactics from Lehman and Haas while under interrogation, they were able to come to an agreement.

"Major. We've been at this for hours. I'm sure we can reach some sort of accommodation," Richter said, now looking visibly tired and worn down from the constant questioning. "What is it you really want from me?"

"What do we want from you?" Lehman mused, "Hmm. Very little actually. I personally don't give two hoots about your business. In fact, I can honestly say we are willing to look the other way and ignore your activities completely. It's not like you're keeping food away from the average German. Your clientele are completely different. They can afford your prices. And under the right circumstances, we might even be willing to help your business thrive. But, just like you, all of this will come at a price."

"And what is that price? What is it you would want from me? A piece of the action perhaps?"

"Oh no. Absolutely not Herr Richter. Nothing like that."

"Then what?"

"Herr Richter," said Haas, who had been sitting alongside Lehman in silence for most of the interrogation, and now finally interjecting herself into the conversation. "What we are looking for is your cooperation."

"Cooperation. Continue, please," said Richter.

"We understand your business dealings take you to Berlin and Potsdam," said Haas. "We have a keen interest in what is going on inside the Soviet Zone of Occupation. So, we might ask you, from time to time, to observe and collect information on our behalf, and then provide that information to us. And since you are in what can be described as the transportation business, we might also ask you to deliver or pick up certain items and bring those items to us. That is our price – a small amount of cooperation on your part. And in exchange for such cooperation, we will look the other way regarding your business activities. We'll keep you safe and out of harm's way from other organizations within the German government or amongst the occupation forces who are not as enlightened as we are and might take a dim view of your activities."

"Yes, I've been approached by the Gehlen people, the former Abwehr officers. They made similar proposals. I turned them down. I'm a businessman, not a spy."

"We're aware of that, Herr Richter," said Lehman, "But we also know you love your country, just as I love mine. You fought against the Russians, and you have no love for them after what they did to your family in Eberswalde, in the East. That's where you're from originally isn't it? That's where you grew up and you saw what the Russians did there on their march to Berlin."

Richter's face grew dark at the mention of his family in the East. His head slumped forward, and he took in several long, deep breaths to compose himself.

"Look, Herr Richter," Lehman continued. "I can't make you do this. But I can make it worth your while. I know the German authorities are planning to put more pressure on you. Your latest transgression has also caught the attention of the British, and I'm afraid they want to throw the book at you. If I were to turn you over to the German authorities tonight, you will face considerable time behind bars, several years by my estimate, and your growing business empire will come crashing down. But we can make all of that disappear. If you were to work with us, we will release you and your men, along with the contents of the lorries we confiscated. No questions asked. And going forward, as long as you maintain a cooperative relationship with us, we will continue to offer our protection and shall we say, our tacit support. You're a businessman, right? Well, think of this as a business deal. But ultimately, I am appealing to your sense of loyalty to Germany, your patriotism. By working with us, you'll be working to make your country stronger."

"I think I've heard this speech before Herr Major. We've all heard it since 1933 and look where that got us."

"Fair enough, but this time your enemy is just across a line on a map. There are hundreds of thousands of Russians on the other side of that line. You've already lost your family to them, and nothing is going to bring them back, so you know what they are capable of. But, by working with us, this is your opportunity to extract a bit of revenge. And really, we're not asking you to do anything you aren't already doing. We're simply asking you to gather information, consider it market research. Gather some information and share it with us. That is something you normally do, isn't it? You always make sure you understand the market for the goods and services you provide?"

"It's true I have no love for the Russians. No German does. But…"

"Then keep doing what you are doing but do it with us. That is all we are asking you to do. You won't regret it, I promise."

"I need some time to think on this, Herr Major."

"Unfortunately, Herr Richter, time is not on your side. The Germans are clamoring for your hide as we speak. If we cannot reach agreement, I'll have no other recourse but to turn you over to them. That's the deal I had to make with them, and it is something I really do not want to do. You see, they want to make an example of you, and you'll lose everything you've worked to build since the end of the war. So, as they would say in sales parlance, this is a limited time offer."

Richter looked across the interrogation table at Lehman and Haas. He gave them each a hard stare, his eyes burned, and then his face lightened, and he smiled. "Very well. I believe I can work with you Herr Major, and Madam," he said acknowledging Haas.

"Good," said Haas. "I think you've made the right decision, but just to demonstrate we are reasonable people, we'll begin our relationship on a trial basis."

"A trial basis?" Richter asked, sounding confused.

"Yes, a trial," Haas continued. "On your next trip to Berlin and Potsdam, we will ask you to collect very specific information for us. And if you are able to do this to our satisfaction, we'll ask you to do it again. Upon your return to the West, we will meet with you. We'll spend some time together, let's say an afternoon. We'll ask you detailed questions about your trip, who you visited, where you went, and you'll pass along the information we've requested. We'll ask you to make several trips on our behalf before we make the arrangement permanent. Understand?"

"Yes, I think so," Richter replied, still acting confused.

"Think of it this way, Herr Richter," Lehman interjected. "A trial period will give us, and you too, a chance to get to know one another. Think of it as a courtship before marriage. Or perhaps a test drive. Try before buy, is the phrase, no? That will give us both the opportunity to see if we can work together. If we all get along, we will continue our relationship. But, if it doesn't work out, you can walk away, we can walk away, at any time. How does that sound to you?"

Richter looked back at Lehman and Haas. "That doesn't change our agreement tonight does it? You'll still release me and my workers? And the cargo, of course."

"If you agree tonight, you'll walk away with your men and your merchandise," Lehman said.

"Then we have a deal," said Richter.

"Excellent," Lehman replied. "We will be in contact with you in forty-eight hours to plan out your next trip to the East. And I'm confident that we will be able to strike a long-term, permanent arrangement that will be very good for you. And for us."

***

Their deal became permanent. Richter became their guy and turned into a highly reliable source for Lehman and Haas. At first, his missions were simple. Gather information on food prices and shortages, or the status of housing construction, the availability of petrol and heating oil. After each mission, Richter was debriefed in great detail by Lehman and Haas. They would grill him for several hours about his contacts and movements with the Russian sector. And they would put him on "the box," the euphemism for the polygraph or lie-detector machine, whose use Lehman first resisted, but then embraced.

Richter didn't like the debriefings initially, and he especially hated the polygraph. But Lehman and Haas made it worthwhile for him. They made sure Richter was invited to top social gatherings and galas whenever he was in Bremen. They would smile and acknowledge Richter with a discreet nod from across the room and watched as he sidled up to top British, German, and American officials, all eager for the products he had to offer. The rigorous debriefings and being put on "the box" were minor inconveniences. His business grew as a result of his agreement with Lehman and Haas, and their relationship morphed from suspicion and doubt to confidence and trust. Over time, Richter routinely, and with great accuracy, provided intelligence information on troop movements, order of battle, and military construction projects. He also successfully delivered and collected packages to and from dead drop sites within the Soviet zone. It became a very solid marriage of convenience.

***

Lehman had Richter's number memorized and he dialed it as soon as he hung up with Haas. It was a special line they had installed in Richter's office that had only one purpose. The phone only rang when his American friends needed something. Richter was startled when the phone rang. He looked at it as it rang once. Then twice. On the third ring he picked up.

"This is Richter."

"Good afternoon, Herr Richter. It's Cap. Cap Lehman, how are you today?"

"Ah, Major Lehman, what a surprise," Richter replied, somewhat nervously. "I wasn't expecting a call from you. Is everything alright?"

"Everything is fine, Herr Richter. There's no need to worry. But I could really use your help. I've been summoned to Kiel, and I need a hotel room for tonight and tomorrow. I know you have connections there. Can you help me with that?"

"Kiel? Of course, I can help," sounding relieved. "I do a good business there, but as you said, you already know that," he laughed. "Herr Major, it would be a pleasure for me to assist you. Tell me, will this room be a room for two?" he asked. Although he couldn't see his face, Lehman could sense Richter's sly smile over the phone.

"Yes, for two people please. And I want the best suite available."

"In that case, I am even happier to assist you, Herr Major."

Within the hour, Lehman had a room booked at the Hotel Kieler Kaufman, a former banker's mansion used by the German Navy's admiral of the Baltic Sea during the war. It was newly renovated and had only recently reopened as a hotel. The manor house had been badly damaged by RAF air raids during the war. But a group of local businessmen, *Der Kieler Kaufmann, e.V.*, the Kiel Businessmen's Association, first leased the property and then was able to buy it, turning the original manor house into a clubhouse and a twenty-room hotel.

All that was left was for him to call Banbury's office. He thought it best not to provide any of the details, but to merely ask them to pass along an urgent message to Haas to contact him immediately. She'd understand the shorthand.

Less than thirty minutes later, the telephone in Lehman's office rang.

"Lehman here," he said with anticipation.

"Cap, it's Luba. Were you successful?"

"Of course. There is a room, a suite actually, waiting for us at the Hotel Kieler Kaufman. The address is Niemannsweg 102. Can you meet me there at say, 7 p.m.? That should give me plenty of time to drive up from Bremen."

"Of course. I'll be waiting for you."

"Great. I'm on my way. It will take me about four hours or so. I have to run by the flat and pick up a change of clothing. Is there anything I can bring you? Is there anything you need?

"Only you. That's all I need."

Lehman drove as fast as he could to Kiel, but once he arrived in the city, he became lost, and the entire trip took him almost five hours. It was nearly 8 p.m. when he finally pulled up in front of the hotel in his jeep, the sight of which seemed to delight the hotel staff. He was the first American ever to stay at the hotel and the doorman made a great show of taking Lehman's bag from the back of his jeep, assuring Lehman he loved Americans and America, and that he had only fought in the East against the Russians.

Lehman entered the lobby and headed directly to the front desk with the door man close behind. Off to his right, Haas sat comfortably in a large wingback chair, her legs folded beneath her, nursing a drink in her hand. Lehman had not noticed her, so she sat and looked on with amusement as the scene unfolded and Lehman checked into their hotel. A tall, rather gaunt man with a pencil thin moustache wearing wire rim spectacles and an impeccably tailored dark gray suit with a red carnation in his lapel came running to the desk when Lehman rang the service bell. Upon seeing Lehman in uniform standing in front of the desk, he immediately began to gush.

"Ah, yes! You must be Major Lehman. I am Herr Kruger, the manager of Hotel Kieler Kaufman, and if there is anything you need, anything at all, please ask for me directly. It is an honor to have you as our guest and I am at your service. You are the first American to stay with us and we intend to make your visit as comfortable as possible. We have set aside our best guest suite for you. It is on the second level and the room's balcony offers a lovely view of the waterfront area" he said as he handed the key to the doorman. "Walter here will help you with your luggage and show you to your room. And I believe, the lady," he said pointing over to where Haas sat, "I believe the lady is waiting for you."

Lehman turned to look to where Kruger was pointing and saw Haas. It was the first time he'd seen her since she left for London, more than a month ago, and it brought on the biggest smile.

"Luba," he cried out and his eyes welled with joy.

"Hello, handsome," said Haas. "It took you long enough to get here."

***

The accommodations were as advertised. They were given a beautifully appointed suite of two rooms. There was a sitting room with a fireplace, a large leather sofa, a small dining table with a window where they took their meals, and a brightly lit bedroom which included an ensuite bath and another fireplace. Their bed faced a set of French doors which led out onto a small balcony and offered a lovely view of Kiel's harbor area.

The next forty-eight hours were a blur. Lehman and Haas spent the entire time in their suite. They had their meals sent up to the room and were served by two Hungarian waiters, who were brothers, and they wanted to linger while Haas and Lehman ate, but were shooed away by Haas, which only piqued their curiosity and increased the level of gossip amongst the hotel staff.

And in between their lovemaking, sometimes tender and slow, at other times quick and urgent, while entangled in the bed linens and entwined in each other's arms, Haas shared everything that was about to happen once she landed in Poland.

"It will be a quick mission," said Haas.

"That's good. How quick?"

"For me, three days. My job is to confirm we are actually meeting with Lygia, and after that, make sure we're not being double crossed. They had originally planned to have me stay for several weeks."

"Several weeks?"

"Yes, but that all changed after the accident. Betancourt wants me out of the way as soon as possible. She wanted me to return to the E-boat once I confirmed Lygia's identity, but Banbury overruled her. So, I'll watch over the young MI6 agent who's accompanying me. She's very eager, perhaps too much so. And then in three days, I'll return to the beach I landed on where I will be plucked off and then I shall return."

"Three days sounds a lot better than several weeks."

"Yes, I'll be glad to get in and get out."

"Do you have reason to believe Lygia is a double agent?"

"No, but we have to make sure. It wouldn't be the first time an agent was turned. That's my primary mission. And once I determine that, I will gladly turn over control of Lygia to my young protégé."

"How will you know? How can you ever be sure?"

"From the reports we've received, Lygia has been directly involved in the insurgency and has engaged in skirmishes. That's been part of the problem. The insurgents need weapons and ammunition. What they need most are more insurgents. But we don't have the capability to give them what they need. At least not at the present time. That's coming later. So, we're going to deliver a few supplies, just what we can carry. And, of course, we're delivering a satchel full of money. That's supposed to tide them over. I'm supposed to use my powers of persuasion and convince them to keep their powder dry and wait."

"The old slow roll, huh?"

"Yes. Judging from their most recent communication, they are running out of patience."

"Sounds like they're running out of bullets."

"Hmm. Yes, that pretty much sums it up. They're getting desperate. I don't know if they're going to be able to hold out. Anyway, once I confirm Lygia's bona fides, and convince the insurgents to bide their time, I will bow out and come home. Or at least to London, and after I get debriefed there, I will come back to you. And you and I," she said leaning over to kiss him, "You and I will live happily ever after."

"I like the happily ever after part. But can you be one-hundred percent certain Lygia isn't giving you all the double cross? This always had a rotten smell to it. At least to me. It's very risky. But you know me. I'm definitely not a glass half full kind of guy."

"It is risky, but in many ways, that's the easy part. It's easier than convincing men who are fighting and dying to hold on just a little bit longer. I'll also know right away if it's actually Lygia. If the real Lygia is dead, they can't send an imposter. If they do, the operation will be aborted. Terminated immediately."

"That sounds pretty final."

"It is."

***

With their two nights now over, Lehman and Haas finally emerged from their suite on their last morning together. They descended the wide staircase from the second story and entered the dining room for breakfast. The hotel staff were still abuzz about their mysterious guests. They had become enamored with them, obsessed, and speculated about who they were and what they were doing together in Kiel. They even gave them a nickname, and Lehman and Haas became known as '*das schöne Paar*,' or the 'lovely couple.'

They both sat quietly, picking at their food, not wanting their time together to end, but knowing that it was inevitable. It was

9:30 a.m. and in an hour, a car from the BBFPS would arrive to pick up Haas and return her to base. They finished their breakfast in silence and returned to their suite to pack up, which didn't take long. They each only had one bag. They took the stairs back down to the lobby, Lehman paid the bill, and then stepped outside to wait for the car that would take Haas away.

Standing in front of the hotel, Haas clung to Lehman with her arms wrapped tightly around him and her head rested upon his chest. She didn't want to let him go.

"You know I have to do this," she said softly.

"I know Luba. We've gone over it many times. I understand. I'll be waiting for you when you return," said Lehman. "And then," he started to say something more but was interrupted when the dark gray Humber with BBFPS markings on the side pulled up in front of the hotel.

"Oh, that's for me," said Haas. She reached up with both hands, grasped Lehman's face and kissed him hard, nearly knocking his service cap from his head. Finally, she released him, picked up her small duffel, opened the rear door and slipped inside. She didn't want to look at him at first, but when the car began to pull away from the curb, she turned suddenly to Lehman and mouthed the words, "I love you."

Lehman stood on the sidewalk in front of the hotel, numb with sadness, as he watched Haas drive off.

"And then," he whispered, "once you return, I'm never going to let you go. Not for as long as I live," he said, finally finishing his thought as he turned to walk over to his jeep to make the lonely trip back to Bremen.

Chapter Eighteen

Sign and Countersign

Haas sat in silence in the landing boat, jostled by the waves as the landing party headed to shore. She was brought back to reality when she suddenly observed two long flashes of light followed by three short flashes and finally two long. It was the signal from the beach. The signal was repeated once more and a crewman sitting forward on the boat reached into his poncho and pulled out a handheld torchlight. He responded with three long flashes and the landing boats began to slow, awaiting for the final signal giving them the all-clear to proceed. In the darkness Haas could make out one long, a short, and one long flash of light. The boats immediately sped up and headed for the rendezvous and whoever waiting for them on the beach.

Another flash of light appeared from the shoreline, helping the coxswain to guide them to the precise spot where they would land. The sound from the surf grew louder and louder, and Haas knew they were getting closer and closer, until finally the two sailors in front jumped out into knee deep water, each of them taking a line to help bring the boat onto the shore. They were vulnerable. If this were an ambush, now would be the time to open fire and Haas strained to see any movement, any sign of trouble ahead, but it was too dark.

"Keep the noise down," Jenkins ordered. "Load and lock your weapons and wait for my orders," she said as the second boat pulled up onto the beach. "Luba, are you ready to go?"

"I'm ready," Haas replied. Any thoughts she had of Lehman were now gone. She felt her heart pumping and the rush of adrenaline as she readied herself to disembark and move out onto the beach.

"Let's go," Jenkins replied and the two of them stepped out of the boat into the shallow water, which only came up to their ankles. They quickly walked up onto the beach and waited.

Haas strained to see if she could make out anything in the darkness. Finally, she saw movement. She could see two figures moving in their direction, walking down the steep beach. "I'll take the lead," she said to Jenkins. "Stay close behind me."

"Right behind you," Jenkins replied as she released the safety on her weapon.

They continued to move up the beach and could now see two people, one tall and one short, approaching, but it was impossible to identify any facial features. Haas raised her hand, indicating they should stop. They were now less than five meters apart.

"He who knew how to live . . ." said Haas in a firm, loud voice. She awaited the reply, but the pair in front of them didn't respond. "He who knew how to live . . ." Haas said, once more, this time a little louder and with more urgency.

Finally, out of the darkness came the reply, "Should know how to die."

The phrase was a quote from Quo Vadis, and it served as the sign and countersign for the meeting. It was correct and acknowledged. *Now they know. Lygia is a woman*, Haas thought, and then she smiled. *Hmm, Jenkins bet a fiver in the pool Lygia was a man.*

"Wait for me. Don't do anything until I give you the signal," Haas said to Jenkins, and she moved forward to get closer to the two figures who stood before her in the darkness. This was it. There was no turning back now. Haas had to determine once and for all if this was the real Lygia standing in front of her. She stepped forward slowly until she was just an arms-length away from the two figures in front of her.

The shorter figure on the right moved forward and pulled off the hood obscuring her face. Haas looked at the woman in front of her. She struggled to recognize her. It had been four years since they last saw each other, but finally recognition came to her, then shock and finally surprise.

"Ada? Is that you? What are you doing here?" Haas whispered. It was still dark. Sunrise would not occur until after 7:00 a.m. local time and it was difficult to make out the face of the young woman standing before her. Her facial features had changed; this person was more mature, older. Despite the darkness and the years since their meeting, Haas immediately recognized the person on the beach in front of her.

"Felicja? Felicja Nowak? Is that you? I cannot believe you are here after so many years!"

"Yes, it's me. But I can tell you my real name now. Felicja Nowak was my cover name. Call me Luba. Luba Haas." Haas leaned forward and wrapped her arms around her and whispered, "What are you doing here? Where's your mother?"

"She's dead. She died in Warsaw, but I've taken her place in the fight. I will tell you everything," Bialik whispered. "But we need to get off this beach. It's too dangerous for us to be here. The area is heavily patrolled and watched."

"Is this Lygia or not?" Jenkins asked, her voice rising with tension as she watched the exchange taking place on the beach in front of her. "Luba, is it Lygia? I need to know. Luba," she said as she readied her weapon and prepared herself to take action against the woman on the beach.

"Yes," came the reply as Haas stared at Bialik, looking into her eyes in disbelief. "Yes," she said, not really knowing whether or not she was lying to Jenkins. But she knew she had to stay with the mission and discover the truth. "It is she. This is indeed Lygia. Now, we have to move. Fast. Let's get the gear unloaded. We need to move. We need to get out of here."

***

On a tall knoll obscured by sea grass, located one hundred meters to the south of the landing and rendezvous point, two Russian soldiers, members of the NKVD watched the activity on the beach. One soldier, a lieutenant, was using a German-made infrared night-vision device attached to his field binoculars and observed the rendezvous on the beach below. The other, a junior sergeant, crouched in the rocks and sand and manned a radio set. He was waiting for instructions from the lieutenant to transmit.

The lieutenant watched as several large duffel bags and a crate were lifted out of the landing boats and carried up the beach to a small lorry parked along the beach road. He watched as the lorry was loaded and two people, one tall and one short got into the cab while another person jumped into the rear of the lorry. Another person who had been part of the landing party could be observed talking to the men who had carried the gear up from the beach. He surmised this person was likely giving some last-minute orders and instructions, before jumping into the rear of the lorry. The lorry's engine fired up, and it began to move down the road, picking up speed, and driving away while the remaining men returned to the landing boats on the beach.

"Send the message to the chase team," the lieutenant said, turning to the sergeant. "Have the lorry followed, but not too closely. And then notify battalion headquarters to move out to the rally point. Tell them we will relay coordinates once we have pinpointed the insurgent base camp."

"Yes, comrade lieutenant."

The lieutenant resumed looking through the night vision device. "It's time to finally crush the insurgency, once and for all," he said as the two landing boats turned around and headed back out to sea.

Chapter Nineteen

There's Something You Need to Know

It took them nearly three hours, driving over poorly paved roads in a lorry with bad shocks and struts, but finally Haas and Jenkins made it to the forest soldiers' hideout which was nestled within a dense forest southwest of Puck. They sat in silence for the entire journey, and Haas mulled over how she would break the news about Lygia's identity to Jenkins. She decided to wait until they reached their destination.

The sun was just rising as they entered the encampment, and they felt the lorry slow down and make a sharp turn onto a heavily rutted road. Haas pulled the lorry's canvas covering aside and she could see an elaborate system of interlocking trenches and what appeared to be handmade bunkers dug into the earth, all covered with pine branches and camouflage netting in an attempt to hide their presence from aerial reconnaissance. Several of the dugouts had metal chimneys, painted a dark green, which protruded from the ground. Wisps of white smoke mixed in with the dense morning ground fog, further obscuring the encampment. She couldn't see any signs of life above ground and in the early dawn light the camp had a kind of magical appearance to it as if it were the setting for a children's fairy tale rather than a launchpad for violence.

The vehicle finally came to a stop with the high-pitched squeal of brakes. The cab doors opened to the shouts and the sound of men running towards them. *So, there are soldiers here*, Haas thought. Both she and Jenkins reflexively reached for their weapons and made them ready.

"Help us unload the vehicle," they heard Bialik say. A few seconds later, the canvas covering at the rear of the vehicle opened.

Bialik stuck her head in and said, "I know it was a rough ride, but we've made it."

Haas and Jenkins gave each other a quick look. They both relaxed their grip on their weapons and clicked on their safeties.

"You're safe here," she said. "You don't have to worry."

"Instinct," replied Jenkins.

"I understand," Bialik replied. "Do you need any help with your bags and equipment?"

"If you grab my duffle bag, I'll carry the case," said Jenkins. "It contains a new wireless set for you. I'll go over its operation and you'll be up to speed in no time."

"Very well," said Bialik, grabbing one of the bags and slinging it over her shoulder. You're both bunking with me. I'll take you there. The commander, Wulkan, will also meet us there, in about thirty minutes."

Jenkins and Haas jumped from the lorry onto the ground. It was covered with pine needles and the air smelled of pine and burning wood. During their journey, they each had shed the coveralls they had been wearing to reveal the civilian clothing they had worn underneath. They were both dressed similarly; only the colors of their clothing were different. Trousers, heavy pullover sweater, waist length jacket, gloves, and boots. At first glance, they both looked as if they were planning a hike through the woods. But their supply belts with ammo pouches, and the weapons they had draped over their shoulders indicated they had different intentions.

"Goodness," Bialik said when she saw them, eyeing them up and down. "You're both ready for action I see. That's good. Alright, follow me. It's a short walk from here. Your quarters aren't elegant, but they are functional. And they're warm and dry."

They set out onto a forest path and came to a parapet where a soldier stuck his head out. Upon seeing Bialik, he motioned the three of them to climb down a set of steps that led to the trenchworks below.

"Mind your step," said Bialik. "It's steep."

The trenchworks were at least two meters deep, deeper whenever the terrain allowed. The walls where shored up with wood to prevent them from caving in and revetted with sandbags. The trench floor was lined with framed duckboards which provided drainage to keep the area dry.

"This must have taken a lot of work to construct," Jenkins said, huffing as she carried the wireless case, which weighed about twelve kilos. The wireless set itself was small, weighing less than three kilos. The batteries and spare parts made up the bulk of the case.

"Everything you see here, it was all done by hand," Bialik replied. "They are constantly making modifications and fortifying the positions. The forest soldiers have been using this camp for over a year now. But we don't know how much longer we'll be here. There are rumors," she said as her voice trailed off.

After a short walk, they came to the entrance of a dugout with a wooden frame which acted as a door. Bialik pulled the frame aside and entered. Jenkins and Haas followed her inside. It was a surprisingly large space, nearly six meters deep and four meters across. It contained four wooden bunks, a small table with a pair of chairs, and a small wood-fired stove that provided heat and served as a place for cooking.

"As I said, it's not very elegant," Bialik said as she showed them inside. "If you go back out and turn to your left and walk about fifty meters, you'll come to the rear of the trenchworks. You'll also come upon two dugouts which serve as our field latrines. There are nine women here in the camp, eleven now with the two of you here. Wulkan has kindly designated the first dugout you reach as the latrine for the women only. But the quarters here are tight, so we're no longer shy. We gave up our modesty long ago."

"We'll be fine here," said Jenkins.

"Fortunately, there is plenty of firewood," said Bialik. "I've scrounged up some food for you. I have bread and a bit of cheese," she said pointing to a small basket on the table. "And there's a small kettle where you can boil water. There's water in the large pitcher on the table. There's a small stream a kilometer north of where we are. That's where we gather water. I don't have any tea, I'm afraid. I'm sorry for that, but I do have coffee. Ersatz. I think it's leftover from the war, but I'm sure you've had it before, so it won't be a surprise."

"Don't worry about us," said Haas. "We'll be fine."

"Alright then," said Bialik. "I'll fetch Wulkan and bring him to you. You're free to move around the camp of course, but until we've had a chance to introduce you, I wouldn't wander around much past the latrine. The men are a little jumpy as you would imagine."

"Noted," said Jenkins curtly. "Good to know."

"Alright, I will be back shortly," said Bialik as she exited the bunker.

Jenkins watched her depart and when she was sure she was out of earshot, she turned to Haas and asked, "How old was Lygia when you recruited her? She seems awfully young now. She can't be more than what, twenty-two, or three?"

"There's something I need to tell you," said Haas.

"What? What is it?"

"The woman we met on the beach is not the original Lygia."

"What?" Jenkins hissed, glaring at Haas. Her mind raced as she wondered what she should do. Finally, she said, "I should shoot you right now, but I'll wait to hear your explanation. What do you mean? Not the original Lygia. What does that mean?"

"Her name is Ada Bialik and she's the daughter of the woman I recruited. Well, I actually recruited them both. It's a long story. She told me on the beach her mother was killed. So, it appears she took her place. I didn't expect to see her, but I know her."

"Let me get this straight," Jenkins said, as her eyes flashed with anger. "Are you saying there were two Lygia's? And this one is the daughter of the woman you recruited? Is that what you are telling me. Is this the person you recruited or not?"

"I recruited Sofia and Ada Bialik in 1944. They were mother and daughter. Sofia's codename was Lygia. Ada was only seventeen at the time, but she wanted to fight. Her mother was heavily involved in the underground and took part in the fighting, sabotage, whatever was necessary. We mainly used Ada as a courier. She shuttled messages back and forth between members of the underground. But, Sofia, her mother, used her for other things including as her wireless operator. Morse code came really naturally to her. So, she became the radio operator for her mother. She was the one who sent the radio messages during the war, not her mother. That's why they recognized her signature when they picked up her transmission. The reason she has a recognizable fist is she is the same woman. Had her mother survived the war, we would have met her on the beach. But she didn't, and Ada took her place completely. So, for all intents and purposes, this is Lygia. It's as simple as that."

"Can we trust her?"

"I expected to meet Sofia Bialik this morning. But I knew her daughter Ada, and that's who met us. They worked as a team. She could have just had us arrested on the beach. She could have had half the Polish Army waiting for us. She could have had us shot right on the beach. But she didn't. She took us here, at great risk, to meet with the insurgents, the forest soldiers. It was just as you had arranged and agreed to do with her. She's held up her end."

"At this point we don't know where we've been taken."

"Look around you for heaven's sake. She didn't bring us to some UB cell or Soviet prison camp. This isn't a ruse. This isn't some elaborate maskirovka operation. This is a camp and there are soldiers here who are fighting against the communist government. Your mission is to make contact with these soldiers and help them win the fight. You're here now, so carry out your mission."

Jenkins exhaled deeply with her fists clenched and looked down at the dugout floor. She took several deep breaths and attempted to calm herself.

"Natalie, during the war I trusted Sofia and Ada with my life. They both risked their lives and fought the Germans and now Ada is fighting the Russians. My gut is telling me to trust her."

"Right," Jenkins scoffed. "Alicia said you were a loose cannon. Now, I understand what she meant. You should have told me immediately on the beach. You should have told me straight away."

"And if I had, what would have happened. Would you have terminated her on the beach if I had said it wasn't the Lygia I expected to see?"

"Those were my orders."

"Then you would have made a grave mistake."

"Loose cannon," Jenkins replied. She continued to take deep breaths but could not calm down. Finally, exasperated she yelled, "I'm going to find the latrine. Unless I get shot first," and stormed out of the bunker.

***

When Jenkins returned to the bunker, Haas had made a pot of the strong, bitter, ersatz coffee. Haas poured a cup and handed it to her.

"It's just as bad as you'll remember," she said smiling, trying her best to lower the tension between them.

Jenkins looked first at Haas and then at the cup. She took the cup from Haas, let out a deep breath and said, "Thank you." Then she took a sip and frowned. "Ugh, this is vile."

"It is. But it's hot."

"Ugh," Jenkins uttered, taking another sip. "Oh my, I don't think I can handle this," she said and placed the cup on the table. "Look, Luba. I'm sorry I flew off the handle at you. I lost my temper. Not good."

"I understand," Haas replied. She thought for a moment about how, during the war, her reaction to Jenkins would have been so different. She would have become enraged, she would have blown her off completely, and given Jenkins an ultimatum to yield to her authority. But now, several years later, she was practicing patience. *Lehman*, she thought. Always insisting on teamwork. *Well, I guess it's worn off on me. Damn you, Cap*, she thought as she smiled at Jenkins.

"Remember, how I told you I always wanted to parachute into danger?"

"I do," Haas replied, nodding her head affirmatively.

"I thought about what you said, and you're absolutely right. I am going to carry out my mission. We're right in the middle of it now and this is what I've always wanted."

"Plus," said Jenkins as Haas took a sip of coffee, "I had a really good poo, and there's nothing like a good poo to help you focus," causing Haas to spit out the coffee out onto the floor halfway across the dugout. They both burst into laughter when Bialik entered the dugout followed by a man wearing a Home Army uniform. It was Wulkan.

He looked around the dugout and then at the two women.

"The ersatz is utterly vile, isn't it," he said with a deadpan look on his face. Haas and Jenkins broke out in squeals of laughter.

Chapter Twenty

From Disappointment to Desperation

In a hastily erected tent, which served as the command post for the forces mounting the attack on the forest soldier compound, Sokolov stood next to a large table on which a map of a forest preserve near Puck was laid out. Next to him stood the two field commanders who would carry out the operation. On his right was the commander of a motorized rifle battalion from the 20th Guards Army. On his left, stood the commander of an NKVD infantry battalion and together, these two would lead a combined force of over one thousand men into combat today.

The source of the map was significant because it was more accurate than any map possessed by the Red Army. This particular map had been produced before the war by the States Forest, National Forest Holding Association, the organization responsible for managing all of Poland's state-run forests. It was the most accurate map available of the area. At 1:50,000 scale, the map provided relief and elevation information and depicted features such as trails, streams, and huts that were intended to be used as shelter during inclement weather, but now could serve as a place for someone to hide if they were trying to escape. Understanding small details could be the difference between success and failure of the operation they were about to undertake.

Grigoriev stood at the end of the table and addressed the three senior officers in front of him. He had led the chase team that had followed Haas, Jenkins, and Bialik from the beach at Ostrowo to a heavily forested area outside of Puck.

"We lost contact with three members of the chase team in this area, here," Grigoriev said pointing to a spot on the map. "The last report we received before we lost them stated they observed and followed the lorry to this forest road," Grigoriev said as he pointed

244 – KARL WEGENER

out the road on the map. "It is a narrow service road and has a dirt surface, and it is heavily rutted from use. It leads directly to the northern edge of a large compound within this forest," he said, sliding his finger to outline the forest on the map. "Our men were able to scout the area before we lost contact. We believe this is the insurgent encampment where they are hiding. The camp is approximately one and a half square kilometers, and it consists of a series of networked trenches. There appear to be gun emplacements and dugouts throughout. As you can see from the contour lines on the map, the grade in this area is relatively steep. They've built their camp into a hillside, and they have camouflaged their positions. And because of the heavy forest canopy, that is undoubtedly how they've been able to evade detection for so long. The terrain may make it difficult for vehicles to navigate beyond the main entrance road. But, apart from a number of small trails on the southern edge of the camp, there appears to be only one way in and one way out, at least by vehicle. They could possibly try to escape along the southern edge," he said pointing to another location on the map. "They would have to cross over this ridgeline, move through the dense forest, and access this network of very narrow trails, which eventually connect back to the main road leading into Puck, approximately twelve kilometers to the south."

"Very good, Lieutenant Grigoriev. But tell me, what happened to your men? Do you know?" Sokolov asked.

"We do not know yet. It is possible they have been captured or they are attempting to evade capture and have become separated from the rest of their squad. The remainder of the chase squad has been instructed to pull back and await further orders."

Sokolov nodded and turned to the commander on his right, and said, "We have an enemy who is dug in and entrenched. We do not know their exact numbers, but we estimate their strength to be less than one hundred. How do you propose we proceed? And how quickly can we move on the camp?"

"We have been moving in this general direction since we received the order early this morning. Our forces are approximately eight kilometers from the target and moving in. Now that we know the target's exact location, I have ordered them to move forward in combat formation to these positions along the northern perimeter of the camp. I've also ordered our motor company and artillery battery to move forward and assume positions along this line here," he said drawing his hand along a line on the map. "They will be in place within the next ninety minutes and ready to begin the assault. Once you give us the order to fire, we will launch mortar and artillery strikes along the perimeter of the camp. Our two rifle companies will then attack here, and here," he said once again pointing out the locations on the map. "Our third company will move up and assume positions to block any escape from the main road to the camp and flank the enemy. Our NKVD comrades," he said nodding to the second commander, "are deploying two companies along the southern ridgeline and their remaining forces will follow our assault in a second wave. Together, we will hit them straight on with superior numbers and firepower," he said. "We have them surrounded. There will be no escape."

"Be aware, Major, the insurgents captured heavy weapons, machine guns and anti-tank missiles when they attacked our ammunition supply convoy. You can be certain they will use them against you."

"Yes, Comrade Colonel. I am aware of that. But I also have men who chased after the Germans all the way from Leningrad. They are not afraid. They are ready to avenge the loss of their comrades."

"I do not mind if they are afraid. I've found fear to be a great motivator. They can be afraid, as long as they are ready."

"Then they are ready, Comrade Colonel," the MRB commander said emphatically.

Sokolov nodded his head and said, "Very well. You do not need to await any further orders from me. This is now your operation. Once your men are in place, you are to immediately commence the attack. We still have more than five hours of daylight," he added looking at his wristwatch, "Let's mount the attack while there is still light. It will be difficult to find them and capture them in darkness."

"Just to be clear," said the NKVD commander. "Our orders are to destroy the enemy. What about prisoners?"

"I don't believe our enemy will give you many opportunities to take prisoners. They've dug into this location for a reason. They plan to die here. But the three women we observed on the beach this morning? They are British intelligence agents. I am certain they will attempt to escape, and we must not let that happen. While your men sweep through the camp, I want Grigoriev's squad to search for the women. You can destroy the camp and kill the men if necessary but capture any women you find there and bring them to me. Make sure your men, every last one of them, understands this. Do I make myself clear, comrades?"

"*Tak Tochno*! Perfectly clear, Comrade Colonel," came their reply in unison.

***

Jenkins, Haas, Bialik, and Wulkan sat around a table set up in a large dugout which served as the forest soldier's command post. Wulkan tried as hard as he could to conceal his disappointment when he laid eyes on Jenkins and Haas. He had hoped he would receive ammunition, weapons, or medical supplies.

"Please understand me when I say we are grateful for your support," Wulkan said to Jenkins and Haas. "When Ada made contact with us, we were very leery, very suspicious of her. She claimed to be in contact with British intelligence. She told us she and her mother were recruited during the war. It seemed far-fetched and the kind of story that could get one killed."

"You had every reason to be suspicious," Jenkins said. "Even we had our concerns. It had been over three years since we had been in contact with our agent here," she said pointing to Bialik. "And when we received her message several months ago, we were surprised to say the least. We had thought that all of the agents we recruited had been lost, killed in the war. Receiving a message from an agent we had assumed was lost years before came as a complete shock to us."

"It was our mission to remain underground, to remain in hiding, was it not?" Bialik asked defiantly. "Or has the mission changed?"

"No, no," Jenkins stammered. "It's just that. . ."

"I had no other choice but to go to underground," said Bialik. "My mother made it perfectly clear to me. And this is what we were supposed to do, right? We were supposed to go into hiding. What do you call us? Stay behinds? That was our mission. Stay behind, blend in and remain hidden until we receive the signal from London. That message never came. So, I took the initiative. I waited until the situation and circumstances were right, and that is when I decided to come out from hiding."

"Nobody doubts your loyalty," said Wulkan. "You've proven yourself time and again. You've bravely fought alongside us on many occasions and have taken the fight directly to our enemies. I trust you with my life," he added. "We all do."

There was an uncomfortable silence as his words hung in the air.

Finally, it was Haas who spoke up. "We are here to set up a plan to give you the assistance you need. So, if I may suggest, let's discuss next steps."

"Yes," Jenkins echoed. "We've brought a considerable amount of cash in hopes it will help you to procure supplies. I know you need more, but . . ."

"What we need most are fighters. We can always use more weapons and ammunition, but most of all, we need fighters. We've lost men in recent skirmishes. And others have drifted off. It's difficult to keep men when they have wives and children who are suffering. The Soviets are now taking a direct hand against us. They have infiltrated the Polish security service. There is greater coordination now between the Red Army, UB, and Polish forces and it makes it difficult for us. The money will help, but we are outmanned and outgunned."

"Now that we've made contact, our plan is to set up regular supply drops," Jenkins explained. "We already have one shipment ready to be delivered to you. But we'll need to be able to rendezvous out at sea. It's impractical and dangerous to deliver weapons and ammunition in the small landing boats we used. We need your help to make contact with local fishermen who are sympathetic to your cause. We need access to boats, and more importantly, someone who can sail them. Fishing boats are ideal because their presence on the Baltic in the late night or early morning hours could be explained."

"We have supporters and one contact in particular located in Puck who can help," said Wulkan. "We can broker a meeting with him."

"If that is the case, let's plan this out," said Jenkins. "Luba, while I'm working out the details here with the commander, can you take Ada and show her how to set up the new wireless set? She's an experienced operator, so it should be an easy go for her. Give us an hour."

***

Haas opened the case containing the new wireless set and placed all the components on the table. The set consisted of three modules that when connected properly, created a wireless transmitter and receiver set.

"The set is American made," said Haas. "We've tested it extensively, and you're the first field agent to use it. But it works and it's easy to operate. These three modules here are the transmitter, receiver, and power supply," she said pointing them out in succession. "This fourth module contains spare parts and accessories. Each module is watertight, and they're designed to handle a lot of abuse. The entire set can be stored under harsh conditions. The carrying case we've provided is watertight, so if need be, you can bury the entire case. They had a set buried for a month during the springtime in London. Not a drop of water seeped through the case."

"What about power? What options do I have?"

"The power supply we've provided gives you tremendous flexibility. You can run the set off the batteries, but when connected to the mains, and you can connect to any wall socket in Europe; when you do that, you'll also be able to recharge the battery. And using this connector," Haas said, handing Bialik a cable with two wire leads at the end, "You can connect and operate the set using a vehicle battery. Tuning is also much easier. It's done using this single knob. You can tune to the desired frequency by turning the knob. The set covers the HF frequency band from three to twenty-four megahertz."

"This is brilliant," Bialik said. "I've been lugging around the old set for years. It's amazing it still works. This set seems much easier to use."

"It is much easier. I thought so the minute I tried it out in London," said Haas. "Now, I want you to get comfortable with it. I want you to break the set down, return it to the storage case, and then set it up. Let's do it several times. You'll need to be able to do it quickly. Ready? Go!"

For the next half hour, Bialik practiced setting up and tearing down the wireless as Haas watched. Tentative at first, but after assembling and disassembling the set several times, she was able to get the set ready to transmit or receive messages in a matter of minutes.

"That's excellent, Ada," said Haas. "You'll want to practice in the dark, but I don't think you'll have any trouble at all."

"I'll manage."

"So, Ada. How old are you now? Twenty? Twenty-one?"

"I'll be twenty-two in December."

"You were so young. Back then."

"There was no time to be young during the war, because you grow old too quickly."

"Hmm," murmured Haas as she thought about the last time she had seen Bialik. It was in Warsaw just one week before the uprising, when Polish resistance forces mounted a massive attack against the Germans. "I never thought I'd see you again."

"I never thought I would see you either. But when I did, when I saw you on the beach, it brought back all the old memories. I held so much anger. For years I was driven by anger at you. For what you did."

"What I did? What do you mean?"

"I was furious," Bialik said. "I was furious with everyone. With the British, the Allies, and certainly the Russians. They all abandoned us during the uprising in August 1944. We were on the verge of success; we had Warsaw in our grasp. We were so close, but everyone abandoned us. And because there was no other face on which I could place my anger, I blamed you. I blamed you most of all. You were the face I knew, and you left us in Warsaw to die."

"I'm so sorry Ada. That was not the plan, and it wasn't my choice. I was ordered to leave. I begged the British to support you when the Germans counterattacked. I begged them for help. But the Russians just sat there and held their positions. They refused to let the British resupply the Home Army. Finally, Churchill said to hell with it, and he ordered supplies to be air dropped. But it was too late."

"Oh yes, I remember those days well," said Bialik. "I don't know how airplanes would have found us, though. The city was in flames. Every building, every house was on fire. We set up flares at the drop sites, to guide the pilots in, but the sky was clouded with smoke from the fires. There was no way to see our flares. Everything was on fire. I remember as if it were yesterday. I watched bundles of supplies, hundreds of parachutes, all of them floating to the ground. But most of them landed behind the German lines. You did a better job supplying the Germans than us."

"But you escaped."

"Yes. My mother saw to that. She insisted on it. I didn't want to leave but she would not have it any other way. We were cut off in the Old Town of Warsaw. It was one of the last places in the city we held. By the end of August, they made the decision to withdraw, to give up the fight, or at least take it elsewhere. So, while a small group of brave souls, including my mother, covered our retreat, thousands of us escaped from the city through the sewer system. We survived to fight another day while those who remained behind . . . most of them were captured and shot on the spot. I guess the Germans became tired of that, or they didn't want to waste more ammunition, because anyone who wasn't shot was scooped up and sent to the camps. Mauthausen and Sachsenhausen is where they were sent. Mother was one of the lucky ones. We said goodbye on September 2, that's the day I left. She died defending her position with the other members of our battalion two days later, or so I was told. I never saw her again. But I held on to the anger, against you and everyone. Oh, I was able to rebuild my life, I suppose. The war ended less than a year later, and I played the game. I convinced them I was a loyal to the Party. I even became a member, not that it is helping me now. But I convinced them I could be trusted. That's what I was supposed to do, right? Blend in. Adapt. Look like one of them. So, I managed to attend school, university, and become a teacher. That's what I had always wanted to do anyway. But the anger stayed with me. It drove me. It became my reason for being."

"Why did you contact us? What made you do it after so many years?"

"Before I even arrived in Puck, I had heard there was an active insurgency, fighting against the Soviets and the communist government. It was pure luck that I was assigned here to teach. I could have been assigned anywhere in the country, but as fate would have it, I was assigned here. So, I decided if I hadn't heard from London, I would take matters in my own hands. I made contact with the forest soldiers. At first, they were skeptical. But I showed them what I was capable of. On our first mission together, we ambushed a group of militiamen. I had planned it out, just as my mother and I used to do against the Germans. It was a brutal attack meant to show the government, and especially the Soviets we meant business, that we could match their cruelty. And it definitely had that effect. We showed them. And then the fight was on. It was after that when I revealed my connection with British intelligence to Wulkan. I told them I had been trained by British intelligence as a leave behind agent. I told them I could help get more supplies, ammunition, whatever he needed to overthrow the communists. And that is when I made contact. I hadn't heard from you, so I took matters into my own hands. But after I sent the first message to London, I never thought in a thousand years it would be you whom I would meet on the beach. I don't know who I expected to meet, but it wasn't you. But life has come full circle and there you were. And for that, I'm glad. I'm glad it was you."

"So am I."

"So, tell me. Did you doubt my loyalty too, Luba? Like your colleague? Did you think I was working for Polish security or worse, for the Russians?"

"No. Not for one minute," Haas replied. "Never. I knew what you went through after we pulled out of Warsaw. But I didn't think you had survived. Few did. So, when I saw you, I immediately knew we had unfinished business to complete. Together." Haas grasped Bialik's hands and gave them a squeeze.

Suddenly, the door to the dugout burst open and Jenkins, out of breath from running. shouted, "Luba. Grab your weapon and gear. And do you have that wireless working? We need to send a message to London. Now."

"What's happened?"

"There are several large columns of armored vehicles approaching. It's the Russians. We've been discovered. Send the message and send it now. The message is Dunkirk. Dunkirk. Send it. Now!"

Chapter Twenty-One

A Quiet Place to Hide

The camp exploded with activity as soldiers raced through the trenchworks and delivered extra ammunition and weapons to the forward positions. They added more sandbags to reinforce the walls of their firing positions and jumped in and readied themselves for the assault they knew was to come. Inside his command dugout, Jenkins, Haas, and Bialik looked grim as Wulkan explained the situation.

"One of our patrols came across a group of at least seven armed and uniformed men," he said. "They were conducting reconnaissance on our camp. We opened fire and three of them were killed, but the others retreated into the forest and were able to escape. When we searched the bodies of the dead men, we discovered they were *Ubecy.* That is the good news. The bad news is that when we pursued the men who escaped, we discovered a large column of armored vehicles and troop carriers moving towards us. It's the Red Army. The Russians are now only a few kilometers from us. The column is at least battalion strength, quite possibly larger. They have split the column with one group of vehicles headed directly for us, and the other has turned to our east. We believe they are attempting to encircle our positions. They want to trap us and block our routes of escape."

Suddenly, the sound of gunfire erupted followed by three explosions that could be heard in the distance.

"Those are ours," Wulkan said. "We've moved a small number of men down the hill to harass the enemy and slow their advance. With a bit of luck, this will cause them to pause a bit before they attempt to overrun our positions here. But this is not the kind of battle we are prepared to fight. So, the question is, what are we to do with you?" he said looking at Jenkins and Haas.

"I am staying here to fight alongside you," Bialik said defiantly.

"I think they have other plans for you," said Wulkan, pointing to Jenkins and Haas. "You are too valuable to die here."

"No, I intend to . . .," Bialik protested before she was cut off mid-sentence.

"He's right Ada," said Jenkins. "We need to find a way to get out of here and take you with us. There is much more at stake. We cannot risk jeopardizing the entire operation. You're coming with us."

"I don't want to go," Bialik replied.

"Ada, listen to me," Jenkins said. "The message Haas sent was an emergency code requesting immediate extraction. It means our mission here is over, at least for now. And while we're frittering away our time here, a fast boat is preparing to be deployed to the Baltic. They had planned to extract Haas from Ostrowo in three days. But with the Russians moving in, we have to assume our original landing site is compromised. So, we have a new extraction point. We still need to communicate with London and coordinate the exact time, but everything has been moved up. We'll need to get to the emergency extraction site as soon as possible and we're wasting valuable time arguing with you."

"You can't make me go with you," Bialik replied. "I won't do it."

"Ada, you have to come with us," said Haas. She reached out and placed her hand on her shoulder. "Please try to understand," she said softly. "There is a much larger operation going on. The fight here is just one piece of a much larger operation, but it is an important piece. Your knowledge of the situation here on the ground is critical. That is something we do not have. If we are going to roll back the communists in Poland and throughout the Baltic, we need your help. We cannot let everything you've worked for die here today."

"And we can't risk your capture," said Jenkins. "You are too important to us."

"I won't be captured. I'll die here fighting."

"That's enough," said Wulkan. "We may be fighting to create democracy, but we don't have one yet. This isn't a democracy where you get to vote up or down. No, Ada. You need to do as they ask and go with them. That's the only way. And Jenkins is right. There isn't much time. So, you are going. And that is, I'm afraid to say, an order."

Bialik looked into Wulkan's eyes, took a deep breath, and let out a long sigh. "Very well. If that is what you want," she said, giving in, "I'll do what you ask. I'll follow your order."

"Good. It's settled then," said Jenkins. "Now, how are we going to get out of here? We can't very well leave the same way we came in."

"We have a way out for you," Wulkan replied. "Sergeant," he called out. "Enter!"

They all turned to the dugout entrance as a man wearing a Home Army uniform bearing the rank of sergeant entered. He was carrying a canvas satchel, and his weapon was draped over his shoulder. He appeared to be in his fifties, his hair was gray at the temples. But despite his age, he seemed fit. He had a lively step, a wiry, lean frame, and his face had a weathered look of a man who spent most of his lifetime outdoors.

"This is Sergeant Mrozek, and before the war, he tended to the forest here, the very forest in which we have made our camp. He knows every tree, every patch of moss. He will guide you to safety."

"What's the plan, sergeant?" asked Jenkins.

"Please call me Wojchiech. So, based on the information we have, we have to assume they will be searching for you on the trails to the southeast because that is the direction their forces are coming from. It is a logical move on their part because there is an extensive network of hiking trails throughout that region. They were quite popular before the war. They all lead to the main road

258 - KARL WEGENER

which you came in on," said Mrozek, "and it would be a natural means of escape for anyone. But there is another way out."

"Oh? And what is that?" asked Jenkins.

"There is a network of tunnels dug into the hillside. We used to have problems with flooding in this area. So, beginning in the mid-1930s, tunnels were added to help improve the drainage in the area. They aren't large in diameter, only a meter and a half. You cannot walk upright in them, but we can make it through on our hands and knees. It's a little tight. Hopefully, none of you are bothered by confined spaces. The weather has been dry, so the tunnels, though damp, should be passable. That is the plan," he said.

Haas looked at Bialik and said, "Imagine that. Just like Warsaw?"

"Yes, imagine that," said Bialik. "Just like Warsaw."

"What?" asked Jenkins.

"I'll tell you later," Haas replied.

"Why wouldn't they search the tunnels?" asked Jenkins.

"There are three tunnels. Two of them are outside our camp. But, one tunnel is located on the southwestern edge of our camp. That is the tunnel we will use. Most importantly, it's not likely the Russians are aware of their existence," Mrozek said.

"And why is that?" asked Haas.

"Because they are not marked on any Polish topographic maps. If they had the original construction plans created in the late 1930s, they could see where the tunnels were placed. But the Germans invaded before the forest service was able to add them to their topographic maps. The maps are otherwise very accurate, except for this important detail."

"We'll have to take your word for it," said Jenkins. "What else do we need to know?"

"The three of you and Sergeant Mrozek will enter the tunnel located on the far west of the camp," said Wulkan. "Once you are all in the tunnel, we'll seal off the entrance at our end. So, even if the Russians overrun our camp, they won't immediately discover the entrance to the tunnel."

"As I said, we'll have to move through the tunnel on our hands and knees," said Mrozek. "I have handheld torches so we will be able to see, because once we enter, it's pitch-black inside. The tunnel we will use runs for a distance of almost nine kilometers. When we get to the end of the tunnel, we'll have to open a steel gate which blocks access to it. It's locked, but I can open it."

"How? Do you have a key?" asked Jenkins.

"In a manner of speaking," Mrozek replied. "I have this," and he reached into his satchel and pulled out a heavy bolt cutter. "We'll get through. It won't be the most pleasant journey, but while the Russians are searching the trails above us, we'll travel to safety right beneath their feet."

"We've been able to get a runner through the enemy lines and he's reached our contact in Puck. When you exit, you'll be met by our man," Wulkan added. "He'll guide you safely from there."

"We need to transmit another message to our headquarters this evening," said Jenkins.

"Our contact has been instructed to hide you for as long as necessary. And he can also arrange for transportation to your new rendezvous point, wherever that will be."

"How will we recognize our contact? And, most importantly, can we trust him?" asked Haas.

"Sergeant Mrozek knows him. When you exit the tunnel onto the service road, Mrozek will signal to him. He has aided us many times and he'll be waiting for you. He has risked his life for us before and he's placing himself in harm's way today. You can trust him."

Suddenly, the dugout was rocked by three explosions in quick succession, followed by three more which caused some of the packed dirt above their head to fall around them. The camp erupted with the sound of automatic weapons fire as the forest soldiers returned fire from their positions.

"Mortar fire!" Wulkan shouted. "They're shelling us. You need to move out now."

Jenkins opened her duffle bag and began to empty out the case inside. "Wulkan, we're leaving the money and our weapons with you,"

"Leave your weapons but take your clothing. You'll need to change after your trip through the tunnels. And take the money with you too," he replied.

"But you can use the money for supplies after this is over," Jenkins said.

"Where I am going when this is over, I won't need any money there," he replied.

***

"Bloody hell." Banbury cursed as he read the message on the scrap of paper he held in his hand. "Have you notified Kiel? Does Betancourt know?" he yelled, directing his anger at a young, newly minted MI6 officer straight out of Cambridge who stood in front of him.

"Yes sir. She is standing by to speak with you on our secure line."

"Do we have any idea of the situation on the ground? Do we know what happened?

"I'm afraid not sir. The E-boat confirmed the landing party successfully infiltrated into the target area. They reported the landing team met up with Lygia and departed the area. And then, out of the blue, we received the Dunkirk emergency message. Haas sent the message, but she added something to the end of the message that was odd. She asked that we confirm the extraction site at Ostrowo. But that isn't correct. The correct extraction site is a place called the Kaszubski Cliffs. Why would she do this? What do you think it means, sir?

"Hmm. I can't be certain, but if I know Haas, it seems she's trying to do a bit of misdirection; in the event the whole operation has been compromised. She's always looking for ghosts."

"Right sir. Unfortunately, we will have to wait until this evening. They are scheduled to transmit their status by 8 p.m., local time, 7 p.m. London. Assuming they are able, of course. We're standing by, regardless."

"Alright, then. Dammit to hell," Banbury cursed. "Let's get over to the communication center. I want that boat deployed as soon as possible."

***

They had been crawling through the muddy drainage tunnels for over two hours, pausing only occasionally to rest and catch their breath. Mrozek was in front, leading the way. He was followed by Jenkins, Bialik, and then Haas. As they made their way through the tunnel, they could hear the sounds of heavy fighting off in the distance, above them. There was a constant crack and pop of gunfire interrupted by the thud of explosions from mortars and artillery. From the sounds above them, they knew the forest soldiers were in a fight for their lives.

The conditions in the tunnel were exactly as Mrozek had described. It was dark and dank, and it was filled with the muck and god knows what else. The kerchiefs they each wore over their mouths and noses did nothing to block the overpowering stench of the rotting material. Mrozek's instructions to breathe through their mouth helped, but not much. The stench was overpowering.

"I don't want to know what we are crawling through," said Bialik.

"Best not think about it. Besides you've been through worse. And it's better than getting captured. Or worse," said Haas. "Just keep moving."

"What did you mean back there when you said, 'just like Warsaw?'" asked Jenkins.

"We used the sewer tunnels to escape from Warsaw," Bialik replied.

"That had to be worse than this," said Jenkins.

"Ladies," Mrozek said, twisting his body to face the three women. "We have to be as quiet as possible now. I can see the end of the tunnel up ahead. We've less than twenty meters to go."

"Thank god," said Jenkins.

"Stay close behind me," Mrozek said. "As soon as I reach the exit, I'll snap the bolt on the gate. But, please remain as quiet as possible."

Mrozek picked up his pace, and quickly crawled forward, towards the light at the end of the tunnel until he finally reached the steel gate which blocked their exit. A heavy padlock hung on the outside on the right side of the gate. The space between the bars on the grate was just large enough for him to be able to slip his bolt cutter through, grasp the lock with its blades and snap it. He looked through the gate to see if anyone was there, but he could see no one. There was still daylight, but he knew the sun would be setting soon, and they would be able to move out under cover of darkness.

He turned to the three women as he opened his satchel and pulled out the bolt cutter. He brought his index finger to his lips indicating everyone should be quiet while he opened the gate. The steel grate covering the exit had four horizontal bars and Mrozek flipped over onto his back, reached up and slipped the cutter through the top bar. He opened the jaws of the cutter and grasped the shank of the padlock with the blades of the cutter, moving around to make sure he had a firm grip on the lock. He took a deep breath and pressed on the handles with all his strength. He could feel the shank of the padlock begin to give way. He paused for a brief moment, took another deep breath, and pressed again until the padlock gave way with a loud crack, falling off onto the ground. He slipped the bolt cutter back through the grate and gave the gate a gentle push with his left hand. It let out a loud squeak as it swung open. They were through.

"Wait here," Mrozek whispered. "I'll slip out and make sure everything is clear."

Mrozek slid forward through the gate and exited the tunnel. The gate's concrete frame rested a half-meter from the ground and faced the narrow service road. He pulled himself through, grabbed his satchel and weapon and came to his knees, looking in both directions. He saw no sign of their contact. He looked at his wristwatch to check the time. 4:52 p.m. He had estimated well. Their contact was to meet them at 5 p.m. *Better early than late*, he thought.

"What's happening?" It was Jenkins. She was halfway out of the tunnel.

"Shh. Quiet! Stay back," he said waving his hand to indicate she should proceed no further. Suddenly off to his right, he could hear the sound of an approaching vehicle and then a green panel van came into sight. The vehicle slowed and stopped some twenty meters from the tunnel where it sat until the headlights flashed three times. Mrozek reached into his jacket, grabbed his torch and flashed three times.

"Let's go," he said to Jenkins. "He's here. Everyone out!"

Jenkins slipped out of the tunnel onto the forest floor. Bialik, who was right behind her tossed out Jenkins' duffle bag and then said, "Here's the wireless set." Jenkins stood up, turned around and grabbed the set as Bialik slipped through the gate. Haas tossed her bag out, and then clambered out, the last to emerge.

The three women stood and looked at each other. They were a mess, covered with mud and debris, but they had made it.

"Grab your gear," Mrozek said. "We have to move quickly," he said as he moved out and headed towards the van. The three women picked up their gear and quickly followed him. Just as they were about to reach the van, they were not more than a few meters away, the front door opened, and an armed Polish militia officer stepped out and stood before them.

"It's a trap," yelled Jenkins, and she backed up, ready to bolt off in the opposite direction.

"No wait!" the officer shouted. "Don't run!"

Haas and Bialik looked around in a moment panic, but just before they were about to run away, Mrozek turned to them and said, "It's alright. This is our contact. He's our man inside and he's here to help."

The officer stepped forward and extended his hand to Haas and Bialik. "I'm Pawel. Pawel Nawrocki, and I will take you to a safe place for you to hide."

"Don't let the militia uniform fool you. He's one of ours," said Mrozek. He turned and called out to the startled Jenkins who stood off in the distance. "Come, come," he called out, beckoning to her to come closer.

"Hello uncle. It's good to see you, but we must leave here," said Nawrocki. "The Russians are wreaking havoc on the forest soldier camp, and we have to get out of here. It isn't safe."

"Uncle?" said Bialik, her eyes wide with surprise.

"He's my nephew. My sister's boy," said Mrozek.

"I've seen you in town, in Puck. I know you," said Bialik. "It was you I passed the note to. The tip about the soldiers hiding on the collective."

"Yes, that was me. After you gave the note to me, I posted it on the stationhouse where it would be found."

"You weren't wearing your uniform when we met. You were serving in the militia all this time?" Bialik asked.

"Yes. I didn't want you to know of my ties to the militia. For obvious reasons."

"He has been our contact within the government all this time," said Mrozek. "He's been giving us information, intelligence about what the Ubecy are up to, Russian troop movements, and the like."

Jenkins, still wary and unsure walked slowly back to the group and asked, "You could have told us in advance your contact was militia. Where are you taking us?"

"We didn't want you to have that information in the event we were captured," Mrozek said.

"I'm taking you to a safe house. You can stay for a short time there," Nawrocki replied. "Now please, let's go. You need to get into the van. Please." Nawrocki walked to the rear of the van and opened the door to reveal two wooden benches on each side of the van. "Toss your stuff inside. Cover everything up with that tarp," he said pointing to a green canvas tarp on the floor of the van. "Whew, you all smell to high heaven," he said making a face and turning up his nose as they walked past him and entered the van. "Uncle, there is a change of clothing in there for you. I suggest you change but make it quick. We can toss your uniform into the forest here. And give me your weapon. It wouldn't do for you to be caught with it in the back of my van."

"I won't need the clothing. I'll wear my uniform and I'll definitely need my weapon because I won't be going with you," Mrozek said. "I'm returning to the fight."

"But you'll be killed," Nawrocki protested. "I can't let you do this."

"And I can't let my comrades down, nephew. Now, just give me the clothing and you get these women to safety. We're counting on you, Pawel."

"You're a stubborn old man," Nawrocki said.

"Yes, and you're my sister's son. Tell your mother I love her," Mrozek said.

Nawrocki kissed Mrozek on each cheek and said, "Goodbye uncle. I'll make sure they get to safety."

"Yes, now hurry," said Mrozek.

Nawrocki turned his attention to the three women and said, "There's one more thing. There is a check point we must pass through. I'll need to shackle you."

"Now wait a minute . . ." Jenkins protested.

"He knows what he is doing," Mrozek said. "You have to trust him."

The three women sat and glared at Nawrocki.

"Wait here, please. I have the shackles up front," he said. "I'll be right back."

Nawrocki returned with four handcuff sets. "Give me your hands, please," and he dutifully placed the handcuffs on the women in turn. "I'm very sorry I have to do this." When he finished, he said, "alright, it is a thirty-minute drive back to Puck. When we get to the checkpoint, let me do all the talking. The checkpoint guards are required to inspect the van. When they open the door, I want you to act dejected. Act defeated. Act afraid. But above all, do not say a word. I will get you through the checkpoint, but you have to do as I say. Understand?" He looked at each of them, and one at a time they nodded their head in assent. "Good. You'll be safe soon," he said as he shut the door, locking the group inside.

Nawrocki walked up to the vehicle cab and opened the door. Before he slid inside, he turned to his uncle one last time and said, "Goodbye and good luck."

Mrozek simply nodded his head and mouthed the words, "Go now. I love you," and then he turned and walked off into the dark forest.

Nawrocki slid behind the wheel of the van and started the engine. The women in back were jostled as the vehicle slowly moved forward and made a sharp turn to go back in the opposite direction. The group sat in silence as the van lumbered down the forest service road. With their hands bound, it was difficult to maintain their balance and they rocked from side to side as the vehicle moved down the rough road. The vehicle slowed and made a very sharp right-hand turn, down what must have been a steep embankment. Bialik lost her balance and was thrown from the bench onto the van's metal floor.

They were now on a smoother road and Haas stood and balanced herself carefully. She reached out and grabbed Bialik with her tightly cuffed hands and pulled her to get back onto the passenger bench.

"Thank you," said Bialik. Once again, the group sat in silence inside the dark van. They had been travelling for an interminable amount of time, when they felt the vehicle slow down, finally coming to a stop.

"This must be the checkpoint," Haas whispered. "Remember, act the part. Be afraid."

"Who's acting," quipped Jenkins.

They could hear a muted conversation outside the van. The door of the cab opened and a few seconds later, the rear doors opened wide. It was Nawrocki, this time with his pistol drawn in one hand, holding a torch in the other. Another militia officer stood next to Nawrocki as he shined the light on his shackled prisoners.

"I caught them trespassing on the pig farm collective east of Puck. They claimed they were in search of food. I'm taking them in for processing and further questioning."

The militia officer looked at Nawrocki's prisoners. "They are filthy," he said, "and they reek!"

"Yes, they tried to escape and tried to hide in a pigsty. They didn't know it was already occupied. So, when this huge sow went after them, they gladly surrendered to me." Nawrocki was counting on the fact the Russians, who had been deliberately holding information from the militia, had not put out an alert to be looking for the three women.

"Hah! That's a great story for you to tell your children, Lieutenant," the officer laughed. "Very well, there's no need to hold you up any longer."

Nawrocki shut the doors and once again they were plunged into darkness. They could hear some indiscernible conversation, then laughter, and then came the sound of the van's front door opening and slamming shut. The motor revved, they could hear a brief grinding of gears, and the van moved forward, gradually picking up speed.

The van drove on for several more minutes until it slowed and made a right turn. They could hear the sound of gravel and rock when the vehicle left the roadway. The van came to a stop. They could hear the cab door opening and the crunch of heavy boots on gravel. The rear doors to the van swung open and Nawrocki peered inside.

"I hope the ride wasn't too rough for you," he said.

"We're fine," said Haas. "But it will be good to get these cuffs off."

One by one, Nawrocki removed the shackles and helped first Haas, then Jenkins, and finally Bialik out of the van. Bialik looked around and said, "I know this place!"

"Yes, you do," said Nawrocki. "This cottage belonged to a brave patriot who died."

"Ela," Bialik cried as her legs buckled and she fell forward to her knees.

"Yes, we've been using her cottage as a safe house," Nawrocki said. "I'm very sorry for what happened to her. Now, we have to get you inside and out of sight."

"Come Ada," said Haas, helping Bialik to her feet. "I'm sorry, but we need to move. Fast."

"I'll grab your gear from the back of the van and bring it all inside. Here are the keys," Nawrocki said, handing over a set of keys on a leather chain to Haas. "It's this one, I believe," he said, pointing out the key to the front door. "Now hurry! All of you."

Haas led the way, her arm around Bialik as Jenkins followed closely behind them. A sign posted on the door stated the cottage was now property of the state and entry was forbidden, punishable by a fine, imprisonment, or both.

"Well, this won't be the first time I've broken laws," Haas said as she inserted the key, gave it a turn, and pushed the door open.

"Well, here we are," she said.

Nawrocki followed them in. He had draped the straps of their duffle bags over his shoulder but carried the wireless set in his hands.

Nawrocki dropped the duffle bags onto the floor and then gently placed the wireless set on the kitchen table. He then moved to the window, drawing the blackout drapes tightly shut. "Give me a hand please. Close the drapes and shades on all the windows. We don't need any curiosity seekers peeking in while you are here."

They scattered through the house, closed the curtains, and pulled shutters tight. Satisfied no one on the outside would be able to see anything inside, Nawrocki flicked on a switch in the kitchen which turned on a single bulb hanging from the ceiling.

"Here you go," he said. "There's not a lot of space. Here's the kitchen," he said pointing behind him, "There's a gas stove here for cooking. There are some canned goods, fruit, and vegetables in the cupboard. I'll bring you some provisions in the morning."

"We'll make do," said Jenkins.

"There is a single bedroom over there to the right, beyond this small sitting room. There is a lavatory, bath over to the left. There are towels and linens in the bedroom. The water is running so you'll have that, at least."

"I know the place. I've been here many times," said Bialik. "I know where everything is."

"Yes, of course you do," said Nawrocki. "The place is pretty much as Zajac left it before she was arrested. I'm very sorry, but there was nothing I could do to help her. But my mission now is to help you. You're all in grave danger. We have to get you out of here," Nawrocki said grimly. "May I ask. What are your plans?" he asked, nodding towards the wireless set.

"We need to get a message to our headquarters tonight," Jenkins said. "They will be dispatching a fast boat. We have to make it to the extraction point, which is a beach not far from here."

"May I ask where? Which beach?" said Nawrocki.

"I'd rather not say until we have our plans in place," said Jenkins. "But can we rely on your help to get us there?"

"Yes," Nawrocki replied. "I will not let you down. But I have to warn you. The beaches are now very heavily patrolled. Your arrival by sea has prompted a heightened awareness. I'm not saying it is impossible, but there are constant, roving patrols and it will be very dangerous for you."

"I'm afraid that is the plan. It's what we prepared for, and it is our only option," said Jenkins.

"If that is the case, I will do my very best to help. But now, I must leave you before I'm missed. If I am gone too long, it will only arouse suspicion. So, I will return early in the morning. I hope you are all early risers."

"We'll be ready for you," Jenkins said.

Nawrocki walked over to the door and opened it but stopped in the threshold. He turned around and said, "What if you had a boat? Could they pick you up at sea?"

Chapter Twenty-Two

Clearing up a Discrepancy

It was after 2 a.m. and Sokolov stood next to Grigoriev in the trenchworks surveying the scene. They stood in what, just a few hours earlier, had been a Polish defensive position. It had been hit by a mortar shell, or an artillery shell, or perhaps both. The sides of the position had caved in. The sandbags that had lined the walls were torn apart and two forest soldiers lay partially buried by the debris. Their bodies were contorted and mangled by the explosions and shrapnel. The air was still thick with smoke from the heavy fighting, and it hung in the area like an acrid fog. Dozens of trees were uprooted throughout the camp. They had fallen on their side with their trunks splintered and their branches ablaze from the barrage of artillery, illuminating the night sky so brightly it created the illusion of daylight.

"Is this the one they call Wulkan?" Sokolov asked pointing to the body on his right.

"We believe so," said Grigoriev. "It's difficult to make a positive identification."

"Hmm, of course. How many bodies have you counted?"

"Seventy-four, so far. We're still counting."

"And the women?"

"So far, we have identified seven women among the dead. They appear to have died fighting alongside the men. They were all found similar as this. They all fought and defended their positions. They never retreated. But we haven't found the teacher and the two agents yet. We're still searching. The mortar and artillery fire were accurate and very efficient. Too accurate perhaps because it has made it difficult to identify some of the remains. It's possible of course, some decided to use the trails to the south to escape. But we did not observe any retreat. They all held their positions, they fought and died here, except for the three women we are searching for. Nevertheless, we've completely blanketed the area to the south of the encampment. We'll continue our search in the morning, in the daylight. If they are there, we'll find them."

"If they died in this camp, we need to know as soon as possible. If they escaped, we need to redouble our efforts to find them. Search behind every tree to our south and along the trails and find them. They can't get far on foot. Unless, of course, they have been given assistance," Sokolov said. "Contact your compatriots in the UB. Find out if their informants have reported anything. And have them question the militia. We've kept everything secret from the militia but in this case, let's bring them in. The militia routinely stops travelers for identification checks on the roads leading to Puck. Find out if they detected anything unusual, such as three women attempting to pass through a checkpoint. If they've escaped, we have to find out how, and discover who is helping them. And we have to deny them any sanctuary."

"Yes, comrade colonel."

"One last thing. Bury all the dead. But there are to be no grave markers. The last thing we need to do is to create a shrine for terrorists."

***

Nawrocki returned to the cottage in the morning along with a local fisherman named Majewski who, for a price, would take them to rendezvous at sea with their fast boat. Nawrocki was insistent. They should not attempt to escape from the beaches. And then he dropped a bombshell.

"They knew you were coming," Nawrocki said.

"What? How?" asked Jenkins. "How could they know this?"

"I don't know how they knew, but the militia received orders to stay away from Ostrowo on the day of your arrival," said Nawrocki. "We were told there would be a joint UB and Russian operation there and we were to stay out of it. They made up some malarkey about destroying counter-revolutionary forces attempting to infiltrate into Poland. That's all we were told. But they obviously were forewarned of your arrival. They had to know you were coming. There's no other explanation."

"That explains everything," said Haas. "They were likely watching the beach when we landed. Then they followed us to the camp, and then Wulkan's men discovered the patrol reconnoitering the camp. If they knew all of this in advance, they must also know of our plan to escape from one of the beaches. Unless, of course . . . the leak was on this end."

"No absolutely not," Bialik protested. "We didn't compromise the operation. There were only two of us who knew the date, time, and location of your arrival. Wulkan and me. And I certainly didn't reveal anything. Neither did Wulkan. No. If there was a leak, it came from your side."

"Nobody is accusing you," Jenkins said.

"No, we're not accusing you," said Haas. "I am sure the leak came from our side. I've always believed that."

"Betancourt told me you'd say that," said Jenkins.

"Yes, and I'll continue to say it," Haas said defiantly. "But there isn't anything we can do about the leak now. But perhaps we can turn the tables to our advantage. We can create a diversion, perhaps. While we escape by sea, we spread the rumor we are planning to escape from the Kaszubski Cliffs, which so happens to be our original plan."

"How do we do that?" asked Jenkins.

"The pub would be the place to plant such a rumor," said Bialik. "Everyone in town goes there and the gossip is wild and incessant."

Haas turned to Nawrocki and asked, "Can you go there?"

"Yes, I can. I can let it drop I heard a rumor about three foreign agents who are attempting to escape, that they'll be plucked off the coast."

"By submarine," said Jenkins.

"Submarine! Why not?" said Haas. "That's even better."

"I'll mention I heard such a rumor when I return to the station house tomorrow," said Nawrocki. "There are several officers who are in the pocket of the UB. They'll eat this information for breakfast."

"Brilliant!" said Haas.

"When can the fisherman take us? We need to inform our headquarters of this change in plans."

"Tomorrow, I hope," said Nawrocki, "I want you moved out of here as soon as possible. You're safe, for now. But not forever. So, I want the fisherman to move you tomorrow evening."

"Very well," said Jenkins. "Luba, would you and Ada set up the wireless. Send a message stating we have abandoned the Dunkirk location, that we'll meet the fast boat at sea, exact date, time, and coordinates still to be determined."

"Yes, we can do that," said Haas. "But I think we need to be careful. There is still a mole in the operation. Therefore, they should continue to report internally nothing has changed, the operation to meet us at the Dunkirk location will take place as planned, at the Kaszubski Cliffs."

"Agree," said Jenkins. "We can investigate this mole business after we return."

"Assuming we do return," said Haas.

***

Bialik set up the wireless set while Haas composed and coded the outgoing message. Haas pulled out a small pad of paper from her duffle bag. It was a document comprised of two columns of letters, a seemingly hodgepodge of characters on a sheet of paper. The characters in the left column acted as the key, while the characters in the right column acted as a guide and allowed Haas to convert her plaintext message into a ciphertext. Back in London, their message could be decrypted, as long as the same one-time pad was used.

"What's that?" asked Bialik, pointing to the pad.

"It's called a one-time pad," said Haas. "Instead of the book code you used, these charts allow us to quickly convert a plaintext message into a ciphertext, an unintelligible string of characters."

"Show me," Bialik said.

"Just watch me while I encode this message. We don't have a lot of time and we need to transmit, but I will explain everything to you. This will be something you'll need to learn."

***

Her training took over and Jenkins set up a four-hour watch schedule even though they had no way to defend themselves if there was an intruder and there was nowhere to run or hide. She was too wired from the day's events to sleep so she took the first watch which would last until 2 a.m. Then Haas would take over until 6 a.m., when Nawrocki was to return. They decided to let Bialik sleep through the night.

"I can pull my weight," said Bialik, protesting being left out.

"We know that," said Jenkins, "But we need you to be fresh tomorrow."

"Just get some rest," added Haas. "We can handle this, and you'll thank us tomorrow. Take the bedroom."

Bialik looked at them, shrugged her shoulders, and trudged off to the small bedroom. She lay down on Zajac's bed and was asleep within minutes of her head hitting the pillow.

***

Haas woke Jenkins and Bialik at five. At 6 a.m. on the dot, as the three were sitting around the kitchen table drinking the coffee Haas had prepared, a vehicle pulled into the driveway of Zajac's cottage.

"That must be them," Bialik said anxiously.

"Let's hope so," Haas replied.

There were three taps on the door, a brief pause, and then two quick taps in succession. Haas slipped the deadbolt back and turned the door's handle to crack the door open. It was not yet daylight, but she could see Nawrocki standing there.

"Quickly," he said. "Let us in."

Haas opened the door and Nawrocki entered. He was followed by a tall man wearing an oilskin slicker and knit cap.

"This is Majewski," said Nawrocki. "He is the man I told you about and he's agreed to help. But we have to hurry. We need to move you to another location. A safer place."

"That doesn't sound good," said Jenkins.

"The Russians are looking all over for you," Nawrocki said. "You were right about the speed of rumors and gossip. They took the bait. They believe you somehow escaped their attack on the camp yesterday, but they still don't know how. They are searching along the beaches and paying very close attention to the area around the Kaszubski Cliffs."

"What about Wulkan? Have you heard anything? Is there any news?" Bialik asked.

Nawrocki looked uncomfortably down at the floor. "I haven't heard anything officially," Nawrocki said, "But the rumors are the Russians overran the camp late last night. They were mopping up early this morning. I don't think there were any survivors."

"What about your uncle?" asked Haas.

"I don't know. I can only presume . . . "

"Oh god," said Bialik. "I should have stayed and fought with them."

"Then you'd be dead too," said Haas. "But you're alive and you'll be able to carry on for them." Bialik stood with her shoulders slumped, shaking her head. "You can grieve later, but now you have to survive," Haas said as she slipped her arm around Bialik's shoulder. "You'll have your day of revenge, but you have to keep your head. You have a mission. Remember? That's why you are doing this. That's what you said."

Bialik closed her eyes and nodded.

"Supposedly, there is an entire battalion searching the trails to the south of the camp," said Nawrocki. "That's how they think you escaped, that somehow you slipped through."

"So, if they are looking everywhere else for us, why aren't we safe here?" asked Jenkins.

"With all the activity in and around the area, I think you'll be safer somewhere not as close to Puck."

Majewski cleared his voice and everyone in the room turned their attention to him.

"The lieutenant has told me of your situation. I'm prepared to take you this evening. But I need for you to be in a place where it will be easier to move you to my boat. I have such a location and I'm prepared to take you there in advance of leaving tonight."

"Alright, how soon can we leave?" asked Jenkins.

"We'll move you to a new location later today," said Majewski. "You'll stay there until we get you aboard. We'll sail shortly after midnight. I've already plotted a course and a heading, and I can give you the coordinates, The location where I propose we rendezvous with your boat is in international waters, and it is a spot where I fish regularly, so our presence shouldn't draw any attention."

"When will you pick us up?" asked Jenkins.

"At midday today. My son will pick you up. But you have to be ready to go. If you're not ready, he'll leave, and we won't be able to help you."

"We'll be ready," said Jenkins.

"What about the course and coordinates?" asked Haas. "Can you give them to me? We need to let our people know."

"Yes," Majewski said. He reached into his pocket and pulled out a slip of paper and handed it to Haas. "Tell your comrades to meet us here," he said.

"What time will we arrive at this point?" asked Haas. "We'll have to give our people an estimated arrival time, at the very least."

"It will take us about two hours to reach this spot. We should arrive between 2:00 and 2:30 a.m. They will see our running lights.

When we get close, tell them I will put out the forward starboard light. That will let them know it is us."

"Very well," said Jenkins. "How will we know it is your son?"

"He'll be driving a small van. He does deliveries during the day. You'll recognize him. He's tall, only seventeen, although you wouldn't know it. He's almost a head taller than me and sometimes he gets too big for his britches. But he's a good boy, he's smart, and he keeps his mouth shut."

"What's his name?" asked Haas.

"Lech."

"Alright," said Jenkins. "And where will Lech be taking us."

Majewski smiled slightly and said, "I'd rather not say in front of the lieutenant. It's a location I've used for, how shall we say, less than legal activities."

"I don't want to know," said Nawrocki.

"Good, because it is better that way, lieutenant. You don't need to know," said Majewski.

"We'll be ready to go. Midday," said Jenkins.

"The only thing left for us to discuss is payment," said Majewski.

Jenkins stared at Majewski, turned, and then walked across the room to grab her duffle bag. She picked it up, carried it over to him, dropped it at his feet and bent down to open the bag, revealing the cash inside. "We have plenty of money and we will pay you, but not until you rendezvous with our boat."

Majewski's eyes went wide at the sight of money, and he let out a low whistle, "Five thousand," he said. "For each."

***

The moment Nawrocki entered the militia headquarters he knew something was wrong. None of his fellow officers would look at him directly. They cast their gaze downward when he approached and scurried off in the opposite direction, as if he were tainted or infected with some disease they did not want to catch.

The officer at the duty desk called over to him. "Lieutenant. Lieutenant Nawrocki. You are wanted in the interrogation room."

"By whom?" Nawrocki asked.

"I, I cannot say," the officer stammered, looking for the words that would not come out of his mouth.

"Never mind," said Nawrocki, irritably. He walked down the narrow hallway and entered the interrogation room and found a man seated behind the table where he would normally sit when he conducted interrogations. A single chair sat in the middle of the room and behind the chair, against the far wall, two other men stood.

"Ah, Lieutenant. Please come in," said the man at the table, rising as Nawrocki entered the room.

"Please be seated," the man said, pointing to the chair. "Please."

Nawrocki slowly walked to the center of the room, eyeing the two men along the far wall. He turned and faced the man behind the table and slowly sat down.

"What is this about? What do you want from me?" Nawrocki asked.

"It's Nawrocki isn't it? Lieutenant Pawel Nawrocki?" said the man behind the table.

"Yes, that is my name. And who are you?"

"Before we start," the man replied, ignoring Nawrocki's question, "May I ask you to please remove your sidearm and place it on the table in front of me. Do this slowly please."

Nawrocki glanced at the two men standing behind him and could see they had withdrawn their weapons and were taking aim at him.

"Slowly please," repeated the man behind the table. "With your opposite hand please."

Nawrocki reached down with his left hand and unsnapped his holster. He carefully removed his pistol, turned it around in his hand and placed it butt-first onto the table. He glanced behind him and saw the two men slowly return their sidearms to their holsters.

"Thank you, Lieutenant," said the man behind the table.

"I'll ask you again. Who are you and what is this about?"

"My name is Grigoriev. As for what this is about, it seems there is a discrepancy, and we hope you'll be able to clear it up. I'm sure it is only a misunderstanding."

"What discrepancy?"

"According to one of the militia sentries who was on duty yesterday evening, a Corporal Palka is his name," he said referring to a set of notes he had in front of him, "Corporal Palka said you passed through his checkpoint on the main road leading to Puck at approximately nineteen hundred hours, 7 p.m. Is that correct, Lieutenant?"

Nawrocki swallowed hard but said nothing.

"And once again, according to Corporal Palka when he stopped you, he checked your vehicle. That is the proper procedure of course. And when he checked inside your vehicle, he said there were three prisoners in the rear. He said you were transporting three women prisoners," he said emphasizing the word 'women,' "to the militia headquarters here. He also said you told him you had arrested them for breaking into one of the farm collectives, allegedly for attempting to steal food. And he said, 'I believed him when he said you arrested them in a pigsty because they stunk to the high heaven.' Those were his exact words." Grigoriev stared at Nawrocki and waited for a reaction.

"Lieutenant Nawrocki, the discrepancy we have is when we checked the arrest log from yesterday evening, there were no such prisoners listed. And when we checked the cells, we found no prisoners fitting the description provided by Corporal Palka. He was very helpful, by the way. Very helpful. So, we thought we should ask you what happened to them? Three prisoners were in your custody yesterday evening. But today, they are nowhere to be found. So, I ask you Lieutenant, and I want you to consider very carefully how you answer my question, because your life may very well depend on it. Did you misplace them somewhere?"

Grigoriev smiled and leaned back into his chair to await Nawrocki's reply.

Chapter Twenty-Three

The Web of Spies

The women packed up their duffle bags, secured the wireless in its case, and sat around the kitchen table to wait for Majewski's son. Bialik had made tea and a simple breakfast of bread and jam, and they sat in silence eating. When they heard the vehicle enter the driveway, they all bolted upright in their chairs. It was only nine o'clock.

Haas and Jenkins both rushed to the kitchen window, and slowly pulled back the shade so they could look outside. They could see a small delivery van parked in front of the cottage. Two men sat in the front seat, but they couldn't see their faces through the dirty windscreen. Then, the van's door opened, and they saw a man step out of the vehicle. He looked around, checking if anyone was watching, and then he quickly walked up to the front door and rapped three times.

"Who is it? Can you see?" asked Bialik.

"It's Majewski. He's with someone, his son presumably, but I wasn't expecting to see him. He's here. Too early," said Jenkins. She nodded to Haas and motioned to her, "Go ahead, let him in."

Haas quickly walked to the door, unbolted the latch, and opened it. Majewski didn't wait for an invitation. He barged inside. "We need to move up our timeline. I need to get you out of here. Now!"

"What's happened?" asked Jenkins.

"They arrested Nawrocki. Grab your things and come with us. Let's move!"

***

"They want to do what?" Banbury exclaimed. "How the bloody hell did they get a boat?"

"They didn't say, sir," said the young MI6 officer. "They did however transmit the coordinates where we are to meet them. The location is in international waters, and it is an area where the Polish fleet fishes. The message, which was coded and transmitted by Haas, was very clear. It said they would rendezvous with our fast boat at between 2:00 and 2:30 a.m. Local. But the message went on to say we should continue to report internally that we will attempt a landing to pick them up at the Kaszubski Cliffs."

"Who else knows this?" asked Banbury.

"As of this moment, only two people, sir. You. And me."

"And the message was encoded?"

"Yes sir. Using the second of the one-time pad series we created. Even the operator who received the message couldn't read it. It reads as gibberish. But I decoded it."

"Alright. Get me Betancourt on our secure line. I will inform her of these developments. Then, I want you to notify headquarters and notify "C" we will attempt the extraction operation on the beach at Kaszubski Cliffs. But, no one else in the world outside of you and I is to know about this meetup at sea. You will speak of this to no one else. Do you understand?"

"Yes sir, I understand."

"And do you understand what I want you to do?"

"Yes sir!"

"Then get me Betancourt on the line and hop to it."

***

Majewski opened the rear of his small van to reveal a jumble of fishing gear and equipment.

"Lech, help me clear a space for them," he said. The two pushed the equipment to either side of the van, creating a small space for the three women on the floor.

"Get in," said Majewski. "It'll be tight. You'll be like sardines."

The three women piled into the van and laid down next to one another on the floor. Majewski and his son covered them with a canvas tarp that reeked of fish. They placed the remaining contents of the van, the nets, floats, lead weights, several long gaffs, and hand tools on top of the tarpaulin creating a messy jumble, but effectively hiding the women.

"Alright, we're heading out. We'll be driving for about thirty minutes so just hang on," Majewski said.

Once they started moving, the women lost track of time. They couldn't tell how long or far they had traveled when the van suddenly made a sharp right turn onto what felt like a steep, bumpy road. After just a few minutes the van slowed. They could hear one of the doors up front open, they couldn't tell which one, and then they felt the van turn to the left and make a quick stop. They heard a squeaky hinge and what sounded like a door opening. Then, the van slowly backed up and finally came to a stop. They heard the same squeaky hinge, but this time the sound of a door being closed and latched. After a few minutes, the rear doors opened and Majewski and his son quickly removed the gear from atop the women, finally lifting the tarp from them.

"You can come out," Majewski said. Jenkins was first to exit the van, followed by Bialik and then Haas.

"Where are we?" asked Jenkins.

"You're in a fishing shack. It's been in my family for many years," said Majewski. "There are dozens and dozens of these shacks around here. All the local fishermen use them for one thing or another. And before the war, families used them during the summer to be closer to the water. During the war, the resistance used them. In the last year or so, Lech and I added the section where we're standing now. We've turned it into a large shed and made it so we can drive our van inside. I use it mainly for storage now and as you can see, it serves other purposes."

Stacked neatly from floor to ceiling were crates filled with food products, tinned meat, fish, and vegetables. There were also cases upon cases of vodka stacked alongside cigarettes, cigars, and loose-leaf tobacco products.

"So, this is where you conduct your not-so-legal activities, eh," said Haas who smiled as she looked at the variety of products stored along the walls.

"I've been helping to feed Wulkan and his men for months now," said Majewski. "It's a necessary business."

"How so?" asked Haas.

"We got a brief taste of independence after the Great War," said Majewski. "We thought we were finally rid of the Russians and the Germans. Then the Germans and the Russians returned in thirty-nine. And now we have the Russians once more. We can't seem to get rid of them. But if it weren't for them, the communists wouldn't last in power for more than a week. So, this is a necessary business because even though half the population has rolled over, there are plenty like me. I want to see Poland run by Poles, not puppets propped up by Moscow. You may think of me as a mercenary, or worse, a profiteer . . ."

"No, we don't see you that way," said Jenkins.

"That's alright. I saw the look in your eyes when we discussed payment. But don't worry, every last zloty you are paying me will go back into the fight. But hey, we don't have time to discuss politics or philosophy, although I'd love to do that with you properly. Someday, over drinks we can discuss the fate and future of the world. But for now, we have to get ready to move you this evening."

"Where are we, exactly?" asked Haas.

"We're about ten kilometers south of Puck," said Majewski. "We are very near to the village of Rewa."

"I know this place," exclaimed Haas. "I was born in Gdynia and my family came here during the summer months. We'd rent a small boat and sail on the bay."

"Gdynia, eh?" Majewski replied gruffly. "Then you'll undoubtedly know half the people who live around here are my cousins or married into the family, so this is our country. You scratch a Pole here and you won't find a communist, I can tell you that for certain."

Majewski turned and pointed to the opposite end of the shack from where they entered. "Out that door behind us there is a short footpath that leads to a dock. I'll bring the boat around there tonight. I'll arrive just before midnight. In the meantime, you can make yourselves comfortable here. There's an old sofa, a table, and chairs at the other end. There's even a gas stove there. Lech will show you how to use it. As you can see, we have food there, coffee, tea, a lot of canned items. But I also have vodka and plum wine. It's all part of my side business, the not so legal business I didn't want Nawrocki to know about."

"Thanks, we'll take you up on your hospitality," said Jenkins.

"Please do. I'm sorry I had to interrupt your breakfast. Nasty stuff all of this, with the Russians that is."

"How did you know Nawrocki had been arrested?" asked Bialik.

"I heard they arrested him this morning as soon as he reported for work," said Majewski. "Apparently one of the guards at a checkpoint reported seeing you."

"How did you find out? I would think the militia would want to keep Nawrocki's arrest quiet," said Haas.

"No, they like to make examples of people. To answer your question though, news like that travels fast in town, especially when they arrest one of our own. But I also have a cousin who works at the militia headquarters as a charwoman. She tells me everything. She sees everything too and nobody there suspects her. Nobody pays attention to an old charwoman. It's as if she is invisible, but she passes important information on to me all the time. She's very helpful to my business. But you should know it wasn't the militia who arrested him. There were three Russians, all dressed up in UB uniforms. They're running the show at the UB and that was the main reason why I didn't want to tell Nawrocki where I had planned to hide you."

"We're grateful for your help," said Jenkins.

"I know. You've said that and you're very welcome," said Majewski. "Over the years I've learned not to become too attached to things. Or people. But when Nawrocki told me of you, I knew I had to help. The fact is we need you. We need to have hope."

"You'll have more than that if we are able to get out of here alive," said Jenkins.

"I'll do everything I can," said Majewski. "Hopefully, Lieutenant Nawrocki will be able to hold out long enough for that to happen."

***

It had become clear to Grigoriev his prisoner would not willingly reveal any useful information. Nawrocki refused to say anything or at best, he would utter, "I do not know," or "I don't know what you're talking about", or a terse, "No comment."

Grigoriev nodded to the two officers in the back of the interrogation room. Grigoriev didn't feel the intense hatred towards the Pole as some of his comrades felt. He had no strong feelings one way or the other about the Polish people. He was indifferent. He felt neither compassion nor pity for Nawrocki. Unlike some of his comrades, he took no particular pleasure from what he was about to do. He felt no pangs of sorrow, nor did he feel uncertainty or hesitation. He knew what he needed to do next. He was a highly skilled interrogator. He wouldn't lose his temper. He would stay in control. This particular Pole had information he needed, and he was determined to get it.

The UB officers tied Nawrocki to his chair. Then, they left the room, only to return a few minutes later with a large tub filled with water. It was heavy, the two officers struggled with its weight and the water sloshed around, some of it spilling onto the floor. Grigoriev pointed to a spot in front of the desk where he sat. "Place it here please." And, once more, Grigoriev asked the question.

"Lieutenant. What happened to your prisoners? Where are they?"

"What prisoners?" Nawrocki replied. And then it began under Grigoriev's direction. Methodical, measured, and with increasing intensity.

Grigoriev lost track of the number of times they held his head underwater. Each time it was the same. He watched his men carefully as they held Nawrocki's head under water, holding him under until it wasn't possible for his lungs to burn any more, just when he was at the point where his mouth was about to open up, wanting to gulp air because his lungs were empty, but swallowing water instead, swallowing enough water to make him believe he would drown. And then they pulled him up. Grigoriev watched Nawrocki carefully and let him catch his breath just long enough to ask the question once again.

"Where have you hidden them?"

"I haven't hidden anybody."

And then it continued again and again, with beatings thrown in for good measure to make sure he wasn't getting too used to the water. And now here they were at last. After hours of interrogation, Nawrocki still sat there, still tied to a chair. His face was bloodied from the beatings and his uniform was soiled and he was drenched from being held headfirst underwater to the brink of drowning. The floor around him was sopping wet and there wasn't even enough water left in the tub for them to dunk him one more time.

The two officers had left the room and only Grigoriev remained. They could do no more. Try as they might, they couldn't get Nawrocki to utter a single word. After everything they did to him, he had said nothing. He uttered not one word about the location of Jenkins, Haas, or Bialik.

Grigoriev sat at the table, scribbling out the written report of the interrogation of Lieutenant Pawel Nawrocki of the Polish Militia when the door to the room opened and Sokolov entered. Grigoriev rose to acknowledge his superior.

"Comrade Colonel!" he said as he stood at attention.

Sokolov looked over at Nawrocki sitting in the chair. Nawrocki lifted his head, squinting to see who had entered the room. Sokolov couldn't tell from where he stood at the door, but he thought he saw a smile register on Nawrocki's face.

"Comrade Grigoriev," said Sokolov, staring at Nawrocki. "What has our friend, our false Polish ally, Lieutenant Nawrocki told us? Has he done his duty and given us the whereabouts of the three spies?"

"I'm afraid," Grigoriev said, shaking his head sadly, "he has refused to say anything. He has not told us where they are."

"Hmm," said Sokolov as he walked over to Nawrocki. He knelt down in front of the chair and stared hard into Nawrocki's face. "You know Lieutenant, when we first met in the forest so many months ago now, I have to be honest with you. I didn't think much of you. There you were, running around in the forest, shouting orders out at your men. I thought you were too young, too inexperienced. I thought you lacked intelligence and above all, I thought you lacked courage. I didn't think you had the courage to do what I asked you to do that day. Do you remember, Lieutenant? I asked you to clean up your own house. Do you remember?"

Nawrocki stared back at Sokolov and this time there was no doubt. He was smiling. "I remember, Comrade Colonel," he replied hoarsely. "I remember it all very well."

Nawrocki's smile startled Sokolov at first, then it angered him, but in the end, Sokolov could only admire the Pole's tenacity. *He's a tough one*, he thought.

"Tell me Lieutenant. We don't have to play games here anymore because I think you know what is going to happen to you. I have to tell you, honestly, I have completely underestimated you. You are a stronger man than I gave you credit for on the first day I met you. So, tell me. And be honest. We can be honest now with one another, can't we? Has it been you all along who has helped these cursed soldiers, these terrorists who hide out in the forest like animals? And now you are helping these three women, these spies to escape."

"I have nothing to say," Nawrocki whispered.

"It was you, wasn't it? You were the one who passed along the anonymous tip? The tip that led to two of your fellow militia being murdered on the forest road. It was you, dammit!" Sokolov screamed. He grabbed Nawrocki's hair, pulled his head upright, and slapped him across the face and bloody spittle flew out of his mouth. "You had your own men butchered."

"They weren't my men," said Nawrocki. He was dizzy and woozy, and his voice was raspy, but he remained defiant.

"They were communists," Nawrocki spat out. "The men I follow want our country back. Can't you get it through your thick Russian skull we don't want you here, Colonel?"

"We are here, Lieutenant and we're here to stay. The men you have followed and supported; do you know what has happened to them? These cursed, forest soldiers. They're dead, Lieutenant. Every last one of them. Gone. You have no one left."

Nawrocki took in a deep breath and cleared his throat. "There are many of us, Comrade Colonel. I'm not alone. You have your informants and spies, and we have ours. There is an entire web of spies spinning a trap around you and you'll never be able to exterminate all of us. No matter what you do, you'll never get us all. We're everywhere."

"Hmm," Sokolov scoffed. "We Russians play the long game. We've endured a millennium of suffering. The Mongols, the Tsars, the Germans, and even ourselves. I have been at this for a very long time, and I will tell you time is on my side. We will outlast you. We will prevail and will dance in joy on your grave."

Nawrocki nodded his head, taking in Sokolov's words, trying to understand them and then he looked up and said, "Tell me Colonel. What time is it now?"

It was a reflex reaction. If somebody asks what time it is, the natural reaction is to look at your watch and tell them.

"It is five minutes until midnight. It's been a long day for you, Lieutenant."

"Maybe," Nawrocki replied. "But your time is up. You're too late. You'll never catch them now. The women are gone. They've escaped. You're too late and there is nothing you can do about it."

Sokolov's face darkened. He slowly stood up, reached down to his holster and pulled out his pistol, racked the slide, pointed it squarely at Nawrocki's forehead and fired. The sound of the shot was ear splitting and its impact knocking Nawrocki over. Still tied to the chair, he fell onto his back onto the floor. Sokolov calmly re-holstered his pistol and turned to Grigoriev.

"You'll have to amend your report. Please note the prisoner was shot while attempting to escape."

"Yes, sir, Comrade Colonel," Grigoriev stammered. "I will indicate that is how the prisoner died in my report."

"Good. After you tidy up here, get your men ready. Our source has also said they plan to escape from the beach at the Kaszubski Cliffs. It's not far from here."

"That's the story Nawrocki was passing around last night at the pub. He said they would be picked up at the Kaszubski Cliffs. Do you believe him?"

"Him?" Sokolov said looking over at Nawrocki, "I don't know. It could be a story to throw us off. What is troubling to me is that it all seems a little too easy, don't you think? Our source has been correct about everything so far, and I shouldn't have any reason to doubt him. And now this dog comes along," he said pointing to Nawrocki, "and he says the same thing. It gives me pause and makes me wonder if everything is lining up too easily, a little too perfectly. But we have to act upon what we know. So, we will be waiting for them on the beach. I'm told our naval comrades have dispatched a ship to the region. While we wait for them on the beach, if they are not there, our navy will hunt for them at sea."

Chapter Twenty-Four

Slipping through The Net

Majewski and Lech arrived at the fishing shack just before midnight. They tied up at the end of the dock and Lech jumped off to collect the three women.

"Make it quick, son," Majewski said.

"Yes, father," Lech replied.

The boat was an impressive fifteen-meter outrigger trawler with two booms attached to the mast, a forward deckhouse and aft working deck. Built in the 1930s, Majewski meticulously maintained his boat, ensuring it could handle the rough waters of the Baltic, North Sea, and Northern Atlantic.

Majewski had placed a short gangway to make it easier to board. Haas and Jenkins tossed their gear onto the deck and quickly made their way aboard. Lech was next to board, and Bialik handed the wireless set to him before boarding herself.

"I want the three of you and all of your gear below," Majewski said. "You can come above deck once we get out to sea. The hatch is forward," he said pointing to the deckhouse. "You'll see it, just head forward," he said, pointing towards the bow of the boat. "Lech, get the lines. We need to shove off."

The three women walked across the deck until they came to the forward hatch. They climbed slowly down the steep ladder that took them below decks to a dimly lit cabin. Majewski poked his head into the hatch above and called out, "The head's aft, in case you need to use the facilities. There's a galley aft. I've brewed some coffee so help yourself. If you want to rest, there are four bunks in the forward stateroom. We're setting out south by southeast through Pucka Bay and then into the Gulf of Gdansk. From there, we'll turn north by northwest until we enter the Baltic. We have to travel slowly in Pucka Bay. There are speed

294 – KARL WEGENER

restrictions, but once we hit the gulf, I can open her up. She'll do a little more than twenty knots. There's always a chance we'll be hailed by a Polish patrol boat. They generally leave us to our business, but you never know. They know my boat, and they know me and Lech, but the sight of you three would raise alarms. So, we'll just keep you below, if you don't mind."

"Thanks," said Jenkins. "We'll be fine, and we'll stay out of your way until you give us the all clear."

"Oh, one last thing. What am I looking for? What type of vessel will we be meeting?"

"You'll rendezvous with a German fast boat," said Jenkins, "It will be flying Danish colors. Are you familiar with them? You must have seen them during the war."

"Oh yes, I know them well," Majewski replied. "Had my fair share of run ins with them during the war. They are seaworthy though, and fast. I suppose the boat was one of those spoils of war, huh?"

"Something like that," said Jenkins. "But I should tell you our boat is manned by a German crew and captain."

"What?" Majewski said, shaking his head incredulously. "A Danish flagged fast boat manned by a German crew. What's this world coming to?" and then he let out a laugh and said, "Lech will come and fetch you once we are out at sea. So, just make yourselves comfortable. We'll be underway in a few minutes."

Jenkins turned her attention to Haas and Bialik and said, "Alright then, I suppose we had best settle in."

The women left their gear in the stateroom and made their way aft to the galley.

"Who wants coffee?" asked Jenkins as she unlatched a cabinet door and pulled out three enamel mugs. Haas and Bialik sat down behind a table anchored into the deck and Jenkins poured each of them a cup. "I wonder if there is sugar?" she said. "Doubtful," she said, answering her own question. "Well ladies, barring any unforeseen problems, we should be able to make our rendezvous point and we'll be back on Bornholm in a matter of hours."

They could feel the rumble of the engines as the boat began to move. As the boat picked up speed, it began to rock up and down, over and over again. They had only been underway for ten minutes when Haas noticed the rocking motion was having an effect on Bialik.

"Are you alright?" Haas asked.

"I've never been on a boat before. I've never been on the water. I'll get used to it," she replied. "This coffee isn't helping though," and she slid her mug to the center of the table.

"Just try to take deep breaths," said Jenkins. "Take long, slow breaths, in and out slowly. That always helps me."

"I'll try," Bialik replied and for the next few minutes, she focused on her breathing, taking in long, slow, deep breaths. "Feeling a little better. I think," she said, continuing to breathe slowly. "So, what's going to become of me?"

"Become of you? What do you mean?" asked Jenkins.

"Just that. I'm going with you to England. But what's next?"

"You'll meet up with your countrymen and women, and you'll be able to join up with them," said Jenkins. "They've been working with us since the end of the war. You'll help us train them properly, prepare them for what they will face when they return to Poland. We have hundreds of fighters who will be ready to go. Over two hundred. Early next year."

"Hundreds?" Bialik said. "Do you really believe we'll be able to turn the tide with just a few hundred fighters?"

"Revolutions have been started with far less," said Jenkins.

"Hmm," Bialik scoffed. "Started maybe. But, finished? I don't know." She closed her eyes again and focused on breathing, inhaling and exhaling slowly, finally letting out all the air in her lungs. She opened her eyes and looked over to Haas and said, "And what about you, Luba? Will you be returning to England with me? Will we continue to fight alongside each other? Together?"

Haas reached across the table and grasped Bialik's hand. "We will be parting ways once we are safely back in England. I have another life now. At least I think I do. And I want to see if I can live it."

"We'll take good care of you, Ada," Jenkins said. "As I said, we'll train you, equip you, and you'll be back in Poland before you know it. We'll make sure you have everything you need."

Bialik closed her eyes, and began to breathe in slowly, deeply, deliberately. And with her eyes closed she whispered, "Everything I need. Hmm. Sounds almost too good to be true. Luba, you asked me why after all these years I chose to make contact. I told you why. I could have remained silent. I could have just blended in. I could have given up a few freedoms in exchange for personal security. Nobody would have known the truth. I could have hidden my true feelings. I could have buried the pain, the suffering, the grief I felt after my mother died. But I came out of hiding because there was a mission to accomplish. That's the reason I gave you. Now I have to ask you, what about you? Why did you come back after all these years? What was it? What made you do it, Luba?" she said, opening her eyes and looking directly at Haas.

"I . . .I," Haas stammered, "The simple answer is I was asked to come on this mission to verify it was actually you. But the truth is, I came back out of loyalty to you. And to your mother. We had unfinished business."

"And what would have happened if it hadn't been me? What would have happened if the Russians or UB had gotten to me first?"

"The mission would have ended on the beach in Ostrowo," said Jenkins calmly. "I would have ended it. Right then and there."

Bialik's eyes widened. "Really?" she replied with a look of amazement.

"And as for certainty," Jenkins added, "Nothing is ever certain. Our craft is built on lies, piled up one upon the other, until the truth becomes obscured, hidden."

"We both knew immediately," said Haas, "that you hadn't been turned. Natalie and I went through the calculus back at the camp. We decided then and there you were good, that we could trust you."

"Hmm," said Bialik. "And now, Luba, you want to move on, and finally rebuild your life after years of fighting. Is it possible to return to a normal life after years of war, when everywhere you turn, there is nothing but death and destruction? When everything you've come to know and love, family, friends, home, everything we've come to understand is destroyed? Is it possible?"

"I hope so. I have to believe it is possible. And I'm going to find out. I have something now. I have someone now with whom I have a chance to build a future. Together. But I'll just have to see."

"Mm," Bialik murmured. "I want to find that too, you know. Find someone to build a future with."

"We all do." said Haas.

Bialik closed her eyes again and took several deep breaths. "I think I'll feel better if I lie down. I'm going to go forward and close my eyes for a bit. Wake me when it's time to go above." She stood, paused for a moment and turned, "Oh, and by the way. I am very grateful I wasn't terminated on the beach," she said, giving Jenkins a smile.

Jenkins and Haas watched Bialik exit the galley and make her way to the forward compartment.

"I know you have your own way of doing things, Natalie," said Haas. "But I strongly suggest you refrain from telling an agent you had planned to kill them. Whether it's the truth or not, it doesn't matter. It doesn't do much for morale and it certainly won't help you build rapport."

***

Sokolov, Grigoriev, his squad of UB officers, and one-hundred thirty-seven men from an NKVD rifle company had been waiting for hours in the forest overlooking the beach at the Kaszubski Cliffs.

"They could have picked any of the beaches along the northern coast," Sokolov said to Grigoriev as he surveyed the narrow stretch of beach below, "Yet they picked this one. It is an unlikely spot, I should think. It is difficult to reach. You can only access the beach below via a narrow footpath, which is very steep, and the beach isn't very wide. It seems to be an unlikely location for a rescue, don't you think?"

"Perhaps they saw us and decided to attempt their escape at a later time," Grigoriev said. "Or from a different location."

As the first glimmer of daylight began to shine from the east, Sokolov raised his field glasses and looked out onto the sea. He watched as a ship; a destroyer named the Lieutenant Ilin moved slowly across the water. The destroyer was operating several miles out at sea. But Sokolov also could see two small Polish patrol boats stationed closer to the shore, and several other vessels farther out. They looked like coastal patrol boats, but he couldn't tell.

"I think we may have missed them, Lieutenant," Sokolov said to Grigoriev. "We should not only have cast a wider net, but a finer one too. If they are going to be rescued from this beach it won't be today, if at all."

"What are your orders, sir?" Grigoriev asked.

"Maintain around the clock watch on all the beaches from here to Ostrowo for the next week. And please radio the commander of the Ilin. Give him my thanks and ask him to widen his search area. It is a big sea, and they could be anywhere, but if I were to go hunting for them, I would suggest he search the areas frequented by Polish fishing vessels. And please also suggest to him they should stop and search every Polish fishing vessel they encounter."

"Fishing vessels, sir?"

"It's the only possibility, Lieutenant. If the spies are not rescued from one of the beaches, they have to find a way to escape by sea. Polish fishing boats are on the sea all the time, at all hours. If I were a betting man, Lieutenant, I would bet somewhere out there in the Baltic, a Polish fishing boat is sailing to meet a fast boat waiting for them."

***

"There are dozens of fishing boats out here on the Baltic," said the crewman. "How will we identify them in the middle of the night, Herr Kapitan?"

Ruger stood on the bridge of the E-boat. It was a clear night, and the visibility was good. A partial moon provided some light, and the sky was filled with stars. "Once they reach the rendezvous area, they will douse one of their starboard running lights," he said. "That's our cue to give them the signal to approach and pull alongside."

A voice crackled over the boat's intercom system, "Herr Kapitan?"

"Yes," Ruger replied, "What is it?"

"We just received a radio message, sir. Signal intelligence reports there is Soviet naval activity along the Polish coast, some fifteen nautical miles to our south. They report an Orfey-class destroyer, the Lieutenant Ilin, accompanied by three motor-torpedo boats, deployed out of Baltiysk yesterday evening. They also report increased Polish patrol boat activity working the coastal region between Wladyslawowa and Leba."

"Radio confirmation. Request additional information on location of the MTBs. We can outrun the destroyer, but their fast boats, they could be a problem for us. Understood?"

"Aye, Kapitan."

"Keep your eyes peeled for this fishing boat," Ruger said. "And for any other vessel operating near us."

"Aye, sir!"

"Damn it. Where the hell are they?" Ruger whispered under his breath.

***

Majewski climbed down the hatch ladder. It was all quiet below. They had been sailing for over two hours now and were still approximately forty minutes away from the rendezvous point. He looked back to see if anyone was in the galley and it looked empty, so he headed up to the forward compartment. He stuck his head through the forward bulkhead and saw the three women, stretched out on the bunks.

Haas immediately noticed Majewski standing in the bulkhead and sprang to her feet. "I'm a very light sleeper," she quipped. "What's happening. Are we getting close?"

"Close, but not there yet. I had to sail eastward to avoid several Polish patrol boats. I've never seen so many out here. And we detected a large Russian ship, a destroyer or cruiser. It was too far off, and I couldn't tell, but we kept a wide berth, just to be safe. So, I've had to reverse course but we're back on course. We'll arrive at the rendezvous area in forty minutes. I'd wake up your compatriots and get ready."

"I'll get them up," said Haas.

***

"Kapitan. I see something off our port side. It's a trawler. I can make out the outriggers. It's approaching fast. Range is . . . three thousand yards and closing."

"Good eyes," said Ruger. He clicked the intercom switch, "Helmsman, stand ready."

"Aye Kapitan."

"She's just doused the forward running light sir. It's our boat. It's the one we're looking for."

"Signal she is clear to approach us."

"Aye Kapitan, signaling clear to approach."

"Helm, take us to heading one-one-five, ahead two-thirds and bring us alongside that boat."

Majewski and the three women stood on the bridge of the trawler. Haas and Jenkins cheered the moment they saw the signal from the E-boat.

"It's them. It's Ruger," shouted Jenkins. "We've made it."

"We're not there yet," said Majewski, "But we will be shortly."

Majewski pushed the right throttle level all the way forward and the trawler lurched ahead, its engines now at full power. The distance closed between the two boats and when the boats were fifty meters from each other, Majewski steered to starboard, the E-boat moved to port and pulled alongside the trawler. Majewski slowed his vessel to match the speed of the E-boat, each boat slowing until they were at full stop. On board the E-boat, a crewman tossed over a line to the trawler.

"Lech, grab that line," shouted Majewski to his son. "Tie us down and pull us closer." Lech grabbed the line and tied it down on one of the forward cleats. The crewmen aboard the E-boat tossed successive lines, all of which Lech tied down, forward, amidships, and aft. Two sailors from the E-boat carefully jumped over the rail onto the deck of the trawler and helped secure the lines, lashing the two boats together.

"I believe I've held my end of our agreement," Majewski said, "I'd like for us to settle up before you transfer over."

"Yes, you have held up your end," said Jenkins. She reached down into her duffle bag and pulled out three bundles of cash. "I've already counted it out, but you should count it yourself to be sure," she said as the handed the bundles to Majewski.

"I trust you," he said.

"Very good," Jenkins replied. "So, let's go, ladies. We'll be in Denmark shortly and I'll buy the first round."

Haas and Jenkins began to walk out of the bridge to the deck where the E-boat crew was waiting for them. They paused and looked back at Bialik. She hadn't budged from where she stood.

"Ada, let's go," said Haas.

"Yes. We can't stay here all day," said Jenkins.

Bialik stood fast and said, "I'm sorry. I can't do this. I'm not going."

"What?" screamed Jenkins. "You most certainly are going with us, or I'll . . ."

"Or you'll what? Terminate me?"

Another sailor from the E-boat jumped over onto the trawler and headed for the bridge where the standoff was taking place. "Miss Jenkins, Miss Haas. Is there a problem?" he asked.

"I didn't think there was, but we seem to be at an impasse," Jenkins replied. "Ada, we are leaving now, and you are coming with us. And there won't be any more discussion about it. I'll have you dragged off this boat if I have to."

"Miss Jenkins, we have to leave the area. Now. Sir," he said to Majewski. "I presume you are the captain of this vessel?"

"Yes, I guess you could call me that," he replied.

"My name is Glos. Lieutenant Glos. I'm the first officer. My captain has asked me to compliment you on your seamanship. It's most impressive. He's also asked me to inform you there is at least one Soviet Navy destroyer and three motor-torpedo boats operating to our south. They appear to be conducting some sort of operation along the coast, no doubt it is a response to our activity. He wanted me to inform you of this so you could exercise caution when you return to your home port, which I presume is Puck?"

"Yes, that's correct. We detected them during the night and steered clear of them. But I appreciate the warning and the information. Lech, my son and I, we'll be out at sea for several weeks though. We're headed for the northern Atlantic. So, I suspect this will all blow over by then."

"Well then sir, I wish you good fishing and Godspeed. Now," Glos said, turning to Jenkins, Haas, and Bialik. "We really must depart the area. Now."

"I'm not going," said Bialik. "And I will jump into the sea if you try to make me."

Jenkins took a step forward, but Bialik lifted her sweater to reveal a scabbard and pulled her knife, the nine-inch Shanghai knife she had kept out of sight, hidden from view, hidden from Haas, from everyone. She crouched slightly and held the knife in her hand menacingly, switching it deftly from one hand to the other.

"I know how to use this, and I'm equally proficient with both hands. You know that, don't you Luba?" said Bialik. "It was you who taught me. You taught me and my mother how to use this. You always said it was your preferred method of killing. Didn't you? Is it still? Is it still the way you prefer to kill?"

"I haven't used my knife for quite some time, Ada," Haas replied.

"This is ridiculous," said Jenkins. "All right, child, and I call you that because you are acting like a child. We'll leave without you. Stay here. But where will you go? What will you do? You don't even have identity papers. A ration card. How will you live?"

"Five thousand will go a long way," said Majewski. "It will get her a new set of identity papers, and more ration cards than a single person can use."

"Are you part of this too?" said Jenkins.

"No, but who am I to tell her what she should do. If she wants to stay here and kill communists, I'm all for it. I'll even help her."

"Miss Jenkins," Glos interjected, "We have to depart. Now. Please."

"Wait. Just one moment," said Haas. "Perhaps there is another way. Perhaps there is a solution that will satisfy everyone."

"And what is that?" asked Jenkins.

"You said five thousand would go a long way. Do you have the contacts who could provide her with a new identity?"

"Of course," Majewski replied.

"What about travel? Could you help her get out of Puck to some other location? Say . . . Warsaw?"

"No. But I know people who could help her with that. They could help her get to Warsaw, or wherever she wants to go, for that matter."

"Fine. Ada, are you comfortable with this? If Majewski helps you, will you return to the fight? In Warsaw? And will you work with us?"

"Yes, of course I will," Bialik replied. "I missed my chance to fight with Wulkan, but I won't be talked out of this now. This is where I belong. It's my country."

"Luba where are you going with all this?" asked Jenkins.

"And what about you?" Haas said to Majewski. "Will you work with us?"

"Of course," Majewski replied. "For a price. But yes."

"Don't you see?" said Haas, turning to Jenkins. "You have the pieces right here. You have an active agent on the ground. And you have the means to ferry arms, supplies, fighters, and support them with whatever they need."

Jenkins looked at Bialik and Majewski and nodded.

"Miss Jenkins," said Glos impatiently. "We need to leave now."

Chapter Twenty-Five

April 1949

An April snowstorm blanketed the ground, shrouding Moscow, an otherwise drab, gray, and dreary city, with a gleaming white, icy blanket. An award ceremony had just taken place inside an auditorium located deep within an enormous neo-Baroque style building which occupied an entire city block stretching from Bolshaya Lyubyanskaya Street to Furkasovski Lane. The building, which before the Revolution housed an insurance company, became the home of generations and iterations of Soviet secret police in 1920. From its prison on the top floor, thousands of Russians were dispatched into the gulag system, sent to Siberia where most of them would remain for the rest of their lives.

After the ceremony concluded, there were still a half-dozen or so people milling around, waiting in turn to congratulate the award's recipient. Aleksandr Vladimirovich Kamenev, who in addition to personally receiving the Order of Lenin from none other than Vyacheslav Molotov, the Minister of Foreign Affairs, had been promoted to the rank of Major in the MGB.

After the perfunctory congratulations, handshakes, hugs, and kisses ended, but before those assembled began to drift off and return to their duties inside the vast building complex, Kamenev clapped his hands to get everybody's attention one final time.

"Comrades! I want to thank you all so much for attending this ceremony today. And I want to remind you to join me at my flat this evening at 8 p.m., where I'll be hosting a small celebration. Nothing extravagant of course, but I hope I will see you all tonight. Thank you so much for coming today."

As the crowd offered up more congratulations, words of support, and confirmations they would indeed be attending his celebratory soiree, a figure emerged from the back of the auditorium and began to make his way down the aisle on the left.

Kamenev looked up and immediately recognized Vitali Serov and called out to everyone, "Thank you all again! Now if you'll excuse me," and he quickly ran down the steps of the stage and rushed over to greet him.

"Comrade Rezident! Vitali Petrovich! It is wonderful to see you again. I did not know you were in Moscow."

"Yes, I am here for a few days to attend my granddaughter's graduation ceremony. It is always good to be with my family and I must say it is good to be with you again, Aleksandr Vladimirovich. I'm very sorry I arrived too late to attend your ceremony," Serov said as he reached over to examine the medal hanging from Kamenev's neck. "The minister himself presented your award! You have done quite well, my friend. You are definitely a rising star."

"I owe it to you, Vitali Petrovich. If you hadn't taken me under your wing in England, and then your support when I was nicked by British intelligence . . ."

"Nonsense. You deserve everything coming to you."

"Thank you Comrade Rezident, but being expelled from a country . . ."

"Is a badge of honor you should wear proudly. Being declared persona non grata is as high an award as the one you wear around your neck. It means you were doing your job, taking risks."

"Thank you, sir, but. . ."

"No buts. It was brilliant. When they picked up your source, the security guard you codenamed Richmond, it deflected their attention away from the more valuable asset, Homer. It was a stroke of genius to sacrifice a low-level source for a highly placed source."

"But that wasn't my . . ." Kamenev protested.

"No. Stop. You were brilliant and that is all there is to it. And that is the way in which I wrote it up in my report to Moscow,"

Serov said as Kamenev shook his head in disbelief. "And do you know the best part?"

"No? What is the best part?"

"Our asset Homer is now moving on. I cannot tell you where, but Homer, the asset you ran, and only because you were the lowest ranking person in the residence, a man nobody wanted has now been promoted to an even higher position, where he will continue to serve us for years to come."

"What?"

"Yes, it's true. And it is all because of you. I included that in my report too,"

"I don't know what to say."

"Tell me, do you recall our conversation in London, the conversation we had the first time we met?"

"Not entirely, Vitali Petrovich."

"Then let me refresh your memory. We talked about the American expression, and about whether it is better to be lucky or good."

Kamenev stood slack jawed in front of Serov, shaking his head in disbelief as he remembered the conversation, but now not knowing if he had been lucky, good, or both.

"Enjoy your celebration this evening, Aleksandr Vladimirovich. I am certain our paths will cross again. Soon."

***

Betancourt sat in Banbury's office on a rainy morning in Chelsea. They were drinking coffee, chatting about the West End premiere of the Rogers and Hammerstein musical, Brigadoon, which opened at His Majesty's Theatre the night before. Their conversation was interrupted by a knock on the door.

"Yes, come in," said Banbury.

Jenkins opened the door and said, "You wanted to see me, sir?"

"Yes, Jenkins. Please come in. Care for a coffee?"

"No, thank you. I'm fine."

"Well, please come in and sit down," Banbury said. Betancourt patted the cushion next to her as she slid over on the sofa to make room for Jenkins.

"So, Jenkins, I just wanted to check in with you. I'm traveling next week, and I wanted to hear from you. Could you just give me a brief run down? Are you and your team ready to go?"

"Yes, we're ready. As you know, we're infiltrating the six agents. We'll meet up with Petronius, the fisherman, and transfer the agents aboard his vessel. He'll take them into Poland. We're just awaiting a confirmation message from Lygia that she's arranged for land transportation to Warsaw where they'll met up with insurgents fighting in the area."

"It was smart of you to keep with the Quo Vadis book code," said Betancourt.

"Well, it's what she knows ma'am," Jenkins replied. "It's a little cumbersome but it allowed us to maintain communication. And one of the new agents will train Lygia how to use our one-time pad system, so we'll be going off Quo Vadis after this mission."

"What about Lygia? What's your gut tell you about her? How's she been to work with?" asked Banbury.

"As you know, we were concerned whether this would work out. And it took her awhile to get set up and reestablished in Warsaw. But she's found employment as a private tutor, she's ditched the name Ada Bialik and now goes by a new name entirely, which we are keeping on extremely close hold. We thought that prudent after last year when the Russians seemed to know our every move. On our side, only Mrs. Betancourt and I know her identity. We did bring in the Americans, the CIA chief of station in Warsaw, into the fold. Purely for coordination purposes. Because we're working in such close proximity with them in Warsaw, we wanted to make sure we weren't treading on each other. But even he doesn't know Lygia's true identity. He only knows we have an asset in Warsaw."

"Good, let's keep it that way," said Banbury. "Awful mess that was. MI5 thought they'd found the mole, and they swear by it to this day. I'm not so sure."

"Yes sir," Jenkins said. "The cash we left with Lygia has helped of course. It's helped her to facilitate the transit of supplies and arms. We're planning to provide a new influx of funds this go 'round."

"How much?"

"Two million."

"Very well. It all sounds like you are good to go. And thanks to you, we're in a better position now than ever. You salvaged the previous mission. You established a relationship with the fisherman, and we no longer have to attempt landings with small landing boats. And keeping Lygia in-country was also smart. I don't know how she does it though. She seems to have nine lives. Thankfully, we'll have more assets in place soon because you never know when her luck will run out."

"She's extraordinarily resourceful sir. A bit of a loner, but very brave, and a law unto herself," Jenkins said, looking directly at Betancourt.

"Hmm. Well, you were able to handle Haas," said Betancourt and smiled at Jenkins. She understood the reference. "You've done a good job keeping Lygia in line. My only advice is, don't get too attached to her, or to any of them. It will be a war of attrition. It always is and you will have losses."

"I'll do my best," said Jenkins.

"There is a lot riding on you, but I know you're up for it," said Banbury. "You'll be taking the first agents in, but they won't be the last. In no time, we'll have hundreds more working across the Baltic."

"Yes sir," said Jenkins. "But I am troubled by one thing."

"What's that?" asked Banbury.

"It was something Lygia said. Do you think a few hundred agents are going to be enough?"

"Let me tell you, Jenkins," said Banbury. "We helped turn the tide in the last war with less. We won that war, and we'll win this one too, this Cold War. Are a few hundred agents enough? The answer is yes."

"Very well, sir. I appreciate your confidence," said Jenkins, rising from the sofa. "Will there be anything else?"

"No, I just wanted to wish you good luck," said Banbury.

"Thank you," said Jenkins. "Um, where are you off to? If you can say?"

"I'm off to the U.S.," he said. "We have a new man who'll be handling our affairs with the CIA. Because the Yanks are still supporting this operation, helping to fund it, it's important they be kept abreast of our progress. And our new man will help us do just that. I'm just going over as a show of support, help him get off on the right foot and what not."

"Right, sir. Well . . . safe travels."

"Right," said Banbury rising and extending his hand to Jenkins. "And Jenkins. I know this won't be easy. So just keep at it. But we will win. Eventually."

***

Springtime had come early to Louisville. The air was warm and humid, and it smelled of honeysuckle. Lehman nursed his drink, a bourbon and cola with ice, and looked out onto the back garden of his sister Rose's house. As he watched his cousin, Katharina Eger, play with her two children, he thought back to the last time he saw her and the children in Hamburg, when they boarded a boat headed for Canada. He had helped them assume new identities and escape their past in the hope they would be able to build a new future. He watched Katharina toss a ball to her son Willi and laughed when he swung a bat nearly as tall as he was, hitting the ball and sending it high over Katharina's head for his sister to chase down.

He took a sip of his drink and placed the cold, icy glass against his forehead to cool himself off a bit. He loosened his tie and the vision of Luba, walking down the aisle flashed in his mind. The wedding was a small affair. Just family. His sisters, their husbands, their kids. And now they were all together, enjoying a warm Saturday in April.

"Penny for your thoughts," said Haas as she sidled up to Lehman, placing her arm around him, leaning into him, and resting her head on his arm.

"I'm just taking it all in," Lehman said. "Taking in everything on what is undoubtedly the best day of my life."

Haas stood on her toes and gave Lehman a kiss on the check.

"Me, too," she said and then turned her gaze back to the children. "Your sister Rose and your family are just as you described. And Therese, sorry, I mean Katharina," she said correcting herself. "They are all looking well and seem to have adjusted to their new life here in Louisville. What is past is now buried."

"I hope so."

"Mmm."

"So, Mrs. Lehman, are you ready to return to Germany?"

"Mrs. Lehman? Who's that? Is that your mother? Oh wait, are you referring to me? You know, I haven't decided if I want to take your name," Haas said, laughing.

Lehman faked a frown but couldn't hold it for very long before he started to laugh and said, "Well, nobody is going to force you. But I believe we have a marriage certificate that says Lehman on it. So, the great state of Kentucky now considers you to be a Lehman. And that fact will make life a lot easier for us. We'll have less explaining to do."

"Why is that? How so?"

"What I mean is, now that we're an old married couple, we move into a whole new world with the United States Army. We're legal. Nobody will accuse us of shacking up together, breaking whatever regulations there are against fraternization. And the best part is we get all sorts of benefits now. Housing allowance. Per diem, more money! All sorts of perks. And, we, as in you and me, we have new orders. A new assignment."

"Orders?" Haas replied, her smile turned into a frown and a serious look came over her face. "Orders to where? Doing what?"

"We're going to Berlin," Lehman replied, his voice turning serious.

"Berlin? What are we going to do there?"

"Well, your job is to keep doing what you have been doing. Keep your network running. Headquarters, specifically General Clay, thought it would be easier for us if we were closer to our target so to speak. So, we'll be taking up residence in the US sector. There is another part of the job, but I can't talk to you about it here. It will have to wait until we return to Germany. But it's called Operation Bliss."

"Oh, I like the sound of that. Does that mean we can make babies? That would make me blissful!"

"We can definitely do that too," Lehman replied. "The army will even give us more money if we have dependents."

"It's settled then. I'm ready, Mr. Lehman. Ready whenever you are."

"Good," he replied. He looked down upon her face and smiled and said, "So, you really don't want to take my name?"

"Of course, I do, silly. But, that's for our private life. For my professional life, they'll still call me Haas. Luba Haas."

"I can live with that," he said as he drained his bourbon and cola. He swirled the glass and the ice cubes clinked. "Want another drink?" he asked.

"I would love one," Haas replied. "I'm parched."

***

Avery slipped his key into the front door, opened it and let it swing open wide. He shook his umbrella several times, attempting to remove all the water it had collected before he brought it inside. He stepped into the foyer, closed his umbrella completely and placed it into the stand. As he slipped off his raincoat, he called out, "Madeline. I'm home!"

"Is that you dear?" came a voice from the kitchen. "May I fetch you a cocktail? Your usual?"

"Yes, please! I'll join you in the parlor. I have some very exciting news."

"News? How wonderful. I'll be there in a second, drinks in hand."

Avery stepped through the foyer and slid open the pocket door leading to the parlor. This was his favorite room in the house, save possibly for their bedroom. Madeline already had a fire going, for although it was April, there was definitely a chill still in the air and it had been raining for three days straight. He reached into his coat pocket and pulled out a letter sized envelope addressed to him, and he hummed a Gershwin tune, 'Nice Work If You Can Get It," as he tapped the letter in his hand.

"Well, you're in a good mood," said Madeline carrying a tray with a shaker and two cocktails, martinis straight up, with three olives, very, very dry.

"I am, my love," he said. "You'll never guess what I have here?"

"What is it?"

"This my dear is my redemption. I've been rehabilitated, reformed, reassigned, and the best part, I've been promoted!"

"That's wonderful, darling. But reassigned? To where? Will we be able to take Caroline?" Madeline asked as she handed a cocktail to Avery.

"Of course, we'll be able to take Caroline! We're all going to the States! You're looking at the new top man in Washington. I'll be handling the American desk there."

***

The radio operator bolted upright when she heard the manual Morse code signal. She was on the graveyard shift at the wireless intercept station near Poundon and had nearly dozed off. But the

Morse code transmission awakened her fully and she immediately switched on her tape recorder and began transcribing the message. After only a few characters, she recognized the sender as Lygia.

When the transmission ended, she replied, confirming the message had been received in full. Then she looked down at what she had transcribed. It was gibberish. Except for the header information in the message, which was sent in the clear, everything else was coded and completely unintelligible to her. But she knew there were others who would be able to decipher the random characters. She rewound her recorder and listened to the transmission once again, checking the accuracy of her transcript and frowned. She listened once more, and once more again. *Something isn't right*, she thought.

She knew the drill. Rewind the tape, remove it, and bring it along with her transcript and code book to her supervisor. She gathered everything up, walked to the end of the long bay of intercept stations, and stood before her supervisor's desk.

"Ma'am. I have a special transcript for you. It's Lygia."

"Excellent. We've been expecting a message from her. So, let's hand it over please?"

"Yes ma'am," the operator said as she handed over the tape, her codebook, and transcription. "But I need to tell you. I feel something may be wrong."

"Wrong? What's wrong?"

"It's Lygia alright. I recognize the fist. But the speed and the cadence of the transmission was off. It was much slower than usual. It just seems off. To me at least."

The supervisor frowned. "Very well. I'll note your concerns in my cover message. Let's package this up immediately. I want this on the next courier to the Citadel."

***

"How did she do?" Sokolov asked the Russian radio operator. They were in a cramped room on the top floor of the UB prison building in Moscow. A wireless was set up on a metal table and

Bialik was seated behind it. She removed her headphones and placed them on the table. She leaned back in her chair and let out a long sigh.

"She transmitted the message exactly as we prepared it, using her copy of Quo Vadis. She included all of the message markers. The message was like the others we monitored before our radio direction-finding units were able to locate her and the transmitter. She repeated the message a total of four times and received a confirmation of receipt of message. So as far as I can tell, Comrade Colonel, she did everything perfectly, precisely as we asked her to do."

"Very good," Sokolov said turning to look at Bialik. "So, you've earned a night's reprieve. No one will bother you tonight."

Bialik nodded.

Sokolov clicked his fingers and a guard emerged from behind him. "Take her back to her cell," Sokolov said. "And get her something to eat. Something hot."

"Yes, Comrade Colonel."

The guard walked around the table and grasped Bialik's arm, helping her to rise to her feet. She stumbled as he led her slowly out of the room. She grasped the front of her dress. It was in filthy tatters and only a single button held the garment in place.

"And get her some new clothing and allow her to bathe and clean herself up," Sokolov added. "We need her to be presentable." He watched as the guard and Bialik shuffled past him. Just as they were about to leave the room, he called out to her once more.

"Miss Nowak?" Sokolov said. "Felicja Nowak? Or perhaps I should address you by your given name, Ada Bialik."

Bialik and the guard paused at the door, and she turned to look at Sokolov.

"I look forward to meeting your friends," Sokolov said. "You'll be there with us to help us identify them and I know it will be happy reunion."

Bialik said nothing but gave Sokolov a cold stare. He nodded and watched as the guard led her out of the room into the dimly lit corridor. *Still defiant? What is it with these people? No matter. For you, it will be into the fog*, he thought. *Into the fog.*

Author's Notes: About the Characters

Operation Nightfall: The Web of Spies is the sequel to my debut novel, *Grown Men Cry Out at Night.* It is a work of fiction and as a novelist, I take advantage of literary license to create the setting, the plot, the characters, and their dialogue. However, the arc of the story is inspired by the true events of Poland's anti-communist insurgency, the Cambridge Five spy scandal, and a covert MI6 operation, which attempted to rollback communism to the borders of the USSR. My goal is to shed light on a lesser-known story of the Cold War and to immerse readers into the shadowy world of counterintelligence and spy versus spy operations.

All of the characters in Operation Nightfall are fictional, but several are based on historical figures. Readers of my first novel will recognize the characters Luba Haas, Caspar Lehman, and James Banbury. They return in Operation Nightfall.

- Luba Haas is a fictional character based on the real-life hero and SOE agent, Krystyna Skarbek, or Christine Granville as she was known in Great Britain. Skarbek was the first woman to serve in the SOE and served in combat longer than any SOE agent. Her exploits are brilliantly told in the biography, *The Spy Who Loved: The Secrets and Lives of Christine Granville.*

- Caspar Lehman is a fictional character, but I based his military record on the service of well-known American author, J.D. Salinger, who served as a U.S. Army Counterintelligence Agent during WWII.

- James Banbury is a fictional character, but his real-life counterpart was Henry Carr. Carr served as Director, Northern European Department, MI6.

- Alicia Betancourt is a fictional character who is head of the Baltic Section, MI6. In real life, Alexander McKibben held that position, but I wanted a woman in that role. After WWII, women holding positions of authority would have been highly irregular given that they were expected to relinquish their careers and return to domestic life. This is another area where I have chosen to exercise literary license. The relationship between Betancourt and Banbury is similar to the one I envision might have existed between SOE Spymaster Maurice Buckmaster and head of the French section, Vera Atkins.

- Ada Bialik is a fictional character whom I loosely based on the life of Maria Zienkiewicz, who served as a captain in the Polish Home Army and was the second wife of Jan Mazurkiewicz, a colonel in the Home Army.

- Natalie Jenkins is a fictional character, but she carries on in the tradition of the brave women who served in the SOE during WWII.

- Yuri Sokolov is a fictional character based on the life of Vasily Blokhin. Blokhin was hand-picked by Stalin to lead a group of executioners and oversaw thousands of mass killings during the Great Purge and along the Eastern Front during WWII. He is purported to have killed more than 10,000 individuals by his own hand, earning him the nickname, "Stalin's Executioner."

- Peter Avery is a fictional character based on Cambridge Five spy, Donald Maclean.

- Vitali Serov is a fictional character based on the life of Anatoly Gorsky, who served undercover as First Secretary Anatoly Gromov, but was secretly the top Soviet spy, the Rezident, assigned to the Russian embassy in Washington DC at the end of WWII.

- Alexi Kamenev is a fictional character.

Acknowledgements

That this book has been written and published is a personal miracle. In October 2022, I was diagnosed with cancer. Over the course of the next year, I underwent an increasingly aggressive and invasive treatment. It included four outpatient surgical procedures, three months of chemotherapy, a marathon ten-and-a-half-hour surgery on October 12, 2023, and after a six-day hospital stay. I finally found myself at home, where I would begin my convalescence. Doctors said my complete recovery would take at least twelve months.

I began writing Operation Nightfall in February 2023, but constant appointments with doctors wreaked havoc on my daily writing routine. By summer, I was already behind schedule. Once I began chemotherapy, its effects were so severe I was forced to stop writing entirely, and I decided to delay publication until 2024.

Recovery does not always follow a straight path. It is full of twists and turns, stops and starts, good days and bad. But I discovered writing gave me purpose. I wasn't able to resume working on Operation Nightfall until mid-November 2023. When I sat down to work, I felt disconnected from my early drafts. It felt almost as if there were two people writing this novel – the pre-cancer writer and the post-treatment writer. But over the course of a few weeks, the old habits began to return. The characters once again began to speak to me and I acted as a faithful scribe, copying down every word they whispered to me. I met my self-imposed deadline, and I shipped a completed manuscript, for better or worse, to my editor in April 2024.

There are so many people whose insights and commentary have made this a better book. I thank the readers of a very early draft, my "alpha-readers," Ed Rober, Donna Shea, Barb Eppley, Carol

Woodfint, Bob Mueller, and Tom Stock. They all dutifully filled out my reader questionnaire, answering my detailed questions, and provided me necessary course corrections to the plot and characters of the book. I cannot thank you enough.

I want to thank my editor Caroljean Gavin. Working with her has been a joy. She has helped to make this book more engaging and entertaining. If you enjoyed reading Operation Nightfall, it is because of her exemplary work. Editors are the secret sauce. They can take an ordinary book and make it special, and Caroljean is among the very best at her craft.

I offer my heartfelt thanks to my brother David. He dropped everything in his life last October to be with me as I underwent surgery. I cannot thank you enough, brother, for all you have done.

And finally, to my wife Jody, the words thank you seem so inadequate. Over the past year, you have been my rock, always at my side, caring for me. You have redefined what it means when we vowed, "in sickness and in health." This book is dedicated to you.

About the Author

Karl Wegener is a former Russian linguist, intelligence analyst, and interrogator who served in the U.S. Army, the U.S. Air Force Reserves, and the Intelligence Community during the Cold War. He currently resides in Delaware with his wife and two dogs. Operation Nightfall: The Web of Spies is his second novel and a sequel to his debut novel, Grown Men Cry Out at Night.

Printed in the USA
CPSIA information can be obtained
at www.ICGtesting.com
LVHW021245041024
792814LV00012B/395